"PROBABLY THE BEST HISTORICAL
ROMANCE EVER PUBLISHED."
Susan Elizabeth Phillips

"MOVING AND MEMORABLE."
Jill Marie Landis

"ONE OF THE MOST PASSIONATE,
POWERFUL, AND PROVOCATIVE
ROMANCES EVER WRITTEN."
Teresa Medeiros

"LAURA KINSALE DELIVERS POWERFUL,
UNIQUE ROMANCE LACED WITH
PASSION, DANGER, AND COMPELLING
CHARACTERS...THE HALLMARK OF A
FIRST-RATE ROMANCE."
Amanda Quick

FLOWERS FROM THE STORM

The poignant, passionate, and unforgettable
masterwork of transcendent love by acclaimed
New York Times bestselling author

LAURA KINSALE

LAURA KINSALE

FLOWERS
FROM THE
STORM

AVON BOOKS
An Imprint of HarperCollins*Publishers*

This is a work of fiction. Names, characters, places, and incidents are products of the author's imagination or are used fictitiously and are not to be construed as real. Any resemblance to actual events, locales, organizations, or persons, living or dead, is entirely coincidental.

AVON BOOKS
An Imprint of HarperCollins*Publishers*
10 East 53rd Street
New York, New York 10022-5299

First Avon Books paperback printing: October 1992

Prologue

*H*e liked radical politics and had a fondness for chocolate. Five years ago, the Honorable Miss Lacy-Grey had verifiably swooned on the occasion of his requesting her hand for a country dance—an example of that category of incidents which one's friends found endlessly amusing and became fond of recalling *ad nauseam* in their cups. The circulating quip had been that a marriage proposal would have crippled the girl for life, and an offer of a baser sort killed her on the spot.

Since Christian lay now with his head pillowed in the smooth curve of her back, his fingers indolently sliding between her stocking and her skin just above a blue-and-yellow garter, he had to assume that his friends had been slightly out in their predictions. She seemed perfectly alive to him. Her ankles crossed prettily, waving gently back and forth in the air above him.

He shaped his palm over her buttock, gave the dimple in the small of her back a kiss and sat up, leaning on his elbow. "When will Sutherland be home?"

"Not for a fortnight. At the very least." The former Miss Lacy-Grey rolled over, smiling, exposing breasts that had grown heavier, the slight, swelling thickness at her waist. They'd been lovers for nigh three months. Christian passed his gaze over the subtle changes and lifted his lashes, saying nothing.

"I wish he would never come," she said, twining her hands together above her head. "It's been wonderful."

"Better than chocolate," he said.

"Really?"

He looked around, having reminded himself. The tall pot sat waiting; the kettle steamed softly on the hob. "Excuse me." He pushed out of bed.

"You odious man."

He gave her a sweeping bow and a wink, and helped himself to the kettle, pouring out boiling water into the cold milk, precisely half-and-half, scraping chocolate shavings into the pot and inserting the mill. The carpet felt cool and silken beneath his bare feet. He rubbed the tall mill handle vigorously between his hands—that ought to have been done over the fire, not in the pot, but conditions in the middle of the night in another man's bedroom weren't always ideal—and poured the frothy mix into a cup.

"How you can bring yourself to drink that without a grain of sugar defies the imagination," she said.

"But you're the sugar, my sweet," he said promptly. He took a sip, standing naked next to the table. "How else?"

She tried to make a jaded pout, but it turned into a smile. She stretched her hands upward again, sighing and arching in a provocative way, sliding her stockinged foot up and down the bed. "Oh, yes, I hope Sutherland never comes home."

"You'd best have him home to bed you, my girl, and soon enough at that."

She stared at her hands, and then lowered them. Her mouth gathered again into that appealing pucker. "He won't care."

"Right-ho," Christian said cynically.

She spread her palm on her increasing belly and slid a glance at him sideways.

He put down the chocolate and leaned across her, kissing her breast, tangling his hands in her hair and kissing her throat. "Worth it?" he murmured, very close to her ear.

She brought her arms up around his shoulders and held him tightly. The softness of her reawakened him. He nuzzled his face into her skin, and while she clung to him as if she were drowning, he took advantage of the moment to tarnish her good character one more time. She seemed to enjoy it. God knew he did.

A single candle guttered at the base of the stairwell, illuminating the left arm and draperies of a marble copy of Ceres gazing down with an excess of sentimentality upon a sheaf of wheat. Christian moved discreetly on the stair, but not stealthily, having made his peace with the butler some weeks ago by the simple habit of leaving a neat stack of three yellow-boys by the candlestick as he let himself out. He was collecting them together in his pocket, feeling for the coins through his glove, when he heard the shuffle of a footstep from below. He paused at the landing, his hand on the rail.

"Edith?" A male voice drifted up, a faint echo in the hall. *The devil take it.*

Christian stood utterly still. Lesley Sutherland walked out from beneath the stair, unbuttoning his greatcoat. "Eydie?" he said again, and smoothed his red sideburns as he looked up.

There was a clock ticking in the hall. Christian had never noticed it before, but at that moment of silence it was like a brazen, irrevocable tally. *One . . . two . . . three . . . four . . .*

At four it happened. The half-smile faded from Sutherland's face. His lips parted. Christian expected nothing to come out, and nothing did: only silence, and Sutherland's face going whiter and whiter, until his mouth clamped shut and color rushed up everywhere but in the carved lines beside his nose and around his lips.

Six . . . seven . . . eight . . .

Christian thought of several things to say, all of them

facetious and directed at himself, except for the classic:
Home early, aren't you?

He kept them between his teeth. Sutherland still looked in
a state of shock. An unpleasant tingling numbness in Christian's right hand made him realize how hard he was gripping
the stair rail through his glove. He let go, but the feeling of
pins-and-needles grew worse and a strangeness seemed to
wash over him, as if the stair beneath him shifted without
moving.

He flexed his hand, open and closed.

The action seemed to focus Sutherland. He stared at
Christian's hand. "Jervaulx," he said in an incongruously
mild voice. "I'll kill you for this."

He even got the pronunciation wrong, the bumped-up Cit;
too much *J* and *X*. In the eerie imbalance of the moment,
Christian's mind absurdly revolved over the proper sounds
of his own title, *Shervoh—Shervoh—Shervoh* . . .

He said nothing, spreading his hand and squeezing his fingers into a fist again, which seemed something difficult to
do. His arm felt heavy, somehow deadened, and his fingers
itched and prickled down inside the bone.

"Your friends," Sutherland said, a little louder, more ag-
gressively. "Name your friends."

"Durham. And Colonel Fane." It was inevitable. But it
surprised him that he felt so strange.

The clock ticked down another ten seconds while they
looked at one another.

"You blackguard. *Get out of my house!*"

The shout came out half-strangled. Sutherland was so
deep red, so throttled, that Christian thought he might burst
and fall down in apoplexy.

"All right," Christian said quietly. He moved down the
stairs, past the other man, deliberately passive and reserved
in his motions. Sutherland might wish to kill him, as was his
right, but Christian had no particular desire to be the cause
of the man dropping dead in his own hallway.

Besides that, he felt himself in need of fresh air. He felt

drunk. His right hand still seemed dead and clumsy as he pulled open the door. He dragged it closed behind him with his left and stumbled, staggering against the iron railing at the doorstep.

The moon was full, lighting a patch of fog that lay at the base of the street: a blue mist fingering against the black row of houses, rising slowly. Christian held onto the rail, staring down the hill. Something definitely was wrong with him. He felt sick and dizzy and . . . strange. A wild thought that he'd been poisoned took hold of his mind.

Eydie? The chocolate. Would Eydie poison him? What the deuce for?

His heart beat at a great rate; he kept swallowing, trying to slow it, trying to think.

After a few moments, he let go of the rail. The cool air seemed to brace him. He drew deep breaths of it, and felt more himself. A dark shape lay at the foot of the front steps; he squinted at it, and realized it was his own hat.

He went down the steps and past it, and remembered again that it was his hat. The carriage waited for him two streets down. He stared uncertainly at the hat, then walked on. He couldn't think why Eydie would poison him. It rather aggrieved him. But he felt better now, walking. Things settled themselves. When he reached his brougham, his coachman got down quickly from the perch and held open the door.

Cass and Devil tumbled out, plumed tails wagging in elation. Christian leaned against the side of the carriage and allowed the dogs a jump apiece on him. He fondled their ears with one hand, called Devil back from sniffing along the coal holes in the sidewalk, and climbed inside. Cass lay down primly at Christian's feet, but Devil inserted a spotted nose beneath his glove and insinuated himself onto the seat.

Christian stroked the setter's head. As the carriage pulled away, he reached up to take off his hat and found that he had none.

He rested his head back on the seat. Sutherland. Sutherland wanted satisfaction.

Christian only wanted sleep. He flexed his right hand against the lingering, leaden weakness there. He thought drowsily that it was for once a convenient thing that he was left-handed, or he'd not be able to lift a pistol.

Chapter One

"I've yet to fathom it. No doubt I never will. How *canst* thou expect any real consideration from a person of his—" Archimedea Timms paused, searching for a suitable word. " —his *ilk*, Papa?"

"Wilt thou pour me a cup of tea, Maddy?" her father asked, in just the sort of amiable voice that left one with no room to start an effective argument.

"He is a duke, for one thing," she said over her shoulder, a parting shot as she marched through the back dining room to locate Geraldine, since the parlor bell was in disorder. The time it took to find the maidservant, see water drawn and set to boil, and return to the parlor was not enough to make her forget the sequence of her thoughts. "A duke can scarcely be supposed to care seriously for such matters—the square is above thy left hand—as must be perfectly clear when his integration has not been prepared for the past week."

"Thou shouldst not be impatient, Maddy. This sort of thing must be done with infinite care. He is taking his time. I admire him for it." Her father's searching fingers found the carved wooden numeral two and slid it into place as an exponent of *s*.

"He is not taking his time, nor a bit of care. He is out and about the town, engaged in creaturely socializing. He has not the smallest regard for thy credit, nor his own."

Her father smiled, gazing straight ahead as he searched out a multiplication sign and added it to the sequence of wooden letters and numbers on the red baize tablecloth in front of him, his fingers floating over the blocks to check each by touch. "Knowest thou certain sure about the creaturely socializing, Maddy?"

"One has only to read the papers. There is not a worldly function which he has not attended this entire spring. And your joint treatise scheduled to be introduced on Third Day evening! I shall have to be the one to cancel it, I know, for *he* won't think of it. President Milner will be most aggravated, and rightly so, for who is to take Jervaulx's place at the podium?"

"Thou shalt write the equations upon the slate, and I shall be there to answer questions."

"If Friend Milner will allow it," she said broodingly. "He'll say that it's most irregular."

"No one will mind. We delight in thy presence every month, Maddy. Thou hast always been welcome to attend. Friend Milner himself once told me that a lady's face brightens the meeting rooms considerable."

"Of course I attend. Should I let thee go alone?" She looked up at the maidservant as the girl brought in the tray. Geraldine set the tea down, and Maddy poured her father a cup, touching his hand and guiding it gently to the saucer and handle. His fingers were pale and soft from all the years of indoor work, his face still unlined in spite of his age. There had always been an air of abstraction about him, even before he'd lost his sight. Truthfully, the set habits of his life had not changed so much after the illness that had blinded him years ago, except that now he leaned on Maddy's arm when he went for his daily walk or to the monthly meetings of the Analytical Society and used carved blocks and dictation in his mathematics instead of his own pen.

"Thou'lt call on the duke again today about the differentials?" he asked.

Maddy made a face, safe to do so when Geraldine had left. "Yes, Papa," she said, keeping her vexation from her voice with an effort. "I'll call on the duke again."

The first thing Christian thought of when he woke was the unfinished integration. He threw back the covers, evicting Cass and Devil from the bed, and shook his hand vigorously, trying to rid himself of the pins-and-needles sensation caused by sleeping on it. The dogs whined at the door, and he let them out. The uncomfortable itchy numbness in his fingers was slow to fade; he worked his fist as he poured chocolate and sat down in his dressing robe to leaf through the pages of Timms' ciphering and his own.

It was easy to tell the difference: Timms had a small, refined hand, a third the size of Christian's inverted scrawl. From his first day in the schoolroom, Christian had rebelled at the insistence on right-handed cursive and used his left, enduring the regular beatings across the offending palm with sullen silence, but it still embarrassed him to write when anyone could see him. This morning Timms' writing appeared so small that it even seemed hard to read; it swam on the page and gave Christian a headache trying to focus on it.

Obviously, he was a little the worse for whatever brandy he'd consumed last night. He took up a quill, already trimmed by his secretary to the special angle that Christian's ungraceful, upside-down hand posture required, and began to work, ignoring what had been written before. It was easy to lose himself in the bright, cool world of functions and hyperbolic distances. The symbols on the page might slide and quiver, but the equations in his head were like unfailing music. He blinked, screwed up his face against the pain that seemed to have settled around his right eye, and kept writing.

By the time he'd calculated the last differential and thought to ring Calvin for a tray of breakfast, it felt as if he were waking from a trance to look up and recognize his own bedroom with its Palladian columns flanking the bed, its plaster frieze and wainscoting, and the blue-patterned wallpaper selected by some lady whose name he did not at the moment recollect. Thinking of ladies, however, brought a pleasant thought of Eydie, and he told Calvin to have a single orchid sent to her before tea.

"As you say, Your Grace." The butler bowed slightly. "Mr. Durham and Colonel Fane are below. They've been waiting to speak to you for some time. Shall I tell them that Your Grace is not at home this afternoon?"

"Do I look as if I'm not at home?" He stretched out his legs and sat back in the chair, crossing his ankles as he glanced at the clock. "By God, it's already half past one. How long have they been down there? Send 'em up, man. Send 'em up."

He didn't bother to make himself presentable for Durham and Fane; two older and easier friends he couldn't have. Rubbing his head against the persistent sharp pressure, he just lay back in the chair, closing his eyes for a moment.

"Egad, what've we got here? Hen-scratching again?" Durham's lazy voice sounded faintly surprised. "At a time like this. You're a regular iceberg, ain't you?"

Christian opened his eyes and closed them again. "Lord save us, it's the clergy."

"Just in time. You look as if you're ready for the last rites, old fellow."

"Oh, do you actually know them?" Christian lifted one eyelid.

"I could look 'em up. Anything for you, Shev." Durham still affected Brummell's style in voice and clothing eleven years after the Beau had fled his creditors to France, but with blond hair and decided movements as a burnished counterpoint to the die-away airs. The morbid dress was his only concession to his reverend calling, and Christian his only sponsor in it—the dukes of Jervaulx holding, among twenty-nine other clerical appointments, the advowson for the living at St. Matthews-upon-Glade, a bounteous ecclesiastical benefice which Christian had seen fit to bestow on his friend. And a particularly obliging favor it had been, too, considering Durham's diverting lack of the character attributes generally required of a rector.

Fane and the dogs followed him in, Devil squeezing past Fane's boots as the guardsman entered blazing in gold lace and scarlet regimentals and twirling a top hat on his finger. He tossed the hat in Christian's direction.

"Sutherland conveys that to you."

Christian caught it. He pushed Devil's forepaws off his lap. "The deuce you say. Sutherland?"

"They claimed you left it on his doorstep last night."

"Who claimed?"

"Well, who do you think?" Fane dropped himself into a chair, scowling. "His bloody seconds, that's who claimed."

Christian grinned in spite of his headache. "What-ho, is he back in town? He's called me out already?"

"Plague take you, Shev, nobody thinks it's funny," Durham said. "Sutherland's the very devil of a shot."

Fane stroked Cassie's head and then picked a black dog hair off his red coat. "He wants it tomorrow morning. Up to you, of course. Pistols, we reckoned—but you might consider sabers, in Sutherland's case."

Christian closed his eyes and opened them. The headache was drowning him; he couldn't even think properly.

"Damned unlucky, meeting him in his own hall that way," Fane added grimly. "I'll swear he didn't have a clue about you and *la* Sutherland. Just plain dumb-dog luck, that's all it was. You'd think the silly bastard would want to keep it quiet, wouldn't you? Just what does he suppose is to come of killing you if he can manage it? A long trip to the continent, or a hanging if he's slow to bolt. By God, Shev—I'll rat on him myself if he kills you."

Christian frowned at Fane uneasily. He thought this must be some elaborate jest, which he was in no mood to take. But nobody was smiling, and Fane looked downright ugly, his jaw set hard.

"Sutherland's seconds called on you this morning?" Christian asked tentatively.

"Cards came at eight." Durham waved his hand. "Nine o'clock, they were on my stair at Albany. He's frothing at the bit, Jervaulx. He wants blood."

"They said—I was in his house?"

"Weren't you?"

Christian stared at his toes. He could not, when he thought of it, recall much of anything about last night.

"God. I must have been roaring drunk."

Durham blew a harsh breath. "Egad, Jervaulx—do you say you don't remember?"

Christian shook his head slightly. He didn't feel as if he'd been drinking. He didn't remember starting to drink. He had this headache, and his hand . . . he just felt strange.

"Hell," Durham said, and sat down in a chair. "What a bungle."

"Doesn't matter." Christian pressed his fingers against the bridge of his nose. "Tomorrow, he wants it? Tomorrow's too soon."

"When?"

"I'm giving a paper tomorrow night. It'll have to be Wednesday morning."

"Giving a paper?" Fane echoed.

"A mathematical paper."

The colonel just gazed at him.

"A paper, Fane," Christian said patiently. "With words on it, by which a message of importance is conveyed. Do you ever read, in the army?"

"Sometimes," Fane said.

"Shev's a regular Isaac Newt', y'know." Durham leaned back and crossed his legs. "Though you'd never think it to see him, would you? You look like hell, Jervaulx."

"I feel like it," Christian said. He caressed Devil's throat with his left hand and sighed. "Damn it all. And I just sent her a bloody orchid."

* * *

The white, elegant, new-built town house in Belgrave Square was an affront to Maddy. Everything about the Duke of Jervaulx was an affront to her. As a born and raised member of the Society of Friends, she supposed that she ought to have a Concern for his state of grace, casting his life away upon dancing and gambling and leisure as he was doing, but in honest truth, her Divine Inner Light did not seem to be much interested in his spiritual condition. Rather, she felt an all-too-earthly antagonism toward the man. Under commonplace circumstances, she would not have expended any thought at all upon him; indeed, Maddy had never so much as heard of the Duke of Jervaulx until he had begun, for his own perverse reasons, writing letters to the Journal of the London Analytical Society, and hence come to occupy such a large and invisible place in the Timms' little house in Chelsea.

She had always read every word of the Journal to her father, and of course it was she who had written out, to dictation, the reply to the duke's published letter inquiring into Papa's monograph upon the Solution of Equations of the Fifth Degree. That had been in First Month. It was now almost Sixth Month, with the window-boxes full of sweet peas and late tulips making a scarlet splash against pale walls, and Maddy had long since become a regular caller in Belgrave Square.

Not that she ever saw Jervaulx himself. She had not once laid eyes upon the man. The duke would not, of course, wait upon a Quaker female of plain and modest standing such as herself, nor attend the meetings of the Analytical Society in person; he had much more aristocratic and questionable ways of spending his time than that. No—Archimedea Timms presented herself at the door of his noble house with a copy of her father's latest work, lettered with painstaking accuracy in Maddy's hand, upon receipt of which the butler Calvin escorted her into an alcove off the breakfast parlor and offered her chocolate, took away her papa's careful proposals, and left her sitting there, sometimes for three hours

and a half at a time, waiting to see if the butler would return
with a note and several sheets covered in casually luxurious
slashes of the pen, rows of equations written as if the letters
and numbers and arcs were an aesthetic rather than a mathematical effort.

Much more often than not, all that Calvin returned with
was the duke's promise that his contribution would be ready
the next day. And when she called the next day, the promise
was for the next, and the next, until she lost all patience with
the man. On top of that was Papa's quiet but rising excitement over what he and Jervaulx were working toward.
Mathematics was her father's entire life, the irrefutable
proof of a theorem the whole goal of his existence—not for
the personal fame of such an accomplishment, but for the
love of the science itself. He thought the duke a miracle, an
amazing blessing upon his life and geometry and the earth in
general, and anticipated the man's irregular communications
with endless patience.

In truth, Maddy feared that she was a little jealous. The
way Papa's face lit up when she finally returned with one of
Jervaulx's new sets of equations and axioms, Papa's look of
shock, and then deep nodding pleasure, when she would read
them out to him and he discovered some particular innova-
tion, some calculation that displayed especial finesse . . . well,
it would not do to begrudge him that happiness, just because
to her it was all nothing but an endless series of symbols, like
a foreign language that one could read and pronounce, but
not really understand. Some people were simply born to it,
and Maddy, in spite of the felicitous hope that her father had
expressed in naming her after Archimedes, was not one of
them.

The Duke of Jervaulx, however, was.

He was also dissolute, reckless and extravagant, a gallant,
a gambler, a womanizer, a patron of creaturely arts—paint-
ers and musicians and novelists—transparently referred to
as the D———— of J———————— in the scandal sheets,
where he and his various exploits appeared with frequency.

She had made it her business to find out about him. Not to put too fine a point upon it, he was a rakehell.

It wouldn't have made any difference to Papa if the man had been a cowherd; the talent was all that mattered. But Jervaulx was a duke, a fact of which Maddy was reminded much more frequently than her papa—to be precise, every time she sat awaiting Jervaulx's royal convenience in his breakfast alcove. And now, having agreed two months ago to co-author this paper with her father and even condescending to offer to make the preliminary presentation himself at the monthly meeting of the Analytical Society, Jervaulx had apparently forgotten all about it and couldn't even be bothered to finish the last crucial step in the calculations.

At least, she hoped he had forgotten, for she had a niggling fear that he might be playing some horrid joke upon her papa. Her worst nightmare was that Jervaulx would come to the Analytical Society with some of his shocking friends, perhaps under the influence of drink, bringing along unsavory women, to make her father and all the members of the Society the object of public ridicule.

She had no real reason to suspect that he would do so, but at best her papa was going to be painfully disappointed and embarrassed in front of his mathematical fellows by the duke's absence, all on account of an aristocrat who was too indolent to live up to his commitments to anything but debauchery. For Jervaulx, this was a mere pastime. For her father, it was lifeblood itself.

She marched up the steps beneath the portico of the white town house, almost of a mind to send in, along with her father's polite and diffident inquiry, a note to the duke containing her own sentiments. Despite the fact that she had never once discovered in her soul the boldness to stand up and speak out in the silence of her own Meeting, she was quite certain that it would not frighten her in the least that he was a duke. It would not bother her at all to speak to him—an indication in itself, she felt, that what moved her met with God's full approval. On the grounds of the biblical spiritual equality of man, she felt that anything which might lay the duke's iniquities before him in a calm and convincing manner must only do him good.

But Calvin was smiling as he ushered her in, and picked up a flat leather case from a table right in the hall. He held it out to her. "To be presented to Mr. Timms, by means of Miss Archimedea Timms, with His Grace's compliments," he said. "The duke has instructed me to impart to Mr. Timms that His Grace will be attending the meeting of the Analytical Society tomorrow night in the company of Sir Charles Milner, and looks with anticipation upon the forthcoming introduction."

Maddy took the satchel into her hand. "Oh," she said. "He finished."

Calvin made no sign of noticing her surprise, but stood with his head tilted expectantly toward the breakfast room. "Would you like chocolate, Miss?"

"Chocolate?" Maddy gathered her thoughts. "No. Indeed, I won't be stopping. I must convey this to my father directly."

"As you say, Miss."

Such a sudden and unexpected attention to his promise by the heedless duke left Maddy rather at a stand, and somehow more vexed than pleased. Odious man, to tumble everyone into a topsy-turvy state of suspense and then think that he could put all to rights merely by consorting with President Milner and finishing the differentials at the very last moment.

"Plainly I tell thee, Friend," she said in the stern accents she'd prepared to use to the duke himself, "I hope that Jervaulx has sufficiently prepared his discourse. I'm afraid there won't be time now for my father to offer any help."

Calvin gave her a bland look. "His *Grace* made no mention of anticipating Mr. Timms' counsel." He put an emphasis upon the honorific, as he always did, which Maddy understood perfectly well was meant to convey his disapproval of her Plain Speech calling of Jervaulx by the title of his temporal office. Maddy didn't give a fig for that. She would have gone further and called him by his surname as an unpretentious Quaker would call anyone else, had she happened to know what it was.

She stood still a moment, tapping her foot silently and quickly beneath her skirt. "May I speak with him?"

"I regret to say that His Grace is not at home."

Maddy's foot tapped harder. "I see. How unfortunate. Thou mayst convey my father's thanks to him, in that case." She tucked the case under her arm and turned down the steps.

Christian lay on the bed, with a cloth saturated in some evil-smelling camphor across his eyes. He grunted when he heard Calvin's scratch at the door.

"Miss Archimedea Timms has called, Your Grace. She took the papers with her."

"Good."

There was a moment of silence. "It would not require the physician a quarter hour to come," Calvin said, "if I were to send for him, Your Grace."

"I don't need a dashed sawbones. It'll go off in a minute or two." Christian swallowed.

His butler made an assenting mumble. The closing door clicked behind him. Christian dragged the musty cloth off his face and tossed it to the floor. He pressed his arm over his eyes and arched his head back, wondering if he was going to die of a damned headache before Sutherland ever got a chance at him.

Chapter Two

The Third Day evening meeting of the Analytical Society was a thundering success. For the Timmses, it began early in the afternoon, with the arrival of a powdered and liveried footman at the door of their modest house in Upper Cheyne Row, bearing a note penned in that arresting style of hand-writing favored by the Duke of Jervaulx. He would send a vehicle to convey Mr. Timms to the meeting rooms, if that would be agreeable, at the hour of half past eight o'clock. And at the conclusion of the meeting, he would be honored if Mr. Timms and his daughter would join him and Sir Charles Milner for late supper in Belgrave Square, after which he would see that they were delivered safely home in his own carriage.

"Papa!" Maddy said in horror, keeping her voice to a fierce whisper in order that the footman outside the parlor door should not overhear. "We cannot!"

"Can we not?" her papa inquired. "I shouldn't think it would be possible to attend the meeting at all, in that case, for what excuse can we offer to refuse to sup with Jervaulx afterward?"

She flushed a little. "It will be nothing but vain leisure and idle talk. He is a bad man. I know thou admirest his science, but his moral character is . . . it is abysmal!"

"I suppose so," he said reluctantly. "But shall we be the first to cast stones?"

"I rather doubt we would be the first." With a little flick, she tossed the duke's note toward the fire. The fine, heavy paper fell short, making a faint chime as it hit the brass fender. "It is not throwing stones, merely to wish not to associate with the man!"

Her father turned toward the sound of the note, and then focused on her voice. "It's but one evening."

"Thou mayst go. I shall come home as soon as the meeting is over."

"Maddy?" Papa had a half-frown upon his face. "Art thou frightened of him?"

"Indeed not! Why should I be?"

"I thought perhaps . . . he has done nothing to impose upon thee?"

Maddy gave a delicate *humph.* "Yes, he has! He has kept me waiting for hours at a stretch in his silly breakfast alcove. I can describe the wallpaper to thee in exquisite detail. It is a trellis-pattern of green on white, with a rose mallow pictured at alternating intersections, consisting of sixteen petals and three leaves, with a yellow center."

Her papa's brow cleared. "I feared he might have said something untoward to thee."

"He has never said anything at all to me, for the simple reason that he has never seen me. But thou mayst take my word that he is all that is worst in the aristocracy. Profligate, licentious and godless. We are plain people, who have no business dining with him."

Her father sat silent for a long moment. Then he lifted his brows and said wistfully, "But I wish for us to dine with him, Maddy."

His fingers toyed with a wooden *Y,* twirling it round and

round on the red baize. The oil lamp at his elbow was unlit
in the dim north light of a cloudy afternoon, the lack of illumination irrelevant to her father.

She pressed her fists together and rested her chin on them.
"Oh, Papa!"

"Shouldst thou mind very much, Maddy girl?"

She sighed. Without saying more, she opened the door to
inform the lingering footman that they would accept the
duke's invitation to supper.

In order to hide her discontent, she left her father to go
upstairs and lay out his Meeting coat and shirt and arrange
the items necessary to shave him. Then she went to her own
wardrobe. Before Jervaulx's message, she had planned to
wear her gray silk, as befitted a special occasion. She was
torn now between the corrupt desire to dress up in a manner
that would demonstrate that she and her father dined out reg-
ularly with dukes and the urge to dress down and appear as if
supping in Belgrave Square held no more appeal to her than
did rooting about in a dustbin.

In addition to the depravity involved in dressing as if one
commonly consorted with noble rakes, certain material re-
strictions made themselves apparent as she perused the dark
recess of her clothes closet. Her family was not of the gayest
orders among Friends: they had always kept to Plain Dress
and Plain Speech. The steel-gray silk, with its wide, stark,
white cotton collar, comprised the zenith of her wardrobe.
Fashioned as the gown was upon strictly pious lines, with
the elevated, out-of-date waistline, it held little hope of mas-
querading as anything more than what it was—a simple
Quaker lady's best morning dress, four years old.

She eyed her black, the one she kept for tasks such as
nursing and marketing. It was neat and proper, but visibly
shabby at the elbows. It would not do to have Papa's associates at the Society think that she cared nothing for the importance of the occasion.

In the end, she decided on the silk. And to emphasize her
personal opinion of the duke's licentious behavior, she re-

moved the white collar, leaving only the unadorned V neckline. Although there were no looking glasses in the house, she was satisfied when she held the altered gown up before her that, with its complete lack of ornament, it was of sufficient austerity.

What to do with her hair presented another dilemma. The starched sugar scoop bonnet she always wore seemed too ordinary for the occasion. Her mother, having undergone convincement to the Friends' faith and forfeited contact with her own family upon marriage, had still passed along to her daughter a few of the ways of society. Maddy thought that some little acknowledgment of the special nature of the mathematical meeting was really a requirement.

She decided to re-braid her hair. Just combing it out was no small task; it had never been cut—her mother's, and now Maddy's, only worldly vanity—growing as long as the back of her knees. After she'd braided it and coiled it around the top of her head, on a whim, she searched out a small box from the bottom of her chest and held up her mother's pearls.

She could not bring herself to be quite so daring as to wear jewelry openly around her neck, but after a little thought and some experimentation, she found that they just circled the base of the crowning braid, an exact fit. She rather thought that the jewelry didn't show at all, which seemed a comfortable compromise between heathenism and zealotry.

But as she came downstairs at quarter past eight after seeing her father suitably dressed, she had a sudden loss of nerve. She was afraid the pearls must look silly—and there was no one to ask but Papa or Geraldine, neither of whom could reasonably be expected to give any dependable advice. Maddy was holding up the silver teapot, trying without success to see herself in the rounded reflection, when her father's slow step sounded on the stairs.

A brisk knock came simultaneously at the door, and she had to rush to the top of the kitchen stair to call Geraldine, as the bell was still in disorder in spite of the landlord's express promise to have it repaired by this afternoon. Then, between seeing that her father descended safely down the stairs and keeping an eye on the footman as he helped Papa into the shining black town chariot—ornamented only by a crest on the door, consisting of a white phoenix surrounded by six golden fleur-de-lis on a blue ground—she found herself suddenly confronted with the footman's bow and offered hand. She had nothing to do but take it.

The lecture room of the Royal Institution in Albemarle Street, a vast semicircle with rising, cushioned benches able to seat nine hundred, was not often very well filled for the meetings of the Analytical Society. Those interested in and able to comprehend the philosophy of pure mathematics espoused by the Society were passionate but few, tending to cluster in the first four rows in the center, around the podium, leaving the rest of the room to echoing darkness.

As the carriage drew up in Albemarle Street, however, the pavement was quite crowded with gentlemen waiting to enter the Institution. Maddy had a horrible moment of fearing that they had arrived on the wrong night—but no, here was President Milner himself, rotund and cheerful, stepping up to the carriage door, giving her papa his support down to the curb. Maddy followed, and the crowd on the sidewalk and stairs nodded and doffed their hats, stepping aside to allow passage.

"Your servant, Miss Timms! We'll just pop into the reading room," Friend Milner said, looking over his shoulder as he guided her papa into the hall. "The duke's there. He's very anxious to meet you both."

Maddy suppressed a snort, doubting very much whether the duke felt any emotion of the kind. She fell behind a moment in the crowded hall, hesitating amid the disorder outside the cloakroom until a polite gentleman, one of the regular Society members, took her wrap for her.

"Who *are* all these people?" she whispered to him.

"I believe they've come to see the mathematical duke."

Maddy made a quick face. "Is that something like the Learned Pig?"

He chuckled and took her hand. "Convey my best wishes to Mr. Timms. I'm looking forward to this lecture."

Maddy nodded and turned away. It would be just like Jervaulx, she thought, to turn everything into a circus. She should have expected it. Her poor papa was going to be a laughingstock.

At the closed door of the reading room she paused, thinking for a distracted moment of the pearls in her hair. No one seemed to have taken any particular notice of them. She put her hand to the braid, to make certain they hadn't fallen loose.

They were still there. She felt as if they must make her look a rather foolish and eccentric old maid, which she supposed that she was, actually—a Quaker, one of the Peculiar People, made even more so by the vain addition of pearls to her tightly braided hair. The thought gave her an odd spurt of amusement at herself: what a picture she must make to this dissolute duke!

Well—so be it, then. She'd give him a shock. He'd probably never had to dine with the likes of Archimedea Timms. With a faint smile at the corners of her lips, she pushed open the door.

At the far end of the dimly lit room, her papa sat in his low-crowned, broad-brimmed hat at one of the tables where the day's newspapers had been shoved aside to make a large space. President Milner was absent. The other man seated there in the pool of candlelight was bent over a sheaf of papers with an intensity that Maddy had last seen in the students she helped teach at the First Day School. His elbows were spread, straining the tailoring of his midnight blue evening coat across broad shoulders, and as she came closer, he pushed back his dark hair impatiently with one hand—giving an excellent impression of some wild poet laboring in a garret over his art.

Suddenly, before she reached them, he threw down the

pen and rose to face her in one swift motion, for all the world as if he wished to hide what he'd been doing.

He looked at her for an instant, and then smiled.

The fervent student, the impassioned poet, both vanished in that seasoned gallantry. "Miss Timms," he said, in just the way a duke would say it—calmly, with a slight bow. His eyes were dusky blue, his nose straight and strong, his clothing perfectly tailored and his bearing well-bred; and somehow, in spite of this polished veneer, he managed very well to resemble a complete and utter pirate.

Precisely as one had expected—although somewhat less decayed, in a physical sense, by his way of life than might have been supposed. He gave the impression of a firmly controlled energy, with nothing dilatory or degenerated about him—no softness at all to his solid and imposing frame. Next to him, her father looked fatally pale, as if he might dissolve into a wisp and vanish at any moment.

"My daughter Archimedea," Papa said. "Maddy—this is the Duke of Jervaulx."

He pronounced it entirely differently from the way they'd been saying it—as if it began with an "sh" and didn't rhyme with "talks" at all, but instead with a sound like "hoe." She felt exceedingly provincial, realizing that their habitual "Jervalks" wasn't even remotely correct and recalling with mortifying clarity the number of times she must have mispronounced it to his butler. She sincerely hoped they had Friend Milner to thank for the information, and not Jervaulx himself.

She offered her hand to shake, abstaining from a salutation or curtsy, or even a nod, as befitted a plain person and a Friend. She'd been brought up to shun such mumbling customs as saying "Good evening," for to wish someone a good day when he was in an evil day was to offend God and the Truth. Nor could she say that she was happy to make the duke's acquaintance, as that would have been another untruth, so she settled for the universal address of: "Friend."

His greeting was not so spare. "It's my wholehearted

pleasure to be at your service, mademoiselle." He caught her hand and lifted it briefly, lowering his eyes, then released her. "I must apologize to Miss Archimedea for all the hours I find I've kept her cooling her heels in my house. I've been cursed with a headache these past two days."

Maddy wondered what his excuse was for all the days before that, but Papa only said, "I hope thou hast recovered," with every evidence of real concern. Her father always told the truth, so of course he would believe the man, poor naive Papa.

"Quite recovered." The duke grinned, and winked at Maddy, as if they were some sort of conspirators together. "Miss Archimedea had her doubts, I know."

Her father smiled. "Yes, she's in a great quake over whether thou'lt shame me beyond holding my head up on Third Nights ever again."

"Papa!"

At that moment, President Milner scratched at the door and came in, spreading his arms and whisking his hands like an enthusiastic shooer of chickens. "Miss Timms, Mr. Timms—it's time. Come and be seated, and then the duke and I shall take our places in front."

"I'll need Miss Timms," the duke said, catching her arm as she started toward her papa. "If you would . . ." He looked into her eyes.

It was, Maddy knew instantly, the kind of look he must use on those women who fell willingly under his influence and into his arms. Even she, who at twenty-eight had only been courted once, by a very conventional doctor who had accepted her refusal with painful regret and then engaged himself to a Jane Hutton and left the Quaker Meeting within the half-year, even Maddy could identify that intense and faintly questioning glance and sense the kind of power it was meant to wield.

Therefore, when he only held out the sheaf of papers toward her and asked if she would transcribe the equations on the slate for him as he spoke, it was something of an anticlimax. She looked down at the papers. "Thou dost not wish to do it? The slate is just behind the podium. Most of the speakers—"

"I don't," he said flatly.

"Come, come." Mr. Milner had the door open, admitting the low rumble from the lecture room. "Let us all go at once, then. Mr. Timms?"

It was Jervaulx himself who took her father's arm, guiding him into the hall and down the steps to the first seat. The president waved Maddy on up to the row of stiff-backed chairs on the podium; the duke followed her, their steps loud and hollow on the wooden platform. He made a gentle adjustment of her chair as she sat and flicked back his coattails in an elegant, relaxed way as he took the place beside her.

The hall quieted as President Milner stepped up to the lectern, turning the shade of the little gas lamp and clearing his throat. Maddy gazed out at the wash of faces, each one underlined by a white collar that seemed to float in a background of uniform black. She'd attended many meetings, of the Analytical Society and the Friends both, occupying a seat in the back benches with her papa, but never had she sat in front of any sort of audience before, let alone one so large. She told herself that everyone was attending to the president, who'd called the meeting to order and begun introducing the paper and describing her father as co-author, but it was easy to recall how one's mind and eyes wandered as a spectator. Several of the gentlemen in the first few rows were most definitely looking past President Milner: at herself or the duke, she couldn't be certain, but she felt agonizingly exposed in her plain silk and pearls.

She felt acutely aware, too, of how real and solid and inescapably large Jervaulx seemed sitting next to her, in midnight blue, his white-gloved hands clasped in his lap, not a bit of quiver or restlessness in them, which made Maddy force herself to stop the squeezing and unsqueezing of her own fingers. He seemed very certain of himself, quite easy and oblivious of the weight of attention focused on him as

President Milner expressed the honor felt by the gathered company in having such a luminary as Christian Richard Nicholas Francis Langland, His Grace the Duke of Jervaulx, Earl of Langland and Viscount Glade, condescend to address the London Analytical Society this night.

The duke rose to applause. He carried no notes, having handed the papers to Maddy. She might have known that he would have a talent for speaking in a pleasant, relaxed voice, which nevertheless carried as he announced gravely that this lecture was dedicated to the memory of his late tutor, Mr. Peeples, an estimable, learned man, a credit to his profession, worthy of his pupil's everlasting regard and respect; and the duke really was sincerely sorry about the dead smelt in the lesson book.

They all laughed, even her papa.

It pained Jervaulx, the memory of that smelt, and somehow the smelt led to the page of the book it had adorned, and that page led to the parallel postulate of Euclid, and differential geometry, and then amid the lingering chuckles from some obscure jest about his passion for examining into the allure of certain irresistible curved surfaces, he was turning to nod expectantly at her.

Maddy jumped to her feet, took up the chalk and began filling the big slate. She was accustomed to the duke's handwriting, but it was difficult to decipher at the best of times. She dared not make any mistakes now, bending her entire concentration to transcribing correctly the order of equations and copying the circles and the lines that transected them. Endless hours of work with her papa had given her a knack for following the sequence under consideration; she listened for certain series as Jervaulx spoke of them, judging when to proceed to the next formula and erase the last to gain more room. She only faltered once, lingering too long on a page, until Jervaulx's pause when he turned toward the slate cued her to her error; she hastily scrubbed off five equations and scribbled out the top half of the duke's next page.

When she reached the last of his notes, she was ahead of him; he was still describing the progression of the proof several steps back. But as Maddy finished copying the final equation, adding a flourish to the integral between zero and r out of pure relief, and immediately sat down, a rustle began to grow within the audience. Jervaulx kept speaking. Slowly, gentlemen in the audience began to stand up—one, then another, then by twos and threes and fives, all gazing at the slate.

Someone started to clap. Others took it up. A rumble developed into a reverberation as more and more stood. The clapping became applause, and the applause rose to a roar, drowning out words.

The duke stopped speaking. Amid the resounding acclaim, he looked back at Maddy with a grin and made a little motion behind the podium toward her papa—but Mr. Milner was already escorting him up onto the floor.

The vigor and sound of the ovation doubled; the gentlemen began stamping their feet, making the room vibrate with noise. Maddy stood up, taking Papa's hand to squeeze it in delight. He patted the back of her palm, and the little quivering smile at the corners of his lips, the exhilaration in his face, was something Maddy had not seen since the day her mother had died six years ago.

Pure energy boomed around them, a tangible throb of tribute. Jervaulx reached out and shook her father's hand, holding onto it when Papa refused to let go. The duke inclined his head a little, with a half-embarrassed smile: a look, if Maddy could have brought herself to believe it, that spoke almost of shyness. For an instant one might nearly imagine him an eager and awkward boy, full of innocent enthusiasm—and then he turned to her and lifted her hand, bending over it with a glance into her eyes that was completely a schooled and experienced man's: a suggestive intimacy that would mark a rogue at fifty paces.

He leaned close to her ear, using her hand to hold her so

near that she could feel the warmth of him and breathe the
faint whiff of sandalwood. "What do you think, Miss
Archimedea?" he said, just loud enough to be heard above
the din.

Maddy took a step back, pulling away. "What have we
done?"

"What have you done?" President Milner bellowed.
"Proved a geometry outside Euclid, m'girl! Burst the parallel postulate! A whole new universe! By God, if this is as
flawless as it looks to be—" He clapped Papa and the duke
both upon the back, shouting amid the clamor. "The pair of
you are wizards, my men! Wizards!"

"The credit must all go to thee, Friend," Papa repeated yet
again. Maddy had counted six times; this one was the seventh. "Verily it must."

Jervaulx shook his head and took a sip of wine. "Nonsense, Mr. Timms." He smiled wickedly. "You're going to do
the hard part. Write the paper."

The four of them sat at a round table in the bay window of
a lovely, cozy room overlooking the darkened square.
Maddy had never penetrated this far into the duke's house
before; the blue chintz and comfortable chairs surprised her.
She had not thought a bachelor would be able to make such
a warm home for himself.

He looked bachelor enough, though, having pushed his
chair back from the cleared table for room to stretch his legs,
dangling his wineglass by negligent fingers at the rim.
Maddy sat primly in her seat, taking only indirect glances
round the room to see how it was fitted up.

Papa was flushed and contented, a little abstracted, as if
he still could not believe that the peak moment of the evening were true: when the Duke of Jervaulx, over an exotic
and delicious creation of fish and asparagus, had casually
asked if her father would consider taking the mathematical
chair at the new college that he and his political associates

were organizing, where there would be no religious tests for entry, but only the express purpose of educating adult students in the whole field of modern knowledge.

It came as something of a jolt to realize that the duke might actually be a supporter of a worthy cause. But indeed, he was so intelligent and persuasive upon the topic, and so committed, that even Friend Milner—who was a High Church Tory if Maddy had ever seen one and who had initially been quite cross when the Timmses had addressed him as "Friend" instead of "Sir Charles," although he had grown used to it in time—even Friend Milner had his initial doubts turned to enthusiasm and recommended Papa consider the proposition seriously.

Papa, Maddy could see, had gone far beyond consideration and plunged ahead into cheerful daydreams. And indeed, when the duke mentioned the endowment that he had already pledged in support of the mathematical chair, Maddy herself felt a bloom of encouragement. It would be unwelcome to have a gazetted rake as a patron, but there need not be more than restricted intercourse, if any at all. She entertained visions of a house large enough to have a garden, and a parlor bell that was always in order.

In the midst of these pleasant fancies, Friend Milner excused himself to smoke. He left the door ajar; within moments, the brisk clip of dog paws on a polished floor heralded the entrance of a setter, its silky white coat flung about with black spots, as if a can of dark paint had been scattered over it. With no more than a sideways glance at the duke, the animal bounded straight to Maddy and cast itself upon her lap, forelegs spread across her skirt and spotted pink nose stretched to lick her chin.

"Devil!" The stern command caused the dog to look inquiringly round at Jervaulx, wagging its tail without removing its feathered front legs from Maddy's lap.

She smiled and rubbed its ears. "What a bad dog," she murmured under her breath, as if it were a secret between them. "What a very bad dog thou art." Devil returned adoring brown eyes to hers, grinning widely at this accusation. Another growled order from the duke made the spotted head sink. With an apologetic wrinkle of his brow, Devil subsided backward onto the floor. Jervaulx gave the animal a protracted stare. After a moment, Devil's tail drooped, and he took himself from the room with the most dejected and dragging aspect. His master, heartless, stood up and shut him out.

The eviction of Devil left a lull in the room. Maddy stared ahead of her at the snowy tablecloth as the duke reseated himself with a brief apology. She had a notion that Jervaulx would think the Timmses very unpolished; there were so many silences that he and Friend Milner had been obliged to fill up. Maddy was not accustomed to idle talk; as a child she had labored too hard to school herself in the biblical injunction "Let your words be few" to find it easy to chatter now. She enjoyed dogs, but had never owned one, nor known any but mongrels, so she had no discourse to offer on the topic to someone like Jervaulx, who most probably was a famous breeder or some such thing and would think her sadly uninformed.

She would have liked very much to inquire into the expense of the pretty fabric that covered the chairs, but held her tongue on that. Plain Quaker homes had no such creaturely baubles as printed chintz upholstery or paintings on display on all the walls. The only picture in the Timms house was a rather awkward painting of a slave ship, approved by the elders as a reminder of the sufferings of their fellow man. As she was gazing at an ornately framed still life hung over a music stand, with the surprisingly demure theme of rough-cut lilac stems thrown down beside a clutch of robin's eggs, Jervaulx spoke.

"How long ago did you lose your sight, Mr. Timms?" he asked.

Maddy stiffened a little in her chair, surprised by such a pointed personal question. But her papa only said mildly, "Many years. Almost . . . fifteen, would it be, Maddy?"

"Eighteen, Papa," she said quietly.

"Ah." He nodded. "And thou hast been my blessing every one of them, Maddy girl."

Jervaulx sat relaxed, resting his elbow on the chair arm, his jaw propped on his fist. "You haven't seen your daughter since she was a child, then," he murmured. "May I describe her to you?"

She was unprepared for such a suggestion, or for the light of interest that dawned in her father's face. Her objection died forming as Papa said, "Wilt thou? Wilt thou indeed?"

Jervaulx gazed at Maddy. As she felt her face growing hot, his smile turned into that unprincipled grin, and he said, "It would be my pleasure." He tilted his head, studying her. "We've made her blush already, I fear—a very delicate blush, the color of . . . clouds, I think. The way the mist turns pink at dawn—do you remember what I mean?"

"Yes," her father said seriously.

"Her face is . . . dignified, but not quite stern. Softer than that, but she has a certain way of turning up her chin that might give a man pause. She's taller than you are, but not unbecomingly tall. It's that chin, I think, and a very upright, quiet way she holds herself. It gives her presence. But she only comes to my nose, so . . . she must be a good five inches under six foot one," he said judiciously. "She appears to me to be healthy, not too stout nor thin. In excellent frame."

"Rather like a good milk cow!" Maddy exclaimed.

"And there goes the chin up," Jervaulx said. "She's perhaps a little more the color of a light claret, now that I've provoked her. All the way from her throat to her cheeks— even a little lower than her throat, but she's perfectly pale and soft below that, as far as I can see."

Maddy clapped her hand over the V neck of her gown, suddenly feeling that it must be entirely too low-cut. "Papa—" She looked to her father, but he had his face turned downward and a peculiar smile on his lips.

"Her hair," Jervaulx said, "is tarnished gold where the

candlelight touches it, and where it doesn't . . . richer—more like the light through a dark ale as you pour it. She has it braided and coiled around her head. I believe she thinks that it's a plain style, but she doesn't realize the effect. It shows the curve of her neck and her throat, and makes a man think of taking it down and letting it spread out over his hands."

"Thou art unseemly," her father chided in a mild tone.

"My apologies, Mr. Timms. I can hardly help myself. Shall we proceed to her nose? That, we shall call a nose of—character. I don't think we can call it perfect: it's a little too aquiline for that. A decided nose. A maiden lady's nose. It goes with the tilt of the chin. But her eyes . . . I'm afraid her eyes ruin the spinster effect again, most emphatically. And her mouth. She has a pensive, a very pretty mouth, that doesn't smile overly often." He took a sip of wine. "But then again—let's be fair. I've definitely seen her smile at you, but she hasn't favored me at all. This serious mouth might have been insipid, but instead it goes with the wonderful long lashes that haven't got that silly debutante curl. They're straight, but they're so long and angled down that they shadow her eyes and turn the hazel to gold, and she seems as if she's looking out through them at me. No . . ." He shook his head sadly. "Miss Timms, I regret to tell you that it isn't a spinster effect at all. I've never had a spinster look out beneath her lashes at me the way you do."

In his house, at his table, she felt that she could not say precisely what she thought of him and his spinsters. Besides that, her father appeared enraptured. "Maddy," he whispered. "Thou hast thy mother's look."

"Of course, Papa," she said helplessly. "Has no one ever told thee?"

"No. No one ever did."

He said it without any particular emotion. But by the candlelight, she could see that his eyes had tears in them. "Papa," she said, reaching for his hand. He only brushed it, and then lifted his fingers, touching her face. He explored

her slowly, intently, over her cheeks and across her eyelashes. She held her hands locked tight, embarrassed and
suddenly close to foolish tears herself.

She had never thought of it: she could have sat and let her
father envision her with his touch in this way any time. He
looked so happy. It was just that life went on, an everyday
thing, and one never considered that Papa had not seen her
face for eighteen years, or might wish to.

"I thank thee, Friend," her father said, turning his face toward the duke. "I thank thee. For one of the finest days of
my life."

Jervaulx didn't answer. He didn't even seem to have
heard, but sat gazing into the shadowed folds of the tablecloth, his dark blue eyes meditative and his pirate mouth
turned grim.

Chapter Three

*N*o pink tinged the dawn fog in the way he'd described last night. Rather poetic of him, Christian had thought, but in reality everything was only whitish-gray, the grass wet and dark, voices uncanny and sharp in the early silence. He could hear his own even breathing as he took the pistol from the case Durham offered and sighted down the slender barrel.

He didn't think he was going to die this morning. He wasn't going to kill anyone, that was certain. Being guilty as the devil in this affair, his only honorable course was to stand fire and then delope. He'd shoot into the air. So—Sutherland might hit him. Likely would. But Christian didn't think he was going to die.

He found it distantly amusing that he was so sure of that. He was old enough to know better. A decade and a half ago, the first time he'd stood up at the fire-eating age of seventeen, he might have been excused for believing himself invincible. But now . . . he looked around at the brightening sky and the new leaves—and still his heart said it was impossible that this was the last moment.

Wounding was nothing to look forward to. He chose not to think ahead about it. He could feel his heart's rhythm rising as he walked out onto the ground without looking at Sutherland beside him.

They stood up and paced off. Christian held the pistol in his right hand, there being no need for accuracy. It gave a better appearance; those who knew him would see that he'd had no intention of firing on Sutherland from the start.

Durham's languid voice called halt and turn.

Christian turned.

Sutherland had his pistol raised already. Christian realized that there was murder in his opponent's face. The man intended execution; he had the skill to do it. Christian's pulse increased suddenly, a fierce thud in his ears.

"Gentlemen," Durham said, lifting his handkerchief.

Pain burst through Christian's skull, agony and strangeness. He stared at Sutherland, blinking twice, wondering why he hadn't heard the shot that hit him.

Durham spoke again. Christian couldn't understand the words. Sutherland's face contorted; he was shouting something at Christian, and Christian couldn't understand that either, but Sutherland was holding his gun at level ready still.

Christian tried to lift his right arm. He squinted at Sutherland, trying to see through the way his vision seemed clear and blurred at once, turning his face to the side to find his opponent. Durham spoke one word. From his fingers, the pale cloth dropped to the ground.

Christian heard the shot and whistle, saw the drift of white from Sutherland's pistol and knew the man had missed, but Christian was falling while he was still standing up. His pistol dropped out of his hand. It went off with a blast as it struck the ground.

Christian stood swaying, staring down, trying to see it.

He'd been hit. Had he been hit?

Durham and Fane came striding toward him. He felt that he was falling, over and over, but he never reached the ground. Their words babbled around him, meaningless. He tried to put out his right hand to lean on Fane's shoulder, but he couldn't lift it. When he looked down, it didn't even seem part of him. He could barely see. He tried to find the blood, couldn't find it, and gazed in bewilderment at his friends.

"What's wrong?" he said.

It came out, *no.*

No, no, no, no.

Fane shook his head and grinned, thumping Christian on the back with a look of triumph. Durham was smiling.

Christian grabbed the colonel's arm with his left hand. "Fane," he said. "What happened?"

No, no, no, no, no.

He heard himself. He closed his mouth in horror, tried to form the right words, breathing hard through his teeth.

"Fane!" he yelled.

And they stared at him, because he still hadn't said it right. He gripped Fane's arm. Half of the other man's face seemed hazy to Christian, blurring off into the gray fog. His heart was a huge drum pounding in his ears. He wanted to let go of Fane, to press his hands over his eyes, but he couldn't command the move. He couldn't say anything at all. He could only pull himself close enough to put his weight on his friend's shoulder, with the world tipping and sliding away from him, the darkness rising up over his brain, coming in from the edges of his vision, taking it all; taking everything . . .

The fineness of the morning could only add to the pleasure Maddy felt in the day. She strolled briskly along the King's Road and past the new construction in Eaton Square, even finding it in herself to admire the architecture of the mansions under construction, designed as they were in the style of the duke's house in Belgrave Square.

This morning, over breakfast, she and Papa had talked of nothing but the chair at the university-to-be. Jervaulx had said it was to open its doors next year, under the admirable name of the University of London, but the professorships and preparations must begin much sooner, possibly as early as Ninth Month. A premises had already been taken in

Gower Street, and Maddy thought that after she called in Belgrave Square, she might go on to Bloomsbury and look into any houses available there.

For this call, she carried no sheets of figures, only a letter that she and her father had composed together, thanking Jervaulx for their supper and his kind attentions, and expressing unqualified praise for his excellent address before the Society last night. After some debate, they had agreed on the proper degree of gratitude and enthusiasm to convey about the mathematics chair—Maddy being inclined to somewhat less effusion than her father, but well aware that an apparent lack of delight in the offer would be fatal.

She turned the corner into the square and paused. Normally there were a few ragged persons loitering about the luxurious houses in hopes of stray coins, but just now a regular crowd of bystanders, very mixed in their appearance, milled around a green curricle in front of the duke's house.

Maddy pressed her lips together. There was straw strewn in the street and the curricle, with its neat pair of grays, had much the look of a physician's rig. As she stood hesitating at the corner, a large coach, drawn by a team of blacks and emblazoned with a raised medallion sporting the full heraldic bearings and crest of the family, motto and all, came dashing round the far side of the square. The cluster of onlookers scattered, and the boy holding the curricle hurried the pair forward to make room as the coach rumbled to a halt before the door.

Even before the footman had jumped down off his perch to lower the steps, the carriage door was being pushed open from inside. An elderly lady groped for the footman's hand and came swiftly down, lifting up her black skirts and advancing with an agitated thrust of her cane. Maddy saw Calvin rush down the stairs to her side; he held her arm up the stairs, as a younger woman descended from the carriage. The footman supported her to the top of the stairs, where this second lady appeared to lose her strength entirely: she faltered and seemed to wilt against the servant. His arm came around her, bracing her into the house. The door slammed shut behind them.

The little crowd stood about, murmuring. Maddy could not seem to think what to do. Her feet took her slowly forward, step by step, as if her mind had relegated the decision to her body.

At the edge of the group, leaning against the wrought iron rail that flanked the house, the crossing boy who usually swept the corner looked up at Maddy and gave her a nod of recognition. She stood uncertainly, and after a moment, he came up to her.

"'Mornin', Miss. Has you heard?"

She glanced up. The windows were all shaded ominously. And straw was spread in the street to muffle carriage wheels, as if there were serious illness in the house . . .

"No. I haven't heard."

"It's His Grace, Miss. Shot."

"Shot?" Maddy whispered.

The boy nodded toward the coach. "Family's been called," he said succinctly. "Too late, Tom says. Tom's in the stables, saw 'em go out before first light; saw his grace brung back on a hurdle. Duel, Miss. Gone and kilt him, Tom says. Dead when they carried him in." He shrugged. "Still—there's the medical man here yet. Waitin' for the family, I expect."

Maddy stared up at the house, beyond words. The murmur of gossip subsided suddenly. They all stood listening to what had stifled it: the distant sound of a woman's shriek—a tearing, rising note—the high-pitched keening moan of denial, cascading down to anguish. Maddy's throat went dry and closed. The wail broke off abruptly as if someone else had hushed it, and the people outside gave one another knowing looks.

She gripped her hands together. She couldn't think. She didn't believe it. Last night, just last night—she had never seen anyone more fully alive, more vibrant with spirit and substance.

A duel. A senseless, futile exchange of shots. An instant, and all that life was gone.

How could that be? Her mind balked at it. She had known him to be what he was: a rake, a reprobate—before yesterday she would have said, yes, I believe it, the Duke of Jervaulx was shot and killed in a duel this morning. But now it shocked her into suspension, so that when she turned away, she didn't know where to go or what to do.

She walked along blindly, clutching her hands together.

He'd known last night, of course. He'd sat there smiling at them, talking of geometry, describing her to her father. All the time, he'd known he was to go out and face this in a few hours.

It was beyond the capability of her mind to grasp. She'd lost her mother, and some friends, all to illness, all much older—not this sudden dizzying turn in reality.

And his own mother—dear God, what she must feel! She was the second of the two ladies, Maddy was sure in her heart, remembering that faltering collapse at the door. Oh, she had perceived it already, had known before they told her, had given that terrible cry when she was sure. The other—in black, the elderly one who had gone in as if to a battle—it would be she who would show nothing, stand stiff and proud, grieving silently.

Maddy felt somehow as if she should be there, offering what help she could to them. She found herself instead inside the door of her parlor, in her own little house. Her papa lifted his head, smiling.

"Home already, Maddy girl?"

"Oh, Papa!" she said.

His smile faded. He sat up. "What is it?"

"I hardly know—I don't—" She gave a little dry moan, holding onto the doorknob. "He's dead, Papa! He was killed in a duel this morning!"

Her father sat very still, his hands poised over his wooden symbols. After a long, silent moment, he said, "Dead."

The word had a hollow sound. Maddy sank to her knees

beside him, leaning her head in his lap. "It is—such a shock."

His fingers rested on her hair. She hadn't put on her bonnet today; she wore her hair in the same braids she'd worn last night. He stroked lightly up and down the nape of her neck. He touched her cheek and caught the single tear that had escaped.

Maddy lifted her head. "I don't know why I'm—why I should be weeping! I didn't even like him!"

"Didst thou not, Maddy girl?" he asked softly. "I did."

He went on stroking her hair. She rested her cheek against his leg, staring off into the corner of the room.

"I can't believe it," she whispered. "I just cannot seem to believe it."

Chapter Four

*B*lythedale Hall looked to Maddy like a handsomely decorated cake, with soft salmon-colored brick set off by straight pilasters and arched curves of pale stone frosting. Cousin Edward's new retreat included a large piece of Buckinghamshire countryside, with a rose garden heavy in Tenth Month blossoms, a herd of fallow deer roaming the open park, and black swans gliding serenely on the lake, all legacies of the impoverished baronet who had sold it and now carefully maintained for the calming and beneficiary effects upon Cousin Edward's patients.

Papa's cousin Dr. Edward Timms supervised Blythedale in the most modern and humane manner. Each of his charges had his own personal attendant; a wholesome restraint was imposed only in the most intractable cases and removed as quickly as practicable. He was dedicated to his work, describing the therapies and management in enthusiastic detail in between cutting up bacon for himself and inviting Papa to take another kipper or more coffee.

Maddy could hear a woman crying—a most disturbing and audible sound—but Cousin Edward seemed not to notice it, and after a while it faded away. She sipped at her coffee, trying to arm herself for the tour ahead: her first view of the place and people, and a description of her position.

Cousin Edward had assured her that the duties were of a supervisory nature, rather than heavy work. There would be an experienced attendant to serve Papa while she was occupied, and altogether it had seemed impossible to refuse Cousin Edward's invitation to come and assume his wife's managerial functions while she was confined with her third child, on the expectation that if all went satisfactorily, the post might become Maddy's permanently. The offer appeared especially propitious after the disappointment of the letter regarding the mathematical chair, from one Henry Brougham, regretting that the funds pledged by the Duke of Jervaulx had been withdrawn and the chair endowed by another source, a gentleman who wished to remain anonymous but who preferred a different candidate to Mr. Timms.

And verily, Buckinghamshire and Blythedale seemed perfect in the autumn morning, with sunlight warming the newly painted marigold-yellow walls of the dining room, sparkling off the silver and fine porcelain plate that had been surrendered by the penniless baronet along with the paintings and furniture. The house smelled of fresh wax and new hangings. Nothing dismal had been allowed to remain, Cousin Edward pointed out.

Everything was peaceful and pleasant, if far too sumptuous for Maddy's notion of Quakerly virtue. But the surroundings were fitted up to the well-bred tastes of Cousin Edward's patients. There was only that distant sound of weeping to mar the opulence, coming again through the closed doors like some lost and grieving daylight ghost.

"Shall we begin, Cousin?" The doctor wiped his mouth and lifted the bell at his elbow. "Janie, call Blackwell to escort Mr. Timms to the family drawing room."

The maid curtsied, spreading her apron, and vanished. Papa's aide arrived a moment later, the whole procedure a clockwork silence. After Maddy had seen him off, Cousin Edward escorted her to his office on the first floor.

"The mail." He nodded toward a basket on his desk. Cousin Edward had the same soft, comfortable, placid features as her father, but his dark eyes were quick and intelligent, his mouth pursing often. He did not strictly adhere to Plain Dress or Plain Speech. Though there was no collar on his coat, it was made of visibly costly fabric. If he seemed pleased with himself, Maddy supposed that he had a right to be, as the most successful member of the Timms family, with a flourishing practice in his medical specialty and his fresh, enlarged and luxurious premises at Blythedale.

"That will be one of your duties," he said, "sorting the post directly it arrives. Open mine and leave it in the basket; whatever is addressed to the patients must be added to their files."

She looked up at him. "Copied, dost thou mean?"

"No need for that. Simply open and file the letters themselves. Or if you feel that the contents are important or unusual, bring them to me. On occasion, an edited version isn't amiss."

"Excuse me—I'm not certain . . ." She touched the pile of mail. "Dost thou intend that the patients aren't to have their letters?"

"It's imperative that we maintain our clients in a state of complete tranquility and quiet at all times. Close communications with families is bound to overexcite. We recommend that the relatives not write at all, but as you can see, they will insist."

"Oh," Maddy said.

"And I remind you that none of the patients presently under care are of our persuasion. I must request that you refrain from using the Plain Speech. Some of them find it offensive to be addressed so familiarly." He flushed slightly under Maddy's grave stare. "We may use it among ourselves, of course—there is no question of that. But perhaps it would be best to have a policy of restricting it to the private rooms."

"I shall try, but—"

"I'm sure you can do it. Take your cue from me. Just let me get my casebook—we'll introduce you to everyone first. We're like a family here; it's important that you always think in that way. I feel myself a father to every poor soul who comes to Blythedale. And you'll find the patients very like children. Think of them as such, and you won't go far wrong."

"Yes," she said. Somewhere in the house, several tenors had taken up a cheerful rendition of some song, while a man began shouting unintelligibly, hysterically, over the notes.

"You'll grow accustomed to it," her father's cousin said, smiling a little. "Some are recovering, but some are very ill."

"Yes," she said, and drew a breath. "I understand."

There were, at present, fifteen patients at Blythedale Hall, fifteen unfortunate ladies and gentlemen who were yet fortunate enough that their families would pay for their residence and treatment at the most lavish private lunatic asylum in the country. With the excellent reputation of Dr. Edward Timms for moral and medical therapy, Blythedale was even more exclusive than Dr. Newington's Ticehurst House in Sussex. Families were not encouraged to visit at Blythedale, but anyone without a personal connection to a patient was welcome at any time to tour the asylum with the attendance of an aide. The house had nothing to hide behind its walls, nothing inhumane or degrading. The most up-to-date treatments of wholesome diet, cold baths, calming routine and rehabilitating entertainment were practiced in an orderly atmosphere at Blythedale.

The ladies sewed and walked in the rose garden, played battledore, took soothing herbal teas, sometimes were allowed to sketch outdoor scenes. The gentlemen followed the same regimen, except that in place of sewing, they had gymnastics and chess and the selection of books provided in the library, and might walk as far afield as the home wood to collect flowers and leaves for the ladies to sketch. Everyone who was capable could attend weekly scientific lectures and play cards, and there was an Anglican vicar who conducted services for all but the most unruly.

Blythedale was singular and forward-thinking among asylums, Cousin Edward informed her, in that a particular effort was made to mix the sexes in a normal social atmosphere, which the one-to-one ratio of attendants made both plausible and safe. He took her first to the drawing room, where the singers were gathered around a flutist. The terrible shouting had stopped, but one of the tenors wore a straitwaistcoat, its white sleeves tied behind his back. His attendant, a wiry, muscular young man with a look of the farm about him, stood close by. As Maddy and Dr. Timms entered, the patient gazed at her hopefully.

"Have you come to take me home?" the man in the straitwaistcoat asked her. "I'm supposed to go home today."

"This afternoon," Cousin Edward said, "Kelly will take you for a walk."

His face began to color. "But I must go home! My wife is dying!"

Cousin Edward glanced at the attendant. Kelly said, "Let's sit down and rest, Master John."

"She's calling me. I am the redeemed of Jesus Christ!" The man flung himself forward. Kelly caught him deftly by a strap on the back of the waistcoat, hauling him reeling off-balance. "I *am* the redeemed of the redeemed of the Lord! My wife died for *me!* She sacrificed her life for *me!* I'm *saved,* do you hear me, sir? *I tell you I'm—*"

His voice kept rising, going faster and higher as Kelly tugged him toward the door. The rest of the patients, three other men and five ladies, appeared unconcerned, except for one of the tenors, who began to laugh. A girl, young and quite lovely, dressed in an elegant gown, sat staring out the window without emotion, while next to her a woman bent over her sewing, rocking and whispering. The tenor's laughter died away, and he bit his lip with an apologetic look at Maddy.

The wild shouting went on, growing distant, but Cousin

Edward began to introduce her to each patient, whether or not he got a reply, and then to the patient's attendant. He made notes in his book, and handed it to Maddy to read the details.

"Miss Susanna's illness is melancholia," he said. "It troubles her very deeply. How do you feel today, Miss Susanna?"

"I'm fine," the girl said listlessly.

"Do you care to sing?"

"No, thank you, Doctor."

Mind is full of apprehensions—Maddy read. *Suffers torments from the most trivial thoughts   poor appetite, restless sleep   talks of suicide, attempted to destroy herself by drowning—formerly was happy and willing in common feminine pursuits—melancholia followed upon disturbances in menstruation brought on by overstimulation of the mind with excessive schoolwork and intellectual endeavors, diverting blood flow from nourishment of female organs.*

He smiled and patted Miss Susanna's shoulder and moved on. Maddy was introduced to Mrs. Humphrey, who suffered from dementia and progressive idiocy. The lady smiled cheerfully and asked Maddy if she were one of the Cunninghams.

"No," Maddy said. "I'm Archimedea Timms."

"I saw you in India." Mrs. Humphrey had about her the slightly sour tang of an unchanged baby. "You took my clothes off."

"Oh, no. Thou art—you're mistaken."

"At half past six." Mrs. Humphrey nodded. "That would be hats."

Does not recognize husband or children, the casebook said. *Dementia and progressive deterioration of intellect precipitated by onset of the climacteric disease of women.*

"Please help Mrs. Humphrey to her room for attention," the doctor said to her attendant. He had a little frown between his brows. "I must ask that you be more vigilant of hygienic concerns."

The patients in the drawing room represented the most

manageable of Blythedale's inmates, Maddy found. Master Philip, the tenor, felt fuzzy, and his food tasted strange. He laughed whenever he heard something sad, he told Maddy, which was very upsetting to him. He giggled as he said it. Lady Emmaline roundly insisted that she was an orphan, a foundling who had lost her family to the guillotine, in spite of Cousin Edward's gentle suggestion that her parents were Lord and Lady Cathcarte, who resided in Leicestershire very much alive. But her navel was disappearing, Lady Emmaline informed him stoutly, as if that proved her case.

Beyond those in the parlor, other patients were confined to their rooms behind doubled doors, the outer of heavy wood, the inner of iron bars. Most of the furniture had been removed except for the patient's bed and a cot for the attendant.

Mania, read the book, *dangerous and destructive— derangement and breakdown precipitated by the overstudy of religion.*

And in another case, *Violent epileptic—restraint required at all times.*

And another: *Dementia—confused speech—hallucinatory—incontinent—atrophy of the emotions.*

Yet even with these patients, Cousin Edward spoke personally, and repeated to Maddy the advantage of strict daily routine, plain, wholesome food and habits of discipline in reestablishing self-control and diverting weakened minds from unhealthy preoccupations.

Maddy tried to believe him. She tried to absorb his matter-of-fact and optimistic humor, but mostly she wished she might curl up in her own bed in Chelsea and weep for these poor creatures. She'd thought herself strong-minded, an experienced sickroom nurse, but the accumulated introductions of the day made Blythedale Hall seem a very comfortable and ghastly sort of purgatory.

"Ah—we're having ourselves shaved," Cousin Edward said, looking through a set of the open bars that replaced doors on the rooms of the most violent patients. He paused before unlocking the door, and leaned over to murmur to

Maddy, "This is one of our most tragic cases, I fear. An example of moral insanity which has blossomed into mania."

She bit her lip, wishing that he hadn't told her. It made her even more reluctant than before to lift her face and look at the next unfortunate inmate of the asylum.

"Good afternoon," the doctor said warmly as he moved inside. "How do you do today, sir?"

The patient made no answer, and the attendant said, "Not a bad day, Doctor. Not too bad."

Maddy finally forced herself to step into the doorway and lift her head. The burly attendant stropped a razor; he looked like a prizefighter, with his hair cut close as fuzz to his head. A few feet away, in pale breeches and white shirtsleeves, manacled by one arm to the bedstead, another man stood silhouetted, staring away from them out the window.

"Friend," she compelled herself to say in greeting, in as normal a tone as she could muster.

He turned around suddenly, the motion caught halfway with a sharp steel clangor, his dark hair falling wildly over his forehead, the deep blue eyes intense, frozen cobalt rage: a caged and bound pirate, a brute at bay.

Maddy lost her voice.

He stared at her, silent. No flicker of recognition. Nothing.

"Thou!" Maddy whispered.

He lowered his face a little, looking at her from beneath his eyelashes. Wariness, anger, a deep and powerful passion— they were all in his face, in his stance, in the concentrated and uneven exhalation with his jaw shut hard and his unbound hand flexing open wide and closed, over and over again.

"Dost thou—not remember?" she asked hesitantly. "I'm Maddy Timms. Archimedea Timms."

"Why, are you acquainted?" her cousin asked in surprise.

Maddy looked away from the barbaric figure at the window. "Well, yes, Papa and I . . . it is the Duke of Jervaulx, is it not?"

The words would hardly come out.

"Well, well. Indeed, it is. Master Christian has come to visit us for a spell."

Master Christian stared at Cousin Edward as if he would like to tear out the doctor's throat with his bare hands.

Her cousin smiled benignly at his patient. "This is a cheerful coincidence." He gestured toward Maddy. "Do you remember Miss Timms, Master Christian?"

Jervaulx's glance flicked from Cousin Edward to her and back again. Then he leaned on the windowsill, resting his head back against the barred panes.

"His understanding is limited," Cousin Edward said. "In the scope of a two-year-old child's. As I say, it appears that he has a history of moral insanity, with a sudden onset of degeneration into dementia. And mania, most particularly when crossed. The apoplexy left him in a state of unconsciousness for two days, and early in the coma his vital signs were depressed to the degree that he was thought lifeless."

"Yes," Maddy said in a constricted voice. "That is—we had understood that he had—been killed."

"It's an interesting story. This is entirely confidential, of course; you must not speak of it abroad, but the event that excited this state in him was an engagement of honor, fought with pistols. He wasn't injured, but the sensation of the moment appears to have precipitated the seizure. The doctor had literally declared him deceased and ordered the body to be laid out, but the duke's dogs created such a frenzy that the mortuary attendants couldn't touch him." Cousin Edward shook his head. "One shudders to think, if those animals hadn't acted as they did. But the noise seems to have reached him in some way—produced enough movement and pulse that life was seen to be preserved. And of course, over time he regained consciousness and the motion of his limbs. But he was left in this state of maniacal idiocy." Cousin Edward made a note in his book, looked up at Jervaulx consideringly, and wrote again. He closed the casebook with a snap and handed it to Maddy. "Of course, you know that indulgence and a lack of moral discipline predisposes the mind to irrationality. He doesn't speak, and his primitive emotions rule him. This is very common in such cases, where the prior foundation is laid in vice and perversity: there's a breakdown, a loss of moral sense that gives free rein to instinctive appetites and desires, in utter violation of former refined habits. Physically, he's quite strong—am I right, Larkin?"

The attendant gave an assenting snort. "Aye, that he is. Barring the right hand. You see I've only got the left tied up—that's the one you have to watch for." He laid down the razor.

"Minimal restraint," Cousin Edward said, nodding in approval. "Physically he's vigorous, but otherwise reduced to the animal nature."

Larkin went to pull the bell. "We'll see how he feels about shaving today. Yesterday we had to go to the waistcoat and a cradle both."

Maddy lowered her gaze, unable to bear it. To meet those potent, silent eyes. She felt flung down, beaten, miserable. That he would be *here* . . .

He would rather be dead. She could look at him and know it.

She held the book against her skirt. "Will he be cured?"

"Ah—" Her cousin drew his lower lip over the upper. He raised his eyebrows. "I won't pretend the case isn't grave. His mother is a very good, benevolent Christian woman, active with great zeal in charities and evangelism in her church. She has suggested to me that her son has a long history of unsubdued self-indulgence and rebelliousness. With such passionate and ill-regulated habits . . ." He sighed. "Well, what I'll say is—that if we cannot cure him at Blythedale, it cannot be done."

Maddy clutched the book. "And what treatments dost— do you follow?"

"The regulated schedule is the most important, of course, to instill a habit of self-discipline and evenness of mind. Complete quiet, frequent exercise to calm him, a progression of therapeutic baths, a course of reading aloud, the sub-

ject matter selected to stimulate the sluggish intellect and inspire temperance. No drawing. Pens and writing instruments
seem to provoke him to the most violent excitations. Nerve
tonics he'll ingest only by force. I'm afraid we haven't seen
any progression toward the point at which he can be trusted
in the drawing room with the orderly patients, but he is soon
to take walks with the other maniacs in order to prevent him
from feeling isolated."

Jervaulx crossed his arms, the chain rattling upward.
Maddy lifted her face and looked at him. His expression had
relaxed, gone from suppressed savagery to a hint of cyni-
cism. He looked back at her with a half-smile, tilted up on
one side.

It was startling. He appeared himself again, the self-
possessed aristocrat; she almost expected him to speak or
nod, but he did neither. He only smiled at her, with an interest that reminded her of the roguish way he'd observed her
that night he'd described her to her father. She felt suddenly
certain that he did remember her.

"Jervaulx," she said, taking a step forward. "My Papa is
here also. John Timms. Thou—you worked together with
him on the new geometry."

His smile faded slightly. He looked at her very intently,
his head tilted a little to one side, the way a dog would look
as it tried to penetrate the mystery of some human behavior.
She noticed that he watched her mouth as she spoke—but he
wasn't deaf; he'd turned instantly toward the sound of a
voice.

"Wouldst thou like Papa to come and call on thee?" she
asked.

He inclined his head politely in assent.

Maddy felt a spurt of excitement. He had responded with
perfect intelligence to that, certainly. She glanced at Cousin
Edward. The doctor only shook his head. "He's trying to
please you. Maniacs can be rather sly, at times. Ask him, in
that same tone, if he's the king of Spain."

She would not do that; it seemed too cheap a trick. She could not believe there was only a two-year-old's mind left behind those eyes. Instead, she said, "Thou never looked to discover me here, didst thou?"

The chain rattled faintly as he shifted. He considered her—and shook his head.

As he did it, she realized that she'd put a negative tone in her question, and cued him to answer no.

"Thou dost not understand me," she said in disappointment.

He hesitated, with a penetrating look, and then only stood silent, his mouth a sullen curve.

"I'm sorry," she said impulsively. "I'm so sorry this affliction hast come to thee."

He gave her that cynical, one-sided smile. Standing straight, he reached out his chained hand, as if to lift hers and bow. Maddy automatically took it. He bent over—and suddenly jerked her up toward him, whirling her into his chest, his chained hand at her throat, his other arm crushing her back into his chest.

"The razor!" her cousin shouted. "Good God—*Larkin!*"

The attendant spun around, holding the water he'd just taken from the maid at the door. He dropped the pail, cascading liquid over the woven rug, and lunged toward them. But Jervaulx made a bloodchilling sound, a guttural snarl, as he held the razor blade at Maddy's jaw.

Larkin stopped short. Maddy could see Jervaulx's thumb against the blade from the corner of her eye, see Larkin and Cousin Edward and the maid at the door, all in a suspended moment. Jervaulx held her, his arm pressing into her waist, ruthless, his breathing a hiss through his teeth at her ear.

"Don't struggle," Cousin Edward said evenly. "Don't do anything."

Maddy had no idea of struggle. It hurt, the way he held her; she could feel herself no match for the strength of his grip. He was tense, a hard, hot, shifting wall against her back, his wrist digging into her as he forced her with him as far as the chain reached and hooked his foot around the shaving table.

He drew it toward them, maneuvering carefully, pausing when it threatened to topple and then nudging it closer again. Cousin Edward began talking in a soothing voice, but Jervaulx ignored it. He took the razor from Maddy's throat; in one wide swing he sent the copper shaving bowl clattering to the floor with his fist. The chain babbled along the edge of the table as he dragged the razor blade in a straight slash up the center of the varnished top, creating a pale incision.

He held Maddy tightly. She felt his muscles move and work as he inverted his wrist and crossed the first line with another. When Larkin took a step toward them, the blade came up instantly to her throat.

She listened to the harsh breath at her ear, felt the heat of it on her skin and the pump of her own heart and his.

"Let him," Cousin Edward murmured. "Let him finish."

Jervaulx waited, holding the razor just touching her skin. Cousin Edward nodded toward him.

"You may go on, Master Christian."

After a moment, Jervaulx's fist curled harder on the razor handle, and he placed the end of the blade at the intersection of the cross. With an effort that Maddy felt all through his body, he drew an even, sinuous S-curve along the axis of the line.

He dropped the razor. It made a loud clump as it hit the table. He put his hand behind her head, forcing her to look down at the carved figure.

His arm loosened. He let her go. Maddy stood still, gazing at the table.

She turned. The intensity of expectation in his face, the concentration . . . he depended on *her* to understand; he wasn't looking at anyone else.

She didn't know the figure. But she knew it was mathematical.

"Wait here!" She gripped both of his hands. "Wait!" She

turned to Larkin and Cousin Edward. "Don't punish him; don't do anything to hurt him!" she exclaimed as she rushed from the room.

She found her father in the family parlor, being read to by his aide. "Papa!" She ran to him and caught up his hand. "What is this?"

Guiding his forefinger, she made the cross on the parlor table's polished surface, and then the sinuous line along it.

"It's a periodic function," her father said.

Maddy released a breath and grabbed up pen and paper. "What's the definition?"

"The infinite series, dost thou mean?"

"Anything! Anything about it. If it were given to thee, thou wouldst answer back what answer?"

"Given to me? What—"

"Papa! I'll explain, but I must go back as quickly as possible! Just tell me—a periodic function, like Monsieur Fourier's? How is it written? Beginning with sin x equals?"

"The sine function series. Or is it the cosine thou'lt have?"

"And the graphs are different, aren't they? For this one—" She bit her lip and closed her eyes, conjuring the scars in the varnish. "The curve begins . . . at the intersection of the axes."

"That would be the sine function. Sin x equals x, minus x cubed over the factorial of three, plus x to the fifth over the factorial of five, minus x to the seventh over the factorial of seven, and so forth."

"Yes. Yes!" Maddy scribbled down the familiar symbols, making them large and clear. "Oh, Papa, thou'lt never imagine! I'll be back to tell thee!"

She ran through the Baroque, marbled front hall and up the staircase. The carpeted floors creaked and thudded beneath her feet. When she came to his barren room, she found that her pleas had been ignored. Larkin and another attendant had Jervaulx shoved with his face up against the wall, holding him there as they finished tying off the sleeves of a strait-waistcoat.

As Maddy stopped in the doorway, they let go of him. He didn't turn or move or struggle, only lowered his head, resting it against the wall, a white figure in the shadowed corner.

"I wish thou hadst not—"

"Cousin Maddy!" Edward turned. "Are you quite recovered? Do you wish to lie down? What a calamity! Inexcusable for Larkin to leave that razor within his reach! When we're using minimal restraint, absolute prudence is required at all times. I should never have allowed you in here."

"It's all right. It's a sine function! Oh, I wish thou hadst not put that on him."

Jervaulx leaned his shoulder on the wall, turning, and Maddy felt that there was accusation in the look he gave her.

"The figure he drew," she said, flourishing her paper. "It's a sine function."

"Yes—as I told you—instruments of writing, of any sort, overexcite his brain. You mustn't expect to wring sense out of what he's done."

"But it is sense! This is the infinite series that signifies it!"

"No. No, I must insist that we leave him to a tranquil atmosphere now. Don't—Cousin Maddy!" His voice became stern as she started past him with the paper. He plucked it from her hand and crumpled it. "Do not show him anything that will cause him further distress."

She stopped. Jervaulx watched her.

"It's a sine function," she said to him, in defiance of her cousin.

If she had expected a reaction, or understanding, she got none. He just looked at her as if there were a wall of glass between them and he couldn't hear her voice.

Chapter Five

*G*one away . . . *gone* . . . *all gone but ruffian shave, dog out-the-doors, sleep room, no privacy, throw down floor . . . made stuff food throat . . . eat or no.*

Cuzzmad.

Cuzz-mad.

Bed, tied hand foot trussed . . . trussed like pa—ba—animal, fat pink . . . curly tail. Word vanish, vanish, always just . . . far. His head hurt to chase the name.

Cuzz-mad. He tried to say it silently, get his tongue around the sounds.

He was afraid of how it would come out aloud. *No, no, no*—that was how it would come out.

Not speak, refuse.

The rage and fear went endlessly around inside him. They all talked too quickly, that was what; they mumbled, they babbled, they wouldn't give him a chance to understand.

Lay hands—ME! by God, no right. Dumb beast, prod force; scheme bath blood, manacles garden strangers watch; fury, fight, SHAME; tied chair; revolting, noisy, ranting madmen—robbed of his friends, his own house, his life.

He lay staring at the dim shadows of the finely plastered ceiling, following the oval pattern to where it met the wall and was sliced rudely off by the partition that created this cell from what must once have been an elegant chamber. Across the hall, one of the madmen was groaning, a sound that terrified Christian somewhere far deep in his throat and chest, because it was the same sound he wanted to make, the despair that only pride and cold fury held inside.

Lock here long enough . . . long enough . . . lunatic.

Sometimes he'd tried to reckon it, to identify who held him here, who it was who wished to drive him past the brink of sanity. He remembered faces; sometimes he could put names to them, and sometimes he could think of the same faces, but the names weren't there.

That had happened with Cuzz-mad. He'd looked at her: *starch white . . . thing . . .* the word for what she wore on her head danced away. *Talk thee, thou. Know; know.*

Listen. Listen hard, hard, hard.

Cuzz-mad seemed right and not right. Truly, the more he considered it, the more bizarre it seemed, but when he tried to think about it too much, tried too hard to drag the answer out of the emerging and dissolving maze in his head, he felt nauseated.

Footsteps creaked in the hall, a familiar sound; alarming, when he never knew what they were going to do to him next. The light bobbed, casting the barred shadows from the door in wild swings across the ceiling. He heard the sound of the lock, and the thick noises of his warden waking up.

A feminine whisper, then her profile in the candlelight as she leaned over the cot in the corner. She spoke to the shambling form that sat up there. The two of them prattled incomprehensibly for a minute, then the Ape got up and shuffled out of the room.

She set the candle on the windowsill, turning toward him. It was intolerable to be seen by her in this state of abject humiliation, this utter enslavement; he closed his eyes and feigned sleep, willed it all away—*wake bedroom; dogs, name, self, WORDS! Words understand, words speak*—this crazy dream would be over.

"Ervoh," she murmured. "Wilthwak?"

She touched his shoulder. Shame made him set his jaw and turn away from her; pride made him clench his fists and jerk once, hard, at the bonds.

The ringing noise startled her; she pulled her hand back and looked down at him nervously. He felt a certain satisfaction in her alarm and stared at her with insolent malevolence.

She smiled tentatively. "Wasign fucshun," she said. "Drotanifiti screes."

She held up a paper. In the candlelight, the ink was dark and clear.

$$\sin X = X - \frac{X^3}{3!} + \frac{X^5}{5!} - \frac{X^7}{7!} + \ldots$$

YES!

Yes, yes, yes, he wanted to shout. *You heard me, you understood; I'm here!*

But he did nothing. Suddenly he was afraid to move, afraid that he would frighten her away after trying to do it an instant before. She became precious, priceless, a jewel beyond measure; he could not, *could not* hazard doing anything wrong now.

He realized he'd begun breathing too fast. He corrected that, contained himself. With a conscious effort, he relaxed his arms and opened his fists, resting his bound hands back against the bed. He looked into her eyes and risked a short, emphatic nod.

"Sign fusha," she said, with a little stress. "Yes?"

Yes, he thought. *Yes.* He thought he might say *yes,* and then didn't chance it. Cautiously, he nodded again.

"Sighn," she said. "Sighn fu shon."

Sighnfushon. Fushon sign. The words went around in his head, *sign fun, fuhn sighn, sign fun signshon, mix tumble, two dice, wheel . . . dizzy.*

"Sign funshun," she said again, kneeling beside him, rattling the paper.

He looked at the symbols. He knew what the series made, he understood its meaning—

And the revolving words fell, dropped into the cup, settling.

Sine function.

Of course.

Sine function. He gave a faint, bewildered chuckle. The candlelight guttered, casting pulsing shadows on her face as she knelt, *prim cap, siren lashes, virtue, Miss.*

He wet his lips. "Sine," he said hoarsely.

"Yes!"

"Yes." The word came explosively, as if he had to push it through, to break a wall. *"Sine,* yes."

She smiled. It was like morning in the shadows; it razed his heart; he found himself in love, in an agony of passion.

"Sine . . . func . . . tion," his beloved said.

Child, not child, silly prim, not child repeat.

"Secant," he grated. "Cosecant."

"No. Sine."

"Tangent. Cotangent. Angle." *Easy. Mathematics, trigonometry.* "Parallel axiom; congruence, co-planar lines, perpendicular lines." God, geometry was easy; why hadn't he remembered how easy? He tried something hard. He gripped the chains above his wrists, fighting to say it. *"Ah . . ."* It was so painful; he knew it, it just wouldn't come. "Ah . . . *she. She!* Cuzz-mad."

He loved her. He didn't want her ever to go away and leave him alone in this place.

She tilted her head quizzically. "Who?"

His open fingers barely brushed hers. He moved his hand to the limit of the chain and stroked his thumb gently up and down the side of her palm. He gazed into her eyes, trying to say it that way. Every word was agony to accomplish: *cling twist slide away silvery fish grab*—shove through the wall. *"Name!"* It burst out of him. *"Name!* She?" He gripped her hand, squeezed it once.

She smiled again. "Maddy."

Yes, that was it. Maddy. Maddygirl. Maddy. *"Mm—,"* it came out, and he gritted his teeth in frustration.

"Maddy," she said.

He nodded. He was afraid that wasn't enough, that she wouldn't know he'd understood. "Sine, yes." He repeated his one success. "Cosine. Tangent." His fingers caressed her hand. He wanted to say "don't go," and instead it emerged, "No . . . no."

She gave a little sigh and started to stand up; he realized she was leaving and shook his head violently. *Don't! Stay here, don't leave yet, not now!*

"No, no, no, no," was what he heard himself uttering, and cut it off, tilting his head back and yanking at the bonds in wrath.

"Peasdon sethee! Clietcliet!" She put her forefinger up to her face, the tip just beneath her nose.

He gazed at her. It meant something, that gesture; he knew it meant something, but he couldn't think what. The echo of the noise he'd made died away, a mere ripple of disturbance in this house full of howling beasts.

Her hand lay on his shoulder. He shifted his head, pressed his cheek against the back of her palm. *Stay here, Maddy. Don't leave me.*

All that got out was, "No. *Mnnh.* No!"

He groaned, turning from her.

She took his face between her cool fingers. She stroked his hair back from his forehead. He closed his eyes, shuddering inside, holding back the tide of feeling. He lay still.

"Weebwell," she whispered. "Vreethin wilvee well."

Wilv well. Will well.

Vreething will well.
Everything will well.

He hadn't really comprehended it; it came after his mind seemed to sift down through the sounds, settling finally on an intuition.

But it was something, anyway. It was something to keep as she turned away and took the candle and paper. One small glass ball to float when he was drowning: she thought everything would be all right, and he'd almost understood her when she said it.

Maddy pursed her lips, carefully folding the brochure about Blythedale Hall into the letter that Cousin Edward had dictated to a Lady Scull, describing in glowing terms the kind and loving treatment that her sister might expect at Blythedale, referring discreetly to a rate of six guineas a week, and inviting Lady Scull for a visit at her convenience. On the brochure, the engraving of the house looked completely serene, with couples strolling beside the willows and the lake and the swans.

Nothing in the letter or brochure hinted at the pounding sound of metal that reverberated through the halls, that had woken everyone this morning and lasted throughout Cousin Edward's stiff and angry lecture on Maddy's folly in sending Larkin away on a made-up pretext and visiting the Duke of Jervaulx in secret, that went on while Cousin Edward read his mail and she filed letters, that went on still while Maddy wrote out her dictation with trembling fingers; the sound and fierce shout that went on and on and on: crash—*Tangent!*—crash—*Distance!*—crash—*Squared!*—crash—*Minus!*—crash—*Y one*—crash—*X two*—crash—*Mah-she!*—crash—*Mah-she!*—*She!*—*She!*—*She!*—outraged, desperate; on and on until the echoing voice was hoarse and grinding; pleading, plaintive, corroding down to an inarticulate syllable between each smash of the barred iron door.

She had not thought him mad last night, but she thought him mad this morning. The truth of Cousin Edward's warnings was patent—she should not have disturbed him, should never have gone to see him in that way. Everyone in the house was agitated, the other patients unnerved; Maddy had heard Cousin Edward instruct Larkin to explain to Master Christian that he would be restrained, taken to the seclusion room and left there if his conduct had not improved by noon.

Maddy already knew about the seclusion room. It was an essential part of the moral therapy practiced at Blythedale, the management of the patients' behavior by an appeal to their dignity, the subtle balance between encouragement and intimidation as the situation demanded. Cousin Edward had given her a copy of Mr. Tuke's *Description of the Retreat,* the famous Quaker asylum at York that had pioneered the humane and moral treatment of lunatics. She'd only had time to read parts of it, but everyone had heard of the Retreat. The brochure about Blythedale emphasized the extensive training and priceless experience Cousin Edward had gained in his eight years of work there under Dr. Jepson. Lunatics were to be spoken to at all times as much as if they were rational beings as possible, in order to cherish the spark of reason. They were to be treated gently and kindly, but made to understand that their circumstances and freedom depended largely on their own self-control. Like children, they were to be secluded if they would not behave after having been given ample chance to do so.

At half past eleven, when Cousin Edward retired to visit with his wife, the halls still rang with the steady *crash* and savage voice that had gone completely wordless now, just a guttural, broken, animal noise in time to the clang of the bars. Maddy felt she could listen no longer. It was her fault; if he was to be punished, she didn't wish to sit in comfortable ignorance of what she'd caused. With no real purpose but to chasten herself for her foolish trespass, she asked a maid to point out the seclusion room. The girl led her to the cellar stairs.

"It's the third door on the right, Miss. Just past the new bath."

Maddy descended the stair. As she turned each corner, the violent sounds from above faded, until she stepped into a silent corridor. The air was cold, but the passage had been whitewashed and a lamp burned steadily at the far end, giving ample illumination. The third door on the right stood open to a small, windowless room with a wooden floor and a bench built into one wall.

It was not the horror chamber that she had expected. It was only a room; quite clean, dry, chill but not cold. A Bible lay on the bench, as if inviting someone to read and meditate in the silence. In the little chamber, Maddy suddenly saw the Quaker in Cousin Edward, the heritage from which he seemed to have drifted so far away in his daily life.

This room was like a meetinghouse. A place to be quiet and listen for the still, small voice, the Indwelling Light. As she stood in the middle of it, she thought that Jervaulx would be all right here.

And yet, the silence of it troubled her. She'd spent a large part of her life in the silence of Meetings and had never felt uncomfortable with it. She'd listened, and waited, and felt at times what she believed to be a true experience of the Inner Light—though she had never been moved by it to speak out or minister in Meeting. And in spite of the blasphemy of presuming to predict such things, she found it difficult to imagine that she ever would feel so moved. She wasn't poised and self-confident, as the duke was.

As poised as Jervaulx had *been.*

She thought of him now. The manacles, the fury in his face. The broken sound of what was left of his voice.

Last night, she had not slept at all. She'd lain awake, as she'd lain awake the night her mother had died, trying to will acceptance out of something that it seemed would never be acceptable.

Silence. There were all kinds of silences: the open, waiting silence of Meeting; the warm silence of home and family where words were unnecessary; the bird- and flower-filled silence of an empty garden.

For months, he'd said nothing. Not one word. The written record so meticulously kept by Cousin Edward repeated it every day: *mute, sullen, uncooperative, violent.*

Cousin Edward called it dementia. Moral insanity; reduced to the animal nature.

She looked at the Bible but didn't touch it. She'd been brought up to think of the Scriptures as a divine word, a useful and necessary word, but never greater than the leading of God in her heart. In the hush of this spare room she felt the slow prickle of truth growing in her, the dawning realization that a charge was being laid upon her, that the man above-stairs who crashed against his cage was calling out for *her,* that to him this room would not be a spiritual place, but a prison, a threat to be used against him. He didn't understand silence; he didn't know it as she knew it.

She lifted her head. He wasn't a two-year-old. He had not lost his reason.

He isn't mad; he is maddened.

The thought came so clearly that she had the sensation someone had spoken it aloud.

She felt that something left her, a presence that she had not even known had been there until it was gone. The room seemed grimmer, less like the clean interior of a meeting-house and more like a little empty seclusion chamber in the cold depths of a cellar.

Jervaulx had not lost his reason. His words had been taken away. He couldn't speak, and he couldn't understand what was said to him.

His banging shouts, his rage and despair, came to seem appallingly rational: not the work of a maniac reduced to lunacy by the sum of his vices, but of a sane man frantic with frustration. He had found no other way to reach out but by violence, this reckless duke who knew periodic functions and Fourier's infinite series, who could create his own geometry, who had been free and eloquent and even generous in his autocratic way, and was now locked up and driven to distraction by it.

Maddy felt humbled. God had never spoken to her in quite so clear a way. She was no minister, not one of those men and women who had the gift of speaking out in Meeting and marketplace; she only went about her life as it seemed she ought to do from day to day.

But this was an explicit obligation laid upon her. What witness it was that God wished to implement by visiting Jervaulx with this affliction, she did not presume to know— although it didn't take much divine insight to hazard a guess. She was not asked to preach to him or judge him in his hardship.

What was required of her was only this: that she not abandon him while he suffered it.

Cousin Edward, Maddy knew full well, would not like it. He had expressly forbidden her the violent corridor. There were all sorts of sensible arguments against what she meant to do.

She thought of a multitude as she walked up the stairs, drawing near Jervaulx's cell, the rhythmic crash growing louder. She was mistaken. She was inadequate. She was unfit for such a task. What did she know of madness or medicine? There was no human voice at all with the crash now. The rest of the asylum seemed strangely quiet, the mumbles and mutterings of yesterday absent as if everyone else hung on the savage clash of metal against metal, listening bewitched.

She turned the corner. Halfway down the hall, Larkin sat on a chair tilted back on two legs to the wall, his skull gleaming beneath the short stubble of hair. He had his pocketwatch out and propped on his knee, flipping the chain idly in time to the clanging.

"Three minutes to go," he declared loudly, to no one in particular. The crashing cadence went on without a pause. He glanced toward Maddy, and the chair came down with a thump that was half-lost in the din.

"Friend Larkin." She raised her voice to be heard. "I've come to talk to Jervaulx."

The crash of the bars fell silent.

The startling lack of noise seemed to ring in her ears. Larkin looked to the door of Jervaulx's room and back at Maddy. He scowled. "You're not to be here, Miss."

His voice sounded strange and hollow, surrounded by imaginary echoes of sound that had already died away.

"Nevertheless, I am here."

"Now—you got me into wonderful trouble last night. I won't be having any more."

"Thou mayst go and speak to my cousin, if thou wilt. Certainly I don't wish to make more trouble for thee."

"I can't do that, Miss. In a minute, I'm to take him down to seclusion. You'll have to leave the corridor."

"Thou wert only to take him down if he was not quieted by noon, wert thou not?" She made a little gesture toward the door. "He is quiet."

As if to prove her, the clock in the hall below began to strike, sending slow chimes echoing up the stairs.

Larkin did not appear pleased with the turn of events. Maddy started forward, and he held up his hand. "Don't, Miss. Do us all a favor and don't get him stirred all up again! Ah, Miss, if you please—"

Jervaulx was standing behind the barred door, his hands gripping the iron. The instant he saw her, the rigid clench of his fingers and jaw relaxed. His lips parted as if he would speak, and then clamped shut again. He stood back from the door in the dim room, making a formal bow, offering his hand through the bars as if she were a lady and there were no metal door between them.

"Don't!" Larkin stepped forward. "He could kill you, Miss! He could strangle you in a minute, if he got hold of you through the bars that way."

Maddy could see very well that this was so. And in the moment of hesitation, she saw Jervaulx recognize her fear. His open hand closed. He drew back and turned away from the door, moving like a ghost, a silent figure that drifted to the window and stood there, gazing out.

And Maddy realized that she had failed. Larkin's voice

had been the voice of the Reasoner, of evil, that would whisper arguments and proofs and make her resist her own Truth. The first test, and already she'd stumbled.

Maddy watched him for a moment, and then turned to Larkin. "Please go thou and ask my cousin to come here. Thou mayst say to him that I have had an Opening, and it is necessary that I speak with him."

"An opening?" The attendant gave her an exasperated look. "I don't know what you mean, Miss, but I'm not going to leave here and let you do something silly."

"I will sit there," she said, nodding toward his chair. "I promise thee, no more than that."

"And what if he gets started again? He's quiet now; you'll agitate him."

"Jervaulx." Maddy went to the door and lifted her hand, offering it through the bars in spite of Larkin's furious protest. "If I stay here, will I disturb thee?"

He looked over his shoulder at her.

"It's on your head, Miss!" Larkin warned. "On your own head be it! After what he did yesterday . . ."

Jervaulx gave the man a look of utter scorn. He gazed for a moment at Maddy—and then he turned away, turned his back on her offered hand in a brusque and disdainful rejection.

A slap across the cheek could hardly have been more pointed. Maddy dropped her hand. "Please go thou and fetch my cousin," she said stiffly to Larkin.

"You won't try nothing while I'm gone?"

Maddy seated herself. "I will not."

"I can't believe you'll last here long, Miss," the attendant muttered, with a shake of his head as he turned away and strode down the hall, disappearing around the corner.

The silence settled.

Jervaulx remained staring out of his window.

"Ape," he said, with that explosive inflection, a discharge of absolute loathing and contempt.

Then, without turning, he slanted a sideways look back at Maddy, speculative, one eyebrow lifted in subtle challenge.

"Yes," she said, nodding emphatically. "A perfect ape."

He crossed his arms, resting his shoulders back against the barred window in his insolent pose, a pale cavalier imprisoned in silence and dusk. A slow smile curved his mouth.

If he was mad, she could not trust him. Yesterday he had leaned back his head on the bars and watched her with just that relaxed and arrogant posture, then a moment later held a razor to her throat.

Be careful, the Reasoner murmured. He's strong; he's intimidating; he is not sane.

Maddy looked back at Jervaulx. She allowed a very faint answering tilt of her lips. "Ape," she repeated decisively.

His one-sided grin seemed a light in the dimness of his little cell.

"Ape," he said, with vicious relish.

Maddy folded her hands. "'Twould appear that we're in agreement."

He said nothing more, but watched her through the iron barrier with that mute and ironic smile.

"I'm afraid that must be out of the question," Cousin Edward said to Maddy. "Leaving aside your inexperience and the impropriety of you acting as the duke's personal attendant, it is—simply absurd. Think of the danger to yourself, Cousin Maddy. You cannot have forgot yesterday's incident."

"I haven't forgot. I have had an Opening."

"Yes, very well, I understand that, but this isn't Meeting, my dear. This is a lunacy asylum."

She looked at him gravely. "Is God not here too?"

Larkin gave a snort. Cousin Edward flushed slightly and frowned at the attendant. "Certainly God is here."

"I have had an Opening," she repeated in a level tone. "I am led."

Cousin Edward pursed his lips. "I hadn't thought you would prefer it, but if you truly wish to work with the patients in a direct way, I can assign you to assist the ladies' matron in the afternoons."

There, the Reasoner whispered. *Do that instead.*

It would be safer. Easier. More proper.

"I would gladly assist the matron in other circumstances," she said, "but I am required to support Jervaulx."

The doctor began to grow pink. "I'm astonished that you even think of such an improper situation, Cousin Maddy. It isn't fitting in you."

"I've attended to nursing duties for much of my life. I'm experienced with patients of both sexes." Maddy kept her voice quiet. "But it's of no moment even if I were not. My leading is concerned with Jervaulx himself."

"Come now." Cousin Edward shook his head and smiled. "Wherever have you got such a fantastic notion?"

"In the seclusion room," she answered simply. "The Light and the Truth were shown to me."

"I'll tell you about light and truth, Miss," Larkin exclaimed. "When he breaks your neck, I'll tell you!"

"He will not hurt me," Maddy said.

"Little you know about it, Miss! He hits out regular; nearly snapped my arm more than once, and I'm a big fellow as ye can see. Slip of a gel like you, he could scuttle in a moment."

Best listen to him, the Reasoner warned. *He knows whereof he speaks.*

"And yet," she said, "when he saw that I had come to speak to him, he was quiet."

Larkin scowled. "There's nothing in that, Miss. You don't know his sort. You ain't been here but a day. Ye can't never turn your back on a maniac!"

"I'm sorry to say that's true, Cousin Maddy. You must not be deluded by an apparent show of wit in a patient of this type. We do our best to encourage reason and civilized behavior, but in sober truth, the duke is not in a state to be relied upon or viewed as a human being."

There was a female minister in Maddy's Meeting, the one who had told her about the Reasoner and how sensibly and subtly he argued, who had the gift of gazing steadily and with great effect into the eyes of the misguided. Maddy looked just so at Cousin Edward, unblinking.

"That is to say—" He cleared his throat. "Perhaps I misspeak myself. He is a human being of course, one of the Lord's children, as are we all. But I'm charged with your welfare."

"Thou art charged with his welfare."

"My dear, you cannot attend him. It is preposterous. I cannot allow it."

She did not disagree. Reason and debate would not be what would convince him. She had not thought ahead of what she would say; if God willed, the proper words would come.

Under her silent gaze, he set his shoulders back and shifted his feet, as if she made him uncomfortable. "It's impossible. I fear that you just don't understand."

"Cousin Edward," she said, "thou art the one without understanding."

He pursed his lips and frowned at her.

"Mind the Light within," she said gently. "Hast thou forsaken it?"

He kept frowning at her. But he wasn't looking at Maddy, not really.

"I don't know about all this 'light' bosh," Larkin said with belligerence, "but a sillier notion I never heard, doctor. I'm sorry to be taking up your time with it, but she wouldn't hear nothing but that you come up here and talk to her about this 'opening' of hers."

Cousin Edward glanced at his attendant. When he looked back at Maddy, she met his eyes steadfastly. Larkin grumbled on about lights and openings and ignorant nonsense, and with every idle word offended a Friend's beliefs to the core.

Cousin Edward stood in the corridor without moving. She saw the moment that he ceased being a lapsed Quaker annoyed by casual contempt for his background and began looking, and listening, elsewhere.

Larkin's comments finally rambled down to an exasperated grunt. Inside the cell, Jervaulx was a shadow watching them through the bars, white and still. The silence filled the house, a very great and waiting silence.

Cousin Edward turned to Larkin and asked him for the key.

Chapter Six

*W*hat say, *argument assertion back and forth prattle rattle gibber* the Ape red-faced and Maddy imperturbable; Christian followed none of it. He was surprised when the one who ran things, the pudgy pale manicured one, unlocked the door and opened it, astonished when she stepped inside alone. She looked a little scared. Perhaps she had reason enough, but he didn't like it. *Not hurt never hurt female damn!*

After a moment's hesitation, she walked across the cell. Her hand startled him; as she held it out it seemed to come from nowhere—things did that, jumped up at him from nothing, *blast sound sudden make noise didn't know—Hide things—Pop out there not there WHY!* It made him furious. It frightened him. He wanted things to stay in place.

He looked at her. Handshake, like a man's, right hand to right hand—but his wouldn't move. He stood helpless, feeling muddled and mortified, opening and closing the fingers of his right hand. He looked down into her eyes, *witless not-move,* unable to explain, breathing harshly, taut with the effort to make his body obey his intent.

Then she grasped his hand firmly and lifted it up and down.

He felt her fingers in his, soft and cool, and like a fog rising from a vista, he knew what he wanted to do and could do it. Something more gallant; he brought her hand to his lips and pressed a light kiss there, squeezing her fingers gently.

Puritan spinster blush prim pretty eyes. He smiled at her. She moistened her lips. The Ape muttered ominously. Christian looked up beyond her and the bars and saw the expression, saw that he'd goaded his keeper past endurance now—and that the time would come when he would pay for it.

The other, *medical blood master bone . . . blood*—the other—only stood there, looking learned and paternal. Christian realized that he was being tested. He transferred his attention back to Maddy, watching her intensely, determined not to botch his chances. The Ape was outside; she was in; it was an improvement he couldn't afford to lose.

When she gestured to him to sit, he sat. When she offered him water, he drank. When she spoke to him, he stared at her mouth and tried to make sense of the collection of sounds that fell from her lips.

It angered him that he could not do it. Everything infuriated him, and had done since he'd come out of the dark and exhausted confusion without words, without himself; he was just barely in control; moment by moment he leashed the urge to grab something and hurl it. But there was nothing to hurl; they'd stripped the cell of anything he could move— Maddygirl looked at him with gentle expectation, and he remembered in time that he must not boil over now.

When the tray came with the same intolerable mutton broth and plain rice, bread pudding and barley water, he sat there glaring at it for long moments, rebelling inside, raging. She stood beside him and finally picked up the spoon.

No.

No, that he would not bear.

He almost sent the tray and soup and everything across

the room. Almost. Instead he reached for her and caught her wrist and held it still, just held it, and then as calmly as he could pressed it downward, until the spoon rested on the tray.

She let go of the spoon. He picked it up and ate their plebeian slops *watch animal zoo damn!* degraded to the bottom of his soul, so full of anger and loathing that every swallow was a battle. But he did it. He did it to keep her there and to gall the Ape in the only way he'd found yet to do it.

And that was the test. He passed. For the first time since he'd woken from the drugged stupor in which they'd brought him here, he'd sat down voluntarily and eaten like human being.

That was how they would look at it.

He thought of his table and his chef at home, of dishes with names that slipped strangely through his head, *les fillets . . . volaille à la marechale,* of chocolate, of *la darne saumon . . . soufflés d'abricots . . .* he looked at the greasy mutton soup and could have gagged on his hate.

But Maddy beamed, which made him feel surly and pleased at once. He could forgive her, he supposed, *plain thee thou can't know better rye bread beer pudding.*

Quaker. Quaker, yes, but he could not say it out loud, nor cared to try.

He passed their bloody test, and they let her stay with him, sitting outside his cell. *Shaky muscle weak . . .* the exhaustion overpowered him, bound him. He leaned on the bars, unwilling to let her out of sight. *Talk . . . can't . . . say Maddygirl . . . stay. Stay.*

Until night at least, when the Ape came back. Christian was wary of him, offering no cause for coercion, lying down on his narrow bed like an obedient dog. Biding his time . . . and he and the Ape both knew it.

In the morning she came again with the blood-man *talk gibberish write book; what's inside book? Lies. Lies. Consult book. Bleed? Bath? God save me.*

Two more keepers came, and he knew it was to be the bath. He looked once at Maddy, just once, putting everything he had of entreaty in his eyes.

She gave him a reassuring smile.

She didn't know. He had to believe that she had no notion—and when he thought of it, he didn't wish her to know what it was they could do to him.

There were three keepers to take him, but this time he controlled his reaction, mastered himself. He allowed them to tie his hands together into leather sleeves—usually it was the jacket, but if he stayed calm they had no excuse for it in front of the manicured medical man. Christian knew. He'd become a connoisseur of bindings, an aesthete, discriminating black degrees of mortification, least down to worst: leather sleeve, manacles, chair, straitjacket, cradle.

He didn't look toward Maddy again. He took himself out of this place in his mind; that was the only hope, the only way to hang on. He went with the keepers down the stairs to the cellars, let them put the full leather mask over his face, undress him, lead him blind and make him stand endlessly, waiting, never knowing when it would come, until they shoved him backwards into the bath.

Ice! Freeze cold hot agony Ice!

They pushed him down, more than once, using a metal bar across his neck to force his head under. The third time, the bar held him down until his chest began to grow tight, until his hands clenched and real fear surged through him— just that long. And when he came up, the Ape bent over and looked through the eyeslits in the mask, through the frigid water dripping down, and grinned.

Christian stared back. The mask was tight against his mouth and nose, wet; he panted with the cold; his body shuddered in uncontrollable seizures. They pulled him out and he stood there shaking, listening to them talk around him, shut out, streaming water, unable to see anything but a slit of light in front of him.

The Ape said something from just behind Christian and

threw a towel over his shoulders. Christian stepped back hard, half-turning, driving his shoulder and elbow against the Ape's body. The calf-high lip of the bath worked just as well on the Ape as it did on Christian—his keeper grabbed at Christian's shoulder in a scramble for balance, fingers slipping on wet skin as Christian stepped away, and then a yell and a splash that sent water flying. Icy drops splattered over Christian's legs.

The other two keepers found it hilarious. The cellar room echoed to their laughter and the sound of oceans of water sloshing. Christian stood still, unsmiling behind his mask— *huge slick flop whale blunder out.* He held his place as he heard the Ape come after him, water pouring and splashing over the stone floor. The metal bar smashed him across the back, exploding pain, stealing his breath, making him stumble for balance—but the other keepers hauled the Ape off and managed to prevent a real bludgeoning.

They constituted a certain check on one another, the keepers. They had their own crude code. They knew the Ape had held him down too long. And Christian was, after all, a lunatic: allowed his little jokes.

So the Ape had gone to dry himself, and Christian, back in his cell in a blue dressing robe that didn't even belong to him, that disgusted him, had Maddy for his valet.

Dress like peasant.

Christian glared at the vulgar clothes laid out for him.

"No," he said. He crossed his arms and set his mouth, clamping his teeth to keep them from chattering, tensing to prevent the shudder that overtook him and sent pain shafting through his back.

The Ape would have gotten help, tied him up and forced the lunatic's jacket on him instead. Christian waited to see what Maddy would do, trying to hide the shiver that came with every deep breath he drew. His hair was wet; he was cold to the bone. He had no intention of carrying any battle of wills far enough to chance getting the Ape back; he wanted Maddygirl desperately, her calm and straight-spined figure sitting in the chair outside his cell: *white stiff . . . cap . . . peace.*

"Whon?" she asked.

He scowled at her. *Wrong?* Wrong, did she mean?

Decent clothes! he wanted to snarl. *No wretched raw bad sew rubbish!*

He grabbed up the coat, meaning to point out the awkward stitching, the ill-matched buttonholes, but he couldn't do it. He just held the coat, muddled again, stuck between the intention and the action.

With a hot sound in his throat, he threw the garment down. A heavy shudder went through his frame.

"Sh'boh?" she said. She touched his hand, caught it between hers, and he couldn't hold himself still, couldn't conceal the cold tremors or contain the catch in his back on each indrawn breath. He pulled his hand away and went to the window, holding on to the bars that seemed hot beneath his freezing palms.

She was silent for a long time behind him. He knew she could see the shaking—what difference did it make? He put his forehead against the bars and let it have him.

The brass lever that controlled the bell creaked. No bell-pull here, too easy for a man to hang himself from the velvet rope. Christian had already thought of it, but they were well ahead of him. They had it all designed, they'd been at it for years; a bumpkin keeper like the Ape had a preternatural ability to anticipate resistance and counter it. Christian was taller, faster, younger; God knew, he hoped he had more brains—but the Ape knew all the tricks. The razor and that incident in the bath had been the first real victories Christian had managed, and his back ached and throbbed where the iron bar had struck him, sparking sharp agony whenever he turned.

He heard the Ape's voice in the hall and tensed, starting another shiver in the depth of his muscles. But there was no sound of the barred door opening. Maddy spoke, the Ape hesitated and then made a grunt of assent. His footsteps thudded away.

Christian turned around. Maddygirl was looking at him, frowning a little, chewing her lower lip. As she met his eyes, she smiled briefly.

"I've runcoles," she said.

Runcoles?

She pointed at the empty grate, hugged herself, and shivered.

Coals. Coals, fire, yes. They'd never done that before, only lit the grate at night.

He wished to say thank you, and could not say it. He nodded briefly.

She picked up the coat where he'd dropped it and offered it to him. As she held it out, he put his hand on the badly made collar, ran his finger down it, pointed at the clumsy buttonholes.

"Donderstan," she said, looking up at him with a helpless expression.

He gritted his teeth and shivered. *All right. Try again.* He touched her sleeve, moved his forefinger up the underside of her arm, where the tiny stitches were invisible, neat and elegant, if plain, as her black dress and white collar were plain. Then he traced the same seam on the coat.

She looked from her own arm to the coat. She shook her head. "I'm sorry," she said. "Doono."

He gave it up, pulling the coat out of her hand and gesturing for her to leave, so he could dress. She just stood there. He took her by one shoulder, turned her, and pushed her toward the door.

"No." She set her feet against him and turned back. "Thamus dress."

Course dress yes, remove she, any female respectability understand. But she stood stubbornly. The Ape came clattering in with a pail of coals. Christian drifted back a little, away from him, prudent. The fire lit, they jabbered together, the Ape shrugged and nodded at whatever she said, gave Christian a carefully neutral glance, and closed the solid door as he left, blocking out the hall.

Christian stared at her. *Not think . . . God's sake . . . not suppose dress here full view she!*

But she did. She walked right up to him and took hold of the buttons on the robe and began to flick them open as if she'd done it every day of her life.

Christian grabbed her wrist and thrust it away with an indignant sound. He gestured at the door, and gave her another light shove.

"Tha ish lark?" she asked.

He took a deep breath, straining for words. "Hunh . . ."

She didn't seem to realize the depth of his disposition toward her—that he would go so far as to try to speak, to allow her to hear it. "Lark?" she said again, with her hand on the bell-lever.

He realized suddenly that she meant to call the Ape. "No!" He shook his head. "No."

"Sikrunus." She laid her hand on her breast. "Ver peryence."

A deep shiver went through him. He kept himself at a guarded distance from her.

"Nuse," she said. "Thow. Nurs."

Nurse.

Oh, dashed nurse, was it? His nurse. And she supposed that just because she imagined herself a nurse, he would let her undress him as if he were some invalid child, did she?

Maddy was secretly relieved when that familiar ironic smile appeared at the corner of his mouth. Clearly he was probing her position; if Larkin and Cousin Edward came back and found him still in the dressing robe, she would look as if she had no authority over the situation. While Cousin Edward's approval of her new responsibility was so precarious, she desperately wished to avoid any impression that Jervaulx was becoming more unmanageable rather than less under her influence.

It was more difficult than she'd expected, to keep plainly in mind that he acted out of adult reasoning which might not be obvious to her. This interest in the seams on her dress and his coat while he stood shaking with cold baffled her. She wished to get him into good warm clothing, with his hair drying in front of the fire—and then later this evening, after Larkin took her place, she intended to examine into the true nature of the therapeutic baths.

This time, when she picked up the shirt and went forward, Jervaulx stood still, allowing her to approach him. Maddy had dressed her father a thousand times; she had her own routine—a system that required him to sit down, which Jervaulx did docilely enough when she motioned toward the bed, though he grimaced a little as he did it.

She began again to unbutton the robe. By the time she had released the first button, she was aware that he was watching her intently, his face near hers as she bent over. By the third, she had become very conscious that this man was *not* her papa, that the solid shape of shoulder and muscle beneath the dressing robe was nothing like. By the sixth, the perception of his breath, soft and steady on her hands as she worked, seemed intimate beyond anything proper or acceptable.

She lifted her eyes. His one-sided smile deepened. He lifted his hand and drew his forefinger down the line of her jaw, catching her chin, raising it a little. Their eyes were at level, inches apart.

His were dark blue.

Maddy pulled herself back. She stood straight, her shoes making a loud sound on the wooden floor as she shifted.

He rose. Without a word, he declared himself ruler of the moment. He lifted his eyebrows a little, as if to ask if she wished to continue. Maddy looked at the open gap in the dressing robe and away from it, having stumbled into something unexpectedly beyond her competence.

He shrugged. The robe slipped from his shoulders and fell at his feet. He held out his hand for the shirt.

She really was very experienced, as a nurse. She'd bathed and dressed a number of patients, not all female; she was frequently called upon when a member of the Meeting needed attendance. And of course, she'd always cared for her father . . .

He was not her father. He was not a child, nor elderly nor ill. He was something she had never in her life seen before: a man in the full—she could only call it glory—of height and bone and strength of adulthood, standing without a stitch upon him, his hand open for his shirt.

Every fiber in her wanted to shove the garment at him and rush out of the room.

But she saw the mocking smile and the anger in it. His body was imposing in the small cell, broad-shouldered and powerful, imposed on *her;* and he knew it. He meant it to frighten her.

It did. At least, it felt something like fear, this mortified agitation. She saw the strength, but she saw too the symmetry, the superb length and shape of muscle. Her flustered alarm was mixed up with a dash of plain creaturely admiration that anyone could stand so: tall and straight and insolent, just the way God had made him.

And God had made him in a striking and brilliant way. A miracle of life breathed into clay. It seemed no more wrong to take note of it than to take delight in the flight of a hawk over the fields outside. That hawk had seemed a marvel to her, a city dweller all her life—and the unclothed figure of a man no less novel and dramatic.

She laid the shirt in his hand. He swept it up and pulled it on, with a faint hiss between his teeth, jerking his head to settle the fabric over his ears. The white cotton fell free down to his thighs. He took a step past her as if she didn't exist and reached for the folded stockings and breeches.

Maddy turned away to the window, having understood his message quite clearly. She gripped her hands together, working her fingers, feeling impelled to apologize but too chagrined to try.

Worldly arrogance and wickedness were not things she'd been brought up to respect, but it was somehow fine that in spite of this place, his affliction, in spite of everything, he asserted his disdain for the circumstances. He was not only a human being; he was a duke, and not about to allow anyone to overlook it. Certainly not one plain Quaker nurse.

She waited until she heard no more sounds of movement behind her. Just as she was about to turn, he startled her into a jump when he laid his hand on her shoulder.

He was dressed—more or less. The waistcoat, breeches and coat hung unbuttoned, and the shirt cuffs seemed to be lost somewhere up inside the coat sleeves. He stood scowling at her ferociously, his jaw working. Then he took a step back and held out both his hands.

It was a strangely vulnerable gesture, abrupt and reluctant. He looked, not at her, but down at his wrists, as a monarch would look at unruly subjects, offended and enraged at once.

Maddy reached out and slipped her fingers inside the sleeves, one after the other, pulling the shirt down and buttoning the cuffs. She looked up at him.

"No," he said, with a brisk nod—which she took to mean yes: she'd done right.

The breeches buttoned on two sides of the fall. Maddy waited to be asked this time, having learned her lesson. He made a brief attempt to close one button on the left side with his left hand, then gave a harsh exhalation and caught her wrist. She took a step closer under the imperious tug and quickly did up the buttons on both sides, closing the breeches over the ample tail of the shirt, stepping back as soon as she'd finished.

For her service, she received another nod. His easy hauteur dismissed any hint of personal intimacy. He picked up the cravat off the table and handed the neckpiece to her.

She tied it, on tiptoe, while he stood with his chin lifted.

When she'd finished, he felt the knot, which was the simple style that she tied for her father, and shook his head impatiently.

"I don't know another way." She lifted her open palms and gave a helpless shrug.

For a moment, she feared that he would grow angry. His frown deepened ominously—but then his mouth flattened. He cast a glance of amused exasperation at the ceiling. With a little flick of his hand at the loose waistcoat, he demanded that it be fastened, too.

Maddy did so. The garment didn't fit him well; it was ill-made and too tight; the buttons pulled in an unsightly manner. She wondered that he tolerated it, as fastidious as she knew he'd been in his tailoring.

He seemed to accept it, though, turning away from her and taking up the damp towel to dry his hair. Next to the metal washbasin, a comb lay: that he used with no hesitation.

Having combed the left side of his head with his left hand, he stopped. He put the comb down on the table and stood still a moment, looking at it. He glanced at Maddy, opening and closing his fingers uneasily. Then he shut his eyes, felt for the comb, and picked it up with his right hand, finishing the other side.

The only sane aspect of this strange little ritual was that he seemed embarrassed to have done it. He glanced at her again, making a defiant jerk of his chin as he tossed the comb with a clatter onto the table.

Warned off so clearly, Maddy behaved as if she'd seen nothing in the least odd about his action. She pointed to the fire which had finally begun to cast effective heat. "Wilt thou sit down and warm thyself, Friend?"

After the small hesitation that seemed to characterize his every response, he went to the chair, pulled it up to the grate and hoisted his leg over the seat, facing the back with one elbow propped on the top rail like some bored and moody porter awaiting orders in a hallway.

Maddy opened the wooden door and went about straight-

ening the room, what little there was to straighten. The clean
bed linens lay in a stack just inside the door—a daily
amenity that was one of Blythedale's choice services.
Maddy made up the bed, embarrassed by the straps and
manacles that had to be draped aside while she changed the
sheets. She was aware of him watching her. Instead of laying
the restraints neatly over the bedclothes, as she'd seen they
were usually left, she lifted the mattress and shoved them
underneath, not without some twisting and stretching and
ungraceful heaving to manage it.

When she stood up, breathless, pushing back a strand of
hair that had escaped her cap, Jervaulx's smile derided her
effort. His jaw tightened; he gritted his teeth and said,
"Ape!" Then he worked to speak again, uttering halfsounds,
unavailing beginnings of the same syllable. Finally he gave
a frustrated exhalation, made as if to pull hard with both his
arms from the direction of the bed, and exclaimed, *"Out!"*

Maddy plumped herself down on the mattress. She
shrugged. "Let him work for it, then."

He tipped an imaginary hat to her and grinned. He looked
very unprincipled and rakish when he did that.

"Wouldst thou like tea?"

"Tea," he said.

"Thou wouldst like?"

He wasn't looking at her. "Tea, tea, tea." He closed his
eyes. "Tea. Tea. Lines in the inversive plane. A point is that
which has no part. A line is a breadthless length. The ex-
tremities of a line are points. A straight line is a line which
lies evenly with the points on itself. Tea, tea, tea." He opened
his eyes, wet his lips as he looked at her. His jaw tensed
again. "Huhnnh . . . *ah!*"

He blew air out of his cheeks fiercely. From some room
down the hall, a patient began yelling at the top of his lungs,
clashing metal, demanding that Dr. Timms and the Holy
Ghost come and wrestle with him.

Jervaulx grasped the rounded finials on the chair and put
his forehead down on the top rail.

He is sane, Maddy told the Reasoner stubbornly. *He is perfectly sane.*

She gathered up the bed linens with the dressing robe and damp towel and went to the door. The mortice lock made a loud clunk as she turned the key. The bars rang as she closed the door behind her. He didn't move or raise his head, but his fingers were dead white with strain where he gripped the chair.

His portfolio contained fifteen letters from a Lady de Marly and sixty-one from the duchess, his mother. Maddy skimmed most of these; the duchess wrote to her son each and every day, and appeared to find that words flowed from her pen with copious ease. She wrote of her evangelical work, and her reverent thoughts and prayerful hopes of his recovery. She expressed complete confidence in Dr. Timms' moral therapy and told of how very much it comforted her to know that Christian was under his care at Blythedale. She begged her son to consider the consequences of his wickedness, to walk in the paths of righteousness, to repent the sins of pride and vanity and idleness, to repudiate the weakness of the flesh, and considerably more along these lines, sentiments which could not in any way be faulted and which succeeded in making Maddy feel quite cross.

She found Lady de Marly more sensible. Her letters were directed not to Jervaulx, but to the doctor, requesting clarifications of his reports and prognosis. In the fourth one that she read, Maddy found what she'd been searching for: a reference to the accompanying trunk and an attached list of the autumn wardrobe that it contained.

She took the list to Cousin Edward where he was completing his daily notations at his desk in the inner office.

"He's quiet," the doctor said, with no need to explain of whom he spoke. "I looked in while you were at dinner." He leaned back in his chair with a sigh. "What am I to think? It may only be coincidence, you know. I can't feel at ease, to leave you exposed to his temper."

Maddy felt it prudent to ignore the vacillation in his tone. "I've finished the filing and the accounts. Wilt—Will you require any dictation?"

"And that is the other thing. What of the post that you're to fill for me?"

"I shall do whatever is necessary. I shan't mind working into the evening, while Papa doesn't need me."

"I don't like it. I don't like it."

Maddy stood silently.

"I'm surprised—shocked—that your father has agreed to allow it. Deeply shocked, considering the impropriety, and the hazard to your person."

"Papa is fond of Jervaulx."

"I'm afraid that the Jervaulx whom he knew is gone. Dead. I've tried to explain it to him, but he's as stubborn as you are."

Maddy had only silence for this, too.

"And Blythedale's reputation. If you were to be injured by a male patient—imposed upon—do you know what I mean?" His face grew crimson. He pulled a key from his waistcoat pocket, examining it closely. "Cousin—it could ruin me."

"I'm sorry," Maddy said sincerely. "But I—how can I turn away from a Concern? I never thought . . . I've never had a leading before, but this one is so deep and strong that everything before it seems . . . spiritless."

He unlocked a drawer, reached into his desk and drew out a pipe, filling and lighting it. The sweet smell blossomed in the neat room. "Well, here then. Take this notebook," he said roughly. "I'll want you to write down your observations on a daily basis. We shall give it a little time. But be careful, Maddy. Be so careful."

"I promise thee I shall."

He took a deep draw on the pipe. "He's to go up to London soon for his hearing."

"Hearing?" Maddy asked diffidently.

"Competency hearing. Before Chancery. It's a common

thing with this class of patient. They have property; they're men of affairs. He has to be declared *non compos,* have a guardian appointed. Confounded nuisance it is, too. Never fails to get them tumultuous beyond any mastery, taking them out into public that way, having questions thrown at them, stood up before a jury and such. I don't look forward to it with *him,* I'll tell you that. I hear he tossed Larkin into the bath this morning. He ought to be disciplined for it."

"Tossed?" Maddy bit her lip. "Art thou certain?"

"Of course I'm certain. Do you think the attendants fabricate these things?"

"Jervaulx was very cold when he was brought back upstairs. He was shivering."

"That is the nature of a cold bath."

"I can't think that such an extreme measure can be good for his health."

Cousin Edward thumped his pipe on the table, emptying the bowl. "And when did you receive your physician's certificate, Cousin Maddy?"

She decided that it was not in the interest of her ultimate objective to answer that. There were times when the injunction to let one's words be few was most fitting.

He cleaned the pipe with a silver hook and looked speculatively at her. "Perhaps, if all goes well, you shall accompany us to London. Do you think you can keep him in order?"

"Yes," she said, and hoped the word came from somewhere and someone else, out of power and knowledge greater than her own.

"We'll take Larkin, anyway."

She held out the list she'd found in the file. "His family has sent clothing. What he's wearing now doesn't fit him."

"We don't give the violent patients expensive clothes. They're too inclined to tear them off."

"Perhaps because they don't fit."

Cousin Edward shook his head. "You'll learn, my dear. You'll learn differently, I'm afraid. Put his valuable clothes on him."

Chapter Seven

In the silence of the deserted family parlor, Maddy found it strange and impertinent to open Jervaulx's safe box—as if she were rifling through someone's home when they were out. Strange, and somehow painful, to touch these things that she never in her life would have conceived of touching. The box accommodated the key to his trunk, a gold watch with a heavy official seal and magnifying glass hung upon its chain, a massive gold signet ring, an ivory-handled razor and a pair of spurs with buckled straps.

Maddy squinted down at the ring, and then held it up to the candle with the magnifier. The metal band was thick, the edges smooth with wear. It fit, without catching, right over her thumb. Beneath the fleur-de-lis and phoenix crest, the carved banner read *A bon chat, bon rat.*

To a good cat, a good rat. Even Maddy's schoolroom French was up to that, and if the meaning were not clear enough, it was spelled out in English, too: *Retaliation in kind.*

A vigorous and rather pugnacious sentiment. She slipped the ring into her pocket with the trunk key. She took the spurs, also. In town, gentlemen wore spurs about everywhere, all the time; they seemed to be a sort of fashionable ornament.

In the attic, among the other boxes and valises, candle-light immediately caught the gleam of the elegantly black-laquered chest with the duke's card inserted in a brass holder. The trunk was packed full with the finest-made clothes she'd ever handled: shirts of choice linen; warm underwaistcoats, soft as the skin beneath her chin; silk-lined coats laid between silver tissue, the buttons mother-of-pearl, the braces embroidered all up and down their length.

It didn't seem so personal to rummage through the trunk as in the safe box. He'd never touched these things; they were all new, smelling of dye and the herbs packed with them. She tried to recall what he'd worn the night she and Papa had dined with him—and searched out a dark green coat as the most similar color.

She'd never dressed in colors herself. Doubt in her choices kept her conservative. She discarded an overwaist-coat embroidered in the most lovely purple and gold hues, deciding that a striped combination of wine and rust and tan was more inconspicuous. Finally she took up the most informal-looking of the pairs of boots and carried it all downstairs to her room.

Having copied out and posted the patients' schedules from Cousin Edward's notes, she knew that no one was to undergo the therapeutic baths because of an outing planned for the orderly patients. After their departure, each of the remaining male patients were listed to be shaved at quarter hour intervals. In Cousin Edward's notes, Larkin had been written beside the duke's name for this operation. Maddy had substituted her own. Since the doctor was going on the outing, she felt safe to do so without precipitating a lengthy and unpredictable conversation on the matter.

However, when she arrived at Jervaulx's room after helping to see off the carriages, Larkin was already there with the basin and towel. He looked in need of a shave himself. Maddy took no notice of his sour mood, but simply lifted the basin from his hand. The razor in it made a metallic sound as it slid against the side of the bowl.

"You'll want help, Miss," he said. "I warn ye."

A drop of water wet her finger. She looked down and saw a sheen of soapy iridescence in the basin. "This is dirty," she said.

"Indeed it ain't! The doctor won't have that. I wiped it clean after Harry finished."

She glanced from the towel slung over his shoulder, visibly damp, to the razor blade. The handle was worn with use, the blade sharp but nicked.

Inside the cell, Jervaulx was already in a strait waistcoat, held by straps around both his upper arms that were tethered to bolts in the wall. His eyes when they met hers were like a wolf's in a cave: blazing, unblinking, silent.

Maddy held herself still. Very still.

Then she said in a painstakingly calm voice to Larkin, "Fetch the hot water, if thou would'st. I shall return in a moment."

The madman's jacket made him frantic, and the Ape knew it. It touched off a nightmare dread Christian had never known he had inside him, a fear that went past reason and pride straight to a well of primeval impulse that made him fight it every time, long after he knew himself damned, long after he'd learned he could not win.

His throat ached where the Ape had used something new this time, an India rubber garrote, adept at his little murders while Christian was still shackled in bed, driving him down to unconsciousness, pure horror, an instant black and he came up gasping, reflexive-struggling, with the side of his face pushed into the floor, a knee on his neck and lancing pain in his back, three keepers leaning over him while they talked to one another in cheerful, ordinary tones. They hauled him up bodily while he was still trying to find himself and air. He discovered the jacket, that involuntary terror, utter helplessness, no way to balance and no way to save himself; an easy push from behind and he was falling whichever direction they shoved him, because with his arms bound across him every move was strange, bewildering. His body lost proper connection with his mind, his limbs defied him, his legs refused to take the step to steady him—a keeper caught him before he fell, with a short, half-laughing exclamation, and shouldered him against the wall.

Christian locked glances with the man, and the keeper instantly looked away. He patted Christian's cheek and said something in a fatherly fashion as the others strapped him into place.

While Christian stood in humiliated, imprisoned frenzy, breathing like an enraged bull, the extra help left and the Ape went about the morning routine. It defiled Christian near to madness. He wished desperately for Maddy and was sick with fear that she would come now, before it was done.

But the Ape finished and wrote his loathsome things in a book and went away and left him alone. Christian was going to kill him.

Someday. Someday.

He didn't think of how. He thought of the look on the Ape's face, the relish of terror, the time it would take; he'd once seen two men hanged and quartered—the expression of the second condemned traitor as he watched the executioner cut down and butcher the first: that was the fear, that was the struggle, the prolonged kicking and spasms, that was the cringing, weeping, purple-faced, swollen-tongued, bloated sickening twitching entrails-sliding agony he was going to inflict.

He thought of that, with berserk pleasure, until Maddygirl came.

She jarred him yet; the transition from night to day, from nightmare vengeance to daylight purity; it was almost more than he could bear. He'd thought himself driven to the limit before, but with each morning she brought reason, then left him to the dark and the Ape, whose mood took a deeper turn now every night. Christian began to see that he'd had it easy. His throat throbbed from the garrote; he prayed to God that his family hadn't forgotten him, that his name protected him, because it would be so simple to keep that stranglehold an instant too long—so easy; and he felt deserted, discarded, disowned; he had no reason to believe there was anything left of the universe but this cell and the hallway and what he could see from the window.

And Maddy. Maddygirl. Standing in the hall in the white scoop bonnet, holding a shaving basin, gazing at him in his shackles.

The Ape hated her. Christian saw it in his eyes when he looked at her from behind, saw it deepen with each small confrontation, the half of them over things Christian couldn't even follow. He was afraid for her, wished her to stay away and craved for her to come, without words to caution her or warn her off—in the end, not brave enough to hope to be left alone here.

She looked shocked, as she had when she'd first seen him. And then her whole figure seemed to grow hushed and motionless. He already dreamed about her voice. It was like a river talking, sliding between serene banks; when she spoke, the sounds made him close his eyes and imagine he understood.

Water? Woods? Retur?

He opened them, and she was gone. The Ape looked at him through the bars. Just looked, without smiling, without frowning, one long knowing moment. Then he winked and whistled low, as if to a dog, and walked down the hall.

When she came back, she would not let the Ape in. She unlocked the door, opened it only far enough to slip inside and pulled it hard out of the Ape's hand as he tried to come behind her with the steaming water bucket. The bars shut with a ringing crash.

Christian saw the Ape's expression as water splashed on

his leg and the floor. Maddygirl set the copper bowl on the table, turned and faced the keeper. Her hands were at her waist, her back rigid.

"Sea adid!" The Ape's ferocity had vanished before she turned. He gave her a hurt look.

"Lee there," she said, in a voice so still and controlled that it even impressed Christian. "Thast her dutees."

The Ape's mouth worked in an ugly way. He dropped the bucket, splashing half the water over the floor, and left.

Without an instant's hesitation, she came to Christian and began to work at the straps that held his arms. She didn't look up at him, but released each one with a sharp pressure and yank. Freed from the wall, he stood balanced over his feet, unable to step forward in the jacket.

"Canuhdoo buckle," she said tartly, still not looking up at him. The angry color was very high in her cheeks.

He closed his eyes. Because it was the only thing he could manage, he lowered himself, bending both his legs at once. He rocked forward onto his knees on the floor, drawing in his breath against the pain where the Ape had hit him, and waited, his shoulders back, staring straight ahead.

She did nothing for a moment. He knew what she must think; how strange he appeared. He gritted his teeth together. *Off! Vile foul loathsome thing off!*

"Untessary the do at," she said, as she knelt behind him and unbuckled the jacket, releasing the taut pressure that held his arms bound across him. She pulled the restraint forward off his shoulders, leaving him bare-chested.

It took several seconds before he could command his hands. He flexed his arms wide, until he hit the shaft of agony in his back. The fingers at the end of his limbs seemed to become his again, instead of objects without purpose, things that had nothing to do with himself or his intentions. As soon as he felt capable of doing it, he pushed up off the floor, wincing. Maddy stood, too, dusting at her skirt with the jacket.

He took her by both shoulders, pulled her close to him, and kissed her mouth.

It was short and hard. He pushed her back away and let go immediately so that the stiff reaction that sprang into her spine wouldn't turn into real fear. It was just surprise, he thought, watching her, watching shock and bewilderment and indignation and chagrin chase themselves across her face.

"Friend!" she said in a confounded tone.

"Friend," he echoed.

It just came, without volition, meaning nothing. But he looked at her, Maddygirl with her red cheeks, her lifted chin, the narrow spinster nose with the stubborn bump in it, and if he'd lain down more times than he could count with women more elegant and comely, he'd never seen anything as beautiful as Maddy in her starched—*thing—white—head— sugar?*—than Maddy in this prison cell.

"Love," he said. *"Love."*

He amazed himself, and her. They stood looking at one another. The thin morning light fell down through the bars on the window, catching her cheek and sultry lashes.

That serious, pensive mouth of hers took on a dry, uneasy curve. She swung the jacket on her finger. "Easy conkest thou."

"Friend," he repeated, with a hesitant smile. *"Maddy.* Friend?"

"Only friend?" She made a mock-pout. "Thotow wert bow!"

Beau?

That, he couldn't say. Or preferred not to attempt. Her color was still high; her teasing had an edge of nerves. He was offended that she'd make a jest of it. With a moody grunt, he turned away.

"Thy back!" she exclaimed. "Astou done?"

He sat down in the chair, facing the rungs. Every move hurt; he was fairly certain that his . . . his—what? *Inside, white, hard, curved, frame.* He was injured. *Crack. Bone.* He looked at her defiantly, silently.

"Dist fall?" she demanded. Moving behind him, she reached toward his bare back. He tensed in anticipation, but her contact was featherlight, tracing the outline of what Christian imagined must be a flaming bruise.

"Hurt?" she asked.

He shook his head. "No."

Her fingers moved; the next touch made him flinch and expel a harsh sound through his teeth.

"Ah," she said, and touched again along the bone. "Here?"

He nodded once. The probe came again, and he made a short, affirmative groan. He held onto the chair and endured the exploration, until one contact shot pain like a stake through his back. His head came up; the involuntary jerk was worse than the touch.

"Fracture," she said. Mercifully, she didn't touch him again. "Cuzzinderd bindoonite. Fall?"

It dawned on him that he could understand her—enough to work meaning out of what she said. He labored for the word, and got it. *"Fall."*

No chance he was going to blame the Ape. He could see easily enough where that would lead.

"How fall?" she asked.

He just looked at her.

With a slight pursing of her lips, a little frown, she regarded him. "Where?"

He shrugged, grimaced at the pain of the unthinking movement.

That dissatisfied her, he could tell. She wished to do something, make some adjustment, remove some hazardous obstacle. That was fine. As long as she didn't go accusing the Ape.

He grabbed the chairback and tilted it beneath him, miming, leaning over perilously. As he let it fall back with a thump that jarred him painfully, her face lit in comprehension.

"Oh, chair! Chair fellver?"

He inclined his head.

"Thamus caerf." She reached out and touched his shoulder. "Move slow. Artipetuous."

Impetuous.

He was that. He shouldn't have kissed her. It embarrassed him now. Look at him; look at him here, in this place, befuddled, as dumb as an animal, with grunts and manual acts for speech. Couldn't even button his own damned—*what, what?—Christ*—he could look down at what he meant, these things on his legs, but the word just hung out of reach, impossible.

Damn.

Damn bloody hell shit damn damn damn. Damn!

Those words he knew. He could have said them, too. He'd tried it, when he was alone, a whole list of curses in English and Italian and German and French. They were like mathematics; they were right there ready when everything else was inaccessible.

She held out the shaving bowl toward him and ran her finger around it. "Clean," she said.

That was a change. He nodded.

She went to the door and opened it, bending over to retrieve the bucket. Christian thought suddenly that it would be easy to stand up and shove past her; it would be easy to escape; and in the same instant that he thought it he was on his feet.

She turned around, pulling the bucket into the room. The lock clashed shut.

Christian stared at her, breathing hard. She didn't even realize it; she didn't know how simple it would have been; the Ape had never—*never*—given him such a clear chance. And she'd do it again, because she didn't know.

He felt dizzy with agitation. Excitement and a strange kind of fear thudded with his heart. If he got out that door, if he left this cell—what would he do? Where would he go? *Run. Run! yes;* his body was ready, but his brain seemed an uproar of confusion. *Left, right*—which way would he turn? He couldn't even be certain of that, and it seemed vitally important. There would be stairs. Stairs, doors, corners; the gardens; walls . . . *damn!*

Maddygirl was looking at him, her expression cautious, daunted. He realized that he was standing with his fists clenched, his whole body taut and explosive.

"Sh'voh?"

He would take her with him. He needed her. The thought of walking out into the world by himself seemed appalling—appalling and sweet; he wanted it so badly that he felt hot wetness burning behind his eyes.

She watched him, waiting.

With an effort that took everything he had, he put his hand on the chair and sat down again. He blinked twice, hard.

She smiled. Christian let go of the breath that fought to leave his chest. He made his arms relax.

"Here," she said. "Brot thy raze."

He looked at her, confounded.

"Here."

It appeared suddenly, almost under his nose. He started back. In her hand lay a razor, not the Ape's dull butcher knife, but one like his own, precisely curved, steel and pearl.

His own razor.

And his own—*finger, gold, family*—

"Ring," she said.

His ring.

He took it from her in his left hand. He held it.

"Dostowmember ring?"

Of course he remembered it. It was his signet, golden and heavy in his palm. He couldn't think what to do with it.

"Not member?" She reached for it.

"No!" His fingers closed hard. If she would just give him time—let him think.

He started to put it on. His hand held it against the back of his other hand. That wasn't right. He spread his fingers out, as wide as they would spread. He kept losing the hand where it should go and then suddenly finding it again. In his mind, he could see the ring on his finger; he just could not seem to reckon how to get it there.

Perhaps he *was* mad. Maybe he only thought he was sane. It was like looking at a box, knowing there was a simple way to open it, and turning it over and over, unable to find a seam.

He began to grow angry. His own goddamned ring!

He closed his eyes; sometimes that worked when he got confused, helped to clear his brain. He felt the ring, rolled it in his left hand, then put it between his palms. He turned his right hand over, and the ring slipped away and thudded on the floor.

Christ!

He stared at it, breathing hard through his nose. The pungent burn behind his eyes began to come back.

Maddy retrieved the ring. She moved as if to put it back in her pocket.

He stood up, seized the chair and swung it, sending it crashing against the table and the wall. A chunk of plaster flew free; the chair fell back, swayed for an instant on one leg, and toppled to the floor.

"No," he said. He held out his open hand.

"Sh'voh—"

"*Give!*"

Her color was high; she put her chin up and pointed at the chair. "Thamusno throw. Set right."

He blew out a hissing breath of fury at this impertinence. She held the ring behind her back; it was nothing to wrench her arm in front of her, and when he couldn't empower his other hand to take advantage of the access, he pressed her wrist between his fingers until she cried out and dropped both the ring and the razor.

He swept the signet up and laid it on the table. He held the edge with his left hand, located his right and put it down flat, slid his fingers until the ring caught on the tip of the third, and by working the band with his right thumb and the seal against the table surface, managed to shove it over his knuckle into place.

That wasn't the proper way to do it. There was another way, but he had the signet on his finger where it ought to be, and he'd done it himself. He looked up at Maddygirl in triumph.

She'd moved close to the door, holding her wrist, chafing her fingers up and down it.

He turned toward her and she backed away.

That stopped him, held him frozen. It dawned on him that he'd hurt her.

What was happening to him?

He didn't know what to do. He stood there a long moment, working the underside of the ring with his thumb. She had that wary look, the worst look; he'd rather have her chin lifted and her meddlesome nurse role than that.

Humbly, he turned around and picked up the chair, set it right; he found the chunk of wall plaster and placed it carefully underneath the hole. He would have repaired it if he'd had the means.

The razor lay on the floor where it had skittered off under the window. He picked it up. She made a faint sound and caught at the door behind her. She had the key in her hand.

So naive. Two steps—he'd have her and the key and freedom; the Ape never gave him such opportunities.

Christian held the razor. She looked utterly terrified, but stood her ground. He didn't like the look; he didn't like it that she was so stupid as to be brave with him. What if he were really crazy? He could kill her in ten seconds. No way on earth she could get that door unlocked fast enough. The Ape knew; the Ape planned every move on that knowledge; that was the reason for the jacket and garrote and chains.

All these madmen in this place—why hadn't anyone told her to be careful?

He frowned down at the razor. Then he put it beside the copper bowl on the table, poured lukewarm water and sat down in the chair, attempting to look contrite.

It was not his greatest forte. If he'd had words, had himself; flowers, notes, diamonds, waltzes—he knew how to disarm a skittish female.

She watched him for a long, long moment.

Then she wriggled her wrist a little, as if testing it. With her small, dry smile, she said, "Look pupdog, Sh'voh."

Well, hell.

"Morlike thou!" she said. She actually laughed, and he realized his repentant expression had turned into a scowl. But her unease had vanished. She dropped the key in her pocket and walked to the table.

He sat quite still as she shaved him. The good razor and her deft touch made it better than the Ape's bloodbath, even with the water gone cold—which he supposed he deserved. Sitting backwards in the chair, he tilted his head for her, lifting his jaw so that she could reach without bending so far.

He began to smile inwardly. Her Quaker clothes, adorned only with a crossed white scarf at the neckline, weren't made to be viewed from this angle. With his lashes lowered, he could see down the front of her plain bodice, an enjoyable view, a schoolboy pleasure, but he was reduced to such small satisfactions. He had no intention of foregoing this one.

She finished all too expeditiously. He watched her clean the razor and the bowl with neat, practiced movements and knew how tigers in the zoo must feel, watching warm temptation pass so close to their cage. Only this enticement was bolted inside with him, until she gathered the shaving utensils and carried them out—another clear chance, so easy—and the bars rang closed.

She would do it again. Over and over again. He had to think. He had to get control of his clouded brain and think.

Chapter Eight

The instant that he saw the new clothes, Maddy could feel the swift rise of his mood. Though he did no more than look at them and touch them, pick up the spurs and hold them, the expectation in his face when he turned to her was something far beyond mere shirt and coat.

She thought he was going to embrace her again. She stepped backwards, but he only pushed at her shoulder, a hint that she obeyed with alacrity, stepping into the hall and closing the solid wooden door behind her. After a few minutes, a single sharp thud from inside signalled her to unlock it.

He held out his hands, impatient while she managed the cufflinks. She tied his neckpiece. He rested his boot on the chair and shoved one of the spurs onto his heel, held the strap and jerked his head for her to come.

She bent over, buckling the leather across the instep, tightening it down against pure black luxury. Supple, shiny, expensive: no months of blisters and dye-stained stockings, no paper-stuffed toes would be required to break in these boots.

She felt his attention, intense and close on the simple task. As she found the tiny hole for the buckle, he touched her hands, a searching contact, the way her father felt over objects to identify them.

She slowed her movement, opening her hands so that he could see what her fingers did as she tucked the end of the leather through its keeper.

He changed legs, shoved the other spur home. His hand hovered over the dangling strap; he laid it across the boot, staring at it.

"Here." Maddy took his hands in hers, closed his fingers around the strap and buckle, guiding one through the other. It was awkward; through five attempts with both of them leaning over his boot, Maddy tried to direct his hands and ignore the increasing rhythm of his breathing, the spiraling of frustration that she perceived in his tensing muscles. Bent so close to him, his size and strength felt substantial, an intimidating potential for explosion.

At last the strap caught through the buckle. She grabbed at it before it slipped out, pressed the end between his fingers, bent it back—simple and complex; his hands like a child's, untutored, and like a man's, firm and powerful, too large for her to direct readily. She pressed his thumb against the catch; miraculously, it found the hole on the first try. He made a sound, a noise in his throat of success and anger.

Maddy guided his hands to finish the task, slide the keeper upward, push the strap through. Another try, another failure. He groaned beneath his breath. But he kept holding the strap and the keeper, a deathgrip that hindered more than helped. She nudged his finger onto the impeding upward twist at the end of the strap, holding down the curl.

"Now push it in," she said.

He did nothing, just held them.

She glanced up at him sideways. His face was close to hers, closer than any man's she'd ever known but her father. He looked at her beneath black lashes.

He closed his eyes, and moved his hands. The strap slipped into the keeper.

"There. Thou hast it."

She let go and stood back. He straightened, his boot still propped on the chair. They were both breathing as if they'd been running hard.

"*Go*," he said, with difficulty. He grinned at her.

It was only then, as she saw him there in top boots and spurs, leather breeches, vented green coat, as smart and rakish as any gentleman who had ever paid court to the ladies' carriages in Rotten Row, that she realized what she'd done. She'd dressed him to ride. And he looked at her, charged with anticipation, ignited in expectation of it.

"*Go*," he said again, the effort a sharp exhalation.

Without speaking, she shook her head.

She had nothing to say. It had been her own ignorant enthusiasm—thinking she knew anything about what he would wish to wear, thinking green would compliment rust and tan. And where had she seen that combination and style every day of her life, pray, but among the gentlemen who rode their burnished mounts in the fashionable squares and streets?

In the silence, his grin failed. He looked at her intently, as if by concentration alone he could find what he desired in her expression.

She pressed her lips together, helpless to repair the blunder now. She shook her head again.

Disillusion chilled his face, turned his aspect to dark ice. He gave her one look, one instant that asked why, and then turned away from her. His hand hovered over the buckled spur. He gazed down at it. With his right hand he worked it free. He propped the left boot up and yanked that spur free with his left hand.

He stood holding the spurs, staring down at the chair.

In profile, a still and intense emotion carved his mouth and cheek. He made no other move, just stood immobile, but Maddy found her feet moving her backward toward the door and safety.

She reached for the key in her pocket. He looked toward

her, and not even when he'd looked at Larkin had she seen that depth of venom and contempt in his face.

A thread of terror formed and spiraled in her throat. She looked down sideways and fitted the key into the lock, apprehensive even to turn her back on him completely. She swung open the bars and slipped through. The iron door never shut softly; it always locked into place with a loud reverberation of metal on metal.

He walked to the door. Without thinking, Maddy moved back, even though protected by the bars. One by one, he held up the spurs and dropped them through. They clanged on the metal and hit the floor with a dead thump.

Christian lay on the bed, listening to the sounds of the madhouse.

He hated her. False thee-thou pious bitch. To join them after all, treat him to her own little crazy-begetting games, nothing so crude as the ice-bath, nothing he might have expected, have armed himself against; oh, no—much subtler than that, but devastating.

To make him hope. To make him believe in her. To make him look a fool, a child: a helpless, inept idiot.

He'd thought they were going. Where, how, why; none of that had mattered. Only to go. Only his freedom. Out of the cage with her for assurance that he could manage in the outside.

He hated her.

Hated her.

Hate hate hate hurt cold blood faithless bitch.

Mixed up with it was the pain, a different rancor from the pure and honest malice he had for the Ape. To the Ape, he was a moving piece of meat, an ox to be trussed and prodded like all the other mad and dangerous dumb beasts in this place. It had been, Christian understood, nothing personal—until Maddy had come and toppled the keeper off his throne. It was personal now, and that too was her doing.

He hated her. He felt ashamed. His back ached with the Ape's punishment, bound now *tight white hard to breath.* That the humiliation of hope and disappointment could be more fierce than anything the Ape had done to him was a bitter revelation. He'd trusted her, let her see his confusion and hear him speak, guide his hands in their awkward futility. She had brought him his own clothes, helped him strap on spurs, made him into a mirage of himself.

Why, why, why Maddygirl?

Why give him that hope? Just to take it from him? Just for the power to shake her head? Stand there with her key, so easy to conquer, and step out into where he could not go?

Could not. Would not. Was afraid to go alone.

He put his hands over his eyes and through his hair, defying the sharp agony in his back. He'd never known he would be a coward, afraid of what he wanted so intensely. He hated her the worse for showing him the reality of himself—that he preferred this animal cell to wrenching the key from her hand and walking on his own out that door.

He rolled off the bed, breathing hard against the hurt. Up, he prowled the room, touched each of the few things in it. He found comfort in the table, precisely in its familiar place, the chair just a hand's width from the fireplace grate. Any changes in the room made him angry. He was afraid only a crazy person cared so much about such things, and tried not to care, and still did.

He looked down at his feet in the top-boots. A madman. Crazy, mute, imprisoned animal. He caught the bars on the door and shook them against the steel frame, filling the room and hall with clanging metal.

Know, Maddygirl? Hear this? Understand feel no self, no pride, sick shame dress coat boots spurs can't go?

Understand?

He jolted the bars violently. He knew she could hear him. He knew she was sitting in her straight-backed chair, just out of his sight.

She didn't come. He sat down, stood up, walked the room again.

A thought came to him, a madman's thought, the kind of thought he would not ever in his real life have entertained. But here there was no such thing as honor. Here there was only brute force and feeling, and he was going to make her understand. He was going to make her know how it felt to be broken down to the last depth of disgrace, to lose every rag of self-respect. Lure her to her own shame, make her bring it upon herself, as she had seduced him so easily into hot humiliation.

Prim thee thou spinster puritan; he knew exactly how he was going to do it.

She did not come back. He spent the long day locked up and dressed as if he were a human being, bored and belittled to a passion. Not only a beast, but now a dancing bear, complete with waistcoat, pearl studs and embroidered braces.

Near dark, the sounds of arrival in the courtyard drew him to his window; he watched three carriages being emptied of their occupants, saw Maddy and the Ape and some other keepers divide and shepherd the group inside. The vehicles rolled away, but Maddy and a young man lingered in the drive. The fellow talked to her earnestly, the words distant and impossible for Christian. He leaned his cheek on the bars, watching her listen, seeing her nod and smile as the young man laughed in a giddy way between his sentences.

Another lunatic. Christian despised her patronizing politeness; she would have smiled and nodded just so at him, wouldn't she? Indulging crazy children and animals.

Not him. She wasn't going to think of him that way.

Instead of Maddy, it was the Ape who brought his dinner. The keeper was in a hurry and appeared to take no note when Christian didn't resist the evening routine. Only when he allowed himself to be shackled without defiance did the

Ape pause and frown at him. Christian met his speculative glance with cold neutrality.

"Choke got think, eh?" The Ape grinned and gave him a push, almost friendly.

Christian thought of all the methodical and bloody ways to kill him. He stared at the keeper, unblinking. The Ape, no fool, grunted and took his hand away. They understood one another.

To lie chained in the dark and plan a seduction required a potent bend of reality. A twist of ferocity and humor, to swallow his affliction whole, to face the truth of himself and then proceed as if it were merely an inconvenience: a husband or a lover, a perverse floorplan of widely separate bedrooms in a country house, an inquisitive aunt or cousin, something to be worked around in pursuit of the ultimate goal. A challenge.

Christian knew women well. He'd frightened her. That would have to be redressed. And he was an inmate. She considered herself his nurse.

As to that . . . he thought of the way she'd looked at him when he'd stood before her naked. *Quaker spinster prudish nurse agog. No shriek run, not her. Shock. Scandal.*

Curious.

He looked up through the darkness with a slow smile. He could do it. Damn him if he couldn't. And enjoy it too.

"We shall take him on a trial outing tomorrow. Up to the village and back in the carriage. Did you put the new clothes on him?"

Maddy stood in front of Cousin Edward's desk. "Yes."

He glanced at her meager sentences in the notebook. "Don't overlook details. Always write down such things, and how he responds. Did he tolerate them well?"

She put her hands together, squeezed them, and pulled them apart. "What dost thou mean?"

"His reaction. Any attempt to remove them? Tear them?"

"No. Oh, no. Nothing . . . nothing of that sort."

"No reaction at all, then?"

"He was—he has difficulty dressing himself. I believe that makes him angry. I helped him to buckle the spurs."

"Spurs?" He sat back in his chair. "Why on earth spurs, dear?"

"With the boots, I thought—all the gentlemen in town—it seems they always wear them."

"Do they?" He grunted. "That's the fashion, is it?" He looked down again at her notes. "Shaved . . . dressed . . . nothing else? He was calm all day?"

"Yes. Except that—he was a little—" She searched for a word, "—restless, in the morning. He banged on the door briefly. But he didn't shout."

Cousin Edward flipped the notebook closed. "I believe you may be starting to exert some calming influence. We're seeing a little of his former personality here, I think. He has more pride at stake in the presence of a lady. We can use that to encourage self-control. Dress him tomorrow to go out. I dislike to restrain him for the entire trip to London, but we'll see how he conducts himself on a short jaunt first. Tell Larkin we'll leave at eleven."

In the morning, Maddy entered Jervaulx's room with her head bent, stepping aside for Larkin to leave. She'd selected the clothes and taken them down early, leaving them in a neat stack on the chair where Larkin would pass in hopes that the male attendant would manage the task of dressing Jervaulx. She'd decided, after long prayer and meditation, that she'd overstepped the true bounds of her Opening— exceeded the divine direction of her Inner Light. She must have, for clearly she was goading Jervaulx to deeper frustration, less acceptance and patience in God's will instead of more.

Part of her wished to stay away entirely, and part of her wished to persist, offering what she could of friendship. Half a night of prayer had not convinced her which part was the Reasoner and which a true leading. She was here because

Cousin Edward had ordered her to see that Jervaulx was ready for his outing, not because she had any certainty anymore about what she was ordained to do.

Larkin stopped, turning back as the bars rang closed. "You put this on him, Miss?" He held up the heavy signet ring.

Maddy nodded.

"If he hit out, wearing this," Larkin said, "he'd mark me for life. And you—he'd crack your jaw like an egg, Miss."

She was silent.

"Don't put it on him," Larkin said.

He walked away, carrying a bundle of linen and clothes.

Maddy turned to Jervaulx. He stood in his place near the window, half-silhouetted. She'd chosen a gray coat this time, with the purple and gold waistcoat, trousers of a darker slate and shoes instead of boots. Larkin had already fastened the buttons, tied the neckcloth in a common, utilitarian square—but Jervaulx had looked an aristocrat even in the asylum's cheap, tight-fitting clothes. Mundane neckcloth or not, he was an absolute duke now.

He gazed at her stoically. Then he made a slight bow, as if she were a lady.

"Friend," Maddy said in greeting.

He smiled a little. She came further into the room. When he moved, however, she stopped at a safe distance from him.

Unexpectedly he knelt, a slow and careful move, reaching beneath the bed, drawing something that looked like a rough white stone from the dark space. Maddy prepared to dart for the door, but he only stood up, unthreatening, and held out the raw object toward her.

It was the chunk of plaster that he'd knocked from the wall. When she hesitated, he took a step closer, lifted her hand and set the broken piece in it. He made a soft sound, touching the flat surface with his finger.

The substance left chalky dust on his hand. Maddy looked down and saw the scratches on the plaster face. A tilt toward the light revealed them—barely—as words. In spite of the

crude abrasions and awkwardly pitched letters, though, she
knew his handwriting well enough. She could read it.

Pretty
Mady
Sory

She gazed down at the crumbly offering.

"All right. Yes. Thou art sorry." She kept her face hidden
as she spoke. She pressed her lips together, holding the
chunk of broken wall between her hands, and whispered,
"Not as sorry as I am."

He touched her chin, lifted her face on his hand.

"I'm so sorry," she said. "About the clothes. Do you understand?"

She couldn't tell. She looked into his eyes, into that dramatic pitchy dark blue. A faint, faint smile seemed to come
into his face. He let her go, with a light hint of a caress along
her cheek. Maddy moved back uncertainly.

"Wouldst thou wish to go to the village today?" she
asked.

His face changed indefinably, lost the faint smile. He
stared intently at her lips.

"Go," she said. "A drive. The village."

"*Go.*"

She nodded. "Drive to the village."

"Maddygirl—*go?*"

"Thou. You. Jervaulx. You go."

He nodded. He touched her arm. "Maddygirl . . . go?"

"Oh. Yes. I'm to go, too. If you like."

He smiled at her openly. Maddy curled her fingers around
the piece of plaster. It was quite a vivid experience to be the
single center of that smile. She returned it with a brief and
nervous one of her own.

Escorted between the Ape and the medical man, Christian
walked outside. He kept his gaze locked on Maddygirl's

chaste figure in front of him, her black dress and white collar, the absurd sugar scoop on her head. He felt the cold sun on his face and shoulders, heard the soft blow of the horses, the creak of harness, the sound of feet on the gravel drive.

He felt overwhelmed by the outside, all the light and open distance, lawns and lake, trees. He'd thought that the moment he ever got the chance, he would break and run, but it was all he could do to keep from turning and retreating to the house and his cell. Maddy and pride kept him moving forward; he would not be a spineless lunatic, not here, not now.

The carriage waited. She climbed inside with a servant's help. Christian followed. Pain lanced through his back as he hiked himself up. He caught a groan between his teeth. The interior smelled of pipe smoke and stale lavender water, a massive vulgarity of rich damask and velvet trimmed purple.

Christian felt panic overtaking him, for no reason but that it was the outside. He was afraid someone would see him; he'd be required to understand jabbering strangers; he'd be expected to talk. He grabbed the balance strap on one side and Maddy's hand on the other, gripping both.

She turned and looked at him. As the Ape and the medical man took the forward seat, Christian held her hand harder, with no intention of letting go.

The medical man smiled benignly. "Bit frite you?" he said. "No dange. Say fuzz."

Christian met the pudgy simper with disdain. If he chose to hold on to what seemed solid to him, it was none of this jumped-up commoner's business. The man was ridiculous in a gentleman's breeches and spurred boots this morning—as if he'd ever in his miserable provincial life got out of his country dogcart and mounted a blood horse.

Amid the sounds of harness and the low resonance of the team's hooves, the carriage made the familiar lurch and began to roll. Christian let it press him back against the cushions, creating a dull ache in his injury. He concentrated on controlling himself, watching the landscape, not trying for words to name the things he couldn't name. The driveway was long and smooth; of everyone in the carriage, he was the only one hanging on to the balance strap as if to a lifeline. He made an effort, commanding his hand to let go, trying to remember that this was all ordinary to him: a carriage, the outside, the grass, the trees just beginning to turn bright for the autumn.

The carriage reached the gates of the property, passed through and began a winding tour among hedge-rowed lanes. Against the pale gold of grain fields, the pastures were still brilliant green. He stared out the window, feeling uneasy.

Harvest, work, tenants, day men, swinging metal things, steady rhythm . . . not there!

He had a shock, a terrible intense recollection of Jervaulx Castle, the Welsh marches and wild country, nothing like this manicured view. He should have been there. He'd forgot it. How could he have forgot? *Sheep wool . . . work . . . tenants—tenants—tenants . . .*

The harvest at Jervaulx—who was managing it?

They came upon the village suddenly: a few red-roofed and plastered cottages, a church, a public house under the sign of a black bull. The vehicle slowed. It stopped before the tavern, swayed as the footman climbed down to open the door. Christian felt taken by surprise, flustered, still trying to follow the new thought of his home and the harvest.

He caught the balance strap again, squeezed hard on it and Maddy's hand. The medical man got out. He stood at the steps and looked at Christian with that bland and expectant smile. The landlord came to the door of the tap-room, wiping his hands on his apron, good-humored with his easy greeting, as if he'd expected them.

Christian didn't move. He wouldn't get out here, expose himself as a lunatic in public.

"Come?" the medical man said.

Christian glared at him.

"Get on," the Ape said and stood up, bent beneath the low ceiling. He motioned to Christian to go in front of him.

Christian braced back in the seat in spite of the pain of it. He hung on to the strap and to Maddy, made a low growl in his throat. He didn't want to get out; he didn't want to start a fight that would end in worse humiliation for him. He looked desperately at Maddy.

She smiled at him, just that sort of reassuring smile that she'd given the laughing young madman the day before, like a patient nursemaid for her children. Christian saw abruptly what it all was: a charade, a little play in which everyone knew their part. The landlord awaiting the carriage, the quiet village, the Ape standing by—a pretense of the real outside when Christian wasn't outside at all. He was still locked in the madhouse. They had only expanded the walls.

There was no public to humiliate him here. They already knew he was a lunatic. They expected it. He could burst into howls of insanity, and they would only smile those gentle smiles at him and wrestle him into the chains.

Maddy's hand worked restively in his, in spite of the encouraging expression she maintained. Christian knew she was afraid of what he would do: she wasn't overly good at hiding it. That, of anything, made him release her hand and stand up and let himself down from the carriage like a civilized man—because he didn't want her afraid of him. He wanted her afraid of herself, *little patronizing patient thee-thou spinster.*

Outside the carriage, she smiled at him again. Christian bore it. He was the prize pupil, subdued and compliant. He was calm.

He was a very, very good boy.

Maddy slowly relaxed as the occasion seemed to be proceeding smoothly. Jervaulx's initial tension had vanished; he looked about the village with casual interest, as if he'd never been wrought up at all, though her hand still held the afterache from the strength of his grip in the carriage.

"Shall we take a walk?" Cousin Edward asked. "Her

Grace requested that Mr. Pember have an introduction to Master Christian. The vicarage is across the common."

As Maddy gathered her skirt and reticule in preparation to follow, she saw the moment of panic in Jervaulx's eyes. He hesitated, with an intense, sweeping glance. Then in one of the uncanny alchemies she was coming to recognize, he controlled the confusion and held on to himself. With an ironic look toward Cousin Edward, who was already moving away, Jervaulx walked to Maddy and offered his escort.

She felt oddly bashful to have this courtesy expended on her. He took her hand on his arm as if it were utterly natural—perhaps it was, to him, but Maddy had never walked arm-in-arm alongside any man besides her father, excepting only briefly in and out of Meeting when the doctor had been courting her.

Of course, Jervaulx only did it because he was what he was, a duke and a gentleman, and intended Cousin Edward not to forget it. Maddy understood that much. When Jervaulx put his other hand over her fingers, not allowing her to slip them away, it was a demonstration for the benefit of Cousin Edward.

Still, a maiden Quaker lady could feel rather complimented, and perhaps imagine just a tiny sinful hint of what it must be like to be a duchess—even if she was one of the Peculiar People and her duke a lost and disordered spirit.

With Larkin trailing them, she walked with Jervaulx across the common. Somehow it wasn't awkward; she didn't have to shorten or lengthen her steps to match his, as she'd had to do in her fleeting strolls with the doctor. She didn't have to watch her feet: the little beaten path through the grass was hers, while Jervaulx kept to the more uneven turf. How many ladies he must have escorted in this way, to be so pleasant and easy at it! When they came to the lane on the other side of the common, he paused, just as if it were a busy London street and he her dependable escort across. At the vicarage gate, he gave way for her to precede him, leaning

forward to hold it open as it began to swing closed behind
Cousin Edward.

She passed through. Jervaulx released the gate to the
weight of the suspended ball and chain that caused it to fall
rapidly shut. At the sharp bang and Larkin's grunt behind
them, Maddy glanced aside at Jervaulx. He lifted his eyebrow and looked down at her with an expression of aristocratic languor.

Mr. Pember was already in his hallway to greet them,
primed for the occasion by the note Cousin Edward had dictated to Maddy in advance. He was a vicar of the sort she'd
been brought up to think the very worst of his breed: obse-
quious and comfortable, his home full of stuffed sofas, carpets, dishes of sweetmeats and too many beeswax candles
and lamps.

A few minutes' conversation, and she decided him to be
amiable, kind, and perfectly disagreeable. It was no wonder
that the dowager duchess had found him worthy of an introduction to her son: he was full of just the sort of pious sentiments that the lady had discoursed upon at such length in her
letters.

Mr. Pember began talking at Jervaulx about the wages of
vice and moral turpitude from the moment that everyone had
been introduced, speaking of a just punishment in the most
genial and mild voice, looking at Jervaulx from behind
square spectacles, with frequent resort to a handkerchief between pinches of snuff. Maddy hoped that Jervaulx understood none of it; she hoped that he thought it was only
country gossip, which was precisely the tone in which the
vicar delivered his sanctimonious pronouncements of divine
judgment.

She didn't think Jervaulx comprehended Mr. Pember's
words. The duke merely looked at his host with an expression of polite boredom, as if he'd been through this sort of
thing many times before. He accepted tea from the housekeeper, glancing over his cup and the woman's plump shoul-

der as she poured for Cousin Edward, giving Maddy a secret smile, perceptive and subtle.

Sitting in the front parlor between the vicar and her cousin, Maddy felt closer to Jervaulx than she had felt alone with him in his barred room. There, she was the stranger, miles and lifetimes different from him, unable to understand or be understood. Here, communication between them seemed perfect: an instant agreement on this little society and its annoyingly pious mummery.

Jervaulx picked up his cup and saucer and stood, looking out the window into the back garden. The vicar's sermon paused. Apparently even he was unable to go on in the face of such obvious indifference.

In the little silence, Jervaulx said, *"Cat."*

The expression on Mr. Pember's face was almost comical. Maddy could see him rapidly revising his estimation of Jervaulx's intelligence downward. The vicar nodded and chuckled uneasily. "Oh, yes. A pretty kitty, isn't she?"

Jervaulx looked at Maddy. He set his teacup on the windowsill and made a gesture with his hand for her to come.

"Oh, dear—is it quite the thing?" Mr. Pember asked, as Jervaulx walked to the door. "Does he wish to go outside?"

The duke stopped beside Maddy's chair. He turned to Mr. Pember and in the sort of tone that could command regiments, uttered. *"Cat."*

His hand fell on Maddy's shoulder. He gave her a hard nudge.

"It's all right. Go outside with him, Cousin Maddy. Let him look at the cat if he wishes. Just stay inside the garden wall."

She rose, happy to comply. The housekeeper led them to the back door that opened into a pleasant kitchen and cutting garden. Inside a high brick wall, asparagus was going to feathery yellow and seed. Carrots had been planted in short, even rows. It wasn't until Maddy had stepped outside a few feet that she saw around the corner. There, against the side wall, a bushy plot of dahlias made an amazing sight: brilliant huge platters of blossoms, red and orange and pink-hued white, staked full seven feet tall and blooming at their autumn peak.

It was just the sort of garden Maddy had always wished to have herself—mostly practical, but with a corner saved for something vivid and wondrous, something not at all useful save in its own joyous fantasy.

The vicarage cat, a plain yellow tabby with a crooked tail, disappeared behind the dahlias. Maddy hadn't thought Jervaulx really interested in the animal; she'd supposed that he'd only used it for an excuse to escape the parlor, but he walked away from her, following the cat into its shadowy alley behind the flowers.

Maddy stood waiting. His passage rustled the plants. The top-heavy blooms swayed cheerfully, moved by an invisible hand.

The cat appeared suddenly atop the wall, balancing from the leap. She hissed back at where Jervaulx was hidden, then jumped off the other side.

The garden grew quiet. Maddy tilted her head, expecting him to come out, having lost the tabby. She could hear muffled laughter from the group in the parlor and a strange, faint, squeaky noise beneath the light breeze.

She moved forward cautiously, not quite sure of Jervaulx. He wasn't above leaping out to grab her, she was perfectly certain of that. She held her skirt up above the dirt path and leaned forward, peering around the back of the thick bush of dahlias to the space in the shadow of the wall.

He stood leaning against the bricks. In his hand, he held a spotted tortoiseshell kitten, while another three or four crawled and mewled and tumbled over his feet. He stroked the tiny creature's head with his thumb. From the hidden corner, he looked up at Maddy with a beckoning smile.

Chapter Nine

S he hesitated.

In the narrow aisle behind the dahlias, he bent down to scoop up another kitten, holding them together in the cup of one hand, a spotted puff against a black one. They hissed tiny hisses at one another, and then fumbled together, settling in his palm. Maddy moved closer, careful of the others at his feet. He held the pair as she stroked their plumy tips of fur with her forefinger. When he pressed the spotted one toward her, she took it into her own hand, feeling the tiny pinprick claws in the transfer.

The space behind the dahlias made her think of when she'd been a child and crawled beneath the baize cloth on the parlor table, surrounded by folds that hung all the way to the floor, creating a dim room of her own. Here and now, the daydream room was built of plants and brick, not cloth; the green wall rustled. No man-made scents, sweet and vain, but the smells of earth and earthy perfumes.

She lifted her face, looking from beneath her bonnet to Jervaulx. The duke stood leaning his shoulder against the brick, holding the kitten in one hand, moving his thumb rhythmically over the tiny creature's head.

His face still held that faint, knowing hint of a smile. He lifted the black kitten toward her, held it within a breath of her cheek. His hand with its small burden drifted downward, so that the kitten's fur caressed her skin from her temple to her lips.

She could feel the little animal shift in his palm. Its dainty nose touched her, exploring. The kitten eyes, wide and blue, stared into hers from an inch away. A paw came out, reached up, clung to the stiff brim of her bonnet, too weak to budge it but ready to play. Tiny teeth and claws opened wide and tried to sink into the rigid brim.

Jervaulx made a soft sound of amusement. He lowered his palm. With a violent soprano mew of distress, the kitten hung suspended for an instant, pulling Maddy's bonnet forward over her eyes. The others broke into a bantam chorus of cries, but before the victim could fall, Jervaulx caught it safely back into his palm.

Maddy moved to readjust her bonnet. She pushed back the brim, settled it properly again, an awkward job as the kitten in her other hand began to try to crawl up her bodice.

Jervaulx reached out. She thought he was going to rescue her from the tortoiseshell kitten busily climbing her dress, but instead he caught her bonnet-string. He curled it in his fingers and tugged lightly. The tight constraint came free. He lifted the bonnet away and held it dangling in his hand.

Maddy pressed the spotted kitten against her dress, looking down, avoiding the sudden awareness, the disarmed sensation. She reached to take the bonnet, but he leaned his shoulders on the wall and held the prize behind him. When she met his eyes, he began to smile. He lifted his arm, teasing.

As he swept the bonnet upward, Maddy grabbed at it one-handed, unbalanced in her effort to lean forward without endangering kittens by shifting her feet. She missed. He held the bonnet high. Maddy stretched. With a flick, he tossed it over the wall. The spotted kitten gave a little cry as she almost dropped it and fell against him.

He made no move to steady her. She pushed herself awkwardly off the solid brace of his arm and side, standing straight. He grinned; an instant of devastating dark blue eyes and humor slanted at her. A moment later, like a bad schoolboy, he'd composed his features to an earnest and virtuous gravity.

"My bonnet!" Her stout censure met his mischief like a stone flung into mist: much effort and little effect. "Thou art iniquitous!"

He flicked a glance at her. She saw the slight frown pass over his face and disappear into proud neutrality. He didn't understand the words, but wouldn't acknowledge it.

"Wicked," she added, for amplification.

He looked straight ahead into the green tangle of dahlias. He tilted his head, as if considering whether he would accept that assessment.

"A scoundrel," she stated. "A rogue."

That pleased him, the frivolous wretch; she could tell it. He cradled the kitten in his hand, rubbing its black fur with his thumb.

Maddy bent down and deposited her kitten on the ground, pulling the others free of her skirts. As she rose and took a step backward, he caught her arm.

She should not have let it stop her. For the first instant of it, she could have simply turned and walked free of the touch, out of the shadowy hidden place behind the flowers. But she hesitated, and the grip on her arm became something to break. It wasn't tight or hard, but it was real.

He leaned back against the wall, his head turned toward her. The black kitten decided to climb his coat, crawling upward. Maddy gazed at that. She felt she could not look up, take her eyes from its faltering progress. He caught the kitten with his free hand and pulled it away from his chest.

He let go of her, lifted himself clear of the wall. Maddy thought of stepping backwards, and didn't. She watched him as he knelt and scooped kittens into his hands. The spotted one, the black, two yellow tabbies and a funny little fellow with silver tufts at the tips of its ears: five kittens overflowing his hands and clinging to his waistcoat with tiny frantic mews as he rose.

A yellow tabby tumbled free. Maddy gasped and caught it in her skirt. As she straightened, he lifted the black kitten to her shoulder. Pins pricked through her dress. He raised the tortoiseshell to her other shoulder, put the second tabby beneath one ear and the tufted silver beneath the other, plucked the kitten from her skirt and deposited it on top of her head.

Maddy, half-bewildered, half-laughing, caught at kittens as they teetered and whimpered and fell. When she was too slow to save one, he did, replacing it, snuggling the warm bodies against her throat for the moment they would remain there. The one atop her head stayed put, but cried and cried, digging in claws that tickled painfully.

Finally a tabby and the tufted gray retained their purchase on her shoulders. The black and the tortoiseshell capsized off, but he lifted the two, installing them like soft and ticklish mufflers against her throat, kept in place by his hands.

He held them there. Rhythmic, energetic kitten laments filled her ears. The squirming bodies drove minute needles of pain through her dress and hair and skin.

His mouth hovered near hers. Even if she had tried to step back, she couldn't have, without kittens toppling in all directions. She felt herself entrapped by it, frozen into place by him.

He brushed his mouth against hers, so lightly and briefly that it was a mere breath, a warmth, a touch and then gone before her lips parted to object. He was smiling at them, at her, holding kittens at her ears, caressing the protesting animals along her cheeks. She sucked in a quick breath as pins burrowed into her forehead and the kitten on top tried to scamper down her nose.

Jervaulx stepped back. He caught the falling tabby with a laughing sound in his throat. His hands washed over with wriggling fur. The others began to slip, dislodged by her startle, driving desperate needles through her clothes to hang on. Maddy ducked, scrambling to break their fall. A small shower of kittens overturned into the soft soil as she fell to her knees. Jervaulx knelt beside her and let his handful tumble out. They picked themselves up and scampered with comical unsteadiness after the others, into the dark between the thick stalks of dahlias.

"Cousin Maddy?"

The doctor's call made her turn, instantly guilty as she and Jervaulx knelt behind the flowers.

"Cousin Maddy?" The voice sharpened. "Where are you?"

She stood up, brushing dirt from her skirt. "Here." She walked quickly from behind the dahlias. "We're back here."

Cousin Edward came in haste, brushing past her to get to Jervaulx. "Is it an attack? Is he having visions?"

"No! Wait—it isn't—" Maddy tried to hold him back from trampling down dahlias in the narrow space. Beyond him, Jervaulx stood up, but she couldn't see his face.

"Irrational?" Cousin Edward snapped, without turning from Jervaulx.

"No! It's nothing like that."

Cousin Edward relaxed a little. He glanced back at her. "Attempting to escape?"

"There were kittens. We were playing with kittens."

"Here?" Her cousin kept Jervaulx within the scope of his attention, obviously wary of his patient. "You shouldn't have gone out of sight of the window. Come now, Master Christian—it's time to go home. Will you come?"

Maddy found herself repelled by the cajoling tone of his voice. She turned away, walking into the house. She retrieved her reticule from a chair in the parlor and stood waiting in the hallway with Larkin and Mr. Pember.

"Your bonnet, Miss?" the housekeeper asked.

"It blew over the wall."

"Oh." The housekeeper seemed a little puzzled. "Should I send next door?"

"It's no matter. If someone finds it, it can be conveyed to

the Hall, please." She kept her face lowered, her shoulders straight: the perfect, quiet, employed assistant.

With Cousin Edward close behind, Jervaulx came striding into the hall from the garden door. He picked up his hat and gloves from the side table, gave Mr. Pember a bow of flawless condescending authority, and turned to the front door. The housekeeper hustled to hold it open.

Jervaulx paused next to Maddy. She hesitated between her role as attendant and his offered arm, between Cousin Edward's justifiable and proper expectations and kittens at her throat, Jervaulx's face laughing silently so close above hers. He looked down at her now with an assumption that had rightfully belonged to him in another time and place: a gentleman in command of a lady's entire existence—her hand on his arm, her clothes and her amusements, her time and sentiment and livelihood.

In a moment of revelation, Maddy realized that this was the Devil looking at her out of gentian eyes: that her Opening to serve Jervaulx was not without its real and dangerous temptations.

She had been foolishly vain to think this affliction entirely a divine lesson for the duke, with nothing in it to humble herself. It was easy to be virtuous—and deceitfully proud of it—across the abyss of their stations in life: the nobleman and the maiden Quaker lady from Chelsea. But God had taken the Duke of Jervaulx right down to the level of Maddy Timms. From an equal vantage, the Devil smiled at kittens and at her . . . and Maddy felt the prick of it on her heart like a tiny claw that seized at her for safety.

She made no move to take his arm. The comprehension of that seemed slow to come to him; he stood there too long before he looked down and then placed his hat on his head. He held the gloves. Maddy knew he couldn't put them on alone. She reached to help him, but he stopped her with a murderous look, gripped the elegant yellow kidskin in one hand, and walked ahead of her out the door.

* * *

Cousin Edward stood at his desk, sipping noisily at his tea as he read over the notes Maddy had made on the day. He nodded, set the cup on his desk, and slapped the notebook down on the polished surface. Golden liquid spilled over into the saucer.

"I do believe we've stumbled upon something. I believe we have! He is much improved. I never thought we should have such a successful day on our very first attempt."

Maddy picked up the book. "Have I written it out properly?"

"Very adequate. Better than yesterday. You need to add considerably more detail of how he conducted himself on your walk in the garden. It's clear that he followed the cat into the flowerbed, but you might add a bit of description about his attention to the kittens. Was he aggressive or gentle with them? Did he try to speak at all? Did he seem to prefer a particular animal, and if so, describe it. That sort of thing."

"I see."

The doctor took another gulp of tea. "I have an intuition about this, Cousin Maddy. This trial of using you as his primary attendant. It's unprecedented—but I'm beginning to see that it might be the natural extension of our social therapy. If a harmonious mix of the sexes is useful in promoting control in the nonviolent patients, why then should it not have a similar, perhaps an even more powerful benefit, in the treatment of the violent patient?"

His voice had begun to take on a sing-song quality. He looked off into the far corner, his chin raised a little, as if envisioning the paper he might write on the topic.

He looked back at Maddy. "We've had some aspersions cast on our policy of social mixing of the sexes here. I believe it's professional jealousy, but a case study of the usefulness of the technique with a truly intractable patient—that should leave little room for doubt. Tomorrow, you may take him out and about the house and gardens." He tapped rapidly on the edge of his desk. "And I think perhaps we'll keep Larkin's presence at a greater distance. We've had him within a moment's reach—but that might become too obvious outside of the duke's room."

Maddy wasn't so certain she was ready to do without Larkin nearby. She slipped her forefinger inside the pages of the notebook, squeezing them together on it. "Perhaps—rather than the gardens—I might take him to visit my father."

"An excellent notion. Begin with that, a call in the family parlor. And try to make him understand what an award that is. Very, very few of the patients are ever invited into the family parlor, and then only the best behaved. If he responds well, you must continue right on to the outdoors. It's important to provide an immediate reward for good behavior. To take him back to his room too soon would counter the positive effect."

"Oh."

He glanced up at her. Maddy was afraid that her expression must convey her doubt, for he paused and frowned at her. She thought of her Opening and her duty to Jervaulx. This was for his benefit. She could not turn away from it because she suddenly found herself afraid to be alone with him.

Cousin Edward pulled open a desk drawer. He took out a silver chain and pushed it toward her. "Just keep this whistle about you."

His pride was in it now. He was determined. Christian saw that he'd made progress, not so much by her bemused reaction to the kittens, but in the way she wouldn't touch or look at him afterward.

Just as well. He'd been tired returning, moving on determination alone. They'd all talked faster, garbling sounds; he'd felt his tenuous hold on comprehension slipping. He'd let it go, *weary blurred transparent head ache, fade. Not care sometimes, just . . . not.*

With the morning, he got energy back, and Maddygirl. From his chair, he watched her bend over his bed, smoothing it to a pointless precision. He sat thinking of pleasures, his arms crossed over the rails. With satisfaction in reach, he permitted himself imagination—a luxury he'd not ventured to indulge in this place.

Let her pretend to be the nurse, offer to assist him with his gloves in front of the others. He'd allowed his temper to get the better of him in his reaction to that yesterday, he knew: it was only native female defense—natural retreat from his first move. In a ballroom it would have been a tap with a fan and giddy flirting with other men, slow stalk and response, a pastime he knew down to his bone and sinew.

She straightened up and turned to him. He smiled at her lazily, which had just the effect he wanted: a flustered little transfer of her attention to some foolish task, in this case wiping her apron over the already dusted table. She wore no sugar scoop on her head today. The sun made a rainbow on the tight sheen of her ale-gold hair trapped in its thee-thou spinster knot.

He allowed himself one fantasy of it showering free across her bare shoulders.

She smoothed down her skirt. "Udst thou likall tims ismorn?"

The vision fell apart in frustration. He gripped the bars of the chair. *"Slow."* He managed to get it out, scowling at her.

"Favver," she said. "Tims."

"Tims," he echoed, damnably, when what he intended was to command her to speak more slowly.

"Mathematics. Tims."

Enlightenment dawned. He struggled to say the name. "Mah—*Timms.* Euclid; the . . . the—ah . . . the parallel axiom is independent of the other Euclidean axioms. It cannot be deduced from them."

Her look at him labeled him crazy. But he wasn't crazy. He could talk about mathematics, that was all.

"Go?" she asked. "Timms?"

Go to her father? He made a sound of amazed assent and stood up. The Ape had dressed him again in decent clothes, Christian's own clothes. Maddygirl had fastened his cuffs.

He felt hopeful and uncertain, afraid that they would make him count on this new whim of being treated as something close to a human being.

She unlocked the door, stepped out and held it open. He followed her. The man across the hall mumbled angrily as they passed, reaching out toward Maddy through the door of his cage. Christian thrust himself forward, but she'd already stepped neatly out of reach. The lunatic caught Christian's arm instead.

The fingers dug in, then suddenly released him, patting, plucking at his sleeve. The man's furious expression had gone to bewilderment, as if he couldn't understand why Christian was standing there. Some attendant had combed the man's hair down, but on one side it stood up straight and wild, as if he'd been pulling at it.

He began to mutter something Christian couldn't understand, a litany of "Jees-dev, jees-dev," whispering under his breath. His blank eyes stared into Christian's, a tempest, lifeless and alive at once.

Christian stared back.

Look like this?

This?

He was horrified.

Not this . . . not! . . .

He gave Maddy a distraught look, wrenching his arm from the lunatic's grasp. He wanted to tell her, to make her comprehend that he was not mad, but nothing at all would come: not the tortured syllables he'd achieved lately, not even the simpleton echo of what he heard. It all left him, everything that had begun to come back. When she spoke, it seemed meaningless, no sense at all in the tangle of sounds.

Not mad not not no no not!

He couldn't move. She was talking to him. He made nothing of it; he only knew that he had to subdue the frenzy inside him. Had to act like a sane man; *had* to do it, had to. It was at that instant the most crucial thing in God's creation:

that he move forward down the hall, calm and rational in his actions.

The square of the hypotenuse of a right-angled triangle is equal to the sum of the squares of the other two sides.

The theorem gave him a hold.

He was sane. He was himself. He was going with her to call on her father.

The sum of the squares of the projections of a plane figure upon three mutually perpendicular planes is equal to the square of the area of the figure.

Effortless to generalize Pythagoras, more challenging to move into analytical geometry. He could walk forward calmly. He could think beyond projectives to his own passion: the imaginary geometry outside Euclid.

Through a point C lying outside a line AB there can be drawn in the plane more than one line not meeting AB.

It existed: a logical geometry that described the properties of physical space, built in direct conflict with the parallel postulate. The Euclidean parallel axiom did not stand, though mathematicians had been trying to find a rigorous proof of it since the Greeks. He knew of men far madder than he, men who'd burned out their whole lives in search of an unassailable demonstration, wasted themselves and their families and their health in the quest. The wiser ones gave it up—and he and Timms had gone at it backward and found an answer in reverse.

He remembered something, something at the edge of a great confusion . . . *rain sky dark sound . . . thunder!* He remembered faces, hands together, moving . . . *sound, the sound of hands together* . . . hands at the Analytical Society.

Timms. Paper, yes. Yes.

Timms. Christian found himself able to move. He walked beyond the madman. He was demonstrably in possession of himself, passing down the stairs of a luxuriously furnished country house. Timms would understand, and Christian was going to see him.

* * *

"Papa, he is here. The duke."

Maddy closed the parlor door behind them. Before she could do more, Jervaulx strode past her to Papa's chair. He looked down at the scatter of wooden letters and numerals on the table. He stared for an instant at the precise arrangement of a trigonometric equation. He grasped her father's hand.

"Friend!" her papa said, with a smile and a depth of warmth that made something change in Jervaulx's face. "I've missed thee sorely."

The duke got down on his knees. He held her father's hand in both of his and pressed his forehead against them.

He knelt there, silent. Her father turned his face toward him. Papa reached out with his free hand and traced their clasped fists, spread his palm and moved it down the side of Jervaulx's face.

"Friend," he said again.

Jervaulx made a sound in his throat, a low growl that somehow conveyed more of love and pleasure than any words Maddy had ever heard. He opened his eyes, stood up, releasing her father's hand. He touched the wooden formula. His forefinger caressed it.

He said, "Tangent of half the boundary angle *pi. X* here, negative exponent." He placed a minus sign. "Yes?" He looked toward her father.

Papa immediately felt over the carved symbols for the correction. "Yes. I agree."

"Calculate for one. *X* equals one." He was silent a few moments, studying the table. "Boundary angle, forty degrees, twenty-four minutes." He looked toward Papa again, intensely.

"For the paper?"

"Pa—" Jervaulx clenched his jaw. *"Pah-huh."* He flung himself away from the table, pacing the room. *"Yes, yes, yes.* Pah-*huh."*

"*X* equal to one," her father said impeturbably. "I shall calculate it out in the paper."

Jervaulx stopped at the window. Beyond him, cloud shadows rolled along the drive and the lawn. They fell over his face and moved on. He appeared to be watching the shapes or the sky.

He cast a glance at Maddy. Then he wandered the room again, but closer to the table, as if it drew him. He stopped at the trigonometric equation again. "Calculate in physical space. Not theory. Parallax. Application. Physical space."

"With what example? The distances are too large."

Jervaulx worked at speaking. Nothing came. He strode to the window and pointed out, upward, looking toward Maddy.

"The sky?" she ventured.

He nodded abruptly. "Sky. *Dark.*"

"Ah," her father said. "Stars, then?"

"*Stars,*" Jervaulx said.

Chapter Ten

The *Mécanique céleste* and Laplace in French, *Theoria motus* and Gauss in Latin, with reference to Kepler's *Astronomia nova* and Newton's *Principia*—Maddy had her head bent over one or another of her father's books all morning. Jervaulx couldn't seem to read the words, but he could speak numbers and mathematical equations, even read them aloud if he cared to do so, but he seemed better pleased to take the volume out of her hands, leaf through it impatiently, find the tables he wanted, and hand it back to her to recite while he and her father conferred, forming and rearranging equations for the parallax of stars and arguing hotly about the suitability for publication of distances that must be so preposterously large.

Her father took the conservative view that they would expose themselves to ridicule with such unthinkable numbers, while Jervaulx, for his side of the debate, just banged his fist on the table and made the symbols jump. Predictably, Jervaulx won.

After the first hour, Maddy had made the mistake of suggesting that he might like to walk outside. For this suggestion, she received a sigh of plaintive resignation from her papa—and from Jervaulx, once she made herself understood, an eloquent look of incredulity and scorn, and an imperious thump on the page of Gauss in her lap. She bent her head and resumed reading aloud.

When the maid came to serve her father's luncheon, the men were past the earlier argument and deep in the arithmetical side of their calculation. Neither of them paid the slightest attention to the tray, except that the duke tore off half of her father's bread, sat down at the table and ate it while computing astronomical squares. Maddy looked helplessly at the maid and asked that a meal also be brought for herself and Jervaulx.

She ate hers unaccompanied, during a period of considerable difficulty in the figuring. Jervaulx was aggravated by the wooden numerals; he demanded a pen of Maddy more than once, but she pretended not to understand him, recalling Cousin Edward's rule that he was not to have writing or drawing instruments. She feared that she had already transgressed that guideline in principle with the wooden symbols, for he was certainly in an agitated state with them. It was as if he didn't even wish to look at them, but kept his head turned aside a little as he maneuvered them across the table, or sometimes, scowling ferociously, closed his eyes and felt of them as her father did, turning them over and over in his hand before he placed them.

But he was speaking better, managing fluent phrases sometimes even beyond the mathematics, and his fervor was all focused on the calculations. She suspected that he'd not have conducted himself very much more calmly even before his affliction. Maddy recognized a mathematical obsession when she saw one.

She sat in her chair, a few feet from the table, feeling oddly jealous. With the whistle safely round her neck, she had been rather looking forward to walking outside with Jervaulx.

Cousin Edward looked in once, in the afternoon. Maddy rose quietly and went to the door, standing just inside to speak with him. Their low voices didn't even seem to reach Jervaulx, although her father turned his face toward them, listened for a moment, and turned back. The doctor stood watching as Jervaulx pushed numbers back and forth on the table, viewed them and changed them. Maddy knew that to her cousin it appeared no more than pointless animation, a crazy sort of mental tic. But Jervaulx was composed, and so the doctor was pleased.

Cousin Edward went away. The door closed. To Maddy's surprise, Jervaulx knocked a value for an angle out of place and sat back, looking toward her.

Her father was still working, his hands hovering over his own wooden symbols in that way he had when he was deep in computation. Jervaulx glanced at him, and at her, and rose from his chair.

Her papa's head turned slightly, a recognition of the change, and then he went back to his labor. The duke strolled to the window. He stretched his head back and gave a sign of relaxation. Then he looked over his shoulder at Maddy.

She pressed her back against the door. "Wouldst thou like to take a walk?"

He made no response. The way he continued to look at her made her squeeze the doorhandle in her fingers. It was his pirate look, easy and wicked.

He meandered to the bookcase, tilting his head, frowning for a moment at the titles there. Then he moved on, to the secretary, the reading table. A slow circle of the room, leading inexorably to where she stood at the door.

She could have stepped out. There was nothing whatsoever to prevent it. She could have opened the door to the rest of the house, as if she naturally assumed that he wished to go through. Instead she just stood there, working her fingers round the handle.

Her father bent over his arithmetic, innocent. That he could have identified where she and Jervaulx stood in the room at a moment's request, Maddy didn't doubt. Jervaulx made no particular effort at silence, at least until he paused within a hand's breadth of her. The whole room, and he stopped so close, as near as he had been when she tied his neckcloth and fastened his cufflinks: his breath and his warmth just touching her, the same as they did then.

She didn't have her bonnet, hadn't realized until this moment how the stiff, deep brim was protection, how it had kept his face at a safe distance from hers.

"A walk?" she repeated, her voice too faint.

He only stood there, absurdly close. Blue eyes, black lashes—smiling.

He dropped his gaze to the whistle dangling at her bodice. The smile became cynical. He touched the silver, toyed with it. Then he lifted it and turned it in his hand. He held the mouthpiece just skimming her lower lip, daring her.

Her rapid breath made a tiny sound come from it, like the distant peep of a lost chick. Her father lifted his head, listening.

"Maddy girl?" he asked.

She turned her mouth from the whistle. "Yes, Papa?"

"I think there may be a sparrow in the chimney. Dost thou hear it?"

Jervaulx lifted his arms, resting his fists on the door frame to either side of her. The chain of the whistle slid and tightened at her throat as he kept it in his hand. He held her trapped, his smile growing into a mocking grin.

"I don't hear it." Maddy pressed her shoulders back against the door. "I'll . . . ask the groundskeeper to look."

Her father seemed satisfied, going back to his calculations. Maddy was amazed. It was impossible that she was standing with a man holding her enclosed against the door— incredible that she didn't push him away, break free, call out to her papa.

Jervaulx leaned on one arm. He traced the whistle over the curve of her ear, watching what he did with a fascinated openness. He brought the cool silver along her chin, warming the metal with his fingers. The instrument grazed an arc across her lips to the center of them, and then back the side; to the center, and back again.

He leaned closer. Maddy's breath was singing faintly, unevenly, through the silver alarm. He held it against her lips, his fingers spread across her cheek and chin. He bent his head and pressed his mouth to the silver, a kiss with her protection caught and made useless inside.

The whistle slipped from his fingers. She felt it bounce against her breasts as his mouth came to hers. He touched her as the silver had touched her, just a light graze, but warm.

He took modesty and virtue and salvation away from her so easily. She gave it up so easily.

She stood washed in the sensation of his featherlight contact against her lips, his breath mingling with hers. It seemed as if God's light within her must be shining bright, filling her with wonder. This man, his eyes closed, dark lashes so frivolously long as they rested against his skin: even his eyelashes were unholy in their opulence.

His tongue moved over her as if she were a ginger lozenge, to be tasted in small nibbles. He took her lower lip between his teeth, gently, teasing. A flourish of pure fleshly joy blossomed in her body.

She felt her own will leap up to meet his. Her mouth opened; he answered instantly with a deep and ardent union. His hands drew downward, closing as he leaned into her, bracing his forearms on the door.

He enveloped her. The feel of his kiss was strange and painful and electric. Her hands opened helplessly, trying to find something to touch that wasn't him, but everything was him: all the solid reality within reach. He opened his palms and smoothed her hair—sweetly, over and over like a parent would touch a child—at the same time that he kissed her, pressing hard against her, a forceful intercourse of their mouths and bodies.

He broke it, pulling back to look into her face. They were

both breathing deeply, almost silently—as it had all been silent, in this room with her father just two yards away.

In her ears, her pulse beat frantically. She began to feel what she'd done. Her soul came back from some place it had gone, lost in self-will, sunk in vanity and carnal pleasure.

Jervaulx was watching her. Maddy stared up at him.

He *was* the Devil—smiling a little, tender, a warmth that she'd never foreseen, not in all her everyday prayers to God to keep her soul safe and in spiritual grace. Never once had she imagined that Satan would smooth her hair, would smell of heat and earth . . . wouldn't speak, wouldn't hiss evil promises in her ears. Never once had she thought he would be anything but ugly and corrupt and easy for virtuous Archimedea Timms to scorn.

He looked down at her. The warmth in his smile went to slow irony. He took a curl of her hair that had fallen free and brushed it under her chin, then pushed himself away. The floor creaked under the shift of his weight.

Her father sighed and sat back in his chair. "It's a fearful thing, this." Papa shook his head over the astronomical calculations. "Inconceivable. I shouldn't have believed the results if I hadn't done it myself."

Jervaulx turned. He went to the table and braced his hands against the edge, bent over the computation, his head cocked to one side.

"Dost thou think it holds?" her father asked, after Jervaulx had frowned at it for a long time.

The duke looked up at Maddy. He swept his hand over the formula her father had completed, where the value for the earth's distance from the sun was multiplied by numbers half a million times greater than itself to reach the realms of their new geometry.

"*Stars,*" he said, his face alight with passion. "In . . . *finity.*"

And he smiled at her as if he owned it: distance and space and stars and infinity . . . as if he owned her, too.

* * *

Silence, and Meeting.

The plain walls, the plain benches, simple, stark, silent, awaiting the still, small voice of God. The woman in front of Maddy, dressed in gray wool, had a cracked button at the top of her collar. When she bent her head, a single faint wisp of dark hair escaped the back of her bonnet.

It was a small Meeting, not more than twelve Friends sitting motionless in the square room. No one took the elders' position facing the members. No one spoke. They listened, subdued self-will to the guiding spirit within.

Maddy stared at the woman's wisp of hair. She felt something she'd never felt before in Meeting—she felt herself among strangers. Everyone here was quiet, in a state of spiritual stillness, unadorned and undefiant. As Maddy should be. As she always had been in the past. She looked at the escaped strands of hair and thought of the duke with her bonnet. She looked at the bare and sober walls and saw his smile: mocking, tender, exulting in stars and infinity.

Infinity. Even that seemed somehow immoral. How could anyone but God Himself dare to trifle with infinity? To harness it with numbers and lay it on a baize tablecloth? Perhaps that was why He had struck Jervaulx down with this affliction—for wicked hubris, for daring to turn the universe inside out and make a calculation that wouldn't fit inside the world God had given to Man.

She felt the power of the new geometry without understanding it. She'd heard the awe in her father's voice. Numbers, stars, parallax . . . infinity.

Maddy found herself on her feet. She stood helplessly. A thousand words and thoughts possessed her, none of them spiritual or even rational. Many times in her life she'd sat in silence and heard someone stand up and speak out spontaneously—never once had she done so herself. Never once had she risen from her bench before the rest did so.

But none of the words within her were God's words. They could not be. They were all about a kiss, a man's smile, and infinity as he leaned over her and touched his mouth to hers and she didn't turn away.

The sound of her shoes on the floorboards filled the room. It was only five steps from the last bench to the wooden door. She pushed it open, letting light pour into the dimness, squinting at the sun. The still, waxen scent of the Meeting room vanished in cold open air, in the smell of sun-warmed, white-washed boards and woodsmoke. A single cow, black-and-tan, looked up at her with solemn, pretty eyes and went back to grazing the common.

Maddy dropped down onto the last step, holding her arms tight around herself, bending over her lap. She hid her face beneath her bonnet brim, though there was no one outside to see her—no one who couldn't see past a bonnet and into her heart anyway.

Christian waited for her. She didn't come in the morning.

Only the Ape, not in a pleasant mood. He brought a Bible marked in three places. While Christian stood manacled by one hand, the keeper read verses out like toneless announcements. Christian didn't bother to listen to it, *thud babble,* watching instead the door and out the window for Maddy.

She didn't come all day.

Brutal humiliation, that she could avoid him and he could not seek her out, his intention to humble her turned back against himself.

Worse, he'd awoken a hunger. He'd brought it with him into this cell: an embrace, her body between his and the closed door. He'd brought something that he wanted and could not have, not at his own will. And there was nothing else to think about, no easy distraction as he'd always had before—stupid to crave a woman he couldn't touch . . . he'd always moved on to one available. But there was no obliging substitute now. There was only a new desire, sharp as the throbbing pang in his back. Only the sweet way she'd let him do it, and answered him.

He was afraid that she would not come back. He watched, chained to the bed. The Ape went away. Darkness fell. Still he watched, and still she didn't come.

She was so ashamed, the first time she had to go back she did not look at him even once. She went into the cell and stripped the bed and left.

That was morning. In the afternoon, the schedule said that she was to take him outside in the grounds.

She prayed that it would rain, miserly cowardice and self-will that God did not see fit to satisfy. The day was still and unseasonable, almost warm, the sky a misty blend of cloud and blue coalescing into one another without definition. She walked from the bright yellow of the dining parlor to the up-stairs corridor, hesitating before she came in view of his door.

Her heart was pounding. She could still go back, the Rea-soner whispered; she'd come so quietly that Jervaulx could not have heard her. She could leave him here and finish up with her secretarial duties.

All the other patients were silent—outside for air or sim-ply mute. Moving softly, she peeked around the doorframe.

He stood at the window, looking out, one hand resting against the bar, his fingers curled lightly around it. And sud-denly she saw how contemptible it was to keep him there in the dim cell, when it was her duty to God and to Cousin Edward—to Jervaulx—to take him abroad in the sunlight.

She put her key in the lock. He turned. For an instant he looked at her, an immeasurable look—infinity between them.

Duty had no place in it. Hot blue, his eyes; sable-lashed; the line of his cheek and his mouth so severe and finely fash-ioned. A mystery. Infinity and falling, down and down and down, the way it was in dreams.

He broke it, drowned it in those black eyelashes and a moody glance away. When she entered the cell, he moved back from her, as if there should be some certain distance between them.

"I've come to take thee for a walk in the garden," she said, with a little gesture toward the door.

A faint smile curved his lips. He said nothing.

"Walk. Garden." She held the door open. "Wouldst thou come?"

He extended his hand in a courtly motion, as if to give way to her before him.

Christian respected her reticence, not insisting that she stay too close to him. He allowed her the lead, walking behind her on the gravel paths among the roses.

She moved restively, touching a flower, pushing back her black skirt, bending to collect fallen leaves and pull a tiny weed. The flowers were opulent, full-blown, *topple shower petals at a touch.*

He thought that she might topple that way, falling all at once into his hand, a soft drift of blossom between his fingers. The roses bowed their extravagant heads, nodding, but she was all stiff prim and black, back in her bonnet, so that he could not see her face unless she looked directly at him.

Still, she made it simple. She walked down along the path to a corner arbor, the bench beneath it dusted with withering petals from the red climber arched overhead. She didn't sit; she inspected the flowers as if it were an important office that she needed to perform. Christian didn't have to do anything; he merely moved into the path of escape, flanked on either side by thorns.

She turned around. He saw her realize it.

She looked scared and breathless. A scarlet petal floated downward, avoided the brim of her bonnet and caught on her shoulder.

The scrap of crimson lay there, close to the pale curve of her throat, between the stark collar and the tight upward sweep of her hair. Christian reached out and caught the petal between his fingers. She held stiff, breathing like a frightened doe. He let the moment spin out, his hand suspended near her cheek, not quite touching—not quite, not quite—a whisper away, a restraint as intimate as a kiss.

Color flooded her cheeks. Expectation. Her eyes, those eyes that turned hazel to gold under wanton lashes; her eyes held terror and wonder.

He stepped back and set her free.

With a duck of her head, hiding beneath the defense of her hat, she hurried past him. Christian turned after her, smiling to himself.

Free . . . at his consent. He still had that much power—that he could have kept her there and kissed her, shedding rose petals at a touch.

After that, she didn't linger in the walled rose garden but went quickly to the gate. Christian followed, lazy hunting now, allowing a little distance to open between them. Beyond the garden door was a large courtyard dotted with lunatics and keepers. Nearest was the madman who muttered across the hall from Christian's cell, the Ape behind with his hand on the lunatic's taut shoulder leash.

Christian disliked the open yard instantly. *Not circus beast, animals drag round leash exercise.* He stopped inside the gate, ready to object, but Maddy was gone.

His nerve evaporated. He stood where he was, trying to find her. The Ape and his madman approached, trudging around the track. The lunatic was shaking his head, pulling at the leash, mouthing silent words. The Ape bent close to his ear and said something. The madman looked at Christian, half a foot away, *full-empty eyes, stare void, chilling.*

"Timms!" the Ape said sharply as they passed him. "Takare charge!"

Christian looked after the keeper, and for an instant he saw Maddy beyond. Then a howl—and an impact that hit him from nowhere, took him down, impaled him on pain, while hands ripped at his coat and collar, drawing the neckcloth in a red strangle against his throat. The madman was screaming above him, mouth pulled back, pounding his fists into Christian's head and face.

Christian fought, his hand on the maniac's jaw, fingers forcing it up, rolling off his back with a shove that speared agony through him. He struck, a hard blow to the madman's face that didn't check him. The clutching hands tore at Christian's throat, scrabbling for purchase. The man shrieked, his fingers closing on Christian's neck, pulling him down, trying to sink his teeth into anything in reach. Christian hauled back on his knees and locked his fists, swinging at the lunatic's jaw.

The impact slammed through his arms, made an instant's weakening in the grip on his throat. Christian swung again. The blow knocked the madman insensible. Christian stayed on his knees; he went on hitting, his side an agony, breathing hard and pounding at the still figure beneath him. He hated the lunatic, loathed him, wanted out of this nightmare if it took beating the man to bloody pulp.

But the Ape came—a surprise, a grip from nowhere—hard hands pulling Christian to his feet, people running toward them. He'd completely lost Maddy. His body was aflame, hurting. He tasted blood. *Left me!* He had four keepers dragging him back from the lunatic. *Maddy!* When she finally appeared it was another shock—she wasn't there, and then she was, and he could only stare at her in accusation *leave vanish desert me Maddy! Leave me this, leave animal defend animals fight teeth fist barbarian! Damn you damn you Maddygirl LEFT me!*

Maddy stood speechless. His glare at her was wild, his jaw bleeding from a long scratch, his shirt front torn into three strips and pulled free of his waistcoat. Larkin stood back and allowed the others to pull him toward the house.

"You let him get too far away from you, Miss," the keeper said gruffly.

"Oh God," she said.

"He went after my patient like a bulldog. Unprovoked. Did you see him hit?"

Maddy hadn't seen it start; she'd only turned from her determined stride around the courtyard track when the man's screech had risen, loud enough to curdle blood. They'd been rolling in the dirt, and yes—Jervaulx had hit him, beaten him, even after the poor man was insensible.

"No need for the doctor to know about this, Miss."

Maddy was still hardly able to speak.

"We kinda keep these things to ourselves, the attendants. One of us to the other. Don't let him get so far away from you again."

"No," she whispered, watching as they bundled Jervaulx through the door.

Larkin put his hand on her shoulder. "You see why we don't put fine clothes on the violent patients, Miss." He smiled. "We know what we're doing here, Miss. Tell me if we don't."

Master William, the man Jervaulx had beaten, was awake and tied in the infirmary, repeating, "Jesus is the Devil," over and over again with a muttered vehemence. Jervaulx was in his cell, manacled, sitting bare-chested on the bed with only breeches and the rib bandage for decency. Maddy shut the solid door behind her and stood near him.

"Why?" she asked.

He looked up at her, beautiful and savage, his hair with dust in it, his face still bloody.

She moistened her lips. "Why didst thou hit him?"

He made a groan, shook his head. *"Kill!"*

"No. No—I don't believe that. Thou couldst not have wished to kill him. Why didst thou attack him?"

He gazed at her as if she were some mysterious vision, then shook his head again, looking down.

"Understand?" she asked.

He shook his head, dropped it lower.

Maddy knelt. "I want to understand," she said slowly. "Tell me why."

His jaw worked. *"Kill."* He lifted his lashes, a brief look, an appeal. "Mnnh . . . *Me.*" He made a fist and struck his chest as if he were driving a knife into it. His mouth drew back in a silent grimace. He turned his face away from her.

She did not know if it was an answer or a plea. With an uncertain move, she reached out and touched his temple, smoothing his hair back from his lowered face. He flinched as if she surprised him; then after a moment he relaxed into it, leaning against her hand.

"It will be all right," she whispered.

He made a sound, a strange half-laugh, and shook his head again. Just perceptibly, his body rocked, like a strong tree in the wind—a silent sway, too deep for words.

"Let me clean thy face."

He made no response. Maddy rose and poured water from the tin pitcher into the basin. The towel was fresh—she'd brought it herself. She knelt again and began to sponge the blood from his face. He closed his eyes. When she finished, she took his hands and washed the dirt from the raw scrapes there.

She rose. The manacles rattled as he put his arm round her hips and leaned his face against her. The chain pressed across the back of her leg; the wristband and his fingers pressed harder. She laid her hand on his shoulder.

For a long time, they stayed that way. It might have been all night but for the loud knock on the solid wood door.

Larkin stood outside the bars. "Doctor found out," he said briefly. "I'm to take him down to seclusion until morning."

After breakfast Maddy was called in to Cousin Edward. He sat at his desk, with a large notebook open and a pen in his hand. "This will not do," he said. "I'm disappointed."

"I'm sorry." She was miserably, utterly sincere. "I allowed myself to go too far away from him."

"It's fortunate that Master William seems to have taken no serious hurt. His family is connected to the Huntingtons, of Whitehaven, you know. And the duke . . . well—he seems prone to injury lately. I wonder now if those ribs weren't somehow cracked in an altercation instead of an accident." He gave her a questioning look, as if she might be hiding something.

"On, no. It was Jervaulx himself who showed me that a chair fell."

"That may be, that may be. Still . . . Larkin was slow to report this—and you also, Cousin. I'm afraid that I must give you both a check."

She kept her head down, receiving the reprimand humbly. He wrote in the book.

After a pause, her cousin went on. "Your reports have been positive. The duke has not offered you any violence?"

Maddy didn't lift her eyes. "No violence at all."

"You aren't uneasy in him?"

She raised her head. "He has not been violent toward me."

"Still, I believe we must restrict his movements for a time. You will continue to serve him, but only with restraints or a male attendant present. We shall see if that suits. I had felt it was going so well. Really, I am surprised to have it reported to me that it was Master Christian who provoked the scuffle rather than Master William, who's been in the very midst of a bad paroxysm for the past fortnight." Once again, he gave Maddy a searching look.

"I did not see who provoked it," she said.

"Next time, you will be more careful."

"I will. I will. I'm so sorry."

Chapter Eleven

S he'd tried to explain to Jervaulx where they were going. She had no idea if he understood. He had that look of tautness, of a man frozen but burning inside. With both his hands laced together to the elbows in leather gauntlets, he gripped the strap inside the carriage and stared out the window, as intense as he had been with the mathematics, fixing on ordinary things, a haystack, a millwheel, watching them pass as if they were enemies that might leap upon the vehicle without a moment's warning. He was a mobile explosive ready to set to spark; Maddy sat across from him and her father and prayed from moment to moment that it would not happen.

Larkin rode on top of the carriage, much too distant to provide real security or aid. Having embarked on this course of supporting Jervaulx, Maddy found it beyond her control now, caught up in the doctor's tests and experimental trials. The duke had been so subdued for the past fortnight since his fight that Cousin Edward had decided to allow him more freedom with Maddy in the carriage.

She was, by her mere presence, to elicit civilized behavior from him, nevermind that she was no genteel and noble lady, but only plain Maddy Timms. Nevermind that they tied him in gauntlets that anyone could see drove him to the edge of control. Nevermind that when they came to the first change, a busy posting-house with a yard full of travelers and horses and shouting ostlers, he pushed back in his seat and expelled harsh breath between his teeth, refusing to get out, and looked at her with terror and anger and a rigid-jawed shame, then turned his face away.

Maddy pulled the curtains closed on the carriage. When Cousin Edward came to the door, she told him that the duke did not wish to take refreshment here. Cousin Edward, sometimes foolish and sometimes not, looked from her to the dim corner where Jervaulx sat, his gaze malevolent and silent, like cat's eyes that turned and caught lantern light in a cellar.

"We'll stop a little farther on," her cousin said.

Maddy let go of her breath. "I'll stay here then, if thou wouldst take Papa in to tea."

When they stopped again, it was in a small and ancient village snugged down in a wooded hollow. The midday street was empty, the public house quiet and dark inside its open door. Maddy helped her father from the carriage and turned back, surprised to find Jervaulx rising, awkward in the gauntlets but apparently ready to follow.

He disdained aid in descending. When he stood in the street, he looked up the curve of the road. Half-timbered brick cottages with skewed slate roofs and garden walls seemed to warp themselves to the contour of the hill, a treacle flow of buildings instead of a neat, straight modern line. Jervaulx looked back at Maddy. His jaw tightened with effort. "Pah . . ." he managed, and then, *"Lost."*

"Not at all, not at all, Master Christian," Cousin Edward walked up to them. "You mustn't be concerned about that. We've come a little off the main road, but we know precisely where we are, I assure you. Chalfont St. Giles."

Jervaulx made an exasperated snort. *"Lost."*

"Indeed, we're not lost. Not a bit."

"St. Giles . . ." Her papa mused, as if he couldn't quite recall something.

"Lost," the duke said emphatically.

Cousin Edward was soothing. "No, no. We are not lost. Larkin, you'll see to the duke. Have a care about handling him—I'm a bit concerned about his mood."

Jervaulx stood behind Cousin Edward, looking down on him with a caustic scowl. "Damned blockhead," he said clearly. *"Lost!"*

"We shall find our way," Cousin Edward responded in a level tone. He scanned Jervaulx critically. "We may have a manic episode developing, I fear. Disrespect and invective are frequent early signs. We'll leave the restraints in place."

"Will you follow me, Master Christian?" Larkin took the duke's arm. Jervaulx stepped back, twitching free of the touch. He glanced once at Maddy, a dark look, as if she'd betrayed him, then walked away toward the public house with Larkin trailing like a bulldog behind a thoroughbred.

She moistened her lips. "Dost thou wish to take tea, Papa?"

Her father turned his head, drawn from a thoughtful silence. "Tea? No, not at all. Shall we walk a little way for fresh air, Maddy girl?"

It seemed startling to hear her father's pet name for her spoken so clearly and easily. Somehow, Jervaulx's tortured intonation had become more familiar—or more significant: an effort of will merely to utter the syllables, and therefore each one momentous.

She took her father's arm, still feeling agitated. They walked a little way in silence until Maddy finally exclaimed, "I hope that he isn't about to become disorderly."

"Disorderly? The duke?"

She had never told him about the fight in the courtyard. She smoothed the cuff of her sleeve down, rolling the edge in her fingers. "He did seem . . . rather turbulent. Perhaps—instead of thee and me—Cousin Edward would consent to have Larkin ride with him."

"Thou art frightened?"

Her father's surprise made Maddy feel a little ashamed. "Thou dost not know him, Papa. He's forbidding in a passion. He isn't rational. And he's very strong."

"He sounded to me quite rational," Papa said. "He called Cousin Edward a blockhead."

"Papa!"

He stopped, holding her back with a strange little smile. "Where are we? We've walked up a hill, have we not? Is there a cottage to the left—red brick, with a chimney facing on the street, and a multitude of vines on the garden side?"

"Oh. Yes—one more house up the way. Hast thou been here before?"

"Upon the chimney . . . is there a sign?"

Maddy looked. "Milton's Cottage."

Her father said nothing. She hesitated, gazing at the modest village home. Understanding dawned.

She burst into a laugh. "Oh no—he *is* a blockhead! And so am I! We aren't lost at all, are we?" She made an imitation of Cousin Edward's soothing reassurance to the duke. " 'Why, you mustn't worry, Master Christian. We know precisely where we are, Master Christian. Chalfont St. Giles.' *Paradise Lost.*"

"The very house where Milton wrote it. Thy mother and I stopped to visit among the Friends here when thou wast only a babe in arms."

"What simpletons the duke must think us! His face when Cousin Edward kept saying we weren't lost! Oh, Papa . . ." She bit her lip as the laughter died and her voice broke. "Oh, Papa—how he hates it, what's happened to him."

"He needs thee, Maddy girl." Her father laid his hand over hers. "He needs thy faith. Even when thou art frightened."

"I didn't think—I haven't been sure—I've been praying. I was so certain before, but now . . ." She shut her mouth tightly. Her father stood silent, his hand still.

He kissed me, Papa.

How she wanted to say it, but could not. She would repulse him beyond forgiving. The duke was his friend—and Maddy . . . she hadn't even tried to prevent it. She thought she must have lured Jervaulx, that the Devil had gotten into her, too, and made her look at the duke and see comeliness in his earthy shape. A woman minister had spoken out in Meeting just weeks ago, when it had meant nothing to Maddy, when she had hardly been listening, words that came back now with vivid precision, as if God wished her to recall them in perfect detail: "All our joys, pleasures, profits— all things delightful to the flesh—they be but vanity and vex- ation, We become silent, not answering to obey the lusts of the carnal mind."

Maddy didn't feel silent. Inside her a clamor of vanity and delight and joy and vexation tumbled; she felt wicked and weak, a foreigner to herself. She felt afraid.

"I don't . . . know what to do," she said painfully. "I don't know!"

Her father lifted his head. After a long moment, he said slowly, "Is it so difficult, Maddy girl?"

She couldn't tell him. She could not.

"It seems to be," she said, looking down at his hand on her arm.

"Thou wouldst rather go home, then?"

She thought of doing that. Returning to Cheyne Row and the safe and quiet life there, where the only temptations were small ones: a disposition to scold the maid and a frivo- lous envy of girls who owned pretty clothes. Going home— leaving him to Larkin and Cousin Edward and Master William, to silence and chains and a prison cell.

"I'm sure that I would rather go," she said. "But I—" She made a sound of despair. "I could not."

He patted her hand. "Thou art a good girl, Maddy."

"Oh, Papa," she cried. "I'm not."

He only smiled, as if she were still an impulsive child. But Maddy knew. She wasn't good. She was tied to the earth and the Devil and a man, and she was not good at all.

* * *

They arrived in London at dusk, the city smells and population a jar to Maddy after only a month in the country. The chaise never slowed, but rolled past Hyde Park into Oxford Street, where bright gay lights already gleamed on the row of lacquered carriages standing in wait down the middle while ladies and gentlemen passed in and out of the shops. A silversmith, a spirit booth, jewelers and linen stores and confectioners: a mile of goods and spectacles, everything lit and polished for display.

The duke watched it pass, glancing keenly sometimes at Maddy, suspiciously, as if she had somehow conjured the illusion of it all. She'd tried to explain, to prepare him for the hearing, but she knew he had no notion of what she meant. She could tell by the suppressed elation in him—he thought he was coming home to stay.

When the coach turned out of Oxford Street and began to wind its way through stylish side streets, he held out his bound arms toward her.

"Off," he said.

The carriage came into an aristocratic square. She could hear the calls of footmen and the bustle to clear pedestrians from the passage.

"Please." The word came harshly, the sharp explosion of it in stark contrast to the appeal.

Outside, liveried servants milled about as the vehicles creaked to a halt before the house at the head of the square. The free-standing building dominated its neighbors, white and symmetrical, pristine in its Corinthian pilasters and balanced windows, not so different from the duke's home in Belgrave Square but larger and colder in its isolated perfection, with a small and unwelcoming door just one step up from the street.

That door stood open, showing lights inside. Maddy saw Calvin the butler come down the single step and stand aside. Then came the dowager duchess in a black dress. She took Calvin's help to the sidewalk and hurried toward Cousin Edward's carriage.

Maddy leaned over, pulling Jervaulx's hands into her lap. In the dimness, she struggled with the leather laces and just managed to pull them free as her cousin and the duchess came to the carriage door.

The gauntlets fell into obscurity on the floor. Maddy kicked them back into a corner. Jervaulx made a sound of gratitude, not quite accomplishing a real word. Lantern light poured into the interior as the door opened and the duchess' voice rose above the others.

"Christian!" She paused, as if she didn't know how to go on, staring up at him from the curb. She took a step backward, her black skirts shifting around her. A footman moved close to her side as she closed her eyes and put her hand to her throat. "No—go away. I shan't let myself be overcome." She opened her eyes. "Go away, all of you! People will stare at this bustle; someone might recognize him." She turned to Cousin Edward and gestured toward an alley beside the house. "Drive around to the rear. We shall take him inside there."

"No," the duke said.

His mother looked back, as startled as if one of the horses had spoken. She and Jervaulx were hardly alike at all, different in everything: the dowager's hair graying from blonde instead of black, her skin fair to paleness, her figure slender and far more delicate, in her eyes but a hint of the midnight blue of her son's. But when her face lit with hope, Maddy saw the same intensity that kindled the duke in his mathematical passions, a stubborn, focused ardor as the duchess swept forward and caught the edge of the carriage door. "Christian? Are you—"

She stopped herself again and glanced at Cousin Edward.

"He's made some progress lately," the doctor said. "I think Your Grace will be pleased."

Jervaulx picked up his hat where Maddy had laid it on the seat, and beckoned her and her father to get down. She obeyed, helping Papa to come behind her, while the dowager duchess watched them speechlessly.

"This is Miss Archimedea Timms—and her father Mr. John Timms, Your Grace. Miss Timms in particular has been of assistance with the duke. We've instituted a novel treatment in his case; I shall apprise you of the details at the first opportunity, but as you see, our success speaks for itself."

The dowager was paying no attention to Maddy or her father; instead she was watching her son descend from the carriage. Jervaulx gave his mother a dry smile and a bow.

He said nothing, only stood by the coach as if he were courteously waiting for someone to suggest a direction. The duchess kept staring at him. Her whole body seemed to shudder. Suddenly a sob burst from her and she walked into his arms, pulling herself close to him.

For an instant, he was very still. Above his mother's trembling embrace, Maddy could see the near-explosion, the way his expression went to emotional tempest, all the words that battled for freedom. His left hand closed into a hard fist.

His eyes met Maddy's. Fury came so close to detonation; she could not imagine that his mother didn't recognize it. He had no way to speak, only violence—and violence hovered, vibrating in the genteel square.

Maddy stood in terror, pleading with him silently.

He closed his eyes. With a long, indrawn breath, he lifted his right hand and laid it, tentative, against the dowager's head. She began to weep in earnest, pressing closer.

The moment of hazard seemed to pass. He stood, awkwardly touching his mother's coiffured hair, like a man put upon by an overeager child and uncertain how to deal with it. But his left hand never relaxed the fist, still locked in mute hostility.

The duchess pushed back a little, turning her face up, smoothing his collar with restless fingers. "Christian." She caught his hand as it fell away and held it against her breast. "Praise God. I've prayed for this. It is a miracle."

"Progress, Your Grace," Cousin Edward said. "Progress based on scientific treatment. We are not wholly recovered yet."

"It's a miracle. We should go down on our knees and lift our thanks to Heaven." She gripped her son's hand hard. "You most of all, Christian—in consequence of your sins. Give thanks for forgiveness and for your deliverance." She bowed her head. "Almighty God, who dost bequeath us life and taketh it away, on whose sufferance we—"

Jervaulx freed himself. He turned and walked away from her, as Calvin sprang forward to hold open the door.

His mother finished her prayer quickly, moving her lips in silence, and went after him. She disappeared into the lighted hall with Cousin Edward on her heels. Calvin held the door open and looked back. "Miss Timms? Mr. Timms?"

There was a moment, when he came into the hall, that he found himself alone. He turned at the sound of footsteps, expecting Maddygirl, but it was his mother behind him with her pious gibberish. He'd forgot it, half-forgot her, until she'd wept on his chest in the street, and he'd realized that she must be the one who had abandoned him to the cell and the Ape.

In the hall, he disengaged himself from her again, working for command of himself, waiting for Maddygirl, feeling the world go out of balance until her gray thee-thou figure appeared in the doorway. Once he knew she was there, he could go on: he mounted the mahogany staircase, his hand on the curved banister.

He owned this house. It seemed strange and disturbing and right. How long it had been since he'd walked this stair, this hall, he had no idea, but he owned it. Everyone here would do his bidding; even his mother lived in it at his pleasure.

It occurred to him that he himself didn't live here. Not now. What he remembered best were times far in the past, seasons in the City, balls for his sisters, going home to Jervaulx—that was where he lived—and he felt a surge of sharp longing for its dark medieval silhouette, its convoluted towers and chimneys and endless rooms.

That was where he would go, now that he was free. Home to Jervaulx Castle.

Two of his sisters waited in the drawing room. He stood at the door, watching them before they knew he was there. They talked to one another in low tones, and looked nervous. At the sound of other footsteps on the stair behind him, they turned. They looked at him as if he were not alive. Transparent. Walking dead. In the shock on their faces, another revelation came to him.

He knew what they'd expected. A madman, carried upstairs to be exhibited in chains. No wonder they were nervous.

His mother passed him, taking him by the arm with her into the drawing room. She talked, kept talking so quickly that he felt overwhelmed.

Clementia. He caught the name and remembered *Clem*. With that came Charlotte's. Both of them reached out and kissed his cheek in turn, puffed sleeves and lace, plump hands that caught at his and brushed gently before they were gone. He felt bewildered, uncertain of them and their sudden smiles. Their dresses seemed too bright and elaborate, their hair too much of rolls and ringlets.

He looked back again for Maddy, found only the blood-doctor, and strode to the head of the staircase. She was standing in the hall below with her father, still in her bonnet and cloak.

He went halfway down the stairs and stopped. When she looked up, he made a sound. He watched her face change, felt a vast and forceful relief when she put her hand to the tie on her cloak, murmuring to Calvin as he took it from her. She guided her father to the foot of the stairs. Christian stood waiting for their slow progress until they reached him.

He would not attempt to speak in front of his family and servants who knew him. He walked silently around the edges of the white and gold drawing room while the others talked.

The house pleased him. Everything familiar and in its proper place, the marble tables with their gilded legs, the matching chairs, rich green fabric, all older than he was, standing in the places they had stood for his whole life.

He had to turn sometimes to be certain Maddy was there, because the others didn't talk to her or even offer her or her father a seat. That provoked him. He fixed a look on Charlotte, willing her to show a little courtesy, but she only glanced at him and grew pale and discomfited.

"Shud—shudbe lowed loose?" she asked the bloodman anxiously.

Loose! As if he were some zoo animal, to be locked up. *My house! Own it, own you . . . dress, lace, fancy, trust, all of it.*

He knew these two. They were the ones who needed Christian's write-name pen to get into their equity, who most liked a generous supplement to their husbands' means—a thing which galled those gentlemen to the edge of civility. Christian noticed that *they* didn't seem inclined to make an appearance on his first night home.

He suspected Clem and Charlotte were here for precisely that—allowance—and he didn't know what he would do when they finally asked. Everything before the cell and the Ape was hazy; he couldn't recall what quarter it was or if he'd made arrangements.

He turned away from them, facing the mantel, where a good fire burned in the well-swept grate. He would ask Maddygirl to help him, after they were gone.

"Archu angry thus?" Clementia spoke into a small silence. "Chris?"

He realized that she was talking to him. He locked his hands behind his back and slanted a look toward her.

"Chu angry?" she repeated.

He looked at Maddygirl, still standing a little distance from the others. He walked to the edge of the room, retrieved two chairs, and placed them for the Timmses. He set the gilt pair with thuds that could hardly be misinterpreted, then guided Mr. Timms to one himself. When Maddy hesitated, he took up a position behind the empty chair and bumped it, frowning at her.

She cast down her eyes and sat. His family looked at him as if he were an astonishing puzzle.

Clem started to speak, then closed her mouth abruptly, distracted by the familiar snap and thump of a walking stick. That sound Christian knew to the bottom of his brain—since before the day he'd even learned to talk—the adamant herald of his Aunt Vesta.

With a sardonic smile, he placed a chair for her, too: her favorite, the heavy French-small-birds-flowers with massive gold arms and dragon-claw feet, fit throne for a she-dragon. He looked up from setting it close to the fire, sketched a bow as she stood in the doorway, imposing pale against sable black, in the mourning for father, husband, brother—perhaps even for Christian, who could tell?—that she had never put off. It was a battle of jet and ebony in this house, between his mother and his aunt. He remembered why he didn't live here.

"You look well, Jervaulx," Lady de Marly announced, moving toward him.

Maddy had recognized her instantly, needing no introduction to know that here was the author of those rigorous and pointed letters in the duke's file at Blythedale Hall, the lady who sent fastidiously tailored clothes instead of devout sentiments, who had marched so fixedly into the house in Belgrave Square on that morning when Maddy had stood watching.

With a rush of help from one of the fashionable young women, Lady de Marly seated herself in the chair Jervaulx offered. Her brows were painted onto skin the color of shriveling white petals, her lips and cheeks delicately but visibly rouged. She lifted one thin finger. "I shall have a glass of claret."

The duke tilted his head. After an instant of hesitation, he reached out and used the bell-pull beside the fireplace.

"You will upset your digestion, Aunt Vesta," the young woman said.

Lady de Marly ignored her. She looked to the side, speaking to Jervaulx where he stood behind her. "Come here where I can see you, young man." She gestured with her walking stick, tapping the floor beyond her feet.

He moved into her view. She looked him up and down. Maddy didn't think a more handsome and elegant gentleman could be imagined.

"You look as if you were going to a French musicale in a hunting cravat. Where is the signet?" Lady de Marly demanded.

"Ah!" Cousin Edward fumbled in his pocket. "I've brought that, my lady. I deemed it best to keep it under my own protection until we arrived."

"You need keep it no longer."

He went to her, bowing in a most servile and unQuakerish way, and handed her a small box. She merely took it and held it out to Jervaulx.

Maddy didn't know if the others could see the duke's subtle wariness. He accepted the box, looked down at it in his hand. As Lady de Marly gave orders for wine to the servant who'd just arrived in the doorway, Jervaulx slid a glance toward Maddy.

She surreptitiously closed her hand, as if round an object, and slipped her fist down the side of her skirt.

Jervaulx tightened his fingers on the box and felt for the side pocket in his coat, dropping the case inside. He gave her a covert, one-sided smile.

"You look well, Jervaulx," Lady de Marly repeated. "I don't scruple to say that I'm surprised. How has this been accomplished, Dr. Timms? I understood from your last report that little progress had taken place."

"We've instituted an innovative therapy, my lady," Cousin Edward said eagerly. "It's been successful beyond our expectations."

"Innovative?" She regarded him suspiciously. "What therapy is this?"

"The natural extension of our social and moral treatment. We find at Blythedale Hall that a regulated social commerce between the sexes can be notably effective in encouraging self-control. I described it to you, my lady, you may remember, when I came to escort the patient to Blythedale. But of course a minimum standard of behavior must be achieved before we can introduce a violent patient to the larger group. As I had communicated to you, His Grace had not approached this quality of conduct, but remained sullen, with unpredictable fits of mania, in his behavior toward all attendants and myself. However, we had a fortunate opportunity in the arrival of my cousin Miss Timms. Knowing her to be of mild and steady feminine character, unimpeachable in her moral fiber, I took care to assign her as the duke's primary daytime attendant. I did so in the expectation that under her influence any remaining vestige of self-control might best be encouraged. I think you will agree that this approach has been most beneficial."

He was working hard to govern his triumph and keep to a professional tone, but could not quite conceal his satisfaction. Lady de Marly didn't even look at him as he spoke, but remained watching Jervaulx for a long moment after he finished.

She turned her imperious gaze on Maddy. "You are Miss Timms?"

Maddy stood up. "I am. This is my father, John Timms."

"Be seated."

Maddy felt those dark eyes fixed on her as she sat again. She kept her gaze just a point lower than Lady de Marly's, not bowing like a child of the world, but not taking a stand of open disrespect, either.

"When last I saw my nephew," Lady de Marly said, "he was a bellowing beast. He was tied into a bed, his hand cut down to the bone from putting it through a window before he was stopped. He had broken the arm of the footman in charge of him, who was attempting to prevent him strangling his brother-in-law. He would not feed himself. His speech was that of an idiot. He roared. He howled. He was an animal, Miss Timms. The Duke of Jervaulx was a mindless brute." She stared at Maddy. "I would like an explanation of how you have realized this change."

Maddy lifted her eyes and looked directly at Lady de Marly. "He is not mindless," she said steadily. "Nor a brute."

For a long moment, the old lady did not respond. Then she said, with a little wry wrinkle of her lips, "I must say, Miss, that he had me fooled on the subject."

"I believe—" Maddy glanced at Cousin Edward, who didn't look entirely happy with her, but he hadn't said that she should not speak her opinion. "I believe that he is in his right mind, and no more an . . . idiot . . . than thou or me."

Lady de Marly lifted her eyebrows. "A lofty little Quaker."

"I don't wish to be lofty. I only wish to explain to thee."

"In my day, Miss, we called the way you talk uncivil. Your cousin here don't thee and thou his betters."

Maddy merely kept her eyes up and level, declining to be drawn into a defense of her Plain Speech. She had known old ladies just like Lady de Marly before—there was nothing she would like better than a good rousing argument that might be turned into a scold. Maddy had a certain affection for the type: she sometimes thought that she might turn out to be one herself, held back now only by her Papa's gentle refusal to rise to any baiting.

Cousin Edward pursed his cheeks in a vexed way at her, and she recalled her promise not to use Quaker language with outsiders. But it was too late now, and she had a feeling that if she gave in and apologized, Lady de Marly would only like her the less for it.

"So," the elderly woman said to the duke. "Miss Timms declares that you are perfectly sane."

Jervaulx simply stood looking at her.

"Well, boy? What have you to say to that?"

He turned his head a little, the way he did when he was intent on something, regarding it obliquely instead of straight on.

"Do you understand me?"

He glanced uneasily at Maddy.

"Don't look to her. It's to you I speak. Can you hear what I say?"

His mouth tightened. He nodded, once and briefly, then began an expressive contemplation of a side table. It certainly bore contemplation, as its black marble top was upheld, instead of by mere legs, by two huge golden birds with spreading wings that seemed to dash flames from their tips. It would have been the most rich and gaudy piece of furniture Maddy had ever seen if it hadn't been matched by one precisely like it on the opposite side of the mantelpiece.

Lady de Marly tapped her stick rapidly against the floor. She scowled at her nephew. "This is no time for your willfulness, boy. You've had you a score of years to treat us to your caprice; wild and thoughtless as a red Indian you've been, and paying for it now. No one can tell me that a sensible man would have got himself tangled in that barbarous exchange of shots at all, far less wake up from it a Bedlamite."

Only the duke's tense jaw gave any sign that he even realized that she spoke to him. Lady de Marly sat back in her chair with a sharp sigh.

"Young fool." She fixed an accusing look on Maddy. "What sort of progress is this?"

"If thou wilt perhaps speak slowly," Maddy ventured.

"You said that he wasn't an idiot."

Maddy stood up. "No more an idiot than thou wouldst be set down in China amongst Chinamen. He will understand, if thou hast patience with him."

"Miss Timms, tomorrow at ten o'clock he comes before the Lord Chancellor. I have managed to see that it will be private. No jury has been called—not yet." She sent a withering look toward her two nieces. "The vultures are covetous, however. I suggest that if you don't wish to see your prize subject warranted an idiot under the law, then you'd best bend your moral fiber and steady character rather smartly to the task of making him understand his peril."

Her words died away into a stunned and uncomfortable silence. The servant's door opened, and a footman padded in, carrying Lady de Marly's claret. She took it from the tray and drank a sip, never taking her eyes from Jervaulx. Then she set the glass on a side table and pushed herself out of the chair.

"Miss Timms will stop here tonight. The rest of you— leave us."

The dowager duchess looked shocked. "But Dr. Timms—"

Lady de Marly cut her short. "I understood that he had accommodation? The Gloucester, I believe."

"Yes, my lady." Cousin Edward bowed. Twice.

"I wished to speak with the doctor," the duchess said, rather plaintively. "I wished to find out how Christian's been going on."

"Hetty, dear," Lady de Marly said dryly, "if you have not already discovered in the last quarter hour how he's been going on, there is nothing the man can tell you that will not keep until tomorrow. Will you join us for breakfast, Doctor? Eight o'clock."

"I would be honored, my lady. I'll just call our night attendant to settle the patient in his bed," Cousin Edward said.

"Will that be necessary, Miss Timms?"

Under Lady de Marly's dictatorial eye, Maddy groped for a proper answer. "I—think it would be wise."

"That's as it may be. I find it highly inconvenient to have extra servants in the house this evening. I hope you feel yourself up to the task." She glanced at the footman. "Tell Pedoe to air the bedding for Miss Timms in the duke's dressing room."

Maddy stood rooted to the floor as Lady de Marly began to thump her way toward the door. She stopped and turned back. "You're blushing girl. I thought you was a nurse?"

"Yes," Maddy managed to say.

"And he's an idiot, until you prove me different. See to it that we have no bizarre scenes out of him tonight."

Chapter Twelve

$\mathscr{A}$ s luxurious as Blythedale Hall had been, as comfortable and rich as the duke's house in Belgrave Square had appeared, Maddy had never even imagined that behind the pale facades of houses such as this were interiors beyond commonplace imagination: servants dressed like princes in snowy satin trimmed with blue and silver lace, walls of red velvet adorned by huge paintings, intricate plaster mouldings painted in white and gold, carpets that muffled the sound of her feet, candelabra glowing everywhere.

When the liveried footman showed her into the duke's dressing room, she tried not to betray her astonishment, but as soon as the servant was gone, leaving Maddy alone with her small traveling case, she looked up at the ceiling and couldn't help herself; she choked back appalled laughter.

It was absurd. A dressing room—and it was painted in royal blue, with huge pediments bordered in intricate bands of gold over the doors. Not only that: above the pediments were round portraits of solemn gentlemen surrounded by languishing gilded cherubs draped over frames of flowers, crossed banners, all gold—then blue velvet up to the arched ceiling where a riot of design glittered, stately rows of knobs

and leaves, *more* gold, highlighting every patterned detail.
The narrow room blazed with it. Maddy hardly saw how one
was expected to sleep amid such splendor.

On the far wall, the connecting door to the bedroom stood
open. Maddy heard the duchess' voice from beyond and
peeked around the tall and glossy door panel.

"You'll be all right, Christian?" His mother stood hesitantly near the door from the hall, while a maid worked
quickly at turning down the bedclothes and drawing the curtains. Jervaulx paid neither any mind, but looked about the
bedroom with his painstaking intensity, as if he were memo-
rizing it.

This room was blue also, but not so garish as the dressing
room, a powder color that Maddy thought quite pretty even
if the bed was an outrageous extravagance, with a headboard
that rose all the way to the ceiling and then curved over like
a huge sea wave. Damask silk drapings matched the walls;
the only diversity of color was in the full-length portraits
and a dark blue and green Oriental carpet that covered the
floor from wall to wall.

Jervaulx caught sight of himself in a mirrored bureau-
cabinet. He gazed at the glass, then turned, looking for
something behind him. With a little surprise, Maddy realized that it was her. He smiled when he saw her, and some of
the tension left him.

She stepped out into the bedroom. The dowager duchess
glanced toward her. "Ah. Miss Timms. You don't think you
will need—" She stopped, looking embarrassed. "I don't
suppose—there's no chance that he might—wander, in the
night?"

Maddy realized that the duchess was afraid of him and
wished him restrained. Though Maddy was hardly so certain
of him herself, she found it somehow terrible that his own
mother would offer the suggestion. "Thou canst lock the
doors, if thou wishest," she said.

"Perhaps that would be best. The windows . . ." She let
the thought trail off. "Well, you will ring if you have trouble.

I'll have a footman in the hall all night. But he seems . . . so much better. I don't imagine . . . you don't think he might try the windows?"

Maddy looked at Jervaulx. Even having seen him chained at Blythedale Hall, she could not envision what he must have been like to have inspired this alarm in his own family.

"The windows, Jervaulx?" she asked slowly. "Thou wouldst not break them?"

He shook his head. She wasn't certain he understood her, for he didn't hesitate or attend to the words, but seemed merely to assent to the tone of her voice.

"I'll leave you, then," the duchess said. "Cook is to send up a tea tray." She gave her son a long look. "Good night, Christian. Good night."

He gave a slight bow, an acerbic smile. The maid passed Maddy and went into the dressing room.

"I shall pray," the dowager announced, and pulled the hall door closed behind her. The key turned in the lock.

Christian sat on the bed. He leaned his head back, clasping his hands behind his neck, and let himself fall backwards into the soft down. He sighed in satisfaction.

Home.

No Ape, no chains, no nightmare. He didn't mind a dressing down from the she-dragon; he was accustomed to it— Hell's bells, he almost enjoyed it. And Maddygirl was here, the only thing he would have taken with him from that place if he'd had his own choosing.

Amazing upside down world, in which his family locked him in with a young and pretty female. *Nurse,* Aunt Vesta had said, and Christian grinned at the blue arch of fabric above him.

He drew up his leg and rested his heel on the edge of the bed, indulging in an enjoyable contemplation of the wilder sort of possibilities to which such a convenient designation of one's mistress might lend themselves. He sighed. While it made a pleasant fantasy, things were different now. The reputation of a thee-thou girl might not have occurred to his family—they wouldn't care about it if it had—but while she was entirely within his dominion she was also his responsibility. Seduction was no longer the neat lesson that he'd anticipated. From this perspective, it looked too much like the sort of offensive attentions a man might force on his housemaid.

It was hard to recall, really, why he'd even got the notion in his head to punish her in that way.

He was frowning, contemplating that, when she said his name. He turned his head and lifted his eyebrows.

"Weema stalk," she said.

He made a questioning sound.

"Talk," she said.

Christian sat up. He pushed himself up on the bed, lounging on pillows, and swept a space on the bedclothes to invite her. "Talk." He was pleased with how easily the word came.

Instead of the bed, she chose a straight-backed chair facing him. "Thou unstan hap tomorrow?"

"To . . . morrow?"

"Hear," she said.

"I . . . *hear,*" he said, annoyed that she would question it.

"Hear-ing," she repeated. "Lord Chansore."

He didn't remember a Lord Chansore. Christian knew there was much he didn't remember, but to think of it made him uneasy.

"Chan . . . *dos?*" he demanded. She couldn't mean Buckingham's son. The Marquess of Chandos hadn't any trouble with his hearing that Christian knew, and he knew Chandos well; they'd gambled and raked together from London to Paris and back. Trouble with his ruinous extravagance, oh yes, but not his ears. Not since Christian could remember.

"Hear," she insisted. "Hear-ing."

He had to work for another word. *"Young,"* he said. Chandos couldn't be deaf; he and Christian were of an age.

She shook her head and clasped her hands with a sigh. He knew that he was failing what she wanted. He had an urge to pound something, to smash his fists into stone. With an angry mutter he rolled off the bed away from her.

At a scratch and the sound of the doorlock, she rose. A footman entered, pushing the tea cart. He gave Christian a wary glance, then wordlessly began to remove the covers and pour.

The mince tarts and thin-sliced bread and butter appeared civilized fare. Christian walked toward the tray. The cups rattled as the footman dropped one back into its saucer and turned to face him.

Christian stopped. Never in his life had a servant looked at him with such a suspicious vigilance, as if he were some footpad shadowing the fellow in a back street.

He felt as if he'd been slapped across the face. He just stood there, accused and condemned in silence and a look.

"Shube tie up, miss?" the man said to Maddy.

Christian felt hot amazement rise in his face. Who was this impudent rogue? He looked toward Maddygirl in powerless shock. He didn't even have a recourse, couldn't order the fellow out of the room and out of his employment.

"No," she answered—at least that. Christian thought she should have cast him out on his ear.

"Not fraydim?" the footman asked her.

Afraid of him? Maddy shook her head, and Christian felt a wave of passionate appreciation for her.

The servant picked up the teapot once again, still glancing at Christian. "Broke arm, did."

Christian couldn't prevent it: at this monstrous assertion, a twisted utterance of protest escaped him. *"Out!"* He took a step forward. "Son of a bitch buggering whoreson bastard— *out!"*

He realized at the same moment as the footman what he'd said, and just how well and loudly. The two of them looked at one another; they both looked at Maddy.

She sat in her scoop-sugar bonnet, her fingers locked, her brows drawn together dubiously. She didn't have the vaguest notion of the full insult to her feminine sensibility, that was obvious, but he gave her a short nod of apology anyway, and then glared at the footman, unable to express anything but obscenities.

"Haps bes go," Maddy said, standing up.

The footman replaced the teapot, made a stiff bow, and obeyed her.

She came to the cart and finished pouring tea. With quiet and methodical moves, she prepared a plate and then set it out on the bedside table.

"Not . . . *arm,*" Christian said, determined to correct the record. "Not . . . see . . . never."

"Thowst eat," she said.

Christian scowled. He crossed his arms and leaned on the wall. "Believe!"

"Eat."

He shoved away. "Believe! Maddygirl!"

A little Puritan pinch appeared around her lips. "Thou dustint member."

She didn't believe him. She believed that puling peasant over him. Christian hit his fist against the wall.

The pinch of her lips tightened. "Thou . . . wast . . . ill," she said, very slowly and clearly. "Thou . . . dost . . . not . . . remember."

He swung away from her, pacing the width of the room. "No. *No, no, no!*"

"Jervaulx!"

She said his name so sharply, with such decisive emphasis, that he stopped and stared at her.

"Morrow. Lord Chansor hear. Thamus show cam sense. Reasonable."

"*Who?*" he shouted. "Not . . . *deaf!*"

"Nor I," she said, lifting her chin.

He exhaled, stiff-jawed, nodding once to acknowledge that. "Who . . . lord?" he asked, in a quieter tone.

"Chansore. Lord Chansore. Comesee hear-*ing.*"

He felt the importance of it in the intense way she looked at him. He needed to understand; she wanted him to. "Come . . . see . . . *hear?*" he asked helplessly.

"Hear-*ing*."

He shook his head, gave it up. He was to go and see some deaf old lord trying to hear, and it was important.

She must have slept, because she had the sensation of coming awake; she felt a long and dreadful moment of fright at the monstrous design of bright eyes that seemed to hover too close before she remembered, and recognized the gilt pattern on the ceiling above. She sat up quickly in bed.

"Jervaulx?"

She saw a movement in the dark corner. A black silhouette detached itself from the mass of the door. Real terror rose up to envelop her in the sound of her own heart pounding.

"Maddy," he said, in the silence and the inner thunder of her heart—but in such an uncertain tone that she let go of a breath, relief following on dread, leaving her muscles weak.

"What is it?" she asked, her voice unsteady.

He was barely illuminated by the shielded lamp she'd left lit. "Hearing." He had the emerald green dressing gown around him, loose and open, with nothing on beneath it but his trousers. "Maddygirl. Tell . . . hear-*ing*. Lord Chance. Lu . . . *legal. Legal?*"

She bit her lip. "Yes. A legal hearing. Competency hearing."

In the faint light, his eyes were black, his aspect satanic—and yet dazed. "Comp . . . me?"

"Yes," she said.

He looked down at her, and then at the lamp and the dusky gleam of polished wood that was the dressing table. He shook his head a little. She drew her knees up under her skirt and held them to her breast, watching him.

He focused a look on her suddenly, a demon-look in that strange light. The cot creaked as he grabbed her arm, sat by her, fixing her with a vehement gaze. *"Back?"* he demanded. "Send—*back?*"

His grip hurt. She endured it, giving him that, for she had no other comfort. "I don't know."

He closed his eyes. "Not . . . back . . . mad place." He opened them, glared at her. "No."

She wanted to lie, to say that what was true was false. The best that she could offer him was saying that she didn't know, and even that was half a lie, told outside the light of Truth, against everything she'd been taught all her life.

"Thou must show sense tomorrow," she said. "Speak calmly, and show sense."

He held her arm, sending pain to the bone.

"Thou canst do it."

He looked toward the hallway door. Maddy saw his thought instantly. For an arrested moment they were both still, caught on the edge of his intention.

"Lock?" His fingers grew tighter yet.

She would not lie. Instead, she gave no answer at all.

He let go of her, walked to the door. The knob turned easily under his hand; the hinges moved half an inch without sound.

He held it there and looked back at her. *"Go,"* he said, between his teeth.

She sat helpless, waiting for him to do it.

He stood with the handle beneath his hand. "Two . . . go." With a motion of his head, he beckoned. "Both."

"No," she whispered. "I can't. Thou must not."

He frowned at her, as if she'd put an obstacle in his way. With a careful motion, he cracked the door wider, leaned against the frame and looked through. A ray of light from the hall fell on his face, crossing it in a slice of diabolic contours.

His mouth curved upward in a contemptuous smile. The crack closed silently. "Bone break," he said in the darkness. "Arm."

Her eyes readjusted to the gloom. He'd turned his back to the door and stood looking at her.

"Maddygirl," he said. "Back—" He broke off, and then from deep in his throat said: "Die."

She had no answer.

He came to her, sat again beside her on the bed, grasped her by both arms. "Not . . . back. No!"

"It is not my decision. It is not mine to say."

"Go!" There was pleading in his voice. "Now."

She pushed at him, not knowing what to do. "Go, then! I will not stop thee."

He held onto her, shook her. "Two. Two go."

"No," she said miserably. "That's impossible."

Christian bent his head, made a sound of agony. "Not . . . one go. Maddy!" His fingers drove into her shoulders. "Can't." He pulled her toward him, leaned his face into the curve of her neck. "Maddy. Maddygirl. Not one. Can't." He pressed his forehead hard against her, his jaw taut with silent entreaty. He was disintegrating. It came to this, after the locks and the keepers and the chains. If she had handed him a key, he could not have walked out free.

He didn't have the courage. Not himself, one, without two.

But to go back that place . . . the cell, the Ape.

He held to her, his body paralyzed, frozen, shattering in panic.

"Jervaulx." She touched his hair, her voice anguished. "Morrow, thamus calm. Sense. Showst sense, ashowstme."

"Maddy," he said, muffled into her skin, all he could say. He shook his head, all he could do. He had no sense or sanity. He had to go, to escape, but he was frozen. He was shaking all over.

She bent her head, pressed her cheek to his, her hand moving lightly over his hair. He turned his face into her throat. She seemed the only thing important in the universe, his one hold on reality. He made an impassioned sound, to tell her what words could never have said anyway: the magnitude of his need to have her with him.

He felt her draw a little shuddering breath, and then a wet tumble of water on her cheek. She whispered, "God forgive, Jervaulx—that I sh'dovethee."

That I should love thee.

It broke the spell that held him. Had she said that? He pushed back, gazing at her.

Faint lamplight caught the glistening curve of her cheek, but he couldn't see her eyes. She smoothed her hand over his arm, a touch, and then gone.

He felt confounded, too stupid to compass it. He wasn't certain that he had heard it right.

She turned her face down, drawing away from him. He let her go.

He stood up. She was lost in darkness, unmoving. His brain seemed befuddled; he wanted to go somewhere and lean his face against a cool wall and find his way through the disorder. The worst was that she wept; he felt angry at it—*no pity thee-thou church charity.*

Was that what she meant? Why she cried? Because he was an animal afraid to leave its cage, no words to say what he thought, no thoughts but muddled mad stupid thoughts? He left her there and walked into the deeper darkness of the room where his father and grandfather and great-grandfather had slept in state. He lay facedown on the bed, his arms spread, his cheek against the silken sheets. His ribs ached. If he'd known a prayer, he would have prayed it—coward that he was, to ask for favors now, when he'd never deigned to ask before.

He didn't reckon that God owed him anything. He reckoned that he'd had it all, and wasted it. Burning lakes and howling fiends had just never seemed that convincing, perils hardly fit to frighten naughty children.

He turned over, staring up at the darkness.

Damned . . . having found out now what hell was really like.

Chapter Thirteen

$\mathcal{F}$rom out the window of the chamber, one could imagine Lincoln's Inn a country town, with the leaves slipping down from venerable trees, green lawns, a meetinghouse stillness broken by the passage of one or two men fluttering in black robes through the late afternoon sun and shadows. Here in the middle of London, the loudest sound was a crow cawing in a nearby tree while his sable brothers marched with stately, halting tread across the walks.

Maddy sat with her papa in the window seat, Cousin Edward and Jervaulx standing on either side of her, and Larkin a few steps away.

It was almost crowded in this room where they waited. By the fire, Lady Clementia and Lady Charlotte and two more of Jervaulx's sisters had their chairs pulled up behind Lady de Marly and the dowager duchess. The ladies' husbands clustered near the door, speaking very softly among themselves, conferring sometimes with a bewigged man who stood in the doorway and sorted through papers without entering the room.

Lady de Marly had particularly asked that Maddy and Papa be present, which was daunting. A very somber and low-voiced barrister had already interviewed the Timmses in a separate room, asking all about the duke and his behavior. The advocate made notes and cross-examined Papa at length on the mathematical work, but when Maddy rose and escorted Papa out, she had no very clear idea of what might come of it.

The councillor had gone away then with Lady de Marly and Jervaulx, who came back strung to a higher tension yet, resonating beneath a veneer of stillness. He stood beside Maddy now, impeccably turned out by a valet who had unceremoniously evicted her from the dressing room this morning. No pretty embroidered waistcoat this time, but severe white, unadorned, with white knee breeches and a dark blue coat that Lady de Marly had pronounced suitable. He appeared as severe as a Quaker, but with a look that Maddy had never seen on any Friend's face, save on a man disowned from the Meeting for marriage by a priest to one of the world.

That was what his relations wished to do to Jervaulx, Maddy thought—deny him. Disclaim and renounce him, make him disappear from family and place. As they sat waiting all the long afternoon in the chancery chamber, she came to understand without anyone telling her: it was these, his own kin, his own sisters and the men they had married, even his mother, who urged this inquiry, and only Lady de Marly stood on the other side.

The summons came to attend the Lord Chancellor. Lady de Marly rose, and with her all the ladies, but it was Jervaulx alone who was wanted.

Lady de Marly thrust out her stick and sat back down. "Do not fail me," she snapped at the duke.

At the door, the advocate stood waiting, square-jawed and expressionless beneath his wig. Jervaulx cast Maddy a look of utter desperation. She gripped her hands hard together, unable to say to him what she wished to say not in front of these others, to will him courage and faith.

"Your Grace?" the barrister said. "His Lordship awaits you."

A slow cold blaze of hate came into the duke's face. It made him frightening. He looked at his family, one by one, each of his sisters, his brothers-in-law, his mother—as if he marked them, not to forget this. Then he walked forward to the barrister and the door.

With one of his strange shifts of reality, Christian recognized the man at the table: Lyndhurst, chancellor's robes—*change government*—he remembered that—he remembered— *Canning*. A whole portion of his life suddenly opened to him.

Lyndhurst stopped the rapid tapping of his fingers and looked up from the papers in his hand. A relief seemed to come into his face, replacing nervous restlessness, when he saw Christian standing silently. Lyndhurst rose and came around the table, holding out his hand.

Christian knew him: a notorious womanizer, renegade Whig—a long, long way from Christian's small radical corner of the Lords but not the worst of the old men. Lord Chancellor now! Plum advance. But Christian recalled that, precariously. Tory crisis, talk and uncertainties; he felt adrift, with no notion of how long ago it had been or where the government stood now.

No revolution, at least—not with the likes of Lyndhurst made Lord Chancellor.

He clapped Christian on the shoulder, took his hand—the baffling moment when Christian couldn't lift it dissolved. Christian moved, became a human being able to return the pressure of greeting.

"Lookell, sir! Verwell!"

Christian nodded.

"Come havseet. Wonake long. Spoke laymarly, y'see." He gestured toward a chair by the fire, pulling his own up to it. The lace on his robes flapped. He shook off the full dress, handed it over to a clerk who slipped out the door and vanished with the scarlet prize. Lyndhurst unfolded spectacles and perched them on his nose. The other bagwigs stood by, rustling papers. "Fewsimp quest, all clerup, eh?"

He gave Christian a glance, between hope and embarrassment, and cleared his throat. A bagwig handed him some papers.

He spent a moment making faces at the sheets in his lap. Without looking up, he said, "Staid namesir, ifill."

Christian closed his hands around the arms of his chair. The fire popped. He could feel his heart beating hard.

Lyndhurst looked up. "Name?"

Christian Richard Nicholas Francis Langland.

He could not say it.

He felt a surge of renewed terror. The words would not come out. His breathing began to deepen; he stared at Lyndhurst, trying to turn an exhalation into a sound.

One of the bagwigs said something, but it was a meaningless string of syllables to Christian. They put a parchment book in his lap, gave him a pen.

He set the pen to the sheet. Nothing happened. He laid it down, then picked it up with his left hand. He tried to think of the letters, their shape, how to begin them. He looked up at Lyndhurst and found the man leaning forward, a troubled frown on his face.

"Cantight name?"

Christian pressed his head back against the chair. The Ape, that place—they would lock him there again! Frenzy sent the words farther away yet, scattering them beyond reach, beyond hope.

The bagwigs watched him solemnly. His last time to speak in the House of Lords, he'd stood up to argue education, mechanical societies, science—he remembered Lyndhurst then, writing notes and whispering asides, regular Tory business. And now, like distant relatives at a deathbed, the Lord Chancellor and his minions peered at the Duke of Jervaulx: proper, uneasy, fascinated.

He was one of them, dressed like them, had sat in the Lords with Lyndhurst—and this had happened to him.

Lyndhurst pulled his lip, leaning on his chair. He shook his head, made a notation on a paper.

Mortification seared Christian. He looked down at the notebook in his lap and wrote the algebraic expression of the distance between two points with respect to an orthogonal axis.

"Whatiz?" Lyndhurst peered at the notebook, reaching to turn it without taking it from Christian's lap.

The same square-faced bagwig leaned over and murmured in his ear.

"Ah." Lyndhurst nodded, pushing his glasses up his nose. He looked at Christian. "Wry unt twenty force?"

Twenty? They all watched the notebook expectantly. Christian deduced that he was to write. This time, his hand obeyed him. He transcribed the numeral twenty in his notebook.

"One two twenty, if please."

With more assurance, Christian wrote one thousand two hundred and twenty.

Lyndhurst sighed, and pulled his lip again. Christian's momentary confidence evaporated. He hadn't done it right, that was obvious. He could taste the terror rise up in him again, feeling himself failing.

The other bagwig spoke, and Lyndhurst nodded absently. The door opened; a clerk escorted Christian's mother into the room. Christian rose. She didn't even look at him; she just paused at the door. When the bagwig touched her arm, she turned and left the room. The door closed.

Christian stood a moment, nonplussed. He sat down.

"Nolade?"

Anger rose in him. Just a game—it was a game to them, petty sport to baffle him.

"Hose?"

What?

"Name?" Lyndhurst prodded.

He closed his eyes. He worked at it. It wouldn't come. Nothing came.

"Dunow?"

Nothing! Christian stared at Lyndhurst, breathing fiercely through his teeth.

One of the bagwigs took an unlit candlestick from the mantel, placing it on the table at Christian's side. The man handed him a paper twisted into a candlelighter.

Taper to candle. Paper and flame. But his hands seemed to have nothing to do with one another.

Lyndhurst leaned over and took the twist of paper. He held it to the coals until it began to smoke. A thin flame appeared. He inverted the taper and offered it to Christian.

Christian accepted it carefully. He gazed at the blue and yellow flame, the white stream of smoke that curled from the tip.

Someone spoke sharply. The bagwig leaned over and blew out the paper twist with a quick huff.

Christian frowned. They had to give him time; they didn't give him time enough. The expression on the bagwig's face infuriated him. He closed his eyes and groped for the candlestick, caught it in his hand. He held the half-burned lighter in his other.

He was determined to show that he could do it. He tried. He looked at the candlelighter, held it to the candle, turned his head to see better. His right hand reversed the candle. His left hand ground the smoking taper into the wax. Little flakes of black soot scattered over the notebook and his breeches, but that wasn't right. He turned the candlestick over and pressed the taper to it again. The paper twist crumpled in his hands and fell to the floor. Christian gazed at it in despair.

Lyndhurst muttered to himself, writing. The clerk gently pried the inverted candlestick from Christian's grip. Then he collected a sheaf of banknotes and a handful of coins from the table, gave them to the Lord Chancellor. Lyndhurst reached out, spreading the money across the notebook in Christian's lap. "Tasumis."

Christian picked up a pound note. He looked at Lyndhurst. The Lord Chancellor looked back kindly. Sympathetically. And in that patient pity Christian read his fate.

He crushed the banknote. He came to his feet, hurling the notebook into the fire. Coins cascaded, ringing against the hearth. "No-no-no-*no!*" That was all he could do, that one futile word, over and over. "No-no-no-no-no." He felt like a cornered beast, all their startled eyes on him.

Lunatic, lunatic, back to the mad place and chains. Back to die. Or worse—to live.

Lunatic, oh God. A sworn and signed madman. Lunatic!

They called Maddy and Cousin Edward to calm him. She went with her heart in her throat, expecting a shambles—all she found was Jervaulx beside an overturned chair, with the barristers and the Lord Chancellor himself looking harassed.

Jervaulx saw Maddy. He lifted his hands and dropped them, making a sound of grief.

Cousin Edward went to the chair and set it upright. "There now," he said calmly. "You won't force us to resort to the gauntlets, will you, Master Christian? Not in front of Her Grace and Miss Timms."

Jervaulx hit him.

Cousin Edward went down in a mill of arms, falling back against the chair as the barristers lunged for Jervaulx before he made it past them. For a moment confusion reigned, shouts and the scrape of wood, then Larkin was there, back-handing the duke with a fist that sent him sprawling against the table, the two lawyers still clinging to his arms. Papers flew, sliding in massive sheafs and bundles to the floor. Larkin flung himself on top of the duke, his blunt hands at Jervaulx's throat.

The struggle ceased. Jervaulx dropped his head back against the table, panting. He closed his eyes and turned his face from the rest of them.

Larkin slowly pushed himself away, flipping a big India rubber ring against his palm before he shoved it in his pocket. The barristers had both lost their wigs. They looked flushed and awkward, chagrined when Larkin said, "Stand him up and let him go, sirs. He'll not fight any longer."

They pulled him upright. Jervaulx hardly seemed aware of the grip on his arms; he stood braced against the table, his head down, making no attempt to move when they released him. His fine coat had ripped at the shoulder seam, showing white linen beneath.

Cousin Edward moved forward with the leather gauntlets, slipping them on and securing the laces with the efficiency of long practice. His lip was bleeding, but Jervaulx, who'd taken a far harder blow from Larkin, had no mark on him.

"What is this?" Lady de Marly's voice cut ice through the air.

The Lord Chancellor looked up from examining his cracked spectacles. "M'lady."

Behind her, the dowager duchess and the rest crowded about the door, nudging themselves into Lady de Marly's wake. Maddy found herself edged into a corner as one of the husbands pushed his way past her, begging her pardon without much conviction.

Jervaulx stood with his arms bound, staring at the floor. The rip at his shoulder gaped with the awkward angle forced on his arms by the gauntlets.

The Lord Chancellor glanced around at the family crowding in. "Well," he said, quite dry and little annoyed. "As it falls out that you're all here—let me tell you my decision in the matter of the petition for a writ *de idiota inquirendo* in the case of His Grace Christian Langland, the Duke of Jervaulx."

Lady de Marly thumped her stick in an ominous way. "Lyndhurst—" she began imperiously.

"M'lady," the Lord Chancellor's voice had a warning note within it. "Allow me." He seated himself in a large chair next to the fire, waving Lady de Marly into the one that had been replaced across from him. He held out his hand in expectation.

The clerk hurried to retrieve a scatter of papers from near his feet. The Lord Chancellor took them, rearranged them, holding his damaged spectacles to his nose without putting them on.

"I have examined the duke with a view to his ability to mind his business. I find that he cannot give his name, nor write it. He cannot count from one to twenty. He does not appear to recognize his mother. He had no sensible response upon being given a candle to light. When asked to tell a sum of money, he threw it into the fire. These are—" His voice rose as Lady de Marly attempted to interrupt. "These are the customary criteria we apply to determine *compos mentis,* m'lady."

Lady de Marly had been leaning forward, She met the Lord Chancellor's look and sank back in her chair, her chin lifted. "Your Lordship, he is the Duke of Jervaulx." She gave the Lord Chancellor a glare that would have shriveled stone. "The Duke . . . of Jervaulx."

They were like two elders locked in silent conflict, two massive wills. Everyone and everything else was eerily still, but for the fire rumbling quietly between Lady de Marly and the Lord Chancellor. Such a commonplace sound, while Jervaulx never moved nor lifted his head.

The Lord Chancellor rustled his papers. He cleared his throat. "On behalf of Her Grace the Dowager Duchess of Jervaulx, we have Lord Tilgate, Lord Stoneham, Mr. Manning, Mr. Perceval, jointly and severally, et cetera, et cetera—petition the court—et cetera—writ *de idiota inquirendo*—yes, I thought I was not mistaken." He glanced toward their councillor. "Mr. Temple—there has been an error in the documents. This should not have been submitted as *de idiota,* but as *de lunatico*—as I have satisfied myself from my examination of the duke." He swept his audience with a dispassionate look. "It is perfectly clear to me that this is a case of mental derangement rather than idiocy. If your party should wish to correct the petition and resubmit, Mr. Temple, I will of course take up the question again at a later date."

* * *

Maddy could not understand why Lady de Marly was so ju-
bilant. She appeared to view the postponement as an entire
victory—and indeed, the vehement low-voiced complaints
of the brothers-in-law revealed their dissatisfaction. As Lady
de Marly made her slow and thumping way down the hall
and outside to the waiting carriages, Maddy overheard one
of the husbands mutter, "Good God, man, another half-
year?" His voice rose a little as he caught the barrister's arm.
"The estate'll be a shambles!"

The others hushed him. Maddy walked past them in the
hall. His sisters and brothers-in-law looked behind her,
edged aside, putting their backs to the wall. Maddy paused
at the head of the stairs.

Between Cousin Edward and Larkin, Jervaulx walked
down the row of spectators, bound, as if he were a criminal
led to execution. He gave no sign that he even knew anyone
else was nearby; he only seemed to watch the hems of his
sisters' dresses as he passed. Not until he reached Maddy
did he raise his eyes—and she saw then that he had gone
away.

Nothing was there, no sorrow, no anger, no recognition.
He'd said that he would die if they sent him back. Maddy
thought that he had already. She almost reached out to touch
him, but . . . no.

No. It was better this way. Better not to bring him back,
not to make him feel this moment. The family closed ranks
in the hall behind him, murmuring among themselves.
Maddy lifted her skirt, turning away from him, leading the
way down the stairs.

In a chair drawn close to the fire as always, Lady de Marly
seated herself in her private boudoir, surrounded by furniture in black Oriental lacquer. Every possible inch of space
was covered with blue and white porcelain bottles, tiny and
large, some simple, some painted with grotesque dragons
and mythical beasts. She took a long draught of smelling
salts from one of the bottles, then opened her eyes and

curled the phial in her hand. "Miss Timms." She fixed her look on Maddy. "It is imperative that he comprehend what I have to say. That is why you are here."

"I understand."

"Ill-bred chit. You answer me 'm'lady' when I speak to you."

"It is not our principle," Maddy said calmly.

Lady de Marly lifted her brows. "I daresay."

She appeared content with this caustic remark and turned her attention to the duke. He stood bound in the gauntlets, watching them both like a dark outlaw enchained. Lady de Marly took another deep breath of her salts, then waved the phial.

"Remove those . . . bonds," she said, as if the very word offended her.

Maddy was happy to do so. Jervaulx held still as she unlaced them. Released, he moved his fists apart, spread his fingers, looking down at his hands one by one. Then he lifted his head and nodded once to Maddy, terse thanks.

Lady de Marly thumped her stick for attention. "You, boy—do you know what's happened today?"

"Slowly," Maddy advised.

The old lady made an annoyed grimace. "Jervaulx!"

He looked at her.

"Hear me," she said. "You failed today. Failed."

His jaw worked. He began to breathe faster, making the effort to speak. To Maddy's relief, Lady de Marly waited without interrupting him.

"Vesta!" he burst out fiercely. "Don't . . . *back*. God! If . . . love. If—" He reached and grabbed Maddy's arm, pushing her toward his aunt. He held her in front of him. *"Say."*

Maddy felt his fingers drive into her arms. He gave her a little shake, made a growl in his throat.

"Say," he insisted.

"He doesn't wish to return to Blythedale, Lady de Marly," she said. "I believe that is what he wants me to tell thee."

"Indeed." She didn't even look at Maddy, only at the duke behind her.

Jervaulx expelled a groan, pushing Maddy from him. He strode to the end of the room. "Kill . . . now." He turned on them, gripping the fretted rails of an ebony Chinese chair. "Not . . . *back.*"

Lady de Marly regarded him, nodding faintly. "Back you go, however. Your mother wills it," she said, with a calm cruelty that forced Maddy into speech.

"Perhaps thou might consider—"

"Miss Timms!" Lady de Marly snapped.

Maddy fell silent.

"Miss Timms, you did not mention that he was capable of intelligent speech."

Lady de Marly had a way of making one feel guilty even for improvement. "He's sometimes spoken," Maddy said, "but not often."

"How often? In what circumstances?"

"I think—when he's angry. When he wants something very much. When it is—" She hesitated. "When it is important to him."

"I see."

Lady de Marly wrapped both her hands around the knob of her walking stick. She leaned her head against the chair and closed her eyes.

"Jervaulx," the old lady said. "You *will* go back. Do you understand?"

He held the chair. *"Back?"* Just that word, one agonized word.

"Yes." Lady de Marly opened her eyes. She thumped her stick. "Unless you do as I say."

She set the stick and pushed herself to her feet. The duke didn't move as she walked toward him, each half-step a stiff rustle of silk. She stopped, leaning hard on her support. They looked at one another with the ebony chair between them.

"Not back, Jervaulx. Not . . . back . . . *if*—" She glared up into the duke's eyes. "*If* you consent."

His face was dark with emotion and wariness. "Con . . . sent?"

"Consent to marry."

He turned his head slightly. Maddy could see the hesitation.

"Marry," Lady de Marly repeated, clear and plain. "Marry . . . secure the title . . . and you do not go back. I'll see to it."

Comprehension washed into his face. Comprehension and affront—an instant of aristocratic arrogance, pure duke, amazed offense at this interference—and then the further realization, full grasp of what she offered. He let go of the chair.

"*Yes,*" he ejaculated.

Anything, that one syllable said. Anything not to go back.

Chapter Fourteen

" ' *I* will,' " Maddy read again.

The duke's fingers tightened around the handgrip of a heavy seal. It formed another stamp in the desk blotter as he pressed down in his effort to speak. All day she'd been locked with him in the library, reciting from the marriage ceremony in the Book of Common Prayer. He never looked at the endless phoenix crests he was making in the paper. He never took his eyes from her. "Wmmm . . . *mill*," he managed.

"I . . . will," she corrected.

He stared at her across the desk. Concentration froze all humanity from his face: he was ice and darkness, his eyes the depth of blue winter. No sound came.

Maddy looked down at the book again. She referred once more to Lady de Marly's note of the proper names to insert, though she had them memorized long since. "I, Christian Richard Nicholas Francis Langland—"

"Christian Richard," he said. "Christian Richard . . . nn . . . klas." He swallowed, clenching his teeth. "Fra . . . Lang."

"Take thee—"

"Thnnnh," he said, half a groan.

She went on as if he'd succeeded, though it had begun to appear that he never would. Lady de Marly had set them to this task just after breakfast, and now, after dinner and tea time, Maddy was near despairing of it.

She moistened her lips, exhaling softly, and read again. A tired sing-song crept into her voice. "Take *thee* Anne *Rose*—"

"Take *thee* Anne *Rose*."

He managed that quite clearly. The sudden fluency made Maddy glance up. Surprise caught them both; the duke looked as startled at his success as she.

Maddy broke into a smile. "There!"

He grinned, flushing with achievement. "Take *thee*— Anne *Rose*," he repeated, nodding on each stress.

"Take thee, Anne Rose Bernice Trotman—"

His smile faded. He frowned, and shook his head. "Take *thee* Anne *Rose*—"

"Ber-*nice* Trot-*man*."

"Take *thee* Anne *Rose* Ber*nice* Trot*man*."

"Yes!" She leaned forward. "I—"

He interrupted her, taking up a nodding rhythm. "*Chris*tian *Ri*chard *Nick*'las *Lang*land. *Chris*tian *Ri*chard *Nick*'las Langland. I . . . *Chris*tian Richard Nicolas Langland." He shoved back the chair, flung himself out of it. "I Christian Richard Nicholas Langland. Langland. Christian. I Christian Richard Nicholas Francis Langland. Langland!" He gave a harsh victorious laugh. He grabbed the seal, pounding it down on the blotter with each word. "I *Chris*tian *Ri*chard *Nick*'las *Fran*cis *Lang*land!"

His violent excitement frightened her a little. Maddy closed the book. "Perhaps that would be a good place to stop for the day."

"No!" He came around the desk, took the book from her hand and flattened it open on the table. "Maddygirl! Take *thee* Anne *Rose* Ber*nice* Trot*man*—"

She hesitated. He caught her hand, squeezed it, working it painfully in his.

Maddy nodded. He let her go. She leaned over the priest's book. "—'to my wedded wife.'" That seemed harder to fit to the lilt. She had to force it into an unnatural beat. "To *my* wedded *wife.*'"

"To *my* wed *wife.*"

She thought that must be near enough. "To *have* and to *hold*—"

"To *have* ant *hold*—"

From this day forward, for better for worse, for richer for poorer, in sickness and in health—whatever else might be said of the Church of England's wedding vows, and the Society of Friends had nothing but ill to impart, the lines lent themselves to this simple, heavy cadence that he could repeat. He was far from perfect, slurring over syllables that didn't quite fit into the rhythm, but the improvement made him joyous. He paced the room, nodding in tempo, insisting that she read the lines over and over as he repeated them.

Finally he came and stood behind her, his hands on her shoulders, reciting the whole passage himself. "I *will*. I *Christ*ian *Rich*ard *Nich*olas *Fran*cis *Lang*land Take *thee* Anne *Rose* Ber*nice* Trot*man*. To *my* wed *wife*. To *have* to *hold*. From *this* day fore. For *bet* for worse. In *sick* and *health*. To *love* to chers. Till *death* do *part*." His fingers worked in time. "Ac*cord*ing to. God's *holy ord*. And *there* . . . I *plight* . . . thee *my* . . . Troth. Ha!" He squeezed her, obviously proud of himself for getting through the difficult last lines.

Maddy turned her head to the side, unable to see him for her bonnet. She didn't try, not really. Her bonnet was there, reality and protection, buffer against a man's elation, his beautiful grin and dark midnight eyes.

He was of the world; he would be married by a priest to a child of the world. He would be married, and he would not go back to Blythedale Hall.

With a quick move, she shut the book. She stood up, breaking free of his touch. "I shall tell Lady de Marly then— thou art able to say thy lines."

She was called into Lady de Marly's presence directly. The lady ate her supper in bed from a lap tray, enthroned beneath exotic birds and Oriental figures in the Chinese room. Maddy stood with her hands clasped.

"So you believe that he's capable?" Lady de Marly demanded, between a bite of toast and a sip of tea.

"He will perhaps be better with more work."

"Six months, Miss Timms. Six months, that is what Lyndhurst gave us. And we may not count upon that, although counsel advises me that it would be surprising if the corrected petition should proceed any faster than the original." She dropped her teaspoon on the tray with a careless clatter. "We can't wait upon improvement. Best to have the thing done and get the girl with child. I want no questions of legitimacy. You understand the urgency of this matter?"

"His marriage, dost thou mean?"

"His heir, girl. He's got no heir. He ought to have done years ago, like any reasonable man, but what must his witless mother do but pester him every living minute of his life to reform and marry, with the natural result that wild horses could not drag him to the altar. He flouts her every way he can. Not that I blame him for it, but only a selfish blockhead with illusions of immortality would have left the title unsecured. Which, as I've made no bones to tell him, is precisely what he is. And now—"

Her voice went to an unexpected quaver. She stopped speaking. Her age seemed to descend on her suddenly, leaving her vulnerable: fumbling for her teacup, taking a long trembling sip. The cup rattled when she set it down.

She stared at nothing for a moment, then made a ripe snort. "Well. At any rate, now that he is—what he's become," she continued, with a brittle precision that gained strength as she spoke, as if by saying the thing out loud she brought it under her dominion, "we must retrieve what we can. The dukedom reverts to the Crown without legitimate male issue. *That* is what lies at stake here, my fine miss. He's got no heir. An idiot can't marry, can he? Nor a man judged out of his mind. If we cannot get him wed before he's declared incompetent—it is lost."

Maddy was silent, and a little shocked. She didn't think that Lady de Marly would admire a speech on the vanity of worldly institutions such as dukedoms, but to force her nephew to marry for one, to blackmail him into it with the threat of Blythedale—it seemed iniquitous.

"But—Anne Trotman?" Maddy asked diffidently. "She is wishful to marry him?"

"He is the Duke of Jervaulx, girl."

"Even though—"

Lady de Marly rattled her cup on the tray quite loudly. "Her father and I have arrived at a satisfactory arrangement a month since. The family are gentry. They have an ancient connection to the Dukes of Rutland, but no direct claim to hereditary honors. Mr. Trotman has just been returned MP for some petty borough in Huntingdonshire. The girl's marriage portion is a scant ten thousand pounds, against what I think you must agree is a generous jointure of fifty-two hundred annual for the duke's wife. I believe Miss Trotman may consider herself a most amazingly fortunate young lady."

"She does not know."

Lady de Marly became interested in her toast, slicing a portion with exactitude. "She is aware that he has been ill. Her parents and I have not judged it useful to tax her with the details. Young minds are inclined to overactive imagination."

"Lady de Marly—it cannot be a true marriage before God."

"You are impertinent."

"I am plain spoken."

"Rude and common. A true marriage before God! A ceremony in the Church of England—how much more before God would you wish? Nonsense, girl. What low-bred notions will you prate of next? Bundling? Shall they court in bed, as the country servants do? Hop over a broomstick for their vows? A true marriage indeed. You know nothing of it."

"I know that no truth can be based upon pride of place and falsehood!"

Lady de Marly threw down her silver knife. "Insolent jade! Do you call me a liar?"

Maddy took a stubborn breath. "Thou knowest thine own heart."

"And you would do well to remember it, girl. Enough of your dissenter babble. He is the duke. She will be his duchess. I don't know what objection there can be to that. I can see only one question, and that is tainted blood, but there's been no case of madness or imbecility in his pedigree for centuries—setting aside his silly goose of a mother. You may believe that I have looked into it. And Mr. Trotman will have too, if he is a man of any sense."

Maddy felt distressed. "She will not have him, when she discovers it. She will humiliate him."

"That she will not!" Lady de Marly said crisply. "Miss Timms—I will allow that you are a generous hearted girl— let me be as plain as you. Naturally you are not accustomed to our ways. Miss Trotman will be a peeress. She will have her own house—this house. Her own staff, access to the greatest in the land, wealth beyond her ability to exhaust. By this alliance, her father's political career—nay, her entire family's future—is assured. For all this, she need have no more to do with him than her duty. Her parents understand this, as well they might. Whatever her immediate feelings, I am assured that Miss Trotman, on reflection, can be brought to see the advantages of the match."

"And the duke?"

"The duke will no longer be your affair."

"But—if there should be an heir? She might wish to see him sent away then."

"You strain my patience, Miss Timms. Why think you that I chose the girl? She's biddable enough. His brothers-in-law will not preside. Nor his mother. Miss Trotman is well-enough aware of who has done this for her."

Maddy stood silent, still caught in peculiar anxiety for his future.

Lady de Marly regarded her. "Miss Timms," she said, in a quieter tone than she had yet used. "He is my brother's last surviving son. He is the last of my family whom I understand. Until you have outlived your husband, your children, and all your generation, you cannot know what that means."

"If thou loved him, thou wouldst not ever send him back."

She lifted her painted brows. "Ah. But I did not say to you I loved him. I said that I understood him. He weds, Miss—or back he goes. I vow it. And so you may assure him." She rested against the pillows. "See that he can speak his pledge proper, girl, if you care what becomes of him. Now move this tray, so that I can sleep."

They were all gathered, the Trotmans, Lady de Marly and the dowager duchess, when Maddy entered the drawing room with Jervaulx. Lady de Marly, without rising from her chair, said, "Jervaulx—Mr. and Mrs. James Trotman."

The father, a distinguished, vigorous gentleman with high color in his cheeks, came forward across the carpet instantly. He held out his hand.

Jervaulx looked at it, looked up in the man's face, and made a slight nod. Trotman's hand dropped.

"Sir." He responded with a deep formal bow, quickly covering the awkwardness. "I'm honored. May I present my wife—" He turned slightly. The lady, very fair and small, dropped a curtsy. "And this . . . this is my daughter Anne." With a fatherly gesture, he beckoned her. "Annie, don't hang back. She's a little shy today—perhaps you'll forgive her, sir, under the circumstances. Come here, darling, and make yourself known to the duke."

Anne Trotman obeyed, leaving her mother's side with lowered face. When she reached her father, she glanced up quickly, and then looked down again, lowering herself into a deep curtsy. In that brief glimpse, Maddy saw how young she was, as pale now as Lady de Marly, but with the same apples of pink in her cheeks as her father, the flush of fright in a face just a breath too round to be called beautiful, but still quite pretty. Blonde, dressed in apple green with ribbons and ruches of white, she looked a terrified lamb to Jervaulx's black wolf potency.

Maddy watched him survey her, her elaborately dressed hair, her puffed sleeves, her tiny waist. So young, Maddy thought—she could not have seventeen years yet.

The duke was impassive. He responded to her curtsy with a half-bow of worldly and impeccable politeness. He straightened, still observing her beneath his long lashes.

"She's a very nice girl, don't you think, Christian? A good devout girl." The dowager duchess floated forward. "Mrs. Trotman and her daughter are both active in the Church Building Society."

Lady de Marly groped for her stick and heaved herself to her feet. "I believe Mr. Trotman expressed his wish to view the library," she announced. "Let us leave the young people to divert themselves. Miss Timms—you will stay. Ring for refreshment."

Maddy was glad of this small task, as it gave her something to do. Lady de Marly overcame the dowager duchess' reluctance to leave by insisting that she needed her sister-in-law's arm for support out the door, and the Trotmans filed out in willing subjection. As they passed him, the duke gave them each a nod of recognition, an ironic lift to the corner of his mouth.

The door closed. Jervaulx turned and walked away to the window. He stood there, gazing out.

The girl also stood, her cheeks aflame, gripping her hands together and staring at the floor.

"Thou wouldst sit?" Maddy asked, finding herself hostess.

Anne Trotman peeked at her. She looked quickly toward the duke and away. "Yes," she said, barely whispering the word.

Maddy arranged two chairs near the fire, and placed one for herself a little back. The girl immediately started to take the one at a distance from the others.

"Please," Maddy said firmly, determined that Jervaulx and his betrothed should come to know one another as well as they might before embarking upon an entire life together. "Do have this seat. Next the fire."

Anne Trotman reluctantly took the chair Maddy indicated. She sat straight, her face lowered, her hands in two white fists. Maddy looked up at Jervaulx, who merely looked back at her with that sarcastic half-smile. She frowned at him a little, moving her chin to hint him into the other chair. He lifted his eyebrows and stayed where he was, cool defiance, a complete disavowal of any obligation.

Maddy sat down in her place. She had to lean forward a little to see Anne Trotman's features. "I'm Maddy Timms," she said.

The girl nodded. She gave Maddy one wild glance and then dropped her eyes to her lap again.

Mercifully, the tea tray arrived. For a few moments, that provided distraction, as Maddy poured and inquired about milk and sugar. The young lady would not take a plate.

"I'm afraid I—could not eat," she said in a low voice.

Maddy prepared a cup and carried it to Jervaulx. He leaned against the window draperies, accepting the tea but making no move to drink it.

She went back to her chair. The stilted silence lengthened. Maddy rued her lack of art for idle talk.

"The duke is fond of mathematics," she said finally.

The girl looked at her as if she'd spoken in some language out of darkest Africa.

"He and my father have developed a new geometry," Maddy continued stubbornly. "They received a standing ovation at the Analytical Society. Are you mathematical, Anne Trotman?"

The girl blinked. "Not at all."

"I can give thee some books on the subject. It ought to be

a pleasure for married people to enter into one another's interests, ought it not? I am a gardener, myself. What dost thou enjoy to do?"

Anne Trotman wet her lips. "Go to balls," she said. "And dance. Although—I haven't been to one. I'm not yet out. Mother said—that now I should come out when . . ." She shot a glance toward the duke and away. "Afterward." She lifted her head a little. "I shall be presented at court, with a satin gown and a train. I shall wear feathers in my hair, and diamonds."

Maddy rose. She walked halfway to Jervaulx, stopped and said clearly, "Anne Trotman enjoys dancing at balls."

He looked up from a deep contemplation of his teacup.

"Dance," Maddy repeated. "Anne Trotman likes to dance. She likes balls."

Jervaulx lifted his brows in exaggerated astonishment at this news.

Maddy returned to the young lady at the fire. "The duke has been—quite ill. If thou wilt but speak slow and distinct, he can converse with thee."

"He is mad, isn't he?" Anne Trotman came to vehement life. "His sister called yesterday—she told me that he nearly killed a footman!"

"He is not mad."

The girl was trembling. She exclaimed beneath her breath, "They put him in a madhouse! He was in chains. Isn't that true?"

Maddy pursed her lips.

"It *is* true!" Anne Trotman dropped her cup onto the tray and stood, turning on Maddy. "I can see it by your face!" She looked beyond to Jervaulx. "It's ghastly. I don't want to converse with him. I don't want him to touch me!"

"Then perhaps thou shouldst not consent to marry him," Maddy said quietly.

Anne Trotman tore her gaze from Jervaulx. "Everyone says that I must."

Maddy could not support disobedience, nor argue against

the wisdom of the girl's parents; it would be wicked. She could only hope that the child would find her own way in the Light.

"I must. I will be a duchess," the girl said. "A duchess."

Jervaulx smiled, a slow sneer. He left the window, walked past Maddy, making a leisurely stalk of Anne Trotman as she backed away, her pink cheeks going to burning ruby against white.

"Don't!" She came up against a gilded table. "Don't touch me! *Miss Timms!*"

The duke caught her chin hard between his fingers. He made her look up into his face, held her there as she panted in hysterical dismay. He touched her, spreading his hand at her wide ribbon sash, his fingers strong and dark on white satin. His palm moved upward in a licentious exploration that ignored all the ruche and ruffles, that outlined her bosom in flagrant depravity.

As she tried to slip sideways, he gripped her arm. He forced himself against her, his whole body a barrier pressed to hers. The girl struggled, gasping.

"You are indecent!" she cried. "Let me go!"

He held her fast in spite of her strain. "*Touch* . . . when . . . please."

The brutal inflection of his words froze her. She held her breath, staring up at him like a petrified animal. Maddy came to her feet.

"Jervaulx," she said.

He let Anne Trotman go. She scrambled aside, brushing at her silk and ribbons as if she had been dirtied. With a wordless, frantic glance at Maddy, the girl picked up her skirts and fled the room. The door shut on a resounding boom.

"Anne *Rose* Ber*nice* Trot*man*." His right fist opened and closed rhythmically. He glanced at her beneath dusky lashes.

"Thou frightened her by intent."

"Bitch," he said clearly. An ugly smile curled his lips. He reached to the mantel and picked up a china figurine of a young girl. He dropped it on the hearth. Maddy startled at the shatter, then took a step forward to prevent him as he reached for another of the set.

The second figure smashed against the stone. He caught up a third, held it suspended in his hand, taunting her. Maddy halted.

He dropped the statuette. It burst into fragments that arched and fell at her feet.

"Mine," he said. "Break." He swept a look around the ornate room. "Break *all.*"

Maddy turned away. "Very fine! Thou art the duke! Thou canst break it all!" She looked over her shoulder at him. "And now she will not wed thee, and thou wilt go back."

"Anne *Rose* Ber*nice* Trot*man,*" he jeered, and flicked at the fragments with his boot.

"They will send thee back." Her voice rose with emotion. "Back!"

That caught his attention. He narrowed his eyes. "No."

"No marriage. Back."

He scowled. "No . . . mar . . . ?"

Maddy gestured toward the door where his betrothed had escaped. "She will not wed thee now!"

In a long instant of hesitation, he concentrated on Maddy's face . . . and then suddenly gave a laugh. "No?" He shook his head and sprawled in a golden-legged chair. "Mad . . . ghastly . . . *touch!*" He made a face of revulsion, pushed his palm away as Anne Trotman had done. He laughed again, bitterly. "Maddygirl. Think won't . . . wed?"

The dowager duchess came to Maddy in the wildly ornate dressing room, just as she had finished her tray of supper. The duchess asked that they kneel and pray together. In a long discourse, she thanked God for Miss Anne Trotman, and for Dr. Timms and his assistants Larkin and Miss Timms, who with the permission of kind Providence, without which all human aid would fail, had set her son on the path of restoration.

Maddy recognized that she was meant to accept this as a

personal acknowledgment, which made her feel uncomfortable and subdued. After the final amen, while the duchess took the single chair in the room, Maddy got up from beside her cot and sat on the edge of it.

The duchess laid her hands together in her lap. "Miss Timms, I've had a long interview with your uncle, and I don't scruple to say to you I'm distressed that my son is to be taken from care at Blythedale. I think you must know who is responsible, but we'll say no more of that. I will tell you now, as I told Dr. Timms, that I consider the whole situation an experimental one." Her fingers moved in a restless pulse, as if she were picking out odd notes on a musical instrument. "The duke should be married; there is no question of that. It is the only reason that I allow this plan to go forward. But if there should be the slightest recurrance of ungovernability, then Dr. Timms believes, as I do, that my son should be returned to the asylum. I speak of this to you because it is intended that you will stay with us through the wedding—perhaps even a little after. I believe that Miss Trotman has asked that you not be let go until she is consulted, which I think we can agree is quite wise of her. She seems a steady girl for her age, a good Christian girl. Of course, I had never thought—my son's bride—" She pressed her lips together. "Her background isn't what anyone could have envisioned, but we must count ourselves fortunate in her, considering the situation. Miss Timms, I cannot tell you how many nights I've prayed that he would see the error of his ways. I cannot tell you—"

She lost her voice. Maddy sat quietly. The duchess lowered her face, with silent tears slipping down her cheeks. She stood up abruptly and went to the hallway door.

"His aunt—" she said, facing away from Maddy, "—Lady de Marly thinks only of the title, but I know in my heart that it is too soon. He should return. I really think that he will. Blythedale offers the best of moral treatment. He should be in your care there. Perhaps—under Dr. Timms' supervision— he might visit his wife when it is appropriate." She held the doorknob and looked back. "That would be better for everyone."

"Lady de Marly has promised him differently," Maddy said.

"Well," the dowager duchess said, "we shall see. We shall see. You are to keep me informed of his state of mind, Miss Timms. Lady de Marly has her whims, but I am his mother. I understand his welfare better than anyone. I feel quite certain that I can bring Miss Trotman to agree with me after they are married. It will be her decision then. Even Lady de Marly must admit that. And Miss Trotman is such a good steady girl."

Christian stood and let himself be dressed for his wedding: his court suit, deep brown velvet, silver buttons, a waistcoat long and trimmed with heavy pattern. Breeches, cutaway embroidered tails—and over it all, the blue Garter ribbon and silver starburst of the Order pinned across his chest. Feudal, unremittingly antiquated, right down to the diamond shoe buckles.

Maddy had been wrong. The girl wanted to be a duchess too badly to bolt.

Mad ghastly lunatic. Commissioned mad, tried and hung: he was theirs now; he had no existence. *Strip naked strangle castrate—powerless—dead!*—but he couldn't think of that—the outrage still burned him, scorched heat and shame in his skin.

Didn't want him to touch her, did she? When she was just the sort of silly green giggle calf he most despised, all dress flounce airs, no wit, primed to dance at balls and swoon on cue.

She was his fate and always had been.

He understood his aunt. It was a family matter, cold-blooded business that went beyond Christian's personal inclinations—it was *duty,* rock hard and unforgiving—seven hundred years of the unbroken name of Langland.

Beyond that, it was Jervaulx Castle in the hands of

strangers. It was the mad place, losing himself, the cradle and the straitjacket and the chains.

He'd thought it through, thought about it all night and the night before that, lying in his father's and grandfather's bed. Marry, breed, heir; his own blood at Jervaulx. He wasn't accustomed to looking at himself in that way; he'd always left it to the women in his family, obsessed as they had always seemed with the notion.

Mate with a bought mare. He envisioned bedding Miss Trotman, realized the horse pun in her name. His mouth curled: vicious humor to contain the ferocity he felt. Good reason to be afraid, Trot calf-duchess; good reason to snivel.

He would bed her, get a son—God would remember him that far, surely—and go home to Jervaulx with the boy. She could stay in town and dance her feet off, play duchess till she died. And Maddy . . . Maddygirl he would take. He couldn't live without Maddy. Jewels, kittens, kisses, whatever he had to give her.

Quaker thee-thou, she wouldn't like to be a mistress; he didn't like it himself, but it was crucial. It was necessary. And he would not take her virtue without giving back anything, everything she wanted.

They could live at Jervaulx with him, she and her father and his heir. And Christian thought, with a kind of bewilderment, that it would be all right. It would be a sufficient life. Different, utterly, from what he'd anticipated; existing by halves, as he was half of himself, but the best he could conceive now.

He tried to think of his wedding lines and couldn't find the start. But that was all right, too. When he heard them, he could do it.

The valet began to brush his coat. Christian looked at himself in the mirror. He looked like a half-man there too, not-real on the right side. It made him uneasy, and he looked away.

Duke.

Duchess.

He didn't want her. He hardly knew her well enough to hate her, but he imagined that the day would shortly come when he would. He knew a hundred men who did anything to avoid going home to their wives.

His valet smoothed his shoulder seams and laid down the brush. Christian found himself made ready to become number one hundred and one.

Chapter Fifteen

The church echoed, almost empty, the windows stark and dim with a cold morning fog. Christian had attended all of his sister's weddings. Fashionably private as they had been, this was so small as to be furtive—in a parish chapel he'd never entered before, only his mother and aunt in front, a small scatter of Trotmans, the blood man, the Ape—and Maddy, her face as sober as her plain gray dress and black cloak, in a box pew farther back.

In the hush, Mr. Trotman escorted his daughter to the spartan altar, both of them breathing frost in the shadowy air. Except for the frost and the red spots in her cheeks, the bride looked as inhumanly polished as a stone effigy.

She arrived at Christian's side, all in pale silk, her train hissing behind her. She didn't look at him. The curate began to speak. Christian took a deep breath, turning his head to watch the man read.

He was lost immediately, unable to find a place in the quick flow of syllables. He clenched his hand.

The clergyman paused, looking up beyond Christian and Miss Trotman to the tiny congregation. He waited an instant, and then began to read again, glancing first at Christian, then

the bride. Christian thought it must be the part about imped-
iments and the dreadful Day of Judgment; he had nothing to
say here, but his first moment was coming rapidly.

The air in front of his face grew white with his breath; he
tried to control it, swallowing, concentrating, forcing his
hand to open, then finding it ground into a fist again.

The priest looked at him. Christian heard his name—but
too fast, it went too fast—the sounds slid by like foreign
babble and ended on an upward questioning note. The
church held an expectant lull.

I will.

Christian knew exactly what he was to say.

He'd said it a hundred times for Maddy. He envisioned
her head nodding in time to the cadence. He breathed deeper
and faster, trying for it.

Silence. Nothing. The curate kept looking at him. Miss
Trotman stared straight ahead.

Christian opened his fist. He knew the words. He couldn't
speak. Speak. *Speak!* His fist went hard with the effort. He
felt himself growing dizzy.

"Jervaulx." His aunt's voice reverberated against brick
and carved wood, empty dead glass windows. "*Vow*—do or
turn blythall!"

The mad place. *Strip chains animal no.*

No no no no.

Christian didn't look at her; he kept his eyes on the clergyman. Her resounding voice died away.

She wouldn't do it; she couldn't send him away to that
place again; he didn't believe her; it was a mistake; he was
trying and she thought he was defying her.

I will, I will, I can't no words not back oh God.

He struggled. Silence . . . silence . . . no-word silence. He
couldn't produce *sound sentence word scream nothing,* as
unreal as the half-man in the mirror, impotent. Miss Trotman
ran her tongue round her lips, not moving more than that.

"Unstan, Jervaulx?" The high, peaked ceiling amplified
his aunt's vehemence. "Unstan back blythall?"

He turned his head. She was on her feet. From where he stood, he could see her shaking with rage.

"Bythall," she said. The word echoed and echoed. *Back mad-mad-mad-mad-mad . . .*

Miss Trotman was a monument, like the stone busts and memorials, a walking dead. The curate lifted his book, said Christian's name again, and read. He came to the question a second time, *keeponherlongbothlive?*

Christian tried to respond. He would not go back, but he couldn't form the words; he felt nauseated with the intensity of the effort. In dumb extremity he turned round, searching for Maddy. She sat still, stark and fixed in her prim bonnet and cloak, not answering when he gazed at her, pleading with her to help him, to say it properly, to give him the heavy unmusical tempo he could control.

"Takm vest," his aunt snapped, moving laboriously out of the pew. His mother rose; the clergyman cleared his throat and closed his book. Christian saw the Ape, ludicrous in a rented coat, stand and come striding up the aisle.

Christian moved. He left Miss Trotman, walking toward the keeper. His mother and aunt were coming into the aisle behind the Ape. Christian went as if to them, brushed past the keeper, the blood man, calm calm no excuse to hold him stop him reach his aunt—almost to the she-dragon—and instead he turned into the box pew where Maddy stood.

He took her arm, pushed her lightly, urging her out. He didn't give the Ape a reason—he headed for the vestry where he'd been before the ceremony, keeping Maddy on his arm, holding her hand there by force.

The others followed. Their voices resounded in the church, a little high pitched but not urgent. He let Maddy-girl pass in front of him through the vestry door.

He closed it behind him.

There was no key. Christian shot the bolt. Maddy exclaimed as he yanked her with him past the rows of hanging vestments. The side door was locked, this one a mortise, but the key hung from a red ribbon directly beside the frame. He caught up the ornate brass, but his right hand was too clumsy; the keyhole seemed hard to see—he let go of Maddy to use his left hand and then could not make the transfer from one hand to the other.

The door behind them rattled. A man's voice called out. Maddy turned toward it. The bolt rattled again, and then pounding began. Christian dropped the key trying to get it into the lock. He made a sound of anguish, retrieving it, pulling back her cloak and pushing the key into her hand. Only a minute, maybe two, before they reckoned what he was about and came around the outside to stop him.

He seized her hand, compelling it toward the lock.

"No," she cried. "Can't!"

He held her wrist in both of his hands, pressed it up against the door. She made a sob of frustration. Still Christian held her there, halfway to tears himself, not even able to say her name to beg and plead and grovel for the one trivial move, the small petty commonplace act, a key in a lock and his whole life balanced on it—he would have gone down on his knees to induce her, but he had no time.

He threw his shoulder against the door. The wood crashed on the frame. He smashed himself against it again, battering on a thick solid barrier, ignoring the punishment to his arm and ribs, working for freedom. Maddy cried out, tugging at him, but he defied that too. The door boomed under his assault; the shouts from beyond the other entrance ceased, and he knew he had only seconds now.

Maddy kept calling at him, but he could barely hear her above the thunder of the wood. She caught his arm desperately. "Wait!" Her frantic words finally came clear in his brain. "Wait—thamus wait!" She was pushing at him, struggling to reach the lock.

Christian stayed pressed to the door, watching her hands. She had the key inserted and turned in an instant. He grabbed the handle and shoved it open.

Down into the tiny side yard. He took Maddy, pulled her

so hard that she fell down the steps against him. At the foot, he met a gate and shattered it at the lock with one kick.

Maddy had ceased speaking or trying to pull away. As he pushed through the gate, she came after, her head down except for one brief glance at him. Christian shoved the gate closed and turned to the old burying ground.

Slipping on long grass, Maddy followed him. A single shout of pursuit hung thin and strange in the vapor, then there was nothing but mist and the graves. The duke was a dark figure in the freezing fog, a ghost from another century in his long-tailed velvet wedding clothes, human only when he looked back to see that she was there.

He moved fast, as if he knew his way. She stumbled over a half buried gravestone trying to keep up. An extravagantly untamed rose bush, all thorns and silvery dying leaves, caught her skirt. She stopped to pull it free and tangled her cloak in it too. He came back and yanked at the fabric himself, oblivious to the rip. He caught her arm then, keeping her beside him as he wound between the headstones.

Her hem flapped heavily; her feet were soaked with cold dew by the time a wall loomed out of the fog. He turned and walked along it, dodging ancient graves, ducking around one big monument where angels with broken and chipped wingtips gazed down on mossy epitaphs.

Maddy could hear traffic beyond the wall, street vendors and the city, a weird contrast to the dank silhouettes and wet stones in the burial place. Another forbidding priestly custom, marking graves and setting monuments: she far preferred the Friends' clean and open ground where no spirits seemed to linger.

Jervaulx brought them to a corner. He walked right into it, beating back the wet branches of an overgrown tree, revealing a stone coffin in the fresh clearing. He stepped up onto it, crushing leaves beneath his feet, and held out his hand to Maddy.

This was a boy's trick, that much she recognized. He knew the place, retained some map of childhood mischief through the fog and weedy grass. When she had climbed up onto the gravestone, he hauled himself atop the wall, straddling it, unmindful of the embroidery on his coattails or the heavy medallion that hung from the sash across his chest. He offered his arm to support her.

Maddy wavered, looked back. He made an impatient noise, reaching for her. Foliage clashed and rustled somewhere in the graveyard far behind. Cousin Edward called, but if it was distant or near, she couldn't tell.

The duke's hand closed on her cloak, her arm, a painful coercion as he dragged her up. In a wild and undignified scramble, she made it astride the top. She perched there, the bricks scraping rough on her legs, pulling at her stockings. Her bonnet had come askew, giving her only a glimpse of how far down it was to the alley on the other side. She tried to settle the headpiece back into some semblance of order and keep her ankles under her skirt.

Jervaulx leaned over and untied the string beneath her chin. He tossed the bonnet back into the burying ground, where the ties caught high up on a broken tree branch.

He grinned. For a terrible reckless moment, she was certain that he was going to kiss her, plain peculiar Archimedea Timms, here atop this wall, with Larkin and Cousin Edward in pursuit, with her skirt up to her waist, with people in view in the street at the end of the narrow alley.

He didn't. He hiked his leg over and dropped to the pavement. Maddy bit her lip as he lifted his arms for her.

She hardly knew what she was doing. It had all happened too quickly to think, and here she was like some wild coalseller's daughter, with a duke reaching for her to take her down to an alley that smelled of chamberpots and puddles.

"Go!" she whispered. "Go! I won't let them find thee."

He pulled at her skirt, stretched up and yanked her hand, hauling her off balance. She fought and toppled, biting a shriek to a whimper as the bricks scratched raw across her palms and thighs. He caught her, his chin connecting sharply with her temple in the force of her drop. Maddy stumbled and they went down together, Jervaulx falling back against the building, exhaling a hard grunt, his shoulder a cushion between her forehead and the unforgiving wall.

She pushed herself upright to her knees, her palms on his coat. He did kiss her then, sitting in the dank alley: a short, painful grind of his mouth on hers, holding her to him with his hand behind her head.

Maddy broke away. She stood up. Her dress was in shambles, her bonnet gone, her hair half-down and her hands bleeding . . . and he was smiling at her, which brought her near to weeping.

He rose, brushing down one side of his coat, ignoring the damp leaves that clung to the other. With one hand, he attempted to unpin the silver starburst on his sash, then gave it up with an annoyed mutter. He looked slipshod, like one of those noblemen who wove their way home at dawn, singing, while good modest people swept their front steps and carried out the ashes.

"What now?" She couldn't keep the quaver from her voice. "Go where?"

He put his hand up to her hair, pushing ineffectually at the part that hung untidy. Maddy gave a huff and caught up the fallen braid, searching out the loose pin and coiling it all back into place as well as she could. As she worked, he dusted at her skirt, walking around her and plucking leaves from her cloak as well. The water stains and rip were beyond help—her best steel-gray—and she was going to be rebuked, possibly punished, probably cast out of Friends and sent to prison for abducting the Duke of Jervaulx.

Maddy didn't know what to do with him. She couldn't take him back; it was impossible to let them send him to Blythedale again, immoral to see him forced into marriage for his title. Clearly it wasn't God's will that he wed Anne Trotman, the words had been there before, but when the time had come Jervaulx couldn't say them—a more obvious

Truth than that Maddy couldn't imagine. But what measure she ought to follow at the present moment was beyond her power to divine.

The duke simply took her arm on his, appropriating the decision. With an autocratic determination, he drew her with him, walking out of the alley and into the street.

Lacking her bonnet, Maddy pulled her hood up over her bare head and still felt baldly conspicuous with Jervaulx on the open curb. She didn't recognize the street, never having ventured into Mayfair. The buildings stretched both ways into the fog, not as elegant as Jervaulx House or the new homes in Belgrave Square but still far above anything Maddy had ever been accustomed to. The scent of roasting apples drifted on the mist, their vendor only a disembodied voice, a woman's musical cry. Her call was lost in the echo of horses' hooves as two carriages came down the street with liveried servants on the box and up behind.

The coaches passed on. Another vehicle came out of the fog, the single lame cab horse clopping forlornly toward them along the cobbles. Shouts began to resonate from the unseen corner in the direction of the church. Jervaulx turned his head, his fingers going tight on her arm.

He stepped into the street in the path of the hackney. The horse threw up its head. "Ho there!" the driver cried, jerking the reins as if the poor animal had not already halted of its own accord. "Mind your lady, fine sir!" The man looked over his shoulder at the commotion in the fog behind and then back at Maddy and Jervaulx. "Can I carry m'lord and m'lady?" he inquired, without much expectation. "Fast as lightning, comfortable too."

He looked rather startled when Jervaulx reached for the door, but clambered down from the perch in an instant, helping in the duke after Maddy, showering them with compliments as the yelling and the sound of running feet grew louder in the misty street.

The cabman glanced in that direction, and then back at Jervaulx. "Where to, m'lord?"

The duke squeezed Maddy's hand so hard that she gasped. She caught her breath, and said, "Chelsea. No!" Not there, people knew her there. A voice shouted up the street; she had no time to think. "Oh—hurry!" She seized on the first faraway locale that came into her head. "Ludgate Hill!"

"John Spring'll have you there in a blink, and so you'll see!" He slammed the door, and in a moment she heard him snap his whip at the mournful horse. They rattled at a great pace away from the pursuit, the sound of it lost instantly in the creak and grind of the shabby coach.

Maddy dropped her head back against the squabs. "We should not. We should not!" She put her hand to her mouth.

"Oh—hast thou any money?"

Jervaulx didn't respond, only gripped the strap with a frown, a look of strained bewilderment in his eyes as if he didn't comprehend her, as if his own actions had gone beyond his mastery.

"Money!" she exclaimed, hardly able to contain her distress.

He glanced at her with a hot uncertainty.

Maddy gave a little moan. "I don't even have a shilling in my shoe!"

"*Shoe,*" he said, one of his reflexive repetitions. He made an aggravated sound, turned from her with a scowl. The hackney took a corner, jostling them together in a bump and rattle of wheels. He propped his foot on the opposite seat and braced her with his shoulder.

Abruptly, he laughed. "Maddygirl." He leaned over and tore the buckle from his formal slipper. "*Money.*"

In Ludgate Hill, outside the mercers' and drapers' shops, amid the screeching roar of iron-wheeled traffic, Maddy had to explain to the cabman as he leaned in the door. "We must sell this," she said, handing it across Jervaulx, "and then we can pay thy fare. I'm so sorry to make thee tarry."

The driver held the sparkling buckle, turning it over in his fingerless gloves. A flock of pigeons took wing from the sidewalk at the sudden peal of the bells of St. Paul's, clapping upward into the sooty fog. "You're running away, ain't you, ladyship?"

Maddy moistened her lips, aghast at his intuition. "I'm not a ladyship! Thou must not call me so."

"I heard 'em after ye, back there west. You talk peculiar. You one o' them sort—how do they say it?"

"Friends," Maddy said faintly. "A Quaker."

He looked up at Jervaulx. "You going to marry her for real, then, m'lord? John Spring don't hold with no carrying off."

The duke said nothing. His confusion had vanished; he only seemed haughty, sullen in his silence. He fixed the cab driver with a look of disinterested scorn.

"Thou art mistaken," Maddy said. "We aren't to marry."

"Ought to," the driver grumbled. "Ought to make 'im do right by you, m'lady."

"It isn't—" She broke off. There was no use trying to explain. "Dost thou know a shop where I may sell it?"

"Those three balls hung over the door yonder, that's a pawnbroker's sign. You stay here, m'lady, if you please, so I know m'lord 'll be back with me fare."

"No. I must go. The—" She almost called Jervaulx by his title, then thought better of it. "He will wait." She gathered her skirt in preparation to get down.

Jervaulx plucked the buckle from the cabman's hand. Before Maddy could prevent him, he climbed down from the coach. She scrambled after, but the driver caught her arm as she reached the pavement.

"One of you stays right here, m'lady," he said.

"No! He shouldn't go alone. He can't—"

The duke was already amid the crowd, ignoring both the driver and Maddy's protest, avoiding a donkey that trundled past with two rush baskets of coals hung across its back. He turned in the direction opposite from the pawnshop, up the hill toward the cathedral.

"Thou must let me go!" Maddy stood on tiptoe, dreading to lose sight of him. "I have to go with him!" Though he stood out, tall even bareheaded, his black hair and the blue sash across his coat easy to descry amid the everyday pedestrians, at any moment he must vanish from sight in the swarm.

"Nay—do you think he'll abandon you so easy, m'lady?" As she craned anxiously, the driver pointed after Jervaulx. "Look there. Right into Number 32, me fine lordship," said John Spring in satisfaction. "Rundell and Bridge it is."

Christian stopped just inside the jewelers' door. The assistant who had ushered him across the threshold seemed to recognize him, bowing from the waist with a stream of soft greeting. It was all familiar; Christian came here with some frequency—he remembered an emerald bracelet, a set of earrings to match; who had that been for?

A partner came instantly from the inner precincts. Christian acknowledged the man, unable to recall his name, not needing it. Words were unnecessary. Normally he would have been escorted to a private room to view velvet trays and rainbow fire at his leisure, something he liked, but had no time for now. He could not afford to linger here where he was known.

He laid his buckles on the counter. There was a little pause. The assistant faded backward into obscurity. The partner, well fed and courteous, his cheeks completely hidden behind tall collar-points, gave no indication of surprise. He went around the counter, felt in his pocket, and pulled out a tiny magnifier. Christian watched the evaluation of the brilliants, which was short and professional. The jeweler laid down the buckle.

"Hd three hunded cepul t'grace?"

Three hundred was an outrageous overpayment, the pair couldn't have been worth more than half that together. Christian frowned, afraid he had not understood it right. He fought down alarm, choked it in ice.

"Three twent five," the man said. He smiled. "Yugrace been good tus. Ledus taportunty showsteem return."

The assistant came round the corner of the counter, returning a tray of rings to their drawer. Golden curves, set neat row after neat row. The brief display caught Christian's eye, distracted him.

The partner made a questioning murmur. Christian realized that he'd drifted. He covered it with a quick autocratic nod, agreeing to the price.

The rings disappeared into their slotted drawer. Wedding rings. The assistant lifted the key on a string round his neck and unlocked another tray.

The partner leaned a little across toward Christian. "Cred grace," he asked in a very soft voice, "caspaint?"

The low tone, the question—Christian didn't understand. He felt befuddled, facing the man's expectant confidentiality. In an appallingly long pause, he clung to his ice remoteness, refused to lean close or acknowledge the question, tried to think it through. The merchandise examined, the bargain struck, then . . . what?

They would pay him.

Credit or cash payment. Yes.

His heart accelerated. He could think of no way to respond. He gripped the edge of the counter—then put his white-gloved hand on top. He opened it, palm up.

"Ver'good." The partner nodded. "Moment." He took up the buckles and went briskly toward the back rooms.

Christian watched the assistant at his work. The new tray went down the counter to a man and a young woman in a plain gray dress. And as Christian was standing there with his jaw clamped, his heart pounding, spying on some country couple who murmured solemnly over their meager purchase, it came to him. A revelation, an answer that had been making its way through his numb and wayward brain for longer than he'd even known himself.

Maddy. It was Maddygirl he should marry.

The clarity of it, the beauty, burst on him in perfect glory. Maddygirl would never let them send him back, Maddygirl could understand him; she didn't humiliate him; her father was a talented geometer, she was devoted and loyal—look at the way she'd come with him, even if it had been under a certain amount of force, a very little. She'd come almost of her own accord—ye Gods, he'd even seen her stand up, and damned well, to the she-dragon. And she had said she loved him. He thought she'd said that. He was almost certain.

Maddygirl deserved to be a duchess. It had been a great mistake of nature to make her a thee-thou sugar scoop bonnet.

The partner returned with a slim leather book. He laid it on the counter, circumspect, no sign of banknotes, but Christian knew what it was. He felt urgent, anxious to escape—with an effort he governed his impulse to snatch it up and flee. Instead he went to the ring tray, made a slight bow of apology to the young lady, pulled a ring from its velvet rest, and brought it back to the jeweler.

The partner smiled his affluent smile. He started to take back the money book. Christian clapped his hand over it.

"Billen, course." The jeweler never blinked. "Led jurgrace box." He took up the ring, leaving the book untouched.

Christian slipped the leather wallet into his pocket. He hated the taste of this—a thief with his own money. He felt his control breaking. A skulking, escaped animal, Chancery lunatic, with no right to sell his shoe buckles, to purchase a ring for his future wife.

The partner returned with the box. Christian accepted it. They ushered him out as if he were real, still the Duke of Jervaulx. Still a man and not a beast.

When he returned to the street, he felt dazed, sluggish; his whole body felt like terror trapped inside lethargy. He walked a little way along the pavement, then stopped and leaned on the wall. The crowds flowed past, confusing and loud—alien gibber, horrible mindless sound that should have been sense.

The ice calm of the episode deserted him; late reaction sent his heart thudding with dread—he might not have done it right, he might have forgotten something, he didn't know;

it was all forbidding and strange; what might have happened, how he might have given himself away, made himself ridiculous, put himself in their power to seize and restrain.

He heard Maddy call him. He heard his name through the disorder—*Jervaulx*—solid dear plain no manners Maddy-girl, her hands on his arms, her eyes—sherry eyes, decadent gold—looking up into his, full of fear and question.

He drew in a hard breath, mastering panic. He manufactured a grin. Without looking down, he fumbled the book of banknotes from his pocket and pushed them into her hands.

Chapter Sixteen

$\mathcal{M}$addy had not ever had so much money at once in her possession. She held the wallet in both hands as they walked, afraid to tuck it into her dress. The hundreds of pounds made this preposterous flight seem all too credible— an immediate return became choice, not necessity.

After she'd paid the driver, Jervaulx had looked at her as if she knew what they ought to do. He kept his hand gripped firmly on her elbow, a strange mixture of dependence and protection. With the duke beside her, none of the barrow boys shouted at her that she stopped the way, no quarrelsome pedestrian pushed her into the muddy street rather than give up an inch of space to pass. He was broadshouldered and imperial, and his eyes were the blue spirit of bewilderment—a disquietude like looking into the sky at the last of twilight, straight overhead to a single star, when comfortable illusion vanished and the solid roof of the sky dissolved to betray its real and dizzy distance.

She felt as if her whole solid world had evaporated in that way; it was hard to conceive that Archimedea Timms was standing in the teeming footway on Ludgate Hill trying to decide what was to be done with the Duke of Jervaulx, since he did not appear to have any notion what to do with himself.

She'd begun to walk, having no better idea. A safe haven, that was what she must find for him. No matter the reprisal that faced her, she had to get back to Papa by evening—he would be frantic that she had disappeared with the duke. She had no clear idea of what broken laws and criminal acts she might be taxed with, but Lady de Marly would be sure to know them all. Maddy was certain of that. For herself, she thought with a rather tenuous bravery, she didn't mind so very much—Jervaulx was her Opening, after all, and any Sufferings that came with him must be borne—but she was afraid of what might become of her papa if she were to be sent to prison.

The pressure of his hand pulled her to a stop. Just in front of them, on the loud blast of a horn, a day coach for Brighton clattered out from beneath the sign of the Belle Sauvage, wheeling into the street with the guard blowing enthusiastically for right-of-way.

As soon as it passed, disappearing into the shifting screen of traffic and black mist, Jervaulx drew her toward the inn yard gate. Beneath the passageway, a stableboy wielded a deft rake, scooping dirt and droppings from their path, skipping backwards with a quick muttered salute as they passed.

Travelers stood about inside the yard, waiting next to their trunks and valises and piles of bundled belongings. Another coach was loading, the yellow-and-black for Newmarket, the horses fresh, rattling their shoes against the cobbles and blowing frost.

Jervaulx went directly to the booking office. He handed Maddy in the door, with a little extra push as if she might need encouragement. The crowd inside around the desk barely admitted two more. Even as outlandishly as Maddy and the duke were dressed, no one paid the least mind, the clerks too busy flinging brown-paper parcels into the tower of pigeonholes behind the desk, the customers calling out questions or trying to engage the attention of some porter.

He pulled her into a tight corner, turned his back on the gathering and leaned over to her ear. *"Go,"* he said, not achieving an actual whisper, but it hardly mattered in the common racket.

Maddy looked at him. "Where?"

The question appeared to exasperate him. *"Go,"* he repeated. "Two."

"Not I," she said firmly.

A lady with a pair of little girls on her arms edged past behind him, working her way to the end of the shortest queue. Jervaulx put his hand on Maddy's shoulder. "Two," he insisted.

"I cannot."

His fingers pressed into her. *"Home.* Shere—" He clenched his jaw with effort. "—voh!"

It didn't seem an entirely absurd notion, except that she had no idea where his home might be, or whether he could travel there alone —without being tagged, like a child or a trunk, or an idiot, which was vision enough to chill her. And his home would be no protection from his family's power to send him back to Blythedale.

"Home," he urged. "Maddygirl."

"Where is it?" she asked. "Where?"

That seemed to foil him. He scowled, released her and turned her around bodily. On the wall she'd been leaning against were posting bills and a shellacked and yellowing tourist's map of England, the varnish in the vicinity of London rubbed through and cracking from all the wear. He put his hand on a part of the map that had hardly deteriorated at all, far to the west, where the green of England met the red of Wales.

"No! Thou canst not go that distance alone."

He caught her shoulders again. She felt him move closer against her back, almost an embrace. He pressed his cheek to her hood, dislodging it from covering her hair, and made a sound of insistence. He wrapped his arms around her and held her back against him, right there amid the stagecoach passengers. *"Two,"* he said in her ear. "Home."

She tried to scramble away, but he wouldn't allow it. He let her turn, then trapped her there against the map and the wall. She hardly knew what to do. Some of the customers were looking at them. She imagined their shock and censure, what they must think of her in a torn skirt and no bonnet, locked in a man's arms. He leaned his mouth next to her ear.

"Maddygirl . . . *wed.*"

Several more customers walked into the room, brushing close behind Jervaulx. One of them kept on his hat, the broad-brimmed, unmistakable insignia of a Quaker. Maddy ducked her head in horror. She hadn't caught sight of who it was, but any visiting Friend with business here might know her from Yearly Meeting, and all too many from London itself would know her very well. She buried her face in Jervaulx's shoulder for concealment. He caught her close, with a soft, willing murmur in his throat.

She did not dare look up. She didn't struggle. He was a shield against discovery, large and solid enough to hide safely behind—if only he would not slip his hand up beneath her hood that way, brushing it fully back and wrapping his fingers round the nape of her neck, pulling her closer yet, resting his face against her hair.

She couldn't imagine that everyone in the room didn't turn and gasp and point in condemnation. But the normal sound of business went on about them, the clump of shoes passing in and out the door, the porters' calls, the Newmarket coach's horn as the team turned into the street.

His hand slipped from her waist. She felt him work at something in his coat; all the while she did not venture to lift her head and risk being seen. He groped for her hand and pressed a small box into it.

Maddy held the container, keeping her head down, looking a little to the side to try to see if the unknown Friend had departed yet. Jervaulx made her turn her hand over. With an impatient mutter, he pushed his thumb awkwardly against the box in her palm.

The lid opened. Hiding as she was, her face lowered, she saw gold and multicolored fire. A ring—a wide filigree band with seed pearls around a vivid opal—for Anne Trotman?

He fumbled at it one handed, got his forefinger halfway through the ring, and let the box fall. In this small corner, with their heads lowered together, they created a tiny private world. Maddy watched in perplexity as he worked the ring around into his hand, and then tried to slide it onto her finger.

"Wed." He put his lips against her ear. "Maddy . . . *wed.* Home."

She stared at the ring, at his fingers as he pushed it forcibly onto hers.

"No!" She pulled the opal free and stooped to retrieve the box, yanking her hood firmly over her head. "Thou art—it is not—*no!* However didst thou invent such a scheme?"

She shoved the box into his palm and turned. With the hood clasped close to her face, she forced her way through the press of travelers and hurried into the yard. Outside, she rushed a few feet from the door and stopped, her face burning. She held her hood over her mouth and nose.

The duke came out of the office door. She was in plain sight, but he didn't seem to see her. He halted, a bizarrely splendid gentleman amid the ordinary surroundings: a lost courtier, rich with velvet and heavy embellishment, with his royal blue sash and medallion, lost in more than place and time.

People turned to look at him. Maddy saw the rigid unease in his stance. He stood immobile where he'd stopped, as if one step in any direction might be into a cavern that opened at his feet. His jaw was tight, his dark brows drawn down. Arrested force, alone and alien.

He scanned the yard. Maddy was quite close to him, within a touch of his right hand, and yet she might have been one of the pieces of baggage scattered in piles about the court. He didn't even look her way. He only radiated high-strung tension, a spiraling stillness—a man ready to splinter.

She said his name, muffled behind the cloak. His bearing changed. He turned toward her as if she'd broken a spell, the release like a bright flame in his face. It seemed to startle him that she was so close; he took an aggressive step and moved to catch her by both arms.

"Not . . . *leave!*" he said savagely. "'Lone . . . *can't!* Stay. You . . . *stay!*"

"I don't know what to do with you!" Maddy bit down on the woollen hood as she held it to her mouth. "I can't stay with you! I can't take you back!"

"Sher—" He put his palms against her shoulders and gave her a sharp push. "*—voh!*" He gave her another, making her take a step back. "*Home.*" A push. "*Marry*"—push— "*Maddy*"—push—"*girl!*"—push—"*Yes!*" Under his coercion, she was progessing unevenly backward across the yard. "Not . . . mad . . . *place!* Marry . . . *Maddy!*"

"No!" she said, then sucked in a panicked breath and twitched her hood as far she could over her face to conceal herself. In somber hat and plain coat, the Quaker from the ticket office approached them.

Maddy peered from inside her hood as the stranger laid a hand on Jervaulx's arm. "Think a moment, Friend. Thou are importunate."

Jervaulx gave him a look as if the man had just spit in his face. For a vibrating instant, she was afraid that he would turn and strike out, the way he'd done to Cousin Edward. The Quaker was only a medium-sized man, no older than Maddy herself—clean shaven and clear-eyed, no one whom she recalled seeing before. A good man, courageous to confront Jervaulx, who was so clearly angry and an aristocrat, with nothing insignificant about him, either in conduct or in build.

The duke shook off the restraining hand. He looked hotly at Maddy, as if expecting her to explain.

"I thank thee, Friend," she said quickly, anxious to placate Jervaulx. "But I need no help."

The Quaker gave her a startled glance. Maddy felt her heart drop.

"Thou are in the Life?" he asked.

She looked at the ground. Wicked lies sprang to her lips, immoral deceptions to retrieve the mistake that had revealed her to another Friend more clearly than a Quaker bonnet and Plain Dress would have done. But she could not; he was no threat to Jervaulx, it was only to save her own stature in front of one of her fellow members.

She barely lifted her eyes. "I am."

Jervaulx grasped her elbow. It was a silent touch, not harsh, but firm. He watched the Quaker warily.

"He doesn't bedevil thee?" the man asked. He met Jervaulx's look. "I'd not suffer thee to lift a hand against her. Will thou compose thyself and walk peaceful?"

It was a quiet inquiry, almost kind. Maddy felt a surge of gratitude and affinity. This man seemed an island of sense in a storm of uncertainty, so much more familiar in his broad plain hat and simple coat, so much more trustworthy than an incalculable, angry stranger in velvet and medallion and royal sash.

The Quaker appeared troubled at Jervaulx's lack of response. "Thou will not answer as an honest man?"

Jervaulx's grip on her arm grew painful.

Maddy touched the Quaker's rough broadcloth sleeve. "Friend," she said softly, ignoring Jervaulx's increasing pressure on her arm, his silent attempt to pull her from the newcomer's range. She was forming a new purpose. "I spoke idle words in haste, to say that I need not thy help." She lifted her eyes to the level, steady inquiry in the young man's gaze. "I'm in true want of aid. Canst thou give assistance?"

"Surely," he said—a single word that lifted a thousand pounds from Maddy's shoulders.

While Jervaulx sat disposed in an attitude of majestic disapproval, his chair pushed away from a table in the public dining parlor, his legs outstretched, his arms crossed over starburst and sash, Maddy bent close to the young Quaker and related her difficulty. Richard Gill took a sip of ale and looked thoughtfully at the duke when she'd finished.

Jervaulx, brooding and defiant, glared back beneath his black lashes. He had not wished to come into the dining room; he'd tried to prevent her, but when Maddy refused to be held back, he'd followed, not allowing her to move a step beyond his immediate reach. He didn't speak, and Maddy couldn't tell how much he understood of what she said to Richard Gill, but his whole demeanor was of betrayed dignity, as if she offended him with this new connection.

Richard remained silent, a somber and thinking pause. Maddy waited, glad to be again with a person who was not so quick with words or action but took time to consider. She was content to bide in Richard's contemplation. The young Friend was handsome, with composed moves and a resolute air that invited confidence. His strong face suited the deep-brimmed hat and unadorned coat better than did many a solemn elder's.

Maddy was certain he'd never attended London Yearly Meeting, where Friends met to conduct their annual business and query the smaller Quarterly and Monthly meetings as to their spiritual state. Yearly Meeting gathered Quaker families together from all over England. She would have recalled it if Richard Gill had been a delegate. It didn't require direct attendance at Men's Meeting for all the women to know who was prominent and who was not—and who was unmarried and who was not.

It was axiomatic that if a young woman wished to wed, her best course was to attend London Yearly Meeting, where one of the chief duties of the Meeting of Women Friends there was to look into hopeful couples' clearness for marriage— a process that naturally lent itself to appraisal and ordering by their suitability of the other eligible bachelors in attendance. Richard Gill, Maddy was quite certain, had not yet been brought to the attention of Women's in any regard, nuptial or otherwise. She was not quite certain what his business must be. He'd come to the coach office to retrieve a sturdy small box that he seemed heedful to manage with great care. It sat now on the table beside him, labeled with a series of circles designated by such curious titles as "Claudiana, 4th row, rose," "Trafalgar Banner, 1st row, byblomen," and "Duke of Clarence, 4th row, bizard."

The waiter brought beefsteak pudding and boiled cabbage. Jervaulx made a face at it. He drank deeply of his ale while Maddy busied herself buttering three slices of bread, serving out portions for each of them.

She bowed her head for a moment of blessing. Richard removed his hat. Jervaulx did nothing at all, just watched them malevolently, slouched with crossed arms in his chair.

Richard put on his hat again and began to eat his pudding. Maddy didn't know many young men who kept so strictly to Plain Speech and Dress. She admired him for it. She wished that she might have appeared in a more neat and proper guise herself, instead of lacking her bonnet, and with her skirt torn.

She glanced at Jervaulx. He wasn't eating. He was watching her—and as cleanly handsome as Richard Gill might be, the duke was more, shadow and connection to her—his fine mouth that had kissed hers, his hands that had caressed her hair.

She flushed, feeling a liar and pretender. She had represented Jervaulx as her patient, herself as his nurse. The appearance of it struck her with strong effect—what nurse would run away with a patient against his family's wishes? What nurse would let herself be kissed? What would Richard Gill think of her if he knew? And not to tell him—it was one of those lies of silence and omission. It was not walking in the Way, not at all.

"Thou don't think him mad?" Richard asked.

He startled Maddy with his sudden speech. She looked up. "No."

"He does not seem raving. But he pushed thee, in the yard."

She broke a piece of bread, with a tiny wry smile. "He's a duke. It's not the same as madness, quite."

Richard ate another bite. "That is what dukes do?" He lifted his brows. "Push?"

"That is the least of what this one will do."

At his little distance from the table, Jervaulx tilted his head and looked bored. He flicked a glance from Maddy to Richard, lifted his ale and drank.

"He doesn't understand?" Richard asked.

"I don't know. Some, I think."

"Thou ought to take him back to his family."

Maddy sat up a little. "No."

Jervaulx looked at her. The tedium left his manner.

"It isn't thy place to keep him away, if they wish him to live retired. He belongs to his own, not to thee."

"No. His family doesn't understand. They don't know what 'tis like there."

"It is thy cousin's house?"

"It's a madhouse. He is not mad!"

"He doesn't speak. How is he to live in the world alone?" She pulled her cloak close around her. "Not alone. He can't live alone."

"How, then? Has he no friends but thee?"

"I—" Maddy stopped, realizing that she didn't know. She looked to Jervaulx. "A friend?" she asked. "Hast thou a near companion?"

He looked from her to Richard and back again warily.

"No," she said, "I don't mean Quaker. A friend*ship*. Of *thine*. A companion."

He hesitated. Then he held out his hand to her.

"Jervaulx!" Despair crept into her voice. "Is there not one friend who loves thee?"

His hand closed. His great golden signet gleamed against his fingers. He gave Richard a baleful look, settling back in the chair.

"Perhaps—Jervaulx . . . thou wouldst remain with him?" She nodded toward the Quaker. "With Richard Gill?"

"Archimedea—" Richard began.

"Only until I can go back and tell Papa I'm well," she said

hastily. "If thou wouldst only stop here with him for a little while. A few hours."

"It isn't the stopping. It is that he ought to go back."

"I can't take him back!" she cried, leaning forward. "Thou canst not understand!"

Jervaulx watched her intensely. His right fist worked in rhythm. He closed his left around the tankard of ale, but did not drink.

"Please," she said to Richard Gill.

Small lines of unhappiness marked the Quaker's brow. She saw the misgiving in his lucid gray eyes.

"Please," she whispered, "Wilt thou not make it thy Concern?"

It was a plea that no Friend could take lightly. Richard frowned down at his meal. He closed his eyes. Maddy waited, pleading with God to speak to him, knowing that it was wrong to do so, to beg that her own self-will prevail, but unable to help herself. She couldn't take Jervaulx back—that was the only Truth she knew for certain; it was simply impossible to imagine him again in the cell at Blythedale Hall.

Richard let go of a deep breath and looked at her. "I will make it my Concern. I will consider further if he should go back."

She hardly knew whether that meant he would wait here with the duke or not, but before she could ask, Jervaulx thumped his ale down on the table. He stood, kicking his chair away, and jerked Maddy up from hers. *"Back,"* he exclaimed, with energy burning in his eyes. Then he gritted his teeth and said, *"Friend!"*

He hauled her with him, his grip more than she could break. She heard Richard utter something behind them, saw the waiter come hurrying up to block him at the table as Jervaulx propelled her toward the door with unswerving force.

Maddy fought him, trying to turn back. Jervaulx overmatched her easily, with more strength than she'd ever realized he could command. When she tried to plant her feet, he dragged her off them. She wrenched free, but Jervaulx grabbed her again, his arm around her neck, forcing her ruthlessly with him. His hold locked as she twisted away, his fingers digging hard into the skin at her nape, catching stray hairs. She yelped. "Jervaulx! Richard! I can't—*help* me!"

She had a whirling glimpse of Richard and the waiter, and then lost them, stumbling out the front door under Jervaulx's propulsion, half-falling down the step among the pedestrians.

"Friend!" Jervaulx ejaculated, plowing ahead with her. *"Durm!"*

He stopped a hackney in the same way he'd stopped one before—by walking right into the street in front of it. As the horse half-reared, its hooves striking the pavement inches from his feet, the driver shouted and another cab swerved. Jervaulx grabbed the animal's bridle.

"*Al*ban!" he yelled, with the horse in one hand and Maddy in the other.

"Jehu Christ! All right, *Albany,* ye blinkin' madman!" the driver shouted. "Let me horse loose, then, and get you in-side!"

A paved and covered walkway led into the mist, materializing ahead of them and vanishing behind as they walked between the double rows of long, pale-cream buildings off Picadilly. The duke's footsteps echoed in the quiet; the place seemed deserted at mid-morning, except for a single boot-black hurrying past with a box and a pair of shoes in his hands.

Maddy had given up resisting. She ceased trying to do anything but keep pace with Jervaulx. He would not let her go or allow her to lag behind. They passed another servant, a little potbellied man in a red waistcoat who stepped aside, bowed to the duke and murmured, "Your Grace." Without a pause, Jervaulx turned into a stone staircase and went up two floors with Maddy.

A dog began to bark before he even touched the door.

Another took up the chorus. Jervaulx froze with his hand lifted.

"Devil." His lips pulled back in a fierce grin. His fist came down, pounding. The dogs on the other side went reckless with extravagant noise. *"Devil, devil, devil!"*

"Good God, hold your row!" A muffled voice yelled from somewhere far inside. On a lower landing, another door opened. Maddy looked down to see a curious face lifted, an elderly man in a dressing robe and nightcap. The dogs scraped savagely at the door. The staircase resonated with barks and Jervaulx's pounding knock.

The voice from inside tried to quiet them. "Here, Cass; here, you worthless cur; shut up, shut up—they'll make me shoot you for certain."

Jervaulx stopped banging abruptly, leaning on the door, his cheek against it as if it were solid ground to a drowning sailor. The dogs went on barking while the latch turned. The door opened to a swarm of white and black fur, pink tongues and plumed tails, as the two dogs threw themselves onto Jervaulx.

Maddy looked beyond them to the blond, drowsy-eyed man who stood in the entrance hall, bare chested and in stocking feet, a scrap of shaving soap still spread on his jaw. The barking ceased as the dogs plunged and pressed themselves over Jervaulx. The duke knelt, spread his arms and let them lick his face and scrabble their paws in his hair.

"Shev?" the man in the doorway said, as if he'd just been woken from a sound sleep.

Maddy glanced at the elderly eavesdropper on the landing below, who was still looking up and leaning a little to get a better view. "May we come inside?" she asked.

The blond man had been staring at Jervaulx and the dogs. He glanced at Maddy, seemed to come all at once awake, and stepped back. "Ye gods," he said. That was all, but he threw his shaving towel over his shoulder and reached to urge the duke within. Jervaulx went, the dogs twining themselves lovingly round his legs. Maddy stepped quickly inside and shut the door behind her.

Their host, still dumbfounded, followed them into the sitting room. "Shev," he said.

Jervaulx crossed the room and leaned his hands on the windowsill, looking out into the mist. Then he turned around, his back to the wall with his dogs pressing ecstatic bodies against him. Some severe emotion came into his face; he closed his eyes and slid down to sit on the floor. The black-and-white setter licked his ear. He put his arm round the dog and buried his face in the silky white coat. The black one whined and tried to push between them.

"I thought—oh, God, man—they said you were dying. As good as dead. They gave me the dogs." The disheveled gentleman strode to Jervaulx, then didn't seem to know what to do when he got there. He fell to his knees. "Shev," he said helplessly.

Jervaulx didn't lift his face. He shook his head, his fingers buried in Devil's coat.

The blond man turned to look up at Maddy. "What is it? They told me he was dying. What's happened?"

"Thou art his friend?"

"Certainly I'm his friend! He don't have a better! Out with it, woman—have you got claws into him some way or other?" He looked back at Jervaulx. "Christ—is it opium?"

"He needs thy assistance."

"What assistance? Who are you?"

"My name is Archimedea Timms. He was a patient at my cousin's asylum in Buckinghamshire. I had charge of him there. We are—" She made a little foolish laugh and spread her hands. "I suppose we have broke bounds, and are run away."

The man pushed back a tousled blond forelock. He sat on his heels. "Shev," he said again, in that baffled voice.

The duke raised his head. His eyes were midnight dark, full of moisture. With an angry, abashed move, he raised his arm and wiped one side of his face on his sleeve. "Friend," he said hoarsely. "Dnnh. Dunnrm." He leaned his head back against the wall with a groan.

"Durm?" Maddy said. "Is that thy name?"

"Durham," the blond man said, and added absently, "Kit Durham, at your service, ma'am."

Jervaulx looked at his friend. Devil put a nose to his cheek and temple, wriggling in delight. Jervaulx hugged the animal. "Drrm . . . *thank,*" he said. "Thank . . . *dogs.*"

Durham stared at him. Jervaulx made another anguished sound and shook his head, pushing air between his teeth.

"Right. Dogs. Nothing to it." Durham stood up, set a chair. "Get off the floor, old fellow. Got to think. Can't think with you on the floor, Shev."

Maddy thought the resumption of normality a good thing. Jervaulx had a very strange expression—he was on the edge of shattering. He wouldn't like his friend to see him beyond control. "Perhaps thou ought to finish dressing," she suggested to Durham, hoping to give the duke a moment to compose himself in privacy.

"Oh good God—" Durham began a hasty retreat. "My apologies. I beg your pardon, ma'am—forgot myself! Wasn't expecting—a lady, that is. You stay right there, Shev! Don't leave!"

"We won't leave," Maddy said.

Durham blinked at her, as if it kept surprising him that she spoke instead of Jervaulx. He backed into the other room and slammed the door.

Having disdained cabbage and beefsteak, Jervaulx seemed quite content to share Durham's breakfast of salmon and fresh oysters with bread and lemon. Without asking what he'd like, Durham sent his servant—the same potbellied man who'd spoken to the duke outside—back to the kitchen for chocolate instead of coffee to drink.

Jervaulx sat sipping at the steaming dark liquid and feeding tidbits to the dogs while his friend interrogated Maddy. As they talked, the duke watched them through the vapors from his cup, an unruffled satisfaction in his expression. He seemed to feel that he had done all that could be done, and was satisfied to leave any further decisions in the hands of others.

Durham, at least, had no doubts that Jervaulx ought to be protected from his family's intentions. "That loathsome old hellcat," was his succinct opinion of Lady de Marly, and his comment upon the duke's mother included words that Maddy had never even heard before.

At best, she found his style of speech difficult to comprehend. She hesitated when he demanded whether she was certain that no one could touch on the drag from the church.

"Drag?" she asked dubiously.

"The scent. No one could find where you went?"

"I shouldn't think so. We've been to Ludgate Hill and back in hackneys."

"Ludgate Hill!" He gave a bark of laughter. "Good girl." He grinned at Jervaulx. "Who'd think of you pointing for a lot of drapers, eh?"

The duke turned his head a little, smiling back. He took a sip of his chocolate. Maddy suspected that he understood less than she.

"No one, take my word," Durham answered himself. "More likely they'd have at . . . Egad." He sprang out of his chair, pulling the curtains. "They'll come here. Mark!" He yelled into the next room. "Onto the stair with you! Keep a watch! I'm not at home. Tell 'em—I've gone early to 'Change."

The servant bowed over his scarlet potbelly. "Sir. They won't believe me."

"Hell's bells, can't a man make a purchase in the public funds? I just had—a bequest from my third cousin four times removed, that's the ticket. Six hundred pounds—but mind you, don't part with that morsel for less than half a crown."

"What of the colonel, sir? Should I turn him off?"

"Damn and blast—Fane! He'll be here any minute." Durham chewed his lip. "No percentage in it." He glanced at Maddy. "We can trust Fane. He'd never swallow the tale anyway—think I'd gone batty to put six hundred in funds. He won't have a noddy notion what to do; he ain't the thinking sort—but if you want a good sound fellow at your back, Andy Fane's your man."

Maddy was pleased to have anyone at all at her back; Durham seemed a little flighty, but he clearly meant to help Jervaulx. She was about to mention her need to return to her papa when Jervaulx and Durham both glanced toward the window at the sound of an off-key whistle.

The duke grinned and set down his cup. *"Friend,"* he said to Maddy.

"Beforehand, for once," Durham said, as a handsome clock on the mantel rang a set of melodious chimes. He ducked halfway into the entrance hall. "I'll send Mark down to bring him up quiet. The old General was in on that racket when you came in, wasn't he? We'll put it in his ear about the six hundred pounds." He frowned at Maddy. "You're my—ah—second cousin five times removed. Orphan. Came with the bequest. Orphan always comes with the bequest. Solicitor brought you, couldn't wait, had to catch the mail back to—somewhere. All that pounding to wake me up, right? Barking—his imagination. Dogs ain't allowed. Lord only knows how I've got by with it this long."

He disappeared into the entryway. All these lies and deceptions made Maddy uncomfortable. Even if she weren't speaking them herself, she was participating. Richard Gill's steady, thoughtful gaze haunted her like a conscience—but against it was Jervaulx's clear joy in his friends, both Durham and the officer with the magnificent golden lace and bright facings on his uniform, who didn't say a word to the duke—just took him round the shoulders and pounded his back, and then shoved him away.

The officer looked down and pushed Devil off his knee. "Knew he was too tedious to kill," he said to the dog. "Got a few more papers to write, what?" He gave Maddy a sideways squint. "Brought a girl along, too, wouldn't you know it?"

"This is Miss—ah—" Durham left an expectant pause.

"Timms," Maddy said.

The soldier swept a bow, holding his sword back with one white-gloved hand and brushing her skirt with the tall white plume of his military hat. "Colonel Andrew Fane, at your service, my love."

"Leave off, Fane. She's a Quaker."

Colonel Fane looked startled. He stiffened his spine and put his heels together in a military manner, going quite red in the face. "I beg your pardon, ma'am! Miss? Then it's your fellow waiting out by the street, is it? One who wanted to know if—damn—asked about you, Shev—that was it! Didn't understand what the devil he was getting at, but I see it now. Wanted to know where to find the duke. What duke, says I. Got dukes by the score—"

"Richard!" Maddy clapped her hand to her breast. "It will be Richard Gill."

"Oh," said Colonel Fane.

"However did he—" She bit her lip and turned to Durham. "He'll have followed us. I spoke to him—I asked him to help, and he said that he would . . . but—I'm not certain that he doesn't think I should take the duke back to his family."

"He knows about it?" Durham demanded. "And he's out there now? Here? Lud, miss—why didn't you say?"

"I didn't know. I never thought he could follow, or would. But—he's made it a Concern. I should have known that he wouldn't cast it off easily."

"What the devil is going on?" the colonel demanded.

"Get rid of that ridiculous thing you wear on your head and sit down." Durham yanked a chair from the table. "We're all gone to cover for Shev. Those harpies he's pleased to call a family want to put him away in a madhouse."

"Say *what?*"

"Tell him, Miss Timms. Shev needs us. You tell him what you told me."

Chapter Seventeen

"*C* an't talk?" Colonel Fane gave Jervaulx a look of comical incredulity.

The duke returned a wintry smile. He stroked the black dog Cass. His mouth curled and hardened with brutal effort; his fingers dug into the black ruff. "Dumb . . . *you.*"

The officer appeared to comprehend this comment instantly. "I'm not dumb!" he protested.

"Come along, Fane." Durham poured him coffee. "Everybody knows you're a block."

"I am not dumb! Listen—who thought of selling Shev to the resurrection jarvey? Me."

"And who had to go and pay his bail?"

Colonel Fane grinned. "Kill him—" He smirked theatrically. "I say—" His lips puckered. "Kill him when—" He began to snicker.

"Take a damper, you lobcock." Durham's face was a pink combination of disgust and pent-up amusement. "This is serious."

"Kill him—" The colonel could no longer speak through wheezes of laughter. "I say, kill him—"

"Kill him when you *want* him," Jervaulx said clearly. He grinned, leaning his chair back on two legs.

Durham's smile faded in surprise—but Maddy caught his eye. He made no comment on the duke's speech. The colonel seemed to think nothing of it; he was chortling, banging one fist into his other palm.

"Bless me, what a row that was, Miss Timms! Shev was right bosky, do you see—he was used up. Corned, pickled and salted—"

"Comatose, Miss Timms," Durham explained gravely. "In strong drink."

"Oh, yes, good Oxford word. Comatose!" The colonel seemed to find that description an uplifting one. "Perfectly senseless. And we was having to carry him home, y'see, between the two of us, and he weighs—'S blood, he must weigh fourteen stone! And who might drive by at the very moment but the one they call the resurrection jarvey—"

"Night coachman. Sells bodies to the surgeons," Durham interpreted. "For anatomy lectures."

"Right! So what should I think—and it was my idea entirely, I promise you, Miss—and the fellow took him, and—" Colonel Fane made an expressive revolution with his forefinger. "And, y'know—his clothes, we got those, and the fellow took him in a sheet to old Brooks! In Blenheim Street! Took him there, to the lecturer's door!" He leaned back his head and thumped the table. "And offered—and offered . . . him for . . . f' . . . *sale!*"

The colonel lost the power of coherent utterance in his hilarity. Maddy had lost hers, too. She stared at the officer in scandalized shock.

Colonel Fane spluttered into speech again. "An' the doctor 'xamines 'im—'n says—he says . . . 'You scoundrel—this fellow ain't—*dead!*' "

She looked around at the others. Jervaulx and Durham were both watching Colonel Fane, grinning broadly in anticipation.

" 'N the jarvey says, 'Not *dead?*' " The colonel drew himself up in a semblance of affront. " 'Not *dead?* Why then—sir . . . then, I say, sir . . . you must just . . . k—k—' "

The other two joined in, harmonizing in sonorous unison, " '*Kill* him when you *want* him!' "—a chorus of deep masculine timbre, Jervaulx as fluent as the rest. He was chuckling, rocking back again with his legs outstretched.

"Damn you," he said to the colonel. *"Rob."*

"Oh, right—that was the upshot of it—poor old Shev, the doctor thinks 'tis a burglary attempt, a shot t' get into his house, and cries thief. The jarvey got clean away, but they tied up Shev and sent 'im to Marlborough Street, an' he laid there all night in a sheet, and half the morning, 'til Durham could get a solicitor out of the Old Bailey—to argue not to commit him. Duke of—" He began to lose his composure again. "Duke of . . . of Jervaulx, y'see—for attempt to rob a . . . a . . . *bone-house!*"

They all grew absurd at that, wiping eyes and sighing when the waves of mirth finally died down. Devil jumped up, his forelegs on the duke's lap. Jervaulx rubbed the dog's head vigorously between his hands. He slanted his pirate smile on Maddy, midnight blue and mischief.

"So there you are, Miss Timms," the colonel said, with a self-satisfied groan. "It was all hushed up, but you have it from the horse's mouth."

"I see," she said, unable to add more.

"What a lark. I'm not dumb. No indeed. Lord bless us, what a lark."

"Perhaps—thou might return to the duke's situation," she said.

"Oh, yes. Right ho. The duke's situation. Got himself into another scrape, has he?"

"Bear with us, Miss Timms," Durham said. "We keep Fane about for his muscle, not his brains. Do you think we ought to speak to this man Richard Gill? How much does he know of it? Could he bring the pursuit down on us here?"

"I told him all that I've told thee."

Durham poured another round, coffee for himself and the colonel, chocolate for Jervaulx and Maddy. "I've been considering. I think we've got a little time before they draw our cover. With no one likely to have seen you get away, it might be all morning before they decide to look beyond the streets about the chapel. Even if they think of me so soon, they'll do no more than send a query round, I'll wager—and Mark can fob that off all right. But for the long run, we must smuggle you both out of town."

"Out of town? The duke—yes, I think that's excellently sensible. But I must return to my father."

"Do you think it wise?"

"It matters not if it's wise—I must."

"Well. We'll think of a story then. You tried to keep up with the duke, but lost him."

"But—"

"That should satisfy even this Gill fellow, eh? Pressed upon by the horses and overran the scent. St. James's was his point, but you lost him among the thickets in Picadilly. Leave the rest to us—and a rare great lady you are, Miss Timms, for bringing him out of that fix, if I may be allowed the compliment."

"I thank thee, but—I can't say those things," Maddy protested.

"Why not?"

"They are not true."

"Of course they aren't true. Where would we be if you were to tell them the truth?"

"I can't tell them falsehoods."

Durham gave her a queer look. "You must, my dear. Just a small falsehood. A very white lie."

"I can't. I can't lie."

"You can't lie?" Colonel Fane echoed. He and Durham were gazing at her as if she were a disturbing illusion that had just crystallized out of the mist in front of them.

"No," she said. She might have thought, wickedly, of deceiving Lady de Marly, perhaps even Cousin Edward—but she couldn't imagine lying to her father—or to Richard Gill, whose whole demeanor was a public testimony to walking in the Life. "It's not our way," she said helplessly. "I cannot do it."

"But—what will you say, then?"

She bit her lip. "If they ask me—I must answer truth."

"You can't lie." Durham fixed her with a hard look. "Not even in this one case—to save a man's neck?"

"It should be—what God wills. To lie is to make it my will. But . . . after I leave—thou canst take him away, and I can say truthfully that I don't know where he is."

"Why, thank you. That leaves you quite in the clear, don't it? And when they ask you where you last saw him, I'll find myself hauled up before a magistrate."

She lowered her eyes.

"All right. Just . . . give me time to think. Let me think." He steepled his hands over his coffee cup. "You must go back directly. Why must you go back directly?"

"My papa. He doesn't know what's become of me. He won't even know that I went with the duke of my own will. He might believe I've been hurt, or even—he might think anything!"

"Right. Your father's worried about you. Where is he?"

"He and my Cousin Edward are staying at the Gloucester Hotel."

"There you are. We'll just arrange to slip a note under his door—tell him you're perfectly well, but can't come back at the moment. That's all true, ain't it?"

"He can't read a note. He's lost his sight. And I don't know what he'd think to get a message like that from me. He'd be beside himself. Wouldn't thou be? And how can I not go back? Where else am I to go?"

"Oh Lord," Durham said, and sighed. "Nothing is simple."

He eyed her speculatively, rubbing his chin. The room fell silent, except for the occasional scrabble of the dogs' toenails as they shifted and pushed one another out the way, vying for the duke's attention.

"Fane," Durham said abruptly, "make yourself useful. Go down and invite Mr. Gill in to luncheon."

The colonel rose obediently, restoring his plumed hat firmly to his head.

"And do make certain that he accepts," Durham added, with a lazy lift of his brows.

Colonel Fane bowed, imposing in his uniform and tall plume, his hand resting casually on the gold-and-silver hilt of his sword. "Most persuasive, when I wish to be. My mother always said so."

The duke didn't relish seeing Richard again, that was immediately obvious. He came to his feet with an irritated exclamation as Colonel Fane ushered the Quaker into the room still carrying his curious box. Jervaulx moved to the sofa where Maddy sat, taking up a place behind her. The black setter instantly made a stand at her feet, growling, while Devil jumped up onto the sofa beside Maddy and began barking and snarling at the newcomer.

"Shev," Durham snapped. "For God's sake, shut them up!"

Jervaulx made a hiss between his teeth. The dogs grew quiet. Devil put his paws in her lap and lowered himself into a crouch, half on her and half off, while Cass stood alert, pressed against her knees.

Maddy, barricaded among dogs, gave Richard a feeble smile. "Thou art good, to come again to help."

He looked around at the other men, then said softly, "I followed. I was afeared for thee, Archimedea. There is no harm?"

"Oh, no. No. The duke brought us here—these are his good friends. Durham, and Colonel Fane."

In spite of his dark plain coat and broad hat, Richard Gill seemed in some strange and subtle way not unlike Colonel Fane—the one an easy scarlet brilliance, trimmed in white and gold and blue, the other starkly unadorned, and yet both with a strength about them, something unexpectedly formidable underlying their preposterously different facades and characters.

Durham didn't invite the Quaker to sit. He leaned his hands on the back of a chair. "Let me be straightforward with you, Mr. Gill. We have no intention that the duke shall go back to his family—not under the circumstances that Miss Timms has described to us. She has suggested that you might have some other opinion. I must say, I don't see that it's really your affair, but it so happens that it'd be dashed inconvenient for us if you should go talking abroad, so I thought it best to have . . . shall we say, a little discussion of the matter."

Richard said nothing. Colonel Fane stood behind him, leaning his shoulder against the door frame, not so foolish-looking now as he blocked the way out.

"Miss Timms requested your aid," Durham said. "Are you willing to give it?"

"Archimedea is doing what she thinks right," Richard said noncommittally.

"Well, if it ain't too impertinent, sir, I guess what I want to know is what you think's right. I understand that you've made it some sort of personal concern of yours—that you might even take his family's view of things. Didn't matter in that case, y'see, that you couldn't name this very chambers—if you was to tell 'em he'd got as far as the Albany, they'd be sure to realize who he'd come to." Durham flexed his hands on the chair and added softly, "He's my friend, Mr. Gill. I want you to understand that clear. Very clear. I won't let him be locked up on account of some pious zealotry on your part."

With a slight chink of metal, the colonel shifted his stance, standing upright. "No indeed," he murmured.

"Tell me what I can say to induce you to keep silent in this matter, Mr. Gill." A faint mocking lilt marked Durham's tone.

"There is nothing thou can say."

"Ah. I suppose that only a higher voice than mine could move you?"

Richard gave a nod of assent.

Durham lifted his eyebrows. "Are you sure then, that you've been brought here to no divine purpose? That there's nothing you might be meant to learn?"

"I think," Richard said, "that thou might have some smooth pretty words at hand to convince me there is more."

Durham smiled. "Words? Is that all you think we have to convince you? My dear fellow, do I need to lay it out?"

Richard's expression did not alter. Maddy was really proud of him, that he didn't lose his fortitude, or his serenity, in the face of this thinly veiled threat. "Concerning the Duke of Jervaulx," he said merely, "I'm not certainly persuaded to either course."

"Mr. Gill—I'm a frivolous fellow, as I'm sure you've determined for yourself. I like a good dinner and a bottle; I'm partial to fair ladies and gambling halls and the best tailors. I really don't have anything to recommend me at all—not even as much as Fane there, who can at least say he led his battalion in open order at Quatre Bras and Waterloo. Beyond that, about the best part of either one of us is that we love this man like our own blood; we don't give a damn for his title or his family or what they want; we'll hang before we see him put away against his will—he'd do the same for us, y'see, just like you'd do it for your own. And that's all, Mr. Gill. All the pretty words I know on the subject."

The enamel clock on the mantel chimed, a sweet melody in the silence. Devil put his nose beneath Maddy's hand and licked it.

Richard looked toward her. "Let me beg thee tenderly to come away and leave them to what they wish to do. It is worldly business, and none of ours."

"All right, go now," Durham said quickly, before she could answer. "Go—but stay away from your father. Give us some time, Miss Timms. A few hours, half a day, enough for us to get ourselves safely away. You're in no danger—he'll have you back—please, can you give us just that much? A little time before you return directly to him?"

She bit her lip, imagining her father's fears—balancing that against the lies she would have to tell, or set in motion Jervaulx's seizure. And she had a terrible feeling that she *would* tell lies, even to her papa, that she—like Durham and Colonel Fane—would do almost anything.

She drew a breath. "Until this evening?"

"That's enough."

She rose. The dog thumped to the floor and pressed past her, rounding the sofa to join the duke. "I will stay away from Papa 'til supper, then. At seven."

Durham nodded shortly. "That'll do. Begone, the both of you. And don't look back, or we'll turn you to pillars of salt. I swear it."

Words or no, Christian understood well enough the way Durham and Fane got the dour thee-thou between them— Durham with his sardonic smile and Fane at his best negligent muscle-flexing. The procedure had Christian's full approval. He didn't like it that Maddygirl had so quickly put her trust in the fellow, trotting off without a by-your-leave *heads together whisper look assess talk* plans he couldn't understand—until he'd heard *back* and seen Maddy begin to contend words with the gloomy mule man. Meddlesome bastard, to have followed them even here!

Durham and Fane would take care of it. Christian watched in pleasure, waiting for them to heave the Mule out on his ear. He would have lent a hand to it himself, but didn't want to upset the dance that Durham would be leading. Christian couldn't really follow the discourse; he only knew that Durham made sweet threats in that soft tone and got answers of obstinate brevity. Christian would embarrass himself by a clumsy entry at the wrong time.

He saw the Mule address Maddy. *Lebeg tend comaythen, leave whish do.* Christian heard Durham's quick response with his own appeal to her . . . *ask hours time? Give time?*

Christian couldn't see her face, but her pause alarmed
him. His body went tense. He took a step; she asked Durham
something; Durham answered—*enough?* She rose and
Christian moved, all at once. She was out of his reach;
Durham was speaking to her with a parting tone—urging her
to leave! The Mule turning to go with her, dogs in the way of
Christian's feet . . . he suddenly found himself with no idea
at all of what had just passed, but no one showed a sign of
preventing her.

"*Stay.*" His enraged voice arrested everyone. "Maddygirl!
You . . . *stay.*"

He caught up with her. Without ceremony, he thrust her
back toward the sofa. Her cloak flared around her as she fell
onto the seat.

Christian stood over her. "You . . . *me,*" he said, knowing
it was too little, unable to command the words to tell her that
she must not leave without him and that he wasn't going
anywhere without Durham and Fane and the dogs. Most emphatically she must not leave him and go with the Mule. He
addressed that in particular by standing between her and the
Quaker, the dogs seconding him, ready to counter any attempt to take her away.

Durham dropped into a chair, crossing his arms. He gave
Christian a look that meant he'd bungled the transaction, but
Christian didn't care. Any agreement that required Maddy to
leave him was mistaken.

The Mule looked ice daggers at him with those vapor-
drab eyes; only Fane had an idle smile, as if it were a row
over some ladybird. Maddy herself just sat on the sofa, her
head down, her hands in two fists on her knees. After a moment, she put one tight hand to her mouth, and Christian
realized, like a blow, that she was weeping.

His certainty evaporated. He felt suddenly conspicuous,
the center of incriminating attention. He had made her cry.
They all looked at him, and he could not tell them why it
was important. She had to stay with him. She *had* to. He was

going home with her, marry her and . . . he couldn't think beyond that. Why was she crying?

"Maddygirl," he said hoarsely.

She shook her head, like a quick rejection.

Christian glared at the Mule. He thought this must be his fault, interfering rogue, *creep round steal in your thee-thou coat.* Strangle the fellow. Christian was considering the notion when suddenly something dark passed in front of him, moving quickly past toward the door.

He realized that it was Maddy. He hadn't even seen her stand up; his brain got behind again—making sense out of the hooded shape when she was already beyond him. He was still trying to gather a response from his scattered awareness when Fane straightened up from his indolent pose against the door frame, blocking it.

"Shev wanchu stay, Miss."

She whirled around to Christian. "Papa!" she cried. "Musgodim! Go—him! Understand?"

"Stay." It was all Christian could utter.

"Jervaulx!" Her face was terrible, pleading with him. "Papa need me. Fraid me. Musgo!"

Fear and denial rose in his throat. Her father—*blind old afraid.* But Christian needed her. "Maddy . . ." He gritted his teeth. "Can't." He hated speaking in front of the others: words like a dimwitted beast, the old jokes and easier exchange with Durham and Fane vanished in his dread.

"Please," she said. "Thoumus let me go."

No. No! He looked beyond her to Fane, shook his head emphatically to keep the guardsman in place, preventing her desertion.

Her thee-thou mule touched her shoulder. "Arkedya. I goeth fathee." He looked past her and Christian. "Ike see fathout shspicion. Friend business."

Maddygirl turned to him, her face alight with a joy that incensed Christian. "Thoudst?"

"Y'won't trayus?" Durham's sharp voice came from a

place that Christian had forgotten. It scrambled his focus; he found Durham and tried not to surrender him again.

"No," the Mule said.

"Have word ond?" Durham demanded.

"I have said. Truth dosth work God."

Pious mule, Christian thought.

The sober thee-thou glanced at Maddy. "Thou'll stay tly return. Consid morthen."

She nodded meekly to his command. The Mule, who'd never even taken off his hat, faced the door. Fane stood implacably until Durham said, "Let'im go," and the guardsman made a bow and stood aside.

Maddygirl turned back to Christian. She gave him a look that razed him, a single glance of accusation, and walked past him to sit down on the sofa.

Through the morning and noon, they waited. Colonel Fane left for parade in the afternoon, promising to return by supper. Maddy kept her place on the couch. She deliberately would not look at Jervaulx, though he brought her a cup of chocolate with his own hands. She took it, not even giving thanks. She wished him to know that she did not remain of her own will, but only because he made it impossible for her to leave and Richard had been so kind as to say he would go to her father and acquaint Papa with the case without speaking of where the duke had gone.

Amazingly, Jervaulx actually seemed to have some inkling of her resentful feelings. Instead of his usual aristocratic disinterest, he spent the endless hours standing near her, or sometimes sitting at the other end of the sofa, restrained in his moves, not attempting to speak. He brought her the chocolate. It wasn't precisely an apology, but it was at least an acknowledgment that she was a person rather than a private and exclusive belonging of his.

By supper, still no word had come from Richard, but there was a deadly scare just at teatime, when a servant in silver and white livery arrived wishing to speak to Durham. Mark could not lead the man off; he insisted on delivering his note into Durham's own hand. The dispute below the window became lamentably loud as the servants argued whether the duchess' man ought to wait until Mr. Durham returned home or leave his message with Mark. When it became certain that the other servant would not go away without seeing Durham, that resourceful gentleman went up to the attics and somehow found his way outside.

While Maddy and the duke waited in the bedroom, Durham came back round as if he'd been out all along and interviewed the duchess' servant in his sitting room, full of falsehoods. The servant went away with a convoluted story about Durham's deceased fourth cousin that even Maddy, listening through the door, could not make out clear.

On the subject of the Duke of Jervaulx, Durham was baffled. Did the fellow mean that the duke had recovered? That was excellent news! Durham had thought him dying; the duchess herself had told him so. But now he was out and about? Miraculous! Durham wondered that he hadn't come to call on his friends—he would have thought that would be Jervaulx's first destination, the moment he was back in form. Did the man mean to say—here now, Durham really didn't understand. The duke was missing? Oh—not missing? Well, if he weren't missing or dying, nor calling on his friends, just precisely what the devil was he doing? Nobody had seen him for months. It sounded dashed suspicious to Durham. He thought perhaps the authorities ought to be notified, and damn the scandal.

The servant backed down quite quickly at that point, and went away with Durham earnestly wishing the duchess would inform him the moment they had any clue.

Maddy had turned around in the dimness of the curtained bedroom and seen Jervaulx's set face as he stood with one hand on the bedpost—arrogant and wary, like a hunter cornered by his own prey, galled with the need to hide himself. Durham came to the door and opened it, allowing the dogs to rush in. They greeted Jervaulx joyously, as if they hadn't

seen him just a quarter hour since, and his haughtiness evaporated into a grin and play.

Those were the moments that shook Maddy, those sudden
transitions from imperious pride to affection. She had no defense against them. Her Opening fell into confusion.

She wasn't even certain that it was a true leading any
longer. Richard hadn't been convinced that she took the
right course. Maddy knew that all of her life she'd had to
fight to submerge a strong self-will, to avoid being tempted
by fashions and fripperies, by the urge to dispute and disagree with her elders. She was too often ungoverned and re-
bellious in her heart. Someone like Richard would be better
able to know the prompting of God from the wiles of the
Reasoner.

Maddy wanted to go home to her father. She wanted to be
safe again. The door was there in front of her, with no king's
officer to stop her now. The duke was employed with his
dogs and Durham in setting out glasses and a decanter of
golden sherry.

The door was there. She did not go.

Christian decided to send Maddygirl to bed. She'd fallen
asleep sitting up anyway, waiting for her thee-thou mule
man. Fane had come and gone again, on duty: welcome nonsense and casual acceptance of Christian's flawed speech—
Christian was sorry to see him leave. Durham was not so
easy about it; he kept starting off to talk to Christian and
then realizing halfway into a headlong statement that Christian didn't understand, though he tried desperately to hide it.

It embarrassed both of them. Christian wanted to turn to
Maddygirl for help, but she sat like a stone when he looked
at her—angry at him still because he kept her from her father. Another thing impossible to communicate: the depth of
his dependence on her being there. He was sorry. But the
world was going too fast for him—new things, surprises and
confusions and noise that made hard understanding harder.

She had to stay. The bedroom was all right. Close by, the

door was where he could see it, know for certain she was there.

He woke her merely by walking close. Devil, following, stopped to touch her hand with his nose. When she opened her eyes, Christian held out his hand.

"Has come?" It was the first thing that she uttered.

Christian merely looked at her.

"Not yet," Durham said.

"Bed." Christian kept his hand extended.

"Yes," Durham said from the table. "Goleye down, Miss Timm. Wake moment return."

She blinked back sleep, and then sighed. She laid her hand in Christian's and rose. He would have taken her himself, but she released him immediately and turned away.

A little rush of coals fell in the grate as the bedroom door closed behind her. Durham sat in silence at the table, surveying the remains of supper. "Egad," he muttered. "Bloody caspickles."

Christian walked to the sideboard and took the round crystal hard thing from the top of the decanter of sherry. He poured himself a glass.

"So." Durham held up his empty one, and Christian filled it. "What spect doother, now th've got?"

Christian put his forefinger to his mouth. Quiet. Durham took a swallow of his drink. He leaned his head back on the chair, gazing at the ceiling. Christian let the clock tick down, listening to it instead of watching it, because it was like looking at himself in the mirror, something odd and annoying about it, something not-real in the way the numbers lay around the face. One of the crazy things that he preferred to ignore when he could.

It chimed once, on the half hour. Without conversation, he and Durham sat drinking. Durham poured two more sherries, and Christian felt a pleasant mellowness begin to steal over him. It was familiar and gratifying, to sit here as they'd done so often. Companion.

Sherry made Durham slow. Christian knew him. Three

glasses took the edge from his decisiveness; four made him smart and his speech lazy. Christian waited for four.

He set his glass on the table. *"Wed."* He looked at Durham. "Maddygirl."

Durham frowned. He shook his head. "Sorry, ol man. Don't unstan."

It was much easier when he spoke slowly instead of mumbling too fast.

"Maddy." Christian moved his head, indicating the bedroom.

"Yes. All right. Miss Timms."

"Me." Christian thrust his hand inside his coat pocket, exploring, and found the ring. He pushed the box onto the table and got it open with his thumb. *"Wed."*

His friend gazed at the ring. He seemed not to comprehend. Christian was about to try again when Durham slammed his glass down onto the table.

"God Almighty. Y'losu bloody mind?"

"No," Christian said.

"Marry girl?" Durham half rose. At Christian's quick warning hiss, he dropped back into his chair and lowered his tone to a violent whisper. "Not serious?"

Christian picked up the ring and slapped it down again.

"Nothinba nurse." Durham leaned forward over the table. "Hang it, she's Quaker!"

"Marry." With an effortful curl of his mouth, Christian said, "Go . . . *home."*

Durham shook his head. "Can't go, m'dear fellow. Not safe. Take y'way, shsaid."

"No!" Christian reached across and gripped his wrist. *"Not* . . . wed. Son . . . dragon want . . . 'nough. *Son."*

The meaning seemed to take a moment to strike. Durham's brows went up. He rubbed his hand across his mouth. "Get heir?"

"All."

"All she wants?"

"Deal." Christian let go. "Not . . . *back* . . . place. *Wed."*

"Whn't marrother girl then?"

Christian made a sound of disgust.

Durham put both of his hands on the stem of his glass and rolled it between them, watching the candlelight catch the cuts, spark color and darkness from the liquor.

"Like thisun better?" he asked, slanting a look across the table.

Christian took a swig of sherry. He laid the pad of his thumb up against his lips, kissed it, and lifted it gently away. He smiled past it at his friend. *"Braid . . ."* He stretched his fingers apart, as if he spread them in her hair. *"Down."*

Durham snorted. He made his own fist, thumb up, and thrust it out toward Christian. "So be it. Want her, old son, shallave her. Din't ordain me f' naught."

Chapter Eighteen

"*M*iss Timms." The voice came out of dreams. "Time to wake, Miss Timms."

Maddy sat up all at once. "Papa?"

She was tangled in her cloak. For a moment of confusion, she thought it was a burglary—a strange man stepping back from the bed, holding a candle so that she only saw his face in shadowed profile. But she wasn't home—she couldn't recall at all where she was until suddenly a black-and-white dog trotted into the circle of candlelight and jumped up to put its front paws onto the edge of the bed. The animal made an enthusiastic stretch and licked her nose.

Maddy spluttered and drew back, blinking sleep from her eyes.

"This came for you." Durham held out a note sealed by an uneven splotch of wax. "It's from Mr. Gill."

She fought to keep her eyes open. Sense and memory returned: she accepted the note as Durham set the candle down next to the bed and left her alone.

She tore open the wax, holding the paper close, squinting at the blocky hand.

Miss Timms,

I have spoke with thy father at length. He is in agreement with thee that the Duke ought to be protected from this travesty, and wishes thee to see to it. He urges thee to put thy trust in the Duke's friends and take him out of danger instantly, as the pursuit is very hot. Thee are to remain with the Duke wherever he goes. Thy father commands thee most gravely not to return to him, as it would put thee in peril. I cannot come to thee myself because of the hazard of being followed. There was some suspicion when I called on thy father. If thee has a message for him, send it to the Belle Sauvage, and I will see that he receives it.

Bless thee Friend
Richard Gill

"Oh," Maddy whispered.

She turned the note more to the light, blinked hard, and read it again. It still said the same thing, in the same awkward way.

She was to go away with Jervaulx. She was to stay with him.

Her papa wished it.

It was bewildering. And upsetting. She wasn't to return to Papa! For how long? How much peril could there be?

Maddy sat up in bed. She was to be accused of kidnapping, she truly was. Lady de Marly would not stick at that for an instant.

She closed her eyes and prayed a quick, silent prayer, asking for the strength to face what she must. Then she hurried to find her shoes. As she bent to buckle them, she had to push Devil off four times from jumping on her. Taking up the candle, she went through the dark to the sitting room.

Jervaulx was there, startling in his extravagant formal

clothes, his hair mussed, his face in need of shaving. He gave her a quick look, wary, as if he half expected that she might scold him for something. The clock chimed; Maddy held up her candle toward it and found that the time was only half past three.

From the entrance hall, she heard the door open and the soft sound of Durham's voice in conversation with his servant. The door closed. Durham came into the room, padding in stocking feet, carrying a coffeepot and tray. "Mark's gone to bring a cab round, if he can find one at this hour. So drink up. There's a post coach leaves The Swan at five. You'll want to put yourself in order in the bedroom, Miss Timms, but let me get something else for Shev to wear first."

He looked no better than the duke, and they both looked as if they'd been up all night. Durham set down the tray, yawned, then took the candle and shuffled into the bedroom, leaving the sitting room with only a faint flame from the oil lamp to illuminate it.

"Shev," he called quietly. "Come here, my dear fellow, and see if this will fit you."

The duke gave her another brief glance, and then walked past her into the bedroom.

A looking glass hung over the mantelpiece. Maddy saw that she appeared no better than the men and attempted to make something of her hair, but with no brush or comb it seemed a hopeless task. She would have to keep her hood close.

She poured coffee, hoping that might clear the sleepy disorder from her brain. Durham seemed to have some plan—he'd mentioned a post coach, which meant that he intended for them to travel quickly. Nothing but the mail would be faster, and no mail left before evening. A post coach would be swift and as anonymous as a ticket at the booking office—but to where? She hoped it was not too far. Then again, if she was to be hung for a kidnapper, perhaps she should wish it would be Scotland. Or America. Or the moon.

*   *   *

As it fell out, it was Bath—or the Great Road in that direction, at any rate, in a beautiful black-and-red post coach emblazoned with the device of the Swan with Two Necks and gleaming in the lamplight of a frosty morning. Durham would not reveal to Maddy their final destination; in fact he had become somewhat close in his speech to her. When she protested the distance, he would only say that they weren't bound for Bath itself.

Jervaulx and his friend slept in the coach. They made a disreputable pair, with Durham stretched across the forward seat and the duke propped uncomfortably against the opposite window from Maddy, wrapped in a borrowed great coat, unshaven and hatless, which was Durham's peculiar notion of how a gentleman going into the country "for his health" ought to look. Maddy had agreed to this description of the duke as basically compatible with the truth, but she would not bend so far as to call him "Mr. Higgens" and present herself as his sister. Not even to avoid transportation or hanging. Without going out of her way to volunteer the information, she was his nurse, if anyone should ask, and her name was Archimedea Timms.

As a result of this stance, she wasn't allowed out of the coach except at the busiest inns, where no one paid much mind to any individual traveler amid the clatter and jingle of the horses ready-saddled, the shouts of the arriving postilions and the stage passengers hurrying in and out for a brief refreshment. Even then, she only descended alone or with Durham. He insisted that the three of them oughtn't to be observed all together, in order to confound any pursuit. He'd paid a full fare to secure the fourth seat in the light and graceful post coach so that they would not have to travel with a stranger, and after the first change of horses and postilions no one even looked inside as long as he leaned out the window to bestow the tips. Even the dogs had been left behind with Mark, mightily unhappy, but far too conspicuous to be seen with the duke.

It was a wonder to travel so fast, in a well-sprung vehicle

on an excellent road, ahead of all the stage coaches and sometimes passing even a privately hired chaise. She was not certain that she approved of the post coach. It seemed a prodigious expenditure of effort in the interest of earthly business. It must be a vain thing to go on in such a headlong rush through the early morning darkness. The horses galloped the whole of each stretch and pulled up lathered after half an hour to be replaced by a waiting team within two minutes. With the gentlemen asleep between changes, Maddy had ample time to watch the ghostly white mileposts spin past and to reflect on the speed with which she was plunging into oblivion.

With dawn, long blue shadows from the trees lapped across fields sparkling with frost. She could see glimpses of a huge castle in the distance, bulwarked round with towers and high walls. Banners at the turrets caught the first sun. Maddy leaned forward to watch as the rays turned the stone to pinkish gold.

"*Wind*-sor."

The duke's voice startled her. She turned and found him watching her sleepily, his shoulders braced against the side of the coach in an awkward position.

The vehicle bounced over a rough section of road without slowing a dot. Maddy caught the strap. Jervaulx's head bumped hard against the wall, while Durham almost rolled off his seat. Durham caught himself, cursed, and pushed back into place, bracing with one foot on the floor, readjusting his hat over his eyes.

Jervaulx sat upright. He rubbed both palms over his face, then rested buried in his hands for a moment, his elbows propped on the greatcoat over his knees. The coach swayed along the road. Maddy thought perhaps he would wake up fully now, but instead he turned and lay down again, this time in the opposite direction. Since he was far too tall to fit into the available seat, this position necessitated that he lay his head in Maddy's lap—which he did, brazenly, with no more warning than a deep sigh as he settled into position.

"Jervaulx," she said sharply.

His only answer was a slow smile, perfectly uncivilized viewed in profile against the shadow of his beard, as if he were some indolent Gypsy happy to sleep beneath a hedgerow.

It being impossible to hold her hand in the air for the remainder of the journey, she found it obligatory to rest it on his shoulder. She held it there so lightly that on each bump it lifted, until he reached and caught it, entwining their fingers, and made her bear down solidly on his shoulder. They were both without gloves, Maddy having left hers far behind in the chapel, and Jervaulx's elegant white ones forgotten in the rush.

Maddy watched the countryside grow bright, the castle at Windsor a massive landmark that appeared and disappeared among the hills and hollows of the road. He moved his head restlessly, snuggling closer. With his free hand, he reached and adjusted hers so that her fingers rested against his temple and cheek, just touching his face each time the carriage rolled. Maddy pretended to ignore it. She reasoned that if the duke had been an ordinary patient—an ailing child or a sick neighbor—she certainly would have been glad to provide whatever comfort she could on this fatiguing journey. She told herself that Jervaulx tired easily, and that the events of the past twenty-four hours would have been enough to exhaust even a person in full health. Indeed, Maddy herself felt the fluttery weakness of too little sleep and too much apprehension.

It was just that his hand against hers felt so full of heat and life—firmly locked with her fingers, his shoulder pressed steadily close, his body not quite as passive under the rock of the coach as it should have been.

He made a sleepy mutter, shifting, tilting his chin up as if he could not find the most comfortable position. His skin was scratchy with new beard, rough against her palm. She didn't think he was asleep at all, and she was certain of it at the next change. As the coach rocked to a halt amid the whistles and shouts of the postilions, Durham rolled over and sat up. Jervaulx didn't stir. After a brief glance at him and Maddy, Durham made an exaggeratedly thorough search in his pockets for his purse.

He finally found it. As he got down, Jervaulx kissed her fingers. She snatched them away. The duke sighed and nestled closer in her lap, without ever opening his eyes.

Durham put his hand on the window frame and smiled faintly at her. "I suppose I ought to bring your breakfast out to you, Miss Timms?"

Sometimes, in daydreams, Maddy had imagined a garden. It never had a house with it; it was just a garden, with room for everything she might want to plant. It had lavender around each of the beds and a low wall with the countryside beyond. In the spring, there were peas and asparagus, tulips and hyacinths; in the summer, vegetables and hollyhock, larkspur, sweet williams; in the autumn, the trees in the corners were heavy with fruit, hanging low over Michaelmas daisies and guelder roses. It wasn't formal, this garden, as the straight paths and majestic lawns at Blythedale Hall were formal, meant only for strolling and creaturely talk. It was a working garden, with the flowers planted between more practical things.

The first morning that she woke and looked out the leaded window of the rectory at St. Matthews-upon-Glade, she saw it. Her garden, or the disreputable remnants of it anyway, catching early sun, casting shadows, a thousand stems sparking fire as they bent in graceful arches beneath the dew.

It was a long-abandoned chaos, a disarray of weeds and old growth, the stone footways barely visible under ragged clumps of grass and autumn-dead foliage—but it was her garden. The dry stone walls enclosed half an acre, with fruit trees planted in each corner, and in the middle a simple urn. Beyond the wall, a pasture, vivid green, sloped down to a village. The houses spread out along the valley, all built of the same silvery gray stone, glinting light through the long finger of mist that blew up through the trees.

The rectory was sinfully neglected. Durham was even worse than she'd thought. Not only did he turn out to be one of the false priests—and a more unlikely man of God she'd never met, unless it might have been Jervaulx himself, or possibly Colonel Fane—he'd allowed this garden and this house to fall almost into ruin. Last night they had arrived at quarter past ten, exhausted, the duke so weary that he kept bumping into things that were perfectly easy to see. After Durham had unlocked the dark rectory and thrown open the door as if it were a welcoming palace, Maddy had been obliged to spend half an hour hunting it over for sheets to sleep upon.

They'd dined out of a paper on meat pies and cross buns bought mid-afternoon at Hungerford, where they'd left the Bath Road and struck off in a private post chaise, all three of them crushed together in a vehicle meant for two. Maddy had slept in her dress for the second night in a row, not very deeply, considering the desolate chill of the house and bedding. And now, in the morning, looking out at the abandoned garden in the sun, she didn't suppose there would be anything suitable for breakfast, either.

She made herself as presentable as she could with no water or brush. All the furniture was covered, the hangings over the bed dark with dust. The mattress looked higgledy-piggledy, made up with two layers of sheets and no counterpane. She feared that the little ball of dust underneath the frame had the unmistakable cast of mice about it.

In spite of the neglect, it was a commodious house. She descended the stairs, listening in vain for any sound of the men yet stirring from the bedrooms in the opposite wing. Her steps echoed as she passed through a carved screen into a spacious flagstone hall, its only furnishing a bare table of the antique sort, long and dark and massive, with legs carved in heavy globes of wood.

In the middle of it lay the paper that had held their dinner, folded over beneath a key. Her name was inscribed on the top. She took a deep breath and opened the stained document, smoothing it out.

> *My dear Miss Timms,*
>
> *It's my Misfortune to be forced to leave without Seeing you again, in Order to make my way back to Town with as much Speed as possible. I hope to be there by Tonight, which ought to Confound anyone as to the distance we've traveled should Suspicion light on me. On my way, I will inform Mrs. Digby that I've made the Rectory available to my Ailing Friend and ask her to see to it that you have a Servant at my Expense. Beyond that you will have to depend upon the money from the Buckles until I receive my Ecclesiastical Revenues next month, as you find me sadly Flat at the moment. I hope that You will make Yourselves at Home. If all goes Well, I believe you may be stopping for some little time here. Rest assured that you are doing the Right Thing, Miss Timms, and please, to the Best of your Conscience—and perhaps even a little to the Worst of It—do what you can to Protect Him.*
>
> *Yr Servant,*
> *Kit Durham*
>
> *P.S. If you please, will you tell Him that I will Think of a way to send the Dogs, unless I shoot them first.*

Next month! He expected them to be here as long as that? Maddy folded the letter. She looked round the empty hall. In her bodice was the wallet with most of the duke's three hundred pounds still intact, since Durham had paid for all the fares. She and her father could have lived two years on that.

Loud footsteps sounded on the stair. Maddy looked up

just as the duke appeared in the doorway, disheveled and intense: dressed—but with nothing tied or buttoned. When he saw her, a look of deliverance came into his face. He held the doorframe, then leaned heavily against it, expelling a harsh breath.

" 'Lone." He closed his eyes and shook his head.

"I'm here," Maddy said.

He made a gesture with his head, back toward the wing where he and Durham had slept. "Not."

"Durham has returned to town." She held up the oily note.

Jervaulx pushed away, strode toward her and took it. He frowned down at the words, turning his head a little. The shadow of his beard had become a real darkness. Maddy wondered if there might be a shaving kit in the house or if she would have to go into the village. How safe would it be for them to show themselves? Durham had said that no one would recognize the duke here, but she was loathe to take any risk.

He looked up, smiling one-sided. "Dogs."

Maddy made a face. "Yes. Thy wicked dogs will come."

He grinned, an unkempt barbarian.

She took hold of his wrist and pulled the shirt cuff down from inside his coat. "Links?"

He made an assenting sound, gesturing again toward the bedrooms.

Maddy pulled the other cuff free and reached up to tie the neckpiece that was draped around his shoulders. He stood very still, watching her from beneath lowered lashes as she did it. When she glanced up, he smiled at her.

In his unshaven state, it was oddly boyish. She had to bite her lip to prevent herself from smiling back. Instead, she took a schoolroom tone. "Bring the cufflinks." She touched his wrist and pointed toward the door.

Without hesitation, he turned to go. Maddy noticed the letter still in his hand.

"Jervaulx," she said.

He looked back at her.

"Canst thou read?"

He came back, slapped the paper down on the table and bent over it, leaning on both arms.

"My . . . Timm.   It . . . mis . . . for . . . to   be   for . . . force . . . *leave* . . . see you . . . in order make my way back to . . . tow . . . *town* . . . speed . . . poss." He looked up at her triumphantly. *"Read."*

"Before now? Didst thou read before now?"

"Math," he said.

She remembered him working with her father. "Only mathematics," she said. "Only numbers."

He shrugged.

"Wilt thou not bring thy cufflinks to me?"

With a brief nod, he pushed away from the table and walked out of the hall. Maddy looked after him. She pressed her lips together. A week ago—a day ago—he would not have understood such a long and complicated sentence, especially not as she'd deliberately spoken it at a normal pace.

He returned, carrying the studs. Maddy accepted them. As she fastened his cuffs, she said, "What dost thou think we ought to do for breakfast?"

He picked up the grease-stained paper between his thumb and forefinger. With a little grunt, he let it drop. *"Pie."*

"Jervaulx," she said, "thou art getting better."

He gave her a pirate grin.

Maddygirl had gone into the village. Christian prowled the house, alone and free, uneasy with it. For something to do, he was yanking the covers off the furniture, leaving them in white piles scattered about the floor. When he pulled down the covering from a frame over the parlor mantel, he found himself face to face with a mirror.

Egad. He looked the very devil, as if he'd been three days in drink. And Durham's coat sleeve was too short, showing a vulgar width of cuff when Christian lifted his hand to feel his beard.

Monstrous fine fellow, the Duke of Jervaulx. Just what a young thee-thou prim would like.

It made him light-headed, looking at himself—a wrench of effort to focus on the not-real side, like trying to stop a dream without waking. It was there, but somehow it just kept not being there.

A loud knocking at the front door startled him. Maddy-girl, he thought, turning into the passage—but at the last moment he had a doubt. He stopped with his hand outstretched. The knocker had fallen silent, waiting, but after a pause the banging took up again.

He wanted to find out if it was her, but the words failed him, as they always seemed to fail him when he needed them the most. He tried to calm himself, to get hold of the unreasonable panic. He couldn't simply stand here, delaying forever. Finally he took hold of the ancient handle and wrenched it open.

Muggy wind gusted inside, unseasonable for October, warmer than the air in the house. Storm weather. Under the dark stone porch, a girl in an apron and cap dropped a curtsy beneath her cloak. "If 'a pleasir, mabrunild digy, maid-all-work."

They looked at one another. She had a wide, dark-eyed country credulity about her, too naive not to stare at him as if he looked as bad as he knew he did. She seemed unthreatening enough: he pulled the door wide and stepped back.

Maddy returned with bread and baked mutton and potatoes in a cookshop dish. She got it all through the front door and was hastening to the kitchen with the tepid burden when the sound of a female voice brought her up short. She peered around the doorframe into the kitchen.

Jervaulx and a maidservant sat across from one another at the table, both holding steaming crockery mugs. The girl faced away from Maddy, chatting blithely about her "lad" and how he was to go into the market town at week's end to attend a lecture on "chemical subjects." She repeated that twice, adding "d'y see?" in a questioning tone, as if it were a perfectly normal thing in speaking to make certain that the other party understood—as no doubt it was when the inhabitants spoke to foreign people in these parts.

Jervaulx set his mug down with an emphatic nod of approval. Focused on the maid, he didn't seem to see Maddy, even though she was well within his view.

"Oh, aye—he's wonderful clever, my lad is," the girl said. She drained her mug and pushed back her chair. "I'm sure I don't know what to think of him anymore, since he got to attending that Mechanics' Institute an' all these lectures and things. He's going to make engines. Engines, d'y mark me?" She turned toward the dry sink with the mug and saw Maddy. "Oh! Mistress!" She dropped a deep curtsy and hurried forward to take the dish from Maddy's hands. "Mr. Langland asked me to sit down with 'en, Mistress! I'm Brunhilda Digby. Did ye see m' mother in the village? Did she tell 'ee I 'us to come? Mmm, don't this smell good. Ought I to put it in to warm, Mistress?"

Without waiting for an answer, she set the dish on the table and began working with the iron oven inside the hearth. Jervaulx stood up, his face relaxing into that easy grin that never failed to make Maddy think of worldly and temporal things. She placed the bread and another package on the table.

"Thou lookest a fine rogue," she said sternly. "I've bought a razor and brush."

He inclined his head.

"The water's heated, Mistress," Brunhilda offered. Having been caught idling, she seemed especially anxious to please. "Ought I to bring the basin down?"

The kitchen was already growing warm; Maddy thought of the chilly, damp bedrooms above and nodded. "Yes. Come and discover to me where I might find more linens."

"Yes, miss'us." The girl obeyed quickly, passing out of the kitchen and through the hall in front of Maddy. On the first stair, she stopped and turned, leaning down, smiling. "He's a little touched, in't he?" Her smile deepened. "But he's a darling. And so gentleman handsome! I can surely see why ye'd marry a lad like 'en, Mistress, long-headed or no."

The storm broke after dark, hail and fury, striking with a power that alarmed Maddy. In town, she'd taken a secret pleasure in thunderstorms, snuggling down in bed to listen to the rain pour, but this was a rampage with a roaring soul of its own. The half-empty house seemed to hold thunder in its corners, sending it back out of the shadows over and over again.

Brunhilda had long since gone home. As the fire whipped and smoldered from uneasy drafts, Maddy released the duke's cuffs and waistcoat buttons in the kitchen. He stepped back when she finished, with a look she couldn't interpret, but she knew well enough not to insist on more help than he wished to have. With Maddy in front, carrying a single candle, they went together up the stairs. She paused at the landing where the two wings separated.

"Thou wilt be comfortable?" she asked.

A little suspended moment went by; he stood still, bathed in the dancing gold of candlelight, looking down at her.

He gave her a lazy smile, his eyes indigo blue, half hidden by those outrageously long lashes. Maddy felt a sudden, aching wrench of emotion. It came upon her without warning, a painful fullness in her throat, like weeping, only it was not weeping but something else.

Lightning froze the shadows for an instant; the crack of thunder exploded directly overhead. She jerked and dropped the candle, dousing them in darkness as the sound rolled down the hallway. The rumbling shook the house like a living thing.

"Oh, my," she said foolishly, as it began to die away.

Another flash and split of sound fractured the air. All of Maddy's muscles jumped in a convulsive flinch. She felt the duke's hand touch her, and turned and went into his embrace amid the reverberations—an action that had no more wit or motive than the twitch of her hand when she'd dropped the candle. But his arms came around her, and Maddy instantly knew she'd done a wrong thing, a thing so sweet and dangerous that a point-strike of lightning was as nothing to it.

He leaned back on the wall, his hand against her hair, pressing her cheek into his shoulder. She felt the rise and fall of his chest, breathed the warm incense of a man, tinged yet with the faint flowery aftermath of scent from his wedding. The thunder was a low timbre, still vibrating, a sound like a heavy wagon rolling on and on over a wooden bridge.

He lifted his hand and traced her temple, a light stroke, an exquisite contrast to the steadfast way that he held her. His fingers slid downward, a feather across her cheek, a delicate caress of her lips. He pulled her harder into him, bending his mouth to her hair. "*Fear,* Maddygirl?"

"No," she said. She began to push away. "No, I—am quite all right now. I am quite calm."

She said it as much to herself as to him, for he did not hold her forcibly. She was embarrassed now, flustered as she pulled free.

"The candle," she said, feeling hot and stupid. She bent, trying to search for it in the dark, glad of some task no matter how hopeless. She found the stick just underfoot, but had no way to light it. "I'm sorry!"

He made an amused sound and put his hand under her elbow, drawing her in the direction of her bedchamber. The distant lightning gave only tantalizing and ineffectual illumination, but he seemed more at home in the dark than she. He ran his hand along the wall as they moved, until finally Maddy could see the faint glimmer of firelight falling on the floor in front of her open bedroom door.

She disengaged herself briskly from his hold, stepping ahead into the room. Rain gusted at the window behind the drawn curtains and rumbled in the drains. In the fitful glow of the fire, she crossed the room, knelt and put the candlestick to the coals until it flamed.

"There." She stood and held it out to him. "Thou canst see thy way back."

He did not take it. He looked at her above it. Faint lightning mingled with firelight and candlelight on his face. Gentleman handsome, Brunhilda had called him. Maddy thought him anything but gentle. The candlelight caught his brows and made them villainous, took away the bewilderment that softened his eyes.

A drop of clear wax tumbled down the side of the candle. They both moved at once; Maddy tilted the candlestick to save herself; at the same time, his left hand seized hers. The hot wax fell free, but not far enough, landing on the inside of his wrist.

He swore distinctly. Maddy exclaimed, "Thy hand! Oh— thou shoudst not have!"

He blew out the flame. "Careful!" he said sharply.

"Thou art burnt?"

Her hand was still locked under his. He gave an ironic laugh. *"Burn."* His thumb moved across her fingers in a slow caress. He held hard, then let go of her, his face outlined in fireglow and darkness.

He watched her, as if to see whether she understood him. Here in this house, locked in by rain and thunder and the intensity of his gaze, she was afraid to.

He put his fist against his chest. *"Burn,* Maddygirl," he said. Then he turned and left her in the flickering gloom and thunder.

Chapter Nineteen

$\mathcal{D}$ressing himself in the morning incensed Christian. He'd had enough of wearing Durham's clothes; after a hard day of travel, even his court dress looked better, especially since the linen had been freshly washed by Bruhilt. The stockings, neatly rolled, were easy enough, but by the time he'd got the velvet breeches buttoned, he was furious with himself and his fuddled brain and his hands that would not work together properly and made such a simple thing so confounding.

After unending frustration, he'd just got the last fastening closed, using one hand, when he heard the deep boom of an outside door. He looked out the window and saw Maddygirl, her cloak sweeping out behind her as she headed off over the sheep walk toward the top of the hill. Her direction was away from the village, her pace quick and determined—the deportment of someone leaving.

Christian swore. He abandoned the waistcoat in his hand. Coatless, his shirt open, he strode out of the room.

Maddy did not know quite where she was going. The storm had brought winter, ready-honed. A wind from the north stung her cheeks. The downpour of the night before had made a muddy, sodden embarrassment of the garden, but the turf in the field beyond sprang back beneath her feet, resilient, just beginning to freeze, so that every step had a little wet crunch in it. She held her skirt up, though it hardly made any difference now; her best gray was so mended and stained that "best" was no longer a fair description.

At the top of the hill she stopped and faced north, glad of the icy blow. All night she'd listened to the capricious storm; this morning she wanted only cold steady discipline in her heart.

It was a trial, that was evident. She was tried and tested, and found herself of more common metal than she'd ever imagined.

Even self-censure was quicksand. To tell herself that she ought to take no delight in creaturely caresses was to remember how his hand had touched hers. To disparage the carnal earthy self was to think of his face, underlit by fire radiance, a tempest distilled to silence—midnight blue and flame.

She heard a step behind her, the sound of a harsh exhalation; she turned and he was there. He stopped a few feet from her, all blown about by the wind, in his shirtsleeves, the kind of man that sensible right-walking elderwomen warned the girls not to recognize should he speak to them.

"What is it?" she asked, deliberately curt.

His mouth drew back a little, as if he tried to speak and then could not. He looked away from her, off and down. The wind blew his dark hair.

"Go back. Thou wilt catch thy death."

He lifted his eyes. They were the color of the deepest heart of hurricane clouds, deeper blue than the sky behind him.

"Go back." Maddy turned away and began walking.

He walked alongside her.

For a few yards, she pretended indifference. Then she stopped. "I wish to walk alone." She said it with her face to the wind, not looking toward him.

"Where?"

She knew the violence of the demand was his affliction, that the manifest arrogance was not entirely real—but some of it was, and she turned on that. "Why must thou know?"

He stiffened a little, as a sensitive horse would bridle at a sharp word. He caught her elbow, but Maddy whirled away.

"What dost thou want of me?" she cried. "What?"

His jaw locked. He moved as if to curb her again and then, with a visible check of himself, dropped his hand. With a great effort, he said, *"Friend."*

"I am thy nurse. That is all."

A shadow of mockery came into his face. "Nurse . . . *stay,*" he said, more easily than before.

Maddy drew a breath, checkmated in her argument. It was perfectly true that no honest nurse would hare off across the countryside, insisting that her patient do without her. She pulled her cloak close around her in chagrin.

He smiled slightly, having tallied a credit to his side. "Come . . . back . . . *me.*"

"No. Please. Not now. Just . . . no. I wish to walk. Alone."

The smile became displeasure. "Walk," he said, with a jerk of his chin. "Come . . . *back.*"

She didn't understand him, couldn't find sense in the contradiction, until he left her and went to the dry stone wall that looped its way over the hill. He leaned against the rough structure.

"Walk," he said, with a brief, open swing of his hand.

It was a hopeless thing now, to expect to find peace in the empty fields, but Maddy stubbornly pulled her flaring cloak against herself, turned and began to walk. She went down a hollow and climbed the next slope; she traversed another hill and valley, startling a small flock of sheep on the other side. When she reached the highest point, the wind was bitter; it made her ears ache even inside the hood of her cloak.

It was pointless, this small attempt at escape. He defeated her. What she wished to avoid was inside her; not for one instant as she walked did she think of anything but Jervaulx.

She found that she could not go on. With a renewed determination to act as a proper attendant and see her patient safely out of the unhealthy air, she started back the way she had come, carefully holding up her skirt as she jumped the little rivulets in the bottom of each hollow.

No white shirt and grim forbearance greeted her when she came in view of the rectory and church. The place where he'd waited for her was only a solitary stretch of stone piled on stone. Maddy paused—and then saw him at the crest of the hill, sitting on an outcrop of natural rock. He rose as she came toward him, a strong, elegant silhouette against the early sun.

"Come," she said, halting at a distance that seemed safe from any emotion beyond proper nursely concern. "'Tis time to go in."

He held out his hand. The light behind him caught unexpected color—the long stems of wild Michaelmas daisies stirred by the wind.

He made the offering without expression—neither contrition nor smile. The unexpectedness of it overthrew her, the strange brightness of the daisies in the drab landscape when they should not have been there so late in the autumn, so fresh in spite of the driving storm. She felt confused, unable to command a tolerable response, a mild and impersonal gratitude. Her cheeks, hot with chafing, seemed to grow warmer still.

"What dost thou want of me?" she cried. "I am no scarlet, yielding woman." She snatched the flowers from his hand and threw them to the wind. The gust took them, tossed them end over end, bent the stems and rolled them awkwardly along the ground. "Thou art unkind, to beleaguer me with thy idle attentions!"

He hesitated, his head turned, frowning at her. Then heat came into his face; self-consciousness.

"Beg . . . *pardon.*" His expression was hot and stony. "Timms! Impert-*nent* . . ." The end of the word got tangled with a sound like an angry groan and laugh. He looked away, still trying to speak and failing, as if the words he wanted eluded him in the field beyond her. His lip curled, and he exclaimed, *"Idiot."*

"Thou art not an idiot, no! Thou art a wicked, worldly man. I've known it since I've known thee. And it becomes worse and worse. Thy kisses and embraces!" She was growing feverish. "Thou art abominable."

He looked out across the countryside, his eyes narrowed against the wind that blew his shirt and his hair.

"That cannot be between us, dost thou understand?" she added with abandon, saying aloud what should have shocked her even to think. "I am born a Friend, Jervaulx. Thou art born a nobleman."

She had only sullen silence for an answer.

"Dost thou even know what would become of me? Thou dost not. Thou wouldst not even ask." She exhaled sharply. "Friends would disown me. It is our way."

Still he did not answer. He had that proud blankness about him: his look without center, gone away, as he had gone away in the chancery court.

"I would not be a Friend!" she exclaimed, frustrated by his lack of response. "I would be alone!"

"No," he said unexpectedly. He turned and held his hand to her, palm upward, empty, a simple masculine offering. "Maddygirl. With . . . *me.*"

She gazed down at it. That sharp swelling pain rose up in her, stopped any more words and denials and explanations in her throat. She hurled herself away from him and ran quickly down the field, slipping on the slick green turf, sliding on her heels—almost but never quite falling, except in her heart.

The worst of it was, he made her think of it. He filled her head with falsehood and fantasy; she dreamt not only of the garden that was not hers, but of living here with him—just the two of them and Papa, quietly, in peace and industry, with Maddy working in the house and garden and Papa and

Jervaulx bent with heads together over their numbers and equations. Sometimes she imagined it was Jervaulx as she had known him that one brief night before his affliction, articulate and self-possessed and teasing; more often it was Jervaulx as he was now, except that when he fought with words and frustration, she could take his hand or touch him—and that vision led to vague and not-so-vague imaginings that made her feel stirred and licentious, ashamed.

All day, Maddy avoided him meticulously. She threw herself into airing the bedrooms and cleaning the oak-paneled parlor, keeping Brunhilda with her. She spoke to Jervaulx only once, when she found him in the rector's cold and dusty study using an old pen and leaves torn out of sermon books to make mathematical notes. He had no fire, and the only light was through a vine-covered window. In her vexation at discovering him situated so uncomfortably, she ordered him rather sharply into the kitchen so that she and Brunhilda might make the room habitable.

She would not look at him as he left, busying herself immediately with cobwebs. Brunhilda lingered at the door, and then suddenly turned and went away. She came back a quarter hour later, taking up the broom. She swept out beneath the desk and around the edge of the bookcases without a pause.

"I could give an opinion to 'ee, Mistress, if 'ee was to want it."

"Yes?" Maddy responded, expecting a household hint.

"Ye oughtn't to speak so thoughtless to yer lad. There's some as it don't make any difference to, but there's some as do well with loving-kindness."

Maddy bit down hard on her lip. She went on with her dusting. Brunhilda went on with her sweeping.

"But yer older than me, Mistress," she said at length, "and you know best. Perhaps ye didn't see how he looked at 'ee."

Maddy straightened the sheaf of writing paper that she'd found in a drawer. She set it in the middle of the desk, next to the freshly-cut pen.

Brunhilda bent down. "He loves 'ee well," she said to the dustpan. "Ye ought not to cut at him for no reason, Mistress."

"We need candles here," Maddy said, keeping any inflection from her voice. "Is there a pair of shears? I wish to trim away the ivy from the window."

"Yes, Mistress," Brunhilda said.

Evening brought Brunhilda's mother with fresh trout, a pudding, and cream for Jervaulx's chocolate, "Because Mr. Langland particularly likes it, my girl says." The country-woman sat down with a heave of pink flesh and began cleaning fish. "Will ye be going to church or chapel, Missus?"

"Brunhilda has not told thee I am a Friend?"

"Aye, that she has. Chapel, then."

"Is there not a meetinghouse near?"

"There's a grand Unitarian chapel over at Stroud. Mind you, that's seven miles."

Maddy smiled. "Perhaps I will stay here. I'm not accustomed to things very grand."

"That's a shame, then. Ye'll never want to see our new church in the market town. 'Tis wonderful grand, with a great organ up to the eaves. The duke gave that. He had to, you see, to get the vestrymen to let him put up his library for the Mechanical Society. I must say, there's wise men and there's wise men, and our vestry are rare ones, nobody can gainsay it. It is a perfect spectacle, that organ."

Maddy carefully cut a vegetable marrow. "What duke is this?"

"The Duke of Jervaulx, it is. I blush to repeat it, but a wild bad scamp of a gentleman, so they say, sharp as needles, but for common sense, I can't vouch. All this land ye see still in sheep, that's his. Oh, but it vexes the large farmers, who think they could do better with it. For myself, I don't say I know. I shouldn't like to see it change, not at my age. But I don't mind to say I'm glad to have this old place dusted out. The Reverend Durham is your relative, Missus Langland?"

"He is Francis Langland's friend," Maddy said.

"What a remarkable fashion you people do talk, then. To call your own husband by all his Christian name that way."

Maddy bent over her slicing. "It is a public testimony. Not to give worldly compliments, nor to lie and call a man our master when he is not."

The older woman chuckled roundly. "Ye don't call your husband master?"

Maddy kept her face down. "No," she said, in a muffled voice.

"Don't ye indeed. My girl says he's a powerful handsome lad, very gentleman-like."

"Yes," Maddy said.

"But his mind is weak."

She put down the paring knife. "His mind is not weak. He has been ill."

"Without doubt, without doubt," Brunhilda's mother said in a comfortable tone. "That gawkhammer girl of mine, 'tis her mind needs improvement. But it's a good heart. He's already a great favorite with her, you know. Wouldn't have nothing but that I stop with his cream directly I finished the skimming."

"It's kind of thee."

"Think nothing of it, Missus Langland. I am glad to do it. The rector doesn't come but once a year, and says his lesson to the Widow Small's chickens that have wandered into the old parish church, and troubles nobody. If I can do anything for him, I will do it."

Maddy looked at her uncertainly, not sure if this was meant sarcastically, but the woman was working with a pleasant smile on her round face.

"My William is on the vestry," she added, "and he tells me that a meddling rector is the very worst thing this parish might have. In particular as the duke is a rash clever man and appoints the living, there is no saying what might come of it. We were all on pins, I'll tell you that, but we like the Reverend Durham very well."

*   *   *

The sound of a dog barking plagued Maddy's dreams. It seemed to grow louder and louder, until it was someone pounding on a distant door. She rolled over in bed, opening her eyes to gray dawn filtering through the leaded glass.

The door pounding was real. So was the dog; she heard it clearly. Catching up her cloak for a robe, she hurried across the hall through an empty bedroom to look down in the weak light outside the window.

Squinting through the sleep in her eyes, she could just make out a chaise below, the horses steaming, but the jut of the old stone porch obscured its occupants. Another dog joined the first in barking. The pounding suddenly stopped. Brunhilda, surely—and a man's voice—Durham? But he'd hardly been gone long enough to turn around and come back. Maddy ran out and reached the top of the stairs just as a black and white dog came loping up the stairwell and tangled itself about her legs.

"*Miss Timms!* Instantly!" It was Durham at the bottom, shouting for her as cold air rushed up from below. "They're just behind me! We must go instantly!"

Jervaulx was already down, haphazardly dressed in a farmer's overcoat Brunhilda had got from the ready-made clothes shop at the market town. The maid stood in her cloak and apron as if she'd just arrived, looking as confused as Maddy felt. Durham came up the stairs two at a time and caught her hand, pulling her with him. Maddy had to put all her thought for the moment into keeping her balance; when they reached the foot she saw Colonel Fane, encloaked in blue over his scarlet uniform, standing in the entranceway as dry snow blew in the open door.

Durham propelled her right out into it in her nightgown and shoes with no stockings. The wind hit her, stinging cold, but she had no time to think of it as Colonel Fane grabbed her round the shoulders and forced her to a run with him, half-lifting her from the ground to keep her apace.

"What is it?" she cried, trying to turn behind and look. "Have they come for the duke?"

"Hot pursuit," he shouted, pulling her along, then suddenly sweeping her up bodily as if she were no heavier than a bag of goosedown. "Got to make the church."

The steeplehouse stood black against the cold dawn, little lacings of snow clinging to the stones and sills. Colonel Fane reached the porch and set her down just as Jervaulx and Durham arrived, Brunhilda in tow, a confusion of people and dogs in the entryway until Durham shoved open the heavy arched door and they all stumbled inside in a sweep of wind and snow.

He rammed the massive wooden bar into place, sending booming echoes through the vaulted space. The thin light of dawn was all color and darkness inside, the stained glass bright slits that marched to a glorious round window of rose and gold and blue above a cross and a barren table, leaving everything else in shadow. From somewhere, chickens muttered sleepy cackles, and a white hen fluttered up and balanced on the rail at the front of the church, eyeing them blandly. Devil stared at it, his body quivering with interest.

"Miss Timms," Durham said, breathing hard, "they're not a quarter hour behind us. I met Fane on the road—there's no time to explain, but we only have one hope. One. Ma'am—you've got to marry him. Now. Instantly. I can do it."

Maddy stood in her gown and cloak, speechless.

"I know it's sudden. I'd hoped to avoid it, to find some other way, but they've run us to ground far sooner than I'd expected. Miss Timms—they can take him. I can't stop it, nor Fane—we're nothing to him under the law. They can take him back."

"But—canst thou not hide him? Take him farther away?"

"No time. No time, Miss Timms! Do you hear that? Fane, check the doors—bolt 'em all! That's them—their horses!"

Indeed, over the moan of the wind, Maddy heard what might have been the clatter of hooves on the little bridge below, but a moment later it was gone. Brunhilda was all eyes. "I hear it!" she whispered.

"Please!" Durham said to Maddy. "For the love of God,

Miss Timms—you're the only one we can count on. Five
minutes it'll take—and you'll be his nearest relation under
the law. They can't touch him if you say them nay."

"But—it's impossible! I'm a Friend!"

"I don't care if you're a bloody Hindu. It's our only hope.
A madhouse, ma'am! It was you who brought him out of it.
You know it as no else does."

"Thou dost not understand! I can't be married by a
priest—in a steeplehouse! Only to satisfy a law! I *can't!* We
must try to hide him!"

Durham abruptly walked away. Maddy clutched her
freezing hands under her arms. She glanced at the duke. He
was watching his friends as they checked the other en-
trances. When he looked at her slantwise, their eyes met—
instant raw sensibility—she hadn't known if he understood
what Durham wanted, but in that glance, she knew that he
did. He was stiff and proud; he said nothing, no petition, no
plea for help—as distant as he had been since she had left
him on the hill.

The sound that had been faraway and unreal a few moments before took a sudden shape—the sharp clatter of iron
shoes on stone outside the door, and men shouting. The hens
flapped. Devil barked, and Brunhilda yelped, "Who is it?" as
the great latch rattled, but the wood muffled the voices outside beyond understanding anything more than excitement
and anger.

Durham strode back. "Too late!" he snapped. "God damn
it!"

The pursuers abandoned the main door. A side entrance
shook under their assault, and the obscured voices outside
grew bellicose. The dog Cass ran toward it, growling. There
seemed to be a multitude of them; the other side door rattled
at the same time. The chickens panicked, running about the
floor, ducking in and out of the railings. Devil lost his composure and began to chase them, barking frantically.

Brunhilda gasped. Maddy turned to see Colonel Fane
come down the aisle, drawing his sword. Durham un-

sheathed another from his walking stick, then pulled a pistol
from inside his coat and delivered it to Jervaulx.

"No!" Maddy couldn't get beyond that one word in her
horror. She tried to catch Jervaulx and Durham both at once.
The duke was already beyond her, but she clung to
Durham's sleeve. "Ye *must* not! *No!"*

He jerked away. "What do you suggest instead, Miss?"
He could barely be heard over the sound of the assault on the
doors and the barking dogs. He took up a station at the front,
where the wood shook as if it were alive. Maddy turned
around, saw Colonel Fane defending the left entry and Jervaulx kneeling down behind a box pew, his arm braced on
the side, taking aim at the last door. Devil's yelping barks resounded amid poultry squawks.

She strode to the front of the church, scattering hens as
she mounted the step and turned. *"No!"* she shouted, as
loud as she could shout it. "Ye will not do violence—none
of ye!"

They all turned to look at her. Even Devil scrabbled out
from beneath a pew, silenced, a chicken feather hanging
from his nose.

"Leave those—weapons—where ye are. And come!"

Durham was the first to do it. He dropped his sword to
the floor. Colonel Fane sheathed his; he followed Durham
to the raised place at the railing where Maddy had stopped.
She glared over them at Jervaulx, who finally, with haughty
leisure, rose and laid the pistol down on the wide box rail in
front of him.

The pounding on the doors had stopped. Even the voices
outside grew dimmer, as if they had drawn off to a consultation.

"Jervaulx," Maddy barked, "I have received from the
Lord a charge to love thee. Thou art my husband, and I am
thy wife, helpsmeet, with no rule but love between us."

The three men looked up at her as if she had gone mad.
Brunhilda stood behind them, shivering, pressing her apron
over her mouth, only a red nose and huge eyes visible.

"That is all that I am led to say at present." Maddy glared back.

Durham seemed to come to sudden awareness. He fumbled in his coat and pulled out a little book, stepped up beside her, leafed through it to a marked page, and began to read the priests' marriage ceremony. Someone outside started to pound on the front door again, this time far louder, with an implement more solid than a human hand. Devil crouched, staring toward the door, growling. As Durham came to the part in the vows where the man was to repeat, Jervaulx looked up at Maddy with a wild and bitter arrogance—and for a moment she did not think he would even try.

"Will!" he sneered. *"I . . . Christian Richard Nicholas Francis Langland . . . take thee . . . Maddygirl—Maddy . . . ah . . . Arc . . . ma . . . Maddygirl . . . Timm . . . to have . . . to hold . . . from this day . . . forward . . . for better . . . for worse . . . for rich . . . for poor . . . in sickness . . . in health . . . to love . . . to cherish . . . till death us . . . do part . . . according to God's . . . holy. Thereto . . . I plight thee . . . my . . . troth!"*

Durham shuffled in the book. "Ah—um—that's right, Shev old man." He raised his voice above the rhythmic boom on the wooden door. "Precisely right. Forgot to take her by the hand, but that don't matter. And now—Miss Timms, would you prefer to repeat after me?"

"I have said what I am led to say."

He frowned a little, and then shrugged. "Good enough. All right. The ring part comes next. Fane?"

Colonel Fane had been standing complacently, hand on his sword hilt. When Durham looked at him, an absurd expression of dismay spread across the soldier's face.

"Oh Good God, Fane. You forgot."

"No! Just now . . . I *give*." Jervaulx scowled at him fiercely. "You *think!*"

The colonel looked bewildered, and then brightened. "Got the papers," he said, pulling them out and offering them to Durham.

His friend snatched them. "You hopeless block. We'll have to use Shev's signet." Durham consulted the book, then glanced expectantly at the duke. "You're supposed to hand it to her. She gives it to me, and I bless it."

Jervaulx looked down at his hand, where the gold signet made a dull spot of richness against his dark clothes. There was a pause in the onslaught at the door, and then one sudden strike, crashing sound around the little church. Devil barked once and ran toward it. The chickens clucked excitedly, cowering under pews.

Jervaulx shoved his ring hand out to Maddy, palm up.

The cold made her fingers clumsy. As she worked the signet free, his skin seemed warm against hers, his hand large and steady. The ring fell into her palm. She would have handed it to Durham, but Jervaulx caught it up from her hand and pushed it onto her finger, where it hung so loose that he had to hold it there.

"*Ring . . . I . . . thee wed.*" He looked up into her eyes as if daring her to dispute it.

A single yelp came from somewhere at the back of the church, and a chicken flapped up into a candle stand, leaving Devil standing on his hinds legs in frustration.

"I will wear it," Maddy said, "as God charges me to do."

"I was supposed to bless it first," Durham protested.

"None but our Lord may do that," Maddy said.

"Well, all right. But it's in the book. Let's keep the thing a little straight here." The pounding began again, this time at a side door. Durham raised his voice. "Is it quite acceptable to you if I lead us in a prayer, Miss Timms? I am ordained, if it helps."

The wood of the side door began to give with a piercing crack. Both dogs rushed to it, raging and bristling. "Hurry!" Maddy snapped.

"Oh, hurry!" Brunhilda echoed.

"Eternal God . . . everlasting life . . . Never mind the prayer." He ran his finger down the book. "Hmm . . . hmm . . . ah." He reached down and awkwardly joined

Maddy's hand with the duke's, having trouble juggling the book at the same time. "What God hath joined together, let no man put asunder." He had to find his place again. The side door suffered another strike and cracking rift. "Forasmuch as Christian—Damn, Shev, what's the rest of your bloody name? Christian Richard, et cetera, et cetera, the Duke of Jervaulx and Archimedea Timms have consented together in holy wedlock, and have witnessed the same before God and this company—" The door gave again, and he began to speak faster. "—and thereto have given and pledged their troth—" Another crack of breaking wood. "—each-to-the-other-and-have-declared-the-same-by-giving-and-receiving-a-ring-and-by-joining-hands—" The door shuddered, splitting. "—Ipronouncethattheyaremanandwife-inthenameofthe-Father-andoftheson-andoftheHolyGhost. Amen!"

Just as if it had been a stage play in a street fair, the door gave way. Brunhilda screamed. Their pursuers burst into the church.

Chapter Twenty

"La! Oh, Mistress!" Brunhilda made her way through the pack of men in the rectory hall to Maddy, curtsying at each step. "Oh, m'lady—ought I to call 'ee lady? Oh, Mistress! I didn't know! I swear I didn't!"

Maddy held her cloak tight about herself, terrified that it would be discovered she was in her nightgown. She was feeling odd and unreal, the full impact of what she'd done slowly creeping through her bones. In the church it had seemed a logical action; the need to prevent an outbreak of violence had overridden any other concern. The picture of Jervaulx, his pistol aimed at the door, his face cold and still—Maddy knew he would die before he'd return to Blythedale; in one electrified instant she'd seen what would happen when the men broke through that door—and surely. . . . surely . . . she had done the only thing she could do to prevent it.

And now it must be carried through. She couldn't stand up and announce that it was all a farce, performed in a moment of terror. She must be the Duchess of Jervaulx, and calmly stand by him, and speak for him, and maintain that she would not allow his family—his real family—to over-rule his wishes and hers.

"We did not tell thee," she said to the maid. "I'm sorry for it. 'Twas a wicked deception."

"Oh, no. It don't matter, Mistress. Long as he was pledged to 'ee. Perhaps, you being Quaker, his noble folk don't like it? I don't blame 'ee, Mistress, for wedding in secret. Me aunt 'n uncle did just the same, living tally 'till they could afford to be churched. And you kept separate rooms of a night; I can swear to that myself." She smiled shyly. "Now ye needn't to do that no more, with such a handsome lad to kiss 'ee an' keep 'ee warm! The duke! I don't hardly believe it's true. Mr. Langland—well, he's not what ye'd think, is he? 'Tis blowed about from pillar to post that the Duke of Jervaulx's a clever man. Are ye—" She hesitated. "Are ye certain 'tis the real duke, m'lady?"

"Yes," Maddy said, with at least that to say truthful. "Thou must not call me lady."

"What'm I t'call ye, Mistress?"

" 'Your Grace,' " Durham supplied, shoving two mugs of foaming ale into Brunhilda's hands. "Our guests are thirsty."

"Yes, sir. I'll bring up a tray." She took the mugs and turned toward the cellar. Durham, when he left off his lazy airs and suddenly took to action, gave a person no time to think. Not only had he declared to the dowager's half dozen henchmen that Maddy was the new Duchess of Jervaulx, he'd even managed to march them all, along with horses and dogs, across the churchyard and into the rectory hall, ready to drink a wedding breakfast. For all their shouting and pounding, the men didn't seem very much concerned about the failure of their mission. The promise of strong spirits for celebration appeared to succeed in making them forget it entirely.

In the rectory, Durham had immediately accosted Maddy and Brunhilda in the matter of where to locate this fountain of hospitality, and the three of them came back up from the cellar just as Brunhilda's mother arrived in the midst of everything, red-cheeked from cold and astonished at the company. Jervaulx was nowhere to be seen, but Colonel Fane was loudly informing the bewildered matron of the special nature of the occasion: the nuptials of the Duke of Jervaulx.

"Oh, him," she said, looking a little less perplexed. "Wish'en joy, then. Do 'ee all know Himself, sir?"

"Indeed, my dear. Very well. Ah! And here she is—the blushing bride!" The colonel swept out his arm with a gallant little bow toward Maddy, as if they were spectators at a parade and he were pointing out the King.

The countrywoman turned to him, laughing. "What a humbug! That's only Mistress Langland."

Colonel Fane leaned over and whispered in her ear.

She listened. She put her thumbnail to her mouth and stared at Maddy, turned white and then red. Maddy clutched the cloak tight round herself, painfully aware of having no bonnet, of her hair hanging down her back in its single loose nighttime braid. The woman drew in a breath, seeming to waver between shock and disapproval. "Souls alive!" She finally shook her head. "The wonder of this life. I'd best see to the victuals, then, for that gawkhammer girl won't know what to do with herself. The whole village will come calling 'fore the day's out. Long life and happiness to ye, M'lady. And to Himself." She dropped a curtsy and turned toward the kitchen.

"So where the devil is Himself?" Durham looked at Maddy.

She already knew that Jervaulx was nowhere in the room. "I'll look upstairs," she said, thankful for a chance to get away.

The upper hall seemed quiet after the cheerful babble of male voices below. She found him in his room, dogs at his feet, attempting to shave. He was in his shirtsleeves, wearing his velvet breeches, his collar open, standing at the looking

glass over the fireplace mantel and scowling. His face was
lathered on one side—the other had a few patches of foam,
as if he had only remembered now and then that he had to
put soap there, too.

Maddy stuck her finger outside her cloak and tested the
water in the basin. "Thou ought to have it hot," she said.

He startled, glanced the wrong way in the mirror, and then
found her by turning around. Maddy couldn't bring herself
to look directly at him. They both stood awkwardly for a
moment, and then he moved to his chair and sat backwards
in it, as he always did for her to shave him.

She plunged into the task as if it were mere laundry or
dusting, brisk and efficient; she would *not* think of what she
had done; she would *not* pay attention to how still he sat,
how he watched her, how warm and clean his skin smelled.
Mostly, she would not look into his eyes, because they were
so dark and blue and intent on her as she struggled with the
difficult double task of keeping her cloak closed tight around
her and shaving him at the same time.

She finished. He caught the towel from her and cleaned
his face himself, rising from the chair. Maddy turned to
straighten his coat—he'd got out the brown velvet; the embroidered waistcoat and blue ribbon and star lay beside it on
the bed. She realized suddenly that he thought all the regalia
appropriate for the occasion. And for some reason, that
seemed to make it quite, quite real, this marriage. He had not
wed her in his splendid clothes, but now, as if he knew what
Brunhilda's mother had predicted, that the whole village
would come—now he dressed the duke.

And she was to be his duchess.

Facing away from him, she looked down at herself, still in
her borrowed nightgown under the cloak, her braid hanging
behind her to her knees. They would laugh at her—married
in a nightgown, with no bonnet. Married to a duke. Married
by a priest. Married in a steeplehouse. Married—married—
married . . . to him.

She felt a little dizzy. When she turned about, Jervaulx

was watching her. She took a deep breath, pulled her cloak close, and held up the waistcoat to him.

He caught her hand inside the fabric. *"Wife,"* he said.

"I am no duchess." She hardly knew if she were apologizing or protesting.

He found the massive band of the signet ring under the silk and turned it upright on her finger. *"Mine."*

She pulled her hand away. "As thy dogs are thine? I'm not thy possession, Jervaulx, because I wear thy ring."

With a flick, he took the waistcoat from her hand and shrugged it on. He worked at the buttons with one hand, making little progress but not asking for help. Maddy finally pulled it closed and attempted to button it for him. With her cloak to mind, too, she was having almost as much trouble as he'd had.

After she'd struggled unsuccessfully for a long moment, he made an exasperated grimace. He caught her hands and wrenched the cloak free. He held it out, exposing her. Maddy tried to snatch the wrapper back, but he was stronger; his quick jerk popped the clasp open. Her shield slipped away. He scanned the nightgown—and then leaned his back against the bedpost, carelessly superb in his silk and lace as he made a slow inspection of her.

A very faint smile curled one side of his mouth. "Come," he commanded, standing up. When she didn't instantly obey, he reached out and yanked her with him, escorting her forcefully down the hall past the stair to her own room, the dogs trotting complacently ahead and behind.

Jervaulx flung open the wardrobe himself. He stood looking into it at her silver dress. *"All?"* he demanded, turning with his brows raised, as if Maddy must be hiding a roomful of ball gowns somewhere.

"Yes," she said.

"Dress . . . wife." He made a little bow. "Pleasure."

Maddy's eyes widened. She felt herself growing hot. "I shall dress myself, I thank thee. If thou wilt go!"

He tilted his head—an instant of confusion—and then suddenly grinned. "*Buy* dress . . . say. Dozen. Hundred."

"Oh." She felt mortified. "I—mistook thee."

He went toward the door. Maddy expected him to leave; instead he let the dogs out and closed it, turned about and leaned back. There was no visible expression to his mouth, but the ghost of his pirate smile was in his eyes.

"Thou must go," she said quickly. "It is not seemly."

He made a look of surprise. "Not? Seem . . . nurse . . . *me*. Not . . . husband . . . *wife?*"

"We aren't—truly . . . we are not . . ." She couldn't bring herself to say it.

Something unalterable came into his face, a new and adamant focus. "Before God . . . Maddygirl. I thee . . . *wed*."

She turned away. "I don't see how it could be true. I'm sure it cannot be. It is to dupe the men below only."

He was silent. Maddy looked at the bed hangings, at the venerable red fabric, faded on the outside of each fold, the tarnished trim, the tangle of unmade bedclothes that she'd left in her hurry. She felt hideously aware of herself, of her body inside thin linen, her plait trailing down her back and hips.

The floor creaked. She felt him come behind her, standing close.

She stood still, frozen in place.

He tugged on her braid. He drew it lightly taut, exerting steady pressure on the connection. It didn't hurt. It teased her. She might have pulled away as he idled with it, gentle tugs that courted her, coaxed each tiny yield in his direction. She knew it. She stood with her face averted, burning, aware of how she allowed it. He twitched the plait, sending a ripple up to the nape of her neck.

"Maddygirl," he said softly, with that wicked smile in his voice.

She shook her head, as if it had been a question and she must answer no.

He moved closer. She could feel the warmth of him at her back. He lifted the braid over her shoulder and curled it round her throat.

Slowly, slowly, he increased the pull. Maddy put her hand to her throat, clutching the braid, holding it from growing tighter. Her hips touched him, her back. She grew stiff, frantic and fixed in place.

He caught her shoulders. He held her against him, a domination, his breath rough beside her ear—and then his hard grip turned to a caress. He smoothed his hands down her sleeves, laced his fingers through hers, covering her hands with his palms.

A low hum, deep music, like his laughter: the sound he made as he touched his mouth to her bared throat seemed to touch a note inside her, turning quiver to resonance. He lifted his arms, their hands still enlaced, and crossed them against her breasts.

Her braid lay over her shoulder and their hands. He toyed with the tip of it. He held it in one fist and ran his thumb against it. The single strand of hair, the tiny thread that she'd looped tight to hold it—the strand broke, and the plait came free.

He made a sound, low and hot. And then he released her—before she could find herself in his embrace, before she could say what it felt like—only that he was solid and tall and heated and catastrophic, only that she felt bare and hollow when he let her go.

He moved past her. He lounged against the bed, holding her loosened braid. As he rubbed it between his fingers, the plaiting spread and curled over his hand. He sat on the edge of the unmade bed, smiling down at her hair in his hands.

"Tower," he said, "Girl . . . *tower*."

"I don't understand. I must dress."

He opened his fingers, working the braid apart higher and higher. "Let . . . down . . . thy hair. Shining . . . hair." He shook his head. "Girl. Can't remember . . . *girl*."

"Thou must go away." Her voice was light and shaky. With each fraction of an inch that he moved up the length of the braid, unplaiting it, he pulled her that much closer to him.

"Maddygirl." He worked steadily. "Princess . . . tower. Lock. Lonely. Prince . . . outside . . . no stair." His knee touched her. He had reached halfway, spreading her hair loose below her waist. "Call . . . lonely . . . fairy princess . . . let down thy hair. Beautiful hair. *Long*. Climb up . . . come up to me." He brought her closer. She stood now between his legs, her plait undone higher yet. He leaned forward, blowing against it where it lay over her breast, sliding his fingers into it there, drawing them down the whole length. "Come up to me."

He blew again—and then touched his lips to the fall of her hair, a soft pressure at the tip of her breast, a stolen instant of contact, so brief and exquisite that she shuddered, flinched back when he kissed her other breast as lightly, but his arm was there at her waist to hold her.

"Maddygirl," he whispered, with that heavy moan in his throat, burying his face in her breasts, drawing his hands downward to touch them. "Shine . . . princess." He held his palms to her shape, his hair black against the whiteness of her gown.

She pulled back, refusing. "No. I cannot."

His fingers tightened, locked at her waist. His lips moved over her breasts, her throat. *"Mine."*

He was so close; he shattered her, made her strange to herself. Her body pulsed and ached, wantonly bared to him. She strained away. "I am not thine. It was not a true marriage."

The line of his mouth changed. His grip hardened. "Yes. *True*."

"Not for me."

"True."

"No."

He looked at her, blue flame and blackness, utterly still.

"I told thee," she said, holding her arms close, pressing

back. "I told thee before. It is impossible." Her voice was shaking. Shivers ran down her limbs, and she pulled them tighter yet.

"Church." He let go of her so suddenly that she took a step to catch herself. "Church . . . say . . . husband I . . . *wife.* I . . . say . . . I thee wed. Love, honor, cherish, death. Say." He rose from the bed. *"Lie?"*

She wet her lips.

"Forgot?" His mouth made a scornful curve. He turned away. " 'Jer*vaulx* . . . received . . . Lord . . . a charge. *Love.* Husband I . . . thy wife.' " At the window, he leaned his forearm on the side of the deep, uncurtained recess. Gray light shone on him from the half-open shutter. *"I* . . . remember."

"Thou wouldst have done violence. Thou wouldst have shot at those men. I was afraid . . ." *For thee*—but she did not say it. "I was afraid of violence."

He smiled bitterly. "False word, Maddygirl? All . . . *lies?"*

If she turned her head, she could see her hair unbraided, spreading free over her shoulder in a fan of his making. "I don't know," she said. "I don't know! How can it be God's will, for me to marry thee?"

He stood at the window, lace and gilt and extravagant comeliness, the light falling on his dark hair and lashes, as sensual as his kisses, as his hands on her skin. *"Done. Why . . . not . . . will?"*

A simple question—and there was nothing simple in him. Or in her, anymore. "I don't know," she whispered again.

"Done." He leaned one hand on the headboard. "Marry. *Wife."* He pushed away and went to the door. Before he opened it, he looked back at her. It was a command, that look, and a challenge. He dared her to deny it.

"Jervaulx," she said slowly, "answer me this. In the church—if I had stood between thee and the other men . . . wouldst thou have shot?"

"Between," he repeated, tilting his head intently.

"My body . . . myself . . . between thee and the others."

His face changed, grew watchful.

"If I had stepped between," she asked again, "would I have stopped thee from killing?"

He kept a long silence. And then, clipped, he said, "Yes."

Her heart sank. There had been another way. She had done the wrong thing after all. "Even if—it meant thou hadst gone back to Blythedale Hall?"

"Yes."

She had erred. She should have practiced a submissive nonresistance instead of taking authority into her own hands. She had only substituted one evil for another.

He came to her across the room and pulled her chin up between his fingers. "Maddygirl," he said. "Never . . . stand between. *Never.*"

She pulled her face away. "I cannot promise thee."

"You answer . . . *me,*" he said. "Stand between—don't kill . . . let . . . *take,* Maddygirl?" He caught her again, held her painfully hard. "That place? God's . . . will?"

No.

That answer was clear, so suddenly clear—her inner voice speaking sure.

The turmoil of doubt inside her relaxed. She *had* done right. There had been two choices, two inevitable outcomes: to marry and keep him free, or to forbid strife only—and let him be seized and chained.

She had done what God wished, then: married him—and therefore it must be a true marriage.

"I would not let them take thee, Jervaulx, if I could stop it," she said. "That is the Truth."

His hold eased. She could have told him more. She could have told him that now she was certain that the words in the church were words in the Light, and therefore she would live in their commitment.

She didn't. But she remembered the thing she had said in the steeplehouse better than he. *With no rule but love between us,* she had avowed. And Jervaulx, she thought, even after Blythedale Hall, recognized no rule but his own.

Perhaps there was a reason that God asked this of her. It had been a great commitment, to be made in an instant. But she would wait to explain, because Jervaulx was a duke, and a child of the world, and not yet ready to understand.

Late in the day, as the carriage lumbered up over the top of a steep grade in the Welsh foothills and started down the other side, she came upon the first full consequence of the course she had taken.

"*There,*" Jervaulx said.

Maddy had already seen it from out the carriage window. It burst upon the mind: floating on the ridge across the valley—a white circuit of towers, a dazzling and disorganized necklace strung of stone, half-tangible, huge and yet weightless, cloud drift and shadow and turrets melded into a daydream, a pale and glowing vision of fantastical chivalry.

It was wild and translucent, like a vanishing reverie that somehow did not disappear but became more substantial as they drew closer. The white walls glittered, hundreds of windows in the upper towers catching the late sun as the carriage descended into the valley below.

Durham grinned at Maddy from the forward seat. Colonel Fane stretched out his legs as far as he politely could and asked, "When's supper?"

Jervaulx exclaimed, "*Home,*" in a voice that resonated with love and satisfaction.

Maddy looked at the castle. It was beautiful. Against the sky and the hills, it was a proclamation. It declared power, announced wealth, blazed luxury—not in a shout, but in a song.

There was a reason God had asked this of her, she repeated to herself.

She had done the right thing.

She was terrified.

Chapter Twenty-one

*C*hristian leaned his head against the carved back of a chair that had been given by Queen Elizabeth to his great-grandfather eight times removed. It was something of a throne itself, though made for a shorter man, with an unlucky projection in the claw of the phoenix crest that always poked Christian in the left ear if he was not careful.

The footman took away his plate. He watched the firelight gleam through his wineglass while Fane rambled on about horses—a clumsy topic with a lady present, Christian thought, which reminded him that he was host and responsible to do something about it. For three and a half centuries, the earls and dukes of Jervaulx had presided over the table in the Great Chamber. It was four floors up over the gatehouse, a hundred and fifty feet above the base of the cliff that dropped away below, with a bank of windows that commanded the border for twenty miles in both directions.

He could remember all that, but he could not depend on his own tongue to say something civilized. Maddygirl, seated at the foot of the long table, had her eyes lowered. She looked strangely small and meek. He decided that he had to do something about the overly masculine conversation.

"Tired . . . *day* . . . Maddygirl?" he asked, interrupting Fane mid-sentence, because he couldn't time his words to a pause but had to take them when they came.

She looked up. "Little," she said, barely audible in the large room.

"Course is," said another voice. Christian remembered Durham on his right and glanced that way. He'd known Durham was there; it was just that he sometimes forgot it if he didn't keep looking. "Long fatigue journey, ontop wedding," Durham added. "Won't dawdle port."

"Port," Christian said, "*drawn* room."

"Excellent notion," Fane agreed, nodding sagely, "Port in the drawing room ladies." He cleared his throat. "Retire early."

All three of them looked at Maddy, expecting her to rise. She looked back, absurdly small in her chair that matched Christian's, with the phoenix wings poised above her head.

Durham figured it out before Christian did. "Duchess, fellows can't get uptil give word," he said kindly.

She stood, and the rest of them followed suit. She still appeared hesitant. Christian went down the table and took her arm. He escorted her into the adjacent drawing room, where the shutters had been closed and the drapes let down to hold the heat from the big stone fireplace. The dogs leaped up from their rug before the fire, tails wagging in welcome. With a sharp syllable, Christian made them sit. Maddy appeared to be more concerned with the tips of her toes than with the rich tapestries of bacchanals and war that decorated all the inner walls. She took the chair he offered without the usual compliments on their fineness.

She seemed, in fact, entirely disinterested in her new home. Christian was accustomed to giving the history of the place to house guests; he had his short, medium, and comprehensive discourses on the topic, depending on whether it was merely after-dinner small talk, or a full-scale tour. He was to be spared either, it appeared, which he found rather vexing, even knowing he would have made a hash of the business.

"Fane myself off town morning," Durham said, backing up to the fire.

Maddygirl showed the first sign of life that she'd shown since their arrival, turning to Durham. "Thou take letter me?"

"Certainly. If you wish."

"Please. To my father."

"Father?" Durham hesitated. He met Christian's eyes.

"Thou'lt have to read him," she said apologetically. "If be so good."

Durham had a helpless expression. He fidgeted. "Course—must understand may be short trip—"

"Write," Christian interrupted. He went to the table and found pens and paper; spread them out on the writing desk and carried a candle to it. "Maddygirl write. Durham calling . . . Timms." He gave Durham a meaningful look. "Ask . . . Timm comes here."

The pleasure and relief in her face gratified him. "Oh—can come here?"

"Your . . . *home*. Come . . . live . . . do you want?"

A pink flush rose into her cheeks. "Father—live here?"

"Yes."

She dropped her eyes.

"Want?" Christian asked again.

She lifted them. "Yes! Want him me. Only—so strange. Here? I can't—become accustomed."

Christian picked up the pen. "Write," he said.

She gathered her skirt and took the place he'd created. He stood beside her for a moment, and then walked away. He wanted to write to her father himself, but was afraid he couldn't do it. Not now. It had been mortifying enough to sign his name to the parish register—he wasn't certain yet that he'd spelled all of it right. He'd kept losing part of it in his hurry. In private he would write, when he could take time and make the sons-of-bitches letters come out straight.

The door from the Great Chamber opened and the steward appeared with coffee and port. Christian motioned for him to serve Maddy at the writing table. He would not speak to the staff unless he had to do it. So far it had been surprisingly easy—Jervaulx ran like clockwork: from the moment the carriage had swept beneath the gatehouse, the mechanism had gone into motion. The party had been met in the hall by the steward and housekeeper—Christian had only to present Maddy on his arm with four words that he'd been practicing under his breath from Gloucester to the border. *The Duchess of Jervaulx.*

He had a feeling that he'd forgot the little words, but he'd got out the important ones with a suitable authority. The head servants had instantly responded with proper courtesies and their names. Now Calvin Elder acknowledged Christian's silent nod with immediate compliance, pouring Maddy's coffee and placing it next to her on the table. Christian reckoned he could rely on the fact that a substantial breakfast would be laid at the usual time in the morning, and rooms had been made ready for Durham and Fane.

A thought struck him. As Calvin Elder withdrew to the door, having left the port, Christian followed him into the Great Chamber. He held the door closed behind him.

"Tonight . . . bedchamber," he said. "My . . . duchess . . . *chamber.*" That wasn't right. Christian felt heat in his face. Not his duchess; he'd meant his chamber. She'd sleep there. After an excruciatingly long moment, he got out, "The bed." Christ! Coarse idiot. "The room . . . duchess. She is . . ." Another interminable pause. *"Mine."* Worse and worse. He gave it up, glaring at the steward.

Calvin Elder put his hands behind his back and bowed. "As you say, Your Grace."

Furiously embarrassed, Christian retreated to the drawing room. Fane helped himself to the port, while Durham still rocked on his heels by the fire.

"Anything else want town for you, Shev?" Durham asked, accepting a glass from Fane.

Christian took a breath. It tried him, wearied him, to batter at the wall of his weakness, but he had to keep going.

"Tell." He groped for a way to say it. "Aunt Vest. Maddy . . . I thee wed."

"Right," Durham said promptly. "Ready Philistines up-onu, eh?"

Upon him, indeed. His whole family, beginning with the she-dragon, as soon as they had the word. God's blood—his mother and sisters—they'd be in a frenzy. His jaw hardened into a sardonic smile.

A silence fell. Maddy was oblivious, at work on her letter. Fane fondled Devil's ears assiduously, pushing the dog off his knees at every third stroke. Durham rocked gently before the fire.

"Play me billiards, Colonel?" Durham asked suddenly.

"Aye!" Fane looked cheerful at the notion. "Guinea game?"

"What, think me a nabob?" Durham was already at the door, his port in one hand, the handle in the other. He gave Maddy a little bow. "Will excuse us, Your Grace?"

She looked up at him. "Thou must not call your grace."

"Duchess," he said placatingly. "Duchess, mean."

"Archimedea," she said stubbornly.

"Maddygirl," Christian suggested, with a slight smile.

"Good night," Durham said. "Before dig this hole deeper. Wish you joy, Duchess-Archimedea-Maddygirl. You, Shev."

Fane echoed his sentiment, settling for "ma'am" with reference to Maddy.

"Dogs," Christian said. "Out."

Fane whistled, the Pied Piper of the canine world, and the dogs hopped up and slipped through the open door with him.

"Durham." Christian spoke as it was closing behind them. "Thank . . ." He wanted to say more, but the words would not come.

In the shadow of the door, Durham turned his thumb up and grinned. The handle clicked shut.

Christian poured himself a glass of port and sat down. He closed his eyes.

A relief, to be alone. In his own place. He allowed himself to drift. His right hand tingled, the levy of exhaustion. He listened to the intermittent scratch of Maddy's pen, noting distantly that she didn't seem to be having an easy time with her letter.

The familiarity of everything was bizarre: the way the place functioned even as he mangled and fumbled his orders. He felt at home, and yet an imposter—as if it were the not-real man who lived here, and the real one, himself, the muddled scared wounded one, belonged back in the bare room and the lunatic house with the other broken beasts. And yet the mad place itself had already receded to a bad dream— he was himself, normal, it was just that a part of his head was off in some obscure and misty cloudland, beyond reach.

It was coming back. He had got here to Jervaulx, so it must be coming back. He could remember himself worse than he was now, but the now was so maddening, and the future . . .

He had not until this moment even thought of a future beyond reaching home and safety, each moment unraveling before him, flashing past like a steeplechase, like riding hell-for-leather point to point, over strange country with the light failing and nothing to do but give her her head and pray—he smiled at himself with his eyes closed—but it had seemed that way, all a rush, obstacles and decisions and words that leaped up at him and then were gone, and he was over them and down on the other side.

Over and down. Married.

God.

So far, it was all right. Everything was the way he'd envisioned it: home, safe, quiet. Loyal Maddygirl, hen-scratching at the writing table.

He opened his eyes and looked at her. She had stopped her pen and held it poised, caressing her lips with the feather tip as she considered. She seemed very careful; from where he was he could see that she had not crossed out anything on her page, though there was plenty of paper for her to have composed all the drafts she liked. Christian always used reams of paper to get his thoughts down before he settled on a final version.

He set his glass on the table beside him and watched her cautious authorship. He supposed that it was her Quaker upbringing, not to be extravagant. Or perhaps it was because she had learned economy in difficult circumstances. Or perhaps it was just Maddy, herself, and she was a natural pinchpenny.

It came as a revelation to him that he didn't know, that he had married this young woman, neat and simple and plain except for her hair and her hedonistic eyelashes, and he knew almost nothing of her at all.

Prim and decent, chaste, careful, loyal, moderately brave in some things, a lion in a few, and when he touched her, she fluttered—nice feminine flutter, modesty and passion. As he watched her, she put her tongue to the tip of the feather and stroked it thoughtfully, unselfconscious, all unknowing— and heat began a slow liquid dissolve in his loins.

It could not quite banish the leaden weariness that held him down, but he took pleasure in imagination. He had time. She was his wife. Anytime, any place that he wanted. Here, if he liked.

He smiled. He lay in the chair and pictured himself rising and going to her, taking down that amazing hair and letting it fall in a cascade to the floor—discarding the white spinster collar that hid her throat, pulling fastenings free; her stark dress in a confusion at her waist, her belly and breasts and shoulders all white and soft—and that hair . . .

He drew a breath deep inside himself and let it go, almost but not quite a sound in his chest.

He would take her here, he thought, right here in the drawing room, his duchess. He would push her skirts to her waist and touch her, kiss her; and she would flutter like a soft bird, flutter and sigh and stretch out her legs and lie back in her chair at the writing desk, that hair a sheen of firelight and honeyed ale from the arch of her throat to the Axminster carpet—bare feet and toes that would flex and dig into the silk as he tasted her—so sweet—warm secret curls, bright and saucy.

And inside her, God, inside her . . . he imagined it . . . spreading for him, opening like a flower; in his mind the dress had disappeared and she was perfectly, gloriously naked, slim pretty nymph in the drawing room, eager, arching back in the chair and pulling him into her, her lips parted . . . wanting closer, wanting deeper and deeper and harder . . .

The duke made a faint sound. Maddy finally put down her pen, defeated. She could not explain to Papa, not in any words that she would want Durham to read aloud. When she looked over at Jervaulx, he was sleeping, his head turned a little toward her, his face relaxed, as if he had pleasing dreams.

Maddy could not help herself: he made her smile.

His hands rested on the carved arms of his chair. On her own hand she felt his heavy signet, suspended inside her finger, too large—but not too large for him. His fingers were strong and sound; they made a slight twitch as he slept, a thing insignificant and private, an intimacy. He breathed deeply, quietly, not precisely even, still on the edge of full sleep—but as she watched, the rhythm eased into the cadence of profound slumber. His head declined a trifle lower to the side.

She felt a rush of confusion and tenderness. It could not be true; it simply could not be. She was not his wife—the absurdity of the idea, the magnificence of this place, the food, the servants, the uncountable candles and paintings and crystal bowls of fruit and flowers, the great harp standing in a corner of the room, the endless corridors—there was even a water closet all richly tricked out in marble, and seventeen more elsewhere in the castle, all of the modern patent variety, as she had been informed matter-of-factly by the housekeeper.

She could not be the mistress of this place. Something would happen that would prove it all to have been mistaken. The wedding, so hasty and preposterous—that would not be legal, even if Durham insisted that the special license he'd caused Colonel Fane to procure in anticipation of pursuit was in order. And even if it were, Friends would not accept it. When they found out, she would be disowned: married by a priest, in a church, without her father's permission—worst of all—married to a man of the world.

Yet in his sleep, he did not look so diabolic. Earthly, yes: the sensual line of his mouth, the straight strong nose, the elegant jaw, his hair falling over his forehead—and those dark lashes, as long as a child's, but with a child's innocence made reckless in a man grown.

Her words in the church had come from Quaker weddings she had attended—whether they were her own words or God's words in her, how was she to know? She could reason both ways: as she had reasoned this morning, that to refuse him was to condemn him to Blythedale Hall, or as seemed so apparent now—that there was no possibility she had any power to protect him, or any grounds to belong to this place.

She had never been so unclear before, caught between what Friends would say and what seemed to hold her heart. For a long time, she watched him sleep.

If it weren't for this place. If he were just an ordinary man.

Just an ordinary man, for ordinary Archimedea Timms. A man the Meeting would approve, a practical garden and a bell-pull that worked. The Duke of Jervaulx in Plain Dress. Whenever pigs might learn to fly.

Standing up softly, she pulled the bell-rope that adorned the duke's drawing room, a thick black cord of silk, braided and tasseled in gold. It worked. In a very few moments, the steward appeared, the door opening on oiled hinges. Dressed in long-skirted white satin livery, with his hawk nose and long chin, his stockings as white as his wig and coat, he bore a strong resemblance to the duke's butler in town—Maddy supposed the likeness of Calvin Elder to London Calvin was not coincidence. She gave him a small, embarrassed smile.

"Your Grace wishes to retire?" he asked in a low voice.

So late, in such a circumstance, it did not seem worth-while to argue the title. She glanced uncertainly at Jervaulx, and then nodded.

Calvin Elder turned, holding the door open for her. Maddy followed him, led from the rich warmth of the tapes-tried and firelit room into a frigid corridor illuminated by torches, the smoky light shining down upon polished suits of armor that lined the walls like a mute army. At the end, a broad stone staircase curved downward into blackness. Calvin Elder stopped at a small table, lit a candle that had been provided ready there, and started down.

The candle's bobbing rays illuminated the arched vault overhead as they descended. At the foot of the stair, the ceil-ing abruptly gave way to a huge darkness: a hall, cold and resonating, in the dim candlelight bigger than the biggest meetinghouse she had ever been inside, bigger than a church, its vast space rising into unseen realms above where the peaks of soaring lancet windows were lost in gloom.

Calvin Elder walked across it on soft slippers, but Maddy's sturdy shoes made crude clapping sounds that she could not seem to silence. The noise echoed: It almost seemed as if someone were following them as they crossed the vast floor—a thought that raised prickles on the back of her neck.

At the other end, he led her two floors up a tight winding staircase, the uneven stone steps worn away in the middle by countless feet. Before she had caught her breath from that ascent, they went through a door into another blackness. The floor creaked beneath the carpet, and Maddy startled at the sudden looming up of a white face and staring eyes. Elder Calvin simply walked on, and his candle illuminated a bright haughty figure, a portrait of a man in studded armor and robes. Another rose up beyond it, a rich stilted profusion of jeweled cloth and pearl headdress, with a woman's pale and expressionless face beneath it. Maddy realized she was in a long gallery, icy, lined the whole length by these staring portraits. Their eyes followed her, appearing out of the shadow, lit for a moment by the passing candle, and fading into ghostly silence.

The hairs on her scalp rose. She felt their antagonism like a living presence.

Finally, through a door, another corridor, and Calvin Elder opened a room. He gave her a grave look. "The duchess' boudoir."

Maddy did not think Calvin Elder approved of her much, either. They hid it well, he and the housekeeper Ellen Rhodes, but the staff must be in something of an uproar—perhaps even uncertain of the duke's sanity. Maddy thought she would have questioned it herself under the circumstances.

She stepped meekly through. The room ought not to have shocked her after all the rest of the feudal splendor, but it did. The light from the single candle darted among huge shadows, glowing momentarily on walls hung in rose damask, plaster and gilt at the ceiling, abundant with chairs and plush settees. A fire smoked in the open hearth, helpless to warm the big room much better than the gallery and halls. Calvin Elder walked through and opened another door. "The bedchamber, Your Grace."

Maddy followed him. Another outburst of luxury, this time in a bed with cloth-of-gold hangings lined in pale pink, the walls adorned by tapestries and silver sconces. She was becoming unnerved by it.

Over the upholstered bench at the foot of the bed, her nightgown lay spread neatly, a plain white contrast to everything else in the room.

"The bell-rope is here, Your Grace." He walked across, reaching to pull it. "A woman will come up to serve you."

"Oh no. I need no one. I can . . . serve myself."

He bowed.

"The duke . . ." Maddy made a vague gesture, not sure which direction was the right one after all the halls and turns and staircases. "Is there someone to help him?"

"When he doesn't bring his own man, His Grace has commonly preferred to valet himself on those occasions that he retires late. The staff is not to disturb him. His room has been made ready in the manner that he usually desires it."

She had to make a conscious effort not to bite her lip. There was no guessing what the staff here had been told about Jervaulx's affliction, or if they knew anything at all. It would not be possible to hide for long.

Calvin Elder looked a solemn inquiry at her. "Will a valet be required, Your Grace?"

His expression said that it was unusual, unwelcome, and against all natural expectation—and that such oddities and anomalies were under particular scrutiny in the present circumstance.

"No," she said.

He bowed and withdrew.

As soon as he was gone, Maddy wished he were still there with her. The candle he'd lit for her cast feeble light, doing little more than making the bed seem twice as large by its shadow on the ceiling. She quickly changed into her night rail and carried her dress and the candle into the smaller dressing closet off the bedchamber.

As she was laying out her dress, she heard a sound in the bedchamber. She hastened out, glad of any company, expecting the duke.

There was no one there. Something creaked behind her. She whirled around. The door of the dressing closet stood open, black now, empty. She didn't want to go back in it; she didn't want it to stand open like a gaping mouth. She slammed it shut, refusing to look inside.

She set the candle on the bedside table, knelt down, and prayed very hard for common sense. She tried to find the Inner Light, but strange sounds, faint shuffles and breathings, sounds like nothing she'd ever heard in other houses, kept dashing her attention away from a calm concentration.

She wished for Jervaulx. For Durham and Fane. For anyone.

Using the gilt and bamboo steps, she climbed into the cold bed. It sank beneath her, enfolding her. The candlelight brushed a deep gleam of color on the underside of the canopy.

She heard footsteps. They were above her—a sluggish step that crossed the room, paused overhead, and then moved on. They did not return.

Maddy's eyes watered. She squeezed herself down in the bed.

Oh. She didn't believe in ghosts. She did not.

If only Jervaulx would come.

Christian awoke chilly. The room had gone to shadows, the candles guttering, the fire a red glow of fading coals. It was hard to rouse; he kept drifting back into odd and forbidding dreams, but with a blank habit he got up and spread the coals out with a poker, snuffed all the candles, and went by feel through the door from the drawing room into his bedchamber.

He was half asleep; he vaguely realized it when he couldn't unfasten his waistcoat. But it was too much trouble. In the dark his bed waited, turned down and warmed. He dropped his coat and his shoes and spread himself full length on it. He rolled over and pulled a pillow to him, got his feet beneath the bedclothes, and slid back down into the deep.

Chapter Twenty-two

$\mathcal{I}$n the morning, Maddy found her own way as far as the immense medieval hall with its dark beams and stone walls. It was almost as forbidding as it had been last night, with its ominous height and echoing floor, the silent beams of light that fell down from slits of windows. Fortunately, she encountered Colonel Fane just entering it with the dogs and had their amiable escort and direction to the breakfast parlor. Durham was already there, engaged with porridge, which he was eating standing up, looking out a window that had a commanding view of the countryside.

"Good morning, ma'am," he said cheerfully. "Have some kedgeree? India or China tea? Coffee?"

Somehow, he had her seated at the head of the linen-covered table, serving her himself from the silver dishes on the sideboard, persuasive as always in his active mode. He sat down next to her and motioned Colonel Fane to pull up his chair.

"We can talk private here—servants don't come unless we ring." He passed her cream. "How do you think it's going so far?"

"I don't know," Maddy said. "I feel so—odd."

Fane reached over and patted her hand. "Jitters. Marriage. First night's always the worst."

Durham cleared his throat. "Really, Fane. Have a little delicacy."

"Beg pardon!" The colonel flushed and busied himself with feeding a sausage to Devil. "Forgot myself."

"What do you know about marriage anyway?"

The colonel kept his eyes down. "Sisters. My mother said that to 'em. Begging your pardon, ma'am."

"It's all right," Maddy said. "I would be glad of thy mother's advice. I haven't had my own mother for many years."

"I'm sorry to know it, ma'am." His momentary embarrassment vanished. "Too bad mine ain't here. She'd set you straight on things in a snap."

"Well, she ain't," Durham said. "Thank God." He looked at Maddy. "Shev coming along soon, do you think?"

"I don't know." She looked down at the congealing porridge in her dish. "After ye left, he fell asleep in a chair. The steward said he doesn't usually have help when he retires, so I thought it best—I didn't want to make them wonder about him more than they do already—so I thought . . ." She pushed her plate away. "So I left him there!" she said all at once. "And I shouldn't have done so ! It was because I was afraid of the steward and didn't want to ask where the duke would sleep, so I just went where I was taken, and he didn't ever come, and I couldn't find my way back!"

An uncomfortable silence greeted this information. Maddy stood up and went to the window. Through the expanse of wavy antique glass, she could see all across the valley below, the trees and fields in morning shadow, the twisting glint of a river amid gray and brown.

"Look at this," she said hopelessly. "Look at this place. No one will ever think I belong here. Oh . . . I want to go home!"

She pressed her forehead against the casement. Devil

came and nosed her hand. She pulled it away, hugging herself.

"Archimedea," Durham said. "Shev's getting better, isn't he?"

"Yes."

"I could tell it. Even in a few days."

She stared out the window. "Every day is better. When I first saw him at Blythedale Hall, he didn't speak at all."

"So—perhaps soon—he'll be well. He'll pass their bloody hearing, and this will be over."

She said nothing.

"There are some obstacles directly before us," Durham acknowledged. "His family will come the instant I tell them. Lady de Marly—but you know about her. Shev thinks she won't mind the marriage; I don't know, but you'd best be prepared for anything. The rest of 'em—no doubt about it— I'd be lying if I told you there won't be the devil of a dust- up—but if you will just stand firm—I'm sure there's nothing they can do. Nothing. If they try to haul him away—why, we'll call in the lord-lieutenant."

"Shev is the lord-lieutenant," Fane said.

"Egad, yes—must be. He owns the whole bleeding county. Is he Justice of the Peace too? But never mind—I'll find out. Just stand pluck—and we'll get through it to the other side."

She whirled around. "What other side? There is no other side for me. I cannot be married to him. I cannot be a duchess!"

Durham watched her intently. "You don't want to be a duchess . . . or you don't want to be married to Shev?"

"Thou wilt not understand!" she cried. "I *cannot!* I cannot be either one. I will be disowned when Friends know of it."

He nodded slowly. "I see." He took a breath. "I didn't know that. I knew you were a little disinclined by your be- liefs."

"Disinclined!" Maddy echoed. She turned back to the

window and gave a small laugh. Devil jumped up onto the window seat and pressed himself against her. She could not help but stroke his head; it was the only way to prevent him from planting his paws on her shoulders and licking her face.

"The marriage—" Durham hesitated. "That won't—be solace enough for your loss?"

He asked it gently, but she could hear the argument in his voice. He thought wealth and a castle and being a duchess should compensate for anything.

"Thou dost not understand," she said softly. "Thou wilt not understand." She stroked the dog's silken ears. "I will never belong here."

"You have to give yourself a little time. You aren't accustomed. It's a big old haunt of a place, I know. Bloody cold, too. We've all got lost in it now and then."

"Oh," she said, her voice trembling, "I'm lost right now."

"He needs you."

"Needs me? Dost thou truly think I can stop anyone from doing anything? Look at me. At this castle. No one would listen to me!"

She bit her lip hard. She would not indulge in tears of weakness over what was already done. But if it were not done, not truly . . .

She spoke without turning around. "I ask thee—is there a way to undo this marriage now? Is it too late?"

There was a pause.

"You wish to undo it?"

"Yes."

"Listen to me," Durham said. "Just for an instant, forget your religion. Forget everything but Shev. His family will find out he's here, whether I tell them or not. When they come, Fane and I can do our best, but if he can't speak, if he can't act for himself yet—they can put us out on our ear. But you—the Duchess of Jervaulx—you can put *them* out. You can protect him. Legally. Until he is himself again."

"Art thou certain of that?" She stared at the sparkling river until her eyes began to hurt. Devil left her suddenly, pulling away and leaping down from the window seat.

"It makes sense, don't it?" Durham asked. "Just let the thing stand. At least until he is well enough to protect himself."

"Then there is a way to undo it."

"Possibly."

"Thou must tell me how."

"Will you promise to stay as long as he needs you?"

"Tell me how."

"For God's sake, Maddy. Will you leave him?"

"Tell me!" She gripped her hands into fists. The river made her eyes water, so bright and silvery in the winter landscape. She could not break her gaze away from it.

Durham said in a low, flat voice, "You haven't slept with him."

It was only half a question. Maddy felt her cheeks burning. She shook her head.

"Then don't. Don't consummate it. And when you decide you can't bear with being a duchess and his wife any longer, then come to me, Your Grace." His voice had gone bitter. "And I'll tell you the rest of what you need to know to nullify the vow you made."

She heard the sound of his chair scraping. Then he swore softly.

She turned—and found Jervaulx, with Devil and Cass at his feet, standing in the closed doorway, watching her.

Christian went out on the battlements when he wanted to be alone. He knew them all, kept them in repair and kept them to himself, reserving the keys for every staircase door that let onto the roofs. The higher the better—and the highest tower at Jervaulx put him above anything else he could see.

Muffled in his greatcoat, he leaned on the whitewashed stone embrasure of a crenel. From here he looked down on the circuit of the curtain wall to the Whitelady Tower, oldest, square and squat, a border sentry joined by the Knight's

Tower, and beyond that the tower called Phoenix, circling to the Northwest Tower and its range of Elizabethan lodgings rebuilt and redesigned by Christopher Wren, where they'd put Maddy in his mother's room last night—and Beauvisage and Mirabile, out of sight round the curve of Belletoile that he stood on.

He knew them. He loved them. When he'd awoken this morning, he hadn't even remembered that anything was different, that he was anyone but the Duke of Jervaulx and master of his life and this castle and his own fate. Then he'd tried to speak to the footman who brought his tea.

He was glad that he hadn't been able to say anything at all. He'd passed for surly, no doubt, instead of an idiot. But it was only a reprieve; he couldn't go on silent with the staff forever.

And Maddy. He put his arms on the wall and his head down in them.

In all honesty, it had taken him a little while to remember her. It was when he got out of bed and found himself still dressed that he began to realize. And even then, he'd not been really disturbed, only a little chagrined to have fallen asleep on his wedding night. He'd bathed and dressed, using the services of the footman, who was passably good—and serenely agreeable in the face of Christian's moody silence, obviously having been selected for this impromptu post on the basis of having ambitions to valet.

On the way downstairs, Christian had thought of how he'd make it up to her. Even at the risk of sounding a dimwit, he determined to make it clear where his wife was to sleep. He'd been considering how to accomplish that when he'd walked in and found Durham advising her not to sleep with him at all.

Christian had feigned not understanding. Easy enough. He'd just stood there, and they took him for stupid. Mute. Deaf. Dumb.

She'd looked guiltily at him. But he'd given her a smile, gone to the sideboard and poured himself chocolate.

I understand, Maddygirl.

Between white stone and a sky of watercolor gray and blue, the wind funneled around Belletoile, blowing Christian's collar against him. It was a novel notion, that anyone could dismiss Jervaulx. Not dismiss it—reject it. And him.

He could understand that part—damaged as he was—but it hardly made the wound any less. He had thought—he had assumed—that what he was missing would be amply recompensed by what he had to offer. Jervaulx itself, and all that went with it: no small treasure. He had thought, when she was here, when she beheld it, she would see in it what he saw.

Well, if she did not—she didn't.

Maddygirl. Will you go then?

He stared at the sky. He felt impotent, aching and angry and helpless.

With a curse, he rammed his fists into the pockets of his greatcoat. If she wished to nullify what she'd done, let it be nullified. Durham pleaded with her to stay until she was not needed, but Christian did not even require that. It had been a decision made out of weakness and muddleheadedness, to make her his wife. She was a Quaker. A nobody. She did not, as she so plainly stated, belong here.

Let her go.

He was better. He was going to be perfect. Let her go. He did not need her or what flimsy protection she could offer. He would not miss her. He would hardly know that she had gone, *stubborn little prim kiss sweet.*

He gazed at the winter hills. He'd taken it—this castle, his heritage—for granted in his life. He had tried not to do it, but he had. Trifling in reform, fighting sham battles, all the time safe in his impregnable tower. All the time not knowing what a fortune he had.

He could lose it again. He felt a new and bone-deep chill. Was it even his now? He'd fled to Jervaulx by instinct; the place functioned at his command by inbred custom. But they'd stripped him to nothing in Chancery. If they came here—if they tried to take him—

Imprisoned, chained, defeated. Crushed.

He would not let it happen.

He knew everything there was to know about Jervaulx. He knew that it was two hundred and seventy-three feet from the ramparts of Belletoire to level ground. He kept the tower key.

He found Maddy alone in the duchess' morning parlor, looking up at a portrait of Herodias with the head of John the Baptist. Below it hung a cross of the graphically bloody variety.

"Cheer," he said, with a dry intent.

She looked round at him. "It is a sumptuous room."

"Thank." He dared her to say it had not been meant as a compliment.

She turned to another portrait, of a pair of boys leaning on a mastiff that was taller than both of them. "That one pleasant."

He made a small bow. "Brother."

"Your brothers?"

He looked at the portrait. James was real; it was Christian's own side of it that seemed nebulous, until he made himself concentrate, lifted his hand and indicated the boy in curls and short coat. "I . . . me and . . . brother. Ten. James . . . *six.* Long time . . . gone. Red . . . red . . . scarlet fever." He remembered sitting for that portrait. Oh, the pain, to be still, when there were games and fields and toads. *"Dog* was . . . Killbuck." He smiled. "Never killed . . . that dog . . . not a butterfly."

She gazed at the painting silently. This morning she was severe, her hair tight, as if she wished to be as different from her surroundings as possible.

"You want . . . to *null.*" He could not approach the subject any more subtly than that. "Wedding?"

She looked at him sharply and put her hands behind her back.

"Understand," he said. "Breakfast . . . Durham undo . . . wedding."

"I believe—would be wise." She kept her eyes on him, level. "But I will stay thou art well enough."

"Now. Well enough! Go . . . now."

"Thou wouldst have me leave now?"

He set his jaw angrily at this twisting of accountability. "*I* . . . don't say. You. Breakfast at . . . Durham . . . the wedding undo." He walked past her. "Don't sleep with. I *heard*." He turned. "Bed . . . last night was . . . *not*. So. Undo. Call Durham . . . *now* . . . undo." He reached for the bell-rope.

"They gone," she said. "They waited thee, but thou couldst not found."

"Gone." That checked him, left him suddenly without a practical intent, bereft of action to release the hostility inside him. Christian dropped his hand. "Gone." He realized what it meant. "Too late! They . . . *call*. Say wed. Family. Devil take 'em both!"

"I've thought." She sat down in a chair and laid her hands over one another in her lap. "I believe ought stay—at least until thy hearing. If thou wouldst agree—" Her fingers slid between one another and tightened. He saw the band of his signet ring on her hand. "I ask—if thou wouldst agree we will not—consummate this marriage—then it can be undone when thou art well." She moistened her lips. "Thou wilt not need me then. I would be a burden and a sorrow thee. I do not belong in thy world. When thou art whole again, thou wilt see."

He wanted to argue with her, but he had no grounds. There was a great defeat in him, a distress that he had no words for. "If . . . not well?" he asserted. "What if . . . never whole? Leave?"

"I don't know. I can only say—I will stay until new hearing."

"Until . . . *new*?"

"Thy hearing. Before Lord Chancel again."

His whole body had gone still. "Again?"

"Yes. Thou art go again."

"When?"

"I'm not certain. Several months yet. Lady de Marly will know."

He strode two steps toward her and stopped. "New! Why?"

His aggressive approach seemed to startle her. She sat back in the chair. "Thy brothers-in-law. They insist to try again judge thee not fit."

Christian gazed at her. He had thought—

He had thought it was done already.

He began breathing in a rush, unable to make the words reeling in his head into a question. He thrust himself into a turn, paced the room, and came back.

"Mean fit . . . *now?*"

She didn't seem to understand.

"Now!" he shouted. "Comp . . . *now?* Free . . . *now?*" He grabbed her shoulders and leaned over her. *"Tell!"*

"Until thy hearing," she said, sitting still beneath his hands, "thou art the same as anyone under the law."

He stared at her, unable to let her go, to move.

"How else couldst thou think to marry?" she asked.

Of course. Of course. He'd been too befuddled; he hadn't even questioned it. He'd thought he was stripped of his legal existence, made into an imbecile. He'd been hiding behind Durham and Fane and Maddy and Jervaulx Castle itself, stupid confused hiding, as if any of that could have saved him when they came to take him back.

Another hearing. Months.

"Maddy." He gripped her harder. "Help . . . me. Well. Whole. I want . . . agree . . . no bed. Stay and helping. Agree. You go then . . . when I . . . *whole*. Hearing."

She lifted her eyes to his. "Will not consummate?"

He found her hand, caught it and clenched it. "Not. Hearing. Whole. No . . . con . . . mate . . . *bed*. Undo wed."

She lowered her lashes, those erotic eyelashes. He looked

down at her, gripping her hand, regretting what he promised even before she made a small nod to confirm it.

The agreement made things easier between them. Maddy did not feel so uncomfortable in the surroundings, knowing that it was only an interval and not a real commitment. When the duke suggested that he show her over the castle, she was willing enough to accompany him. She even consented to have one of the dowager duchess' simpler gowns re-fitted for her, as she could not continue to wear her faithful gray silk forever.

The one she chose was a dark blue satin. In the wardrobe closet, it had not looked overly rich compared to the others, especially since she insisted that the maid remove the trimming, but when she had it on and saw herself in the daylight in a looking glass, the opulence of the color was dramatic.

The girl waited. "Very nice, Your Grace," she said, holding the sewing box.

It was beautiful. Maddy had never in her life worn anything like it. She smoothed her hand down the vivid fabric. "Yes," she said, gazing at herself in wonder. "I . . . it is— very nice."

With the hem lengthened, the flounces and trim removed, and a shawl of white India silk over the puffed sleeves and exposed neckline, she was ready to meet Jervaulx in the gallery. When she saw him, she had a moment of hesitation, certain that he would think her foolish to choose such a lavish dress, but he only looked at her longer than he ought to have done, and then smiled with one corner of his mouth as he took her arm. The dress matched his eyes.

"Maddy," he said. "Sorry I . . . consent . . . no con."

She thought she might understand what he meant, but let it pass without inquiry.

The disapproving portraits stared down from the gallery walls, a prickling reminder of the eeriness she'd felt here in the night. He stopped before one of the most imposing, a huge painting of a grave and condescending personage dressed in red robes and a wide white ruff, bejeweled and kingly, holding a wand of high office. "Lord Jervaulx," he said. "First. Rule power . . . great earl."

"He is very distinguished," Maddy said in a small voice.

"Marry seventeen. A girl . . . he . . . got a rich heiress marry. She write before . . . to him . . . *letter*. I have it. She writes my sweet life . . . say my mind . . . consider allowance. Pray beseech thee . . . kind love . . . she wants . . . twenty-six hundred quarter."

"Oh," she said dubiously. "Was that not a large sum for the day?"

"Very . . . *large*." Jervaulx grinned. "Also . . . to make things clear . . . she writes . . . I want three horses own . . . two gentlewomen . . . horse each them, six or eight gentleman . . . two coaches . . . *velvet* . . . four horse each . . . two . . . *footman* . . . gentleman-usher . . . six hundred a quarter for charitable . . . all to be . . . defrayed by him."

"Very sensible," Maddy said, beginning to smile.

"Also . . . yearly . . . she would have twenty gowns . . . eight country . . . six good . . . six excellent good. Also . . . six thousand buy jewels . . . four thousand pearl chain. Also . . . all houses furnish . . . chambers . . . fit . . . beds . . . stools . . . chairs . . . cushions, carpets . . . hanging . . . *canopy*. Also . . . he would kindly pay . . . all her debts. Also . . . purchase land. Also . . . lend no money . . . Lord Chamberlain. Also . . . pray . . . when rise to . . . *earl* . . . allow two thousand more . . . double attendants."

"All this was in the letter?" Maddy was holding back a laugh by the end of this recital, not quite so awed by the poor kingly gentleman.

"Yes. He gave," Jervaulx said. "All. And never lend to . . . Chamberlain. Wise advice. Die earl . . . councillor . . . treasurer to the King. Rich. Power. He building . . . Northwest Tower. Good wife."

She made a face. "Thy idea of a good wife!"

"Yes! Rich. Shrewd. Spoilt. Fine dress. Ambition. *Good* wife."

"Thou hast certainly married the wrong woman."

He gave her a considering look. She felt herself growing warm, and wished she had not said it. As she lowered her eyes, he took her chin between his fingers, bent and kissed her lightly on the lips.

Maddy pulled away, drawing in a quick breath.

He shook his head as she began to protest, smiling like a rogue. "*Bed* . . . only promise."

He took her arm again and walked on as if nothing had happened.

Chapter Twenty-three

*L*ady de Marly arrived without warning five days after Durham and Colonel Fane had left. Maddy and Jervaulx were in the hall—Maddy was lying on her back on the floor next to him, looking up and up and up to the fantastically carved tracery in the timber roof, while he pointed out the heraldic beasts fashioned there, the trefoils and fleurs-de-lis and intricately rendered flowers and foliage shaped in the beams so far above them.

The castle seemed a different place with Jervaulx. He knew it as if it were his own self; he talked about it the way women talked about their offspring, with endless interest in the most minute particulars, with love and humor enough to make even details entertaining. She liked it in the daytime. It was only at night, when she had to retire alone to the duchess' rooms, lying in bed, listening for the footsteps to walk the floor above—it was only then that panic rose in her throat and she wished she had not asked to sleep alone.

"Go up . . . *five* . . . rafter," Jervaulx was saying, describing where she was to look, since they had long ago determined that his ability to point accurately was unreliable. "The dog's . . . face . . . do you see?"

"Mmm—yes. I see it."

"Dog. Dragon. Henry Tudor beasts."

"Which Henry?"

"Henry . . . seven. Lily's."

"Ah." She had become quite familiar with Elizabeth, that lively wife of Francis Langland, the first Lord Jervaulx, who, in return for her husband's docile compliance in the matter of her allowance, had not hesitated to further the family interests by becoming a clandestine mistress to their mysterious and clever king. Between Lily's wealth, discretion and beauty, and her husband's astute loyalty to a monarch who had come from the same mists of Wales as the young knight himself, the dynasty established by Francis Langland enjoyed an auspicious beginning.

"Gray . . . dog. Gray*hound* . . . dragon . . . look to the side." He twisted his head around on the floor. "Lily. See?"

Under the firm guidance of his hand, Maddy contorted herself. "Oh yes!" There was the lily, hidden amid the heraldic carvings until one looked at it at just the proper angle.

"Henry sent a . . . to cut. A man to cut wood."

"A carver."

"Carver."

"Was it a secret trick?"

His head was turned around close to hers. "Secret," he said. He slipped his hand into the curve of her waist. Maddy shrieked at the tickle, her voice echoing around the vast hall. She skittered away, but he caught her, rolling half on top of her, teasing her waist with one hand and clasping her cheek with the other. Maddy struggled, but not too hard. She was about to be kissed, and she liked it.

His mouth touched hers, warm in the cold hall, as velvet gentle as the stone beneath her was hard. He stopped the tickling. Her body softened; she closed her eyes and felt him over her, breathed his heat in the chilly air, heard the low sound of pleasure he made as he explored her. She had not kissed him back; she had not quite yet—but she was going to soon.

It was singular, this being wife and not-wife, free to be kissed, to tussle about the floor like puppies. It was not chaste; she knew that well enough. But he did it so sweetly, so playfully, that she never found a place to demand that he stop. "No bed," he promised her, whenever she drew back— and that eased her. It was only trifling, and pleasant, and if it was a worldly and carnal pleasure, then at least it was only for a little while, and then she would go back to being ordinary, scrupulous Maddy Timms. Exemplary Maddy Timms, with a secret memory of her own to keep, a lily hidden among the dragons of virtue.

She lifted her chin and kissed him back.

He had been her teacher: she knew how to taste his mouth, search the corners while he grew still, his lips parting a little. His body seemed to respond with a slow tautness, a tightening over her; his hands pressed into her skin. Yet he lay motionless, suspended, his mouth acquiescent to hers, as if his whole concentration was on what it felt like. His lips opened more with each contact, allowing her to seek further—inviting it.

She touched him with her tongue. He was foreign and familiar, so close and yet so strange to her. A nobleman, with fairies and Welshmen and kings in his history, lord of this hall and castle, but most alien and potent of all: a man. Sandalwood and strength, an aggressiveness she could feel held in check. His breath mingled with hers, light with anticipation.

Maddy tasted deeper. He met her with his tongue, with a visceral note in his chest and a penetrating answer. He took command of the embrace. His body closed with hers. On the floor of the hall, with his weight pressed down on her, he kissed her wholly, all play and lightness vanished.

And she returned it, opening her mouth across his. The low music beat against her, a primitive sound in his throat.

He responded to her, taking what she surrendered as easily as if he knew her mind, knew the moment that her body and her heart awakened to sensation.

He locked his hands with hers and spread them out on the cold stone. His signet ring drove into her finger, caught between his hand and hers, painful pressure down to the bone, but she wanted it. She wanted it there, as she wanted him. Everything inside her arched upward to meet his kiss. It seemed that she had been bound up, held tight by threads that he had broken with a touch.

She heard herself, like a whimpering child, moaning with the terrible pleasure of it. She moved; she could not help it, taking the rhythm that he gave her with his tongue, arching to find more.

"*Most* edifying." Lady de Marly's voice was like a cascade of ice water.

Maddy jerked. Jervaulx stilled for an instant—but instead of springing away, he held tighter against Maddy's convulsive effort to extricate herself. Without looking up, he kissed her ear. "Calm," he said, muffled against her. "Calm, Maddygirl." Then he kissed her briefly again, and lifted himself away.

She scrambled to her feet. Jervaulx stood. Lady de Marly, with a maid behind her and her stick planted in front, was a white, grim face painted upon a black statue.

"Aunt Vesta," Jervaulx said, with a slight bow. He took Maddy's arm. She could not move of her own accord; he pulled her closer to him and drew her forward. "Welcome," he said, amazing Maddy with his composure. All of her own self-possession had vanished. "Pleasant . . . *trip?*"

Maddy saw the way his speech caught Lady de Marly's attention, a gratifying respite from focus on herself.

The elderly woman stared at him, a long and arctic scrutiny.

"You are recovered," she said at last.

"*Better,*" Jervaulx said. The pressure of his hand forced

Maddy forward. "Duchess . . . Arc . . . *mede*. Honor of . . . *wife*." His speaking had regressed. With Maddy alone, he could already express himself more smoothly than that.

"Not much better," Lady de Marly said dryly. She glanced at Maddy. "And you, Miss. You have outfoxed us all indeed. I had not taken you for an adventuress."

"Duchess," Jervaulx said, with an emphasis more of warning than of effort.

"Where are the documents?"

Jervaulx smiled darkly at her. He said nothing.

"Impudent boy," she snapped.

"Legal," he said. "Age. Resident. Special . . . paper. Church. Witness. Register . . . write sign. No lawful . . . stop."

"Except perhaps your sanity," she responded, but it sounded less a threat than a grumble. "Bedlamite. You might have taken the girl you were offered and saved us both a peck of trouble."

"Miss . . . Trothorse."

"Miss Trotman. Whose father threatens to sue you for breach of promise."

"Me!" He laughed outright. "You promise. You . . . *pay*."

By the set of her jaw, it was obvious that he had made a point. She hit her stick on the floor, and the sharp sound echoed round the hall. Maddy found herself the object of that cold-hearted stare. "I will retire to rest. You, Miss— Duchess. You will attend me in one hour in my chamber."

There was no evading it. Maddy nodded.

Lady de Marly creaked and tapped her way across the hall. The maid, almost as elderly as her mistress, gave Maddy a quick glance, and hurried after. Strangely, it had almost seemed as if the maid had smiled.

"Call you . . . *duchess*." Jervaulx looked at Maddy sideways. "She will . . . conceded."

Occupying all of one of the oldest ranges of the castle, Lady de Marly's customary apartments still had the chill of disuse. Blanketed and swathed up to her chin, she had established herself in the inglenook of a mammoth hearth. The fire was robust, but in most of the room one's breath still frosted.

Lady de Marly might have conceded that Maddy was the duchess, but she gave no extra deference to the fact. Under the all-encompassing title of "girl," Maddy was ordered into a straightbacked chair that did not quite fit into the nook, where in a very short time, her front was roasted and her back freezing.

With no other overture, Lady de Marly said, "I took pains to stop at this St. Matthew's on my way. The marriage is registered in the parish book."

"Yes," Maddy said. She had signed herself there—the worst and most concrete of her offenses, she feared.

"I also inquired into the Notice Book at Doctors' Commons. The issuance of a special license for the marriage of the Duke of Jervaulx and Archimedea Timms is duly remarked. 'Twould appear that it is as he said. All is in order."

"Is it?" Maddy knew nothing of the formalities of the process outside of Friends. She felt an odd relief that Durham had after all been truthful.

"That comforts you, I see. Did you think it was not?"

Maddy looked at her skirt and then up again. "Verily, it would not have surprised me to find it unlawful in some way. It was—done in much haste, at Durham's urging."

"And was it indeed?" Within the hood of her shawl, Lady de Marly's eyes were sharp.

"Yes." Maddy took a deep breath. "Thou knowest that the duke will do anything to avoid confinement. He has done this in order that I may help to protect him from it. I would not have consented—I would have searched for another way, but with half a dozen of thy men breaking in at the door of the church—"

"*My* men? Breaking in? You're mistaken, miss. No one in my service had to do with this debacle."

"There were men there—intent to take him."

"Take him!" Lady de Marly hunched down in her blanket. "His mother is a fool." Her lips wrinkled in contempt. "As if he were a common criminal. I knew nothing of this."

"Durham told us that when he returned to London, hirelings had been asking after him and the duke. He feared that they would follow him out of town, and he could think of no answer but to arrange for the special license in case they should, so that someone might be able to say them nay."

"Cocklehead! He should have come to me! I could have said them nay, and soon enough." Unexpectedly, the old woman chuckled. "But Jervaulx prefers to hide behind a prettier face, does he? His appetites outweigh his judgment. Those jackals that his sisters married will have him yet, if he don't show more wit. Mark me, if there were hired men brought in, we can guess who put that pretty notion into his mother's head. Wretched vulgarians. Hired men, do you believe it! We'll have a reward in the newspapers next. Wanted—the mad Duke! It's a blessing that his father never lived to see this, God rest him." She took a deep inhalation of salts, and then her hand disappeared among the blankets and shawls again. "The new petition for a writ has already been filed. Did he have you first before the wedding, or after?"

"Have me do what?" Maddy asked.

Lady de Marly snorted. "Have relations with you, Duchess," she said in an ironical tone.

As if her body understood before her mind, Maddy grew flushed all over. When full comprehension of the question burst upon her, she had to make a conscious effort to keep herself still in the chair, although it scraped back over the hearth a little with the force of her reaction. She was vividly aware of the maid sitting somewhere further from the fire and Lady de Marly's acid surveillance. "Not before," she mumbled.

"Tell me the truth—and speak up, girl. I'm not interested in your morals. I'm interested in an heir."

Maddy lifted her chin. "Not before," she repeated, with more emphasis.

"When was your last monthly?"

"Thou art intrusive!" Maddy said.

"When one becomes a duchess, my girl, one finds oneself intruded upon in these matters. When?"

Maddy stayed stubbornly silent.

"I wonder at your reserve, considering the public display to which I found myself treated this afternoon." Lady de Marly leaned back and pushed the shawl from her head, revealing a black cap and jet ribbons. "Although I suppose it bodes well for the fruitfulness of the marriage. Tell me about Jervaulx. He is much restored."

Maddy was relieved to go on to another topic. "Yes. He's better even than thou hast heard, when he is at ease."

Lady de Marly nodded. "I'd pondered bringing in another physician—but where's the good of it? We've had a hundred. I think he does well enough with you." She lifted one white, twig-like finger. "Make no mistake, girl. This marriage is a disgrace. I'd have had better for him, but as long as it's been made legal—one breeder's as good as the next in the circumstances." She shrugged. "He seems to like you well enough."

"Your mother sent a letter," Lady de Marly announced in the drawing room after dinner. She produced a paper from beneath her shawl and held it out to Jervaulx. Just as he was about to take it, she held it back a little. "Shall I read it for you?"

He plucked it from her hand. "I . . . *read*." He took it to his chair and sprawled there. He held the sealed missive between his hands, then put it on his knee. Lady de Marly watched him intently, as if to judge whether he was truly going to read it or just make the motion.

He turned the letter over. He pushed it onto his other knee. Finally he stood up, brought it to Maddy, and commanded, *"Open."*

After she'd broken the wax seal, he returned to his chair and read. He took a long time about it, turning his head slightly to the right as if he could not quite see the writing straight on. Finally he sighed, rolled his eyes, and tossed it on the table beside him. Then he gave Maddy a sly grin. "Not . . . coming."

"She says no more than that?" Lady de Marly asked.

Jervaulx picked up the letter again and let it unfold from his fingers. "Pray. Pray. Lots of . . . pray. Set . . . not . . . foot . . . with same house . . . my miss. Mistress." He glanced at Maddy. "You." He consulted the letter again. "Sisters . . . not allow. Unnature . . . son." He crumpled it in one hand and lobbed it into the fire from across the room.

"She is not pleased with your choice," Lady de Marly commented.

"Legal," Jervaulx said. "Not . . . mistress. *Wife*."

"To be sure," his aunt said. "But you leave yourself open, you know. There is the question of whether you are in your right mind. What are the provisions? Is the estate protected? What if Miss Timms is a fortune-hunter who has trapped an imbecile in her web?"

"He is not—"

Lady de Marly interrupted Maddy. "I speak only of questions, Duchess. Your position is weak. This marriage can only tell against him at his hearing. No rational man of his rank would have contracted it."

The duke stood up suddenly. He went to the writing desk, picked up the pen and held it out to her. "Settlement now. Write . . . what you want."

"What I want?" Maddy asked.

Lady de Marly snorted.

Jervaulx smiled suddenly. "My sweet life," he said. "Three horses own . . . two gentlewomen . . . twenty gowns . . . all chambers fit . . . beds . . . cushions . . . carpets . . . six or eight gentlemen." He laid the pen in her hand. "Maddygirl. What you want."

"I want nothing."

Lady de Marly laughed outright, as if she had made a joke. Jervaulx gazed down at Maddy a moment and then knelt beside her chair. "Nothing?"

She shook her head helplessly. "Of course not."

He looked into her eyes, his head tilted a little. He had the ghost of a gentle smile on his lips. "Father?" he asked. "Not you then . . . support father?"

"Oh . . ." She bit her lip, sorely tempted. "No. It would not be right."

Lady de Marly spoke abruptly. "You had best not carry this pretty act too far, girl. If he died tonight, there's not a provision for you anywhere. Not a shilling would you get, and you may believe it. State some reasonable and provident sums, and the court will think the better of you for your common sense. Calvin and I can witness your hand, and the duke's."

"But—" Maddy looked to him. "I want no sums. Thee and me—we aren't to—"

He put his hand over hers, a sharp squeeze. She understood that well enough. For a moment the room was silent.

"Maddygirl," he said. "I owe now . . . everything." He smiled at her, such a smile—it made her heart ache. "Give back . . . you . . . a little."

"Thou dost not owe anything to me," she whispered.

He let go of her and stood up. "How much . . . Trotman?" He looked at his aunt.

"She brought ten thousand," Lady de Marly said.

He made an impatient gesture of his hand. "How much?"

"A jointure of fifty-two hundred. Allowance the same, and life interest in a quarter of the Monmouth rents upon your death. Mind you, Miss Trotman brought ten thousand with her. Fifty thousand to be distributed among female issue on marriage with consent. Seventy-five thousand among second, third and fourth male issue, fifty among any other males, the same terms. Remainder to the heir."

He laughed. "Busy . . . wife."

Lady de Marly lifted her thin brows and scanned Maddy. "She looks in prime health for the task."

"Tomorrow," he said. "I send for . . . Bailey. You tell settlement. Write same . . . what you said. Add . . . two thousand annual . . . *life* . . . Mr. John Timms. Careful . . . mistake. I can . . . read."

"But—" Maddy said.

"Want," Jervaulx interjected. "*I* . . . want."

She sat back in her chair. It was all a parody; she had gone so far into falsehood that it had come to the writing of preposterous documents providing for the children of a marriage that would not exist. With a sudden spirit, she stood up. "I will retire."

Jervaulx bowed. Lady de Marly actually smiled. She held out her hand. "Good night to you, Duchess."

Maddy took it. The old lady squeezed her with gaunt fingers, turning up one cheek. Maddy hesitated, and then bent and gave her a brief kiss. Lady de Marly started to let go, and then grasped the duke's signet, lifting it upright on Maddy's finger. "Is this the best you could do, Jervaulx? For heaven's sake, boy, get her a proper wedding ring."

"*Will*," he agreed.

Maddy withdrew her hand as Lady de Marly released it. She went to the door, already not looking forward to the long walk down dim corridors and across the dark hall.

"It's the other door, girl," Lady de Marly said irritably. "Don't open that one—you'll let the chill in!"

Maddy faltered. She was quite certain that this was the correct door.

"Maddy," the duke said. She looked at him. He inclined his head toward an entrance that she had not used before.

Obediently, she crossed the room and opened that door. It led into a room as magnificent as all the rest—a bedroom, done in the phoenix colors of white and blue. Above the formidable tall bed, a golden coronet crowned the canopy.

Belatedly, she realized what it meant. She stopped in the doorway. This was Jervaulx's chamber.

She turned around and came out. "I prefer—"

Lady de Marly interrupted her. "Nonsense," she said, as if she knew exactly what Maddy had intended to say. "Why should he have to chase you across half the county? Sleep in there, girl. There'll be years enough ahead for your own chamber."

Jervaulx said nothing. He stood in the middle of the room, his hands locked behind his back, tall and elegant. He just looked at her, deep blue eyes and mystery.

"Years enough, girl," Lady de Marly repeated, in a voice that had grown old and timeworn. "You mark my words."

Maddy sat up in a gilt chair with a knobbed and railed back, well calculated to prevent anyone from falling asleep. The duke's bedchamber had a more lived-in look than any of the others she had seen. In addition to the intimidating bed and the coronet, a low case held books that lay tilted and piled on one another as if they were used often; stacks of papers and journals on a writing desk before the window had the look of real work instead of company show.

An oil lamp was lit there. The neat banking of each pile seemed likely to Maddy to be a servant's contribution rather than Jervaulx's. She recalled the quick disarray he had made of the study at St. Matthew's and felt sympathy for the responsible maid, who would have to take care not to displace anything in her tidying, no doubt caught between the housekeeper's standards and the duke's jumble, which he would certainly claim was perfectly organized in his own abstruse system. Maddy was familiar with such arrangements. It would consist entirely of shoving whatever he was not working on out of the way, heaping more work on top of that, creating another stack for a new project, pushing them back and forth as needed, taking the top off of one and putting it onto another when a journal was required from the bottom of the first, and then blaming the servants for their meddling re-arrangements when some necessary paper could not be found.

She looked mostly at the desk, because she felt embarrassed to look at the paintings. They were just what Friends found worst about the vain representation of worldly things. Even the ostensibly religious ones were lascivious—one whole wall was covered with a full-length figure of Eve, the apple at her feet and only a coyly placed hand for covering. There was a panel of women bathing in a stream, with satyrs peeking from the woods around, and one of Lady Godiva riding through the city on a white horse, with her hair spread, concealing more of the horse than herself.

The only work Maddy could observe without blushing outright was a small painting of a young woman in a Dutch headdress, turning toward the viewer as if surprised in the act of observing herself in the looking glass she held. Her smile was a blend of self-consciousness, mischief and welcome, so real, and with such shy pleasure in it that it made one want to smile in return. Maddy looked at that one for a long time, beguiled by the magic of mere paint and flat canvas made into such a living presence.

The table next to her chair held a decanter and glass, and several miniatures, all of ladies. She supposed they must be his sisters, though they did not much resemble the ladies Maddy had seen. Next to one was a watch glass with no watch, but instead a lock of bright yellow hair pressed within it. Not one of his sisters had yellow hair.

She stood up and went close to the little painting of the girl and the looking glass, trying to distinguish the brushstrokes that created the impression. It hung close to the wainscot, so that she had to lean down to look. As she bent there, the door opened softly. Maddy turned around.

Jervaulx closed the door behind the dogs, who both trotted forward, gave Maddy a brief greeting and then leaped upon the bed, curling up at the foot with the familiarity of long possession. Jervaulx stood a moment, looking at her. "Like the girl . . . paint?" he asked.

"It's a very creditable image," she said.

"Credit . . . Rembrandt."

"Oh, yes. He is very famous, is he not?"

"Somewhat." He seemed amused.

"I don't know much of paintings," she said shyly. "We aren't to have them."

"No?" He came close and stood beside her, looking at the portrait. "Why?"

She frowned a little. "The Bible says no graven image. And they are—creaturely." She cast a quick meaningful glance round the room. There was hardly a collection of images conceivable which could have been called more creaturely than his.

"I . . . like them," he said, and smiled, and touched her cheek lightly—and kissed her.

Maddy stepped back, moistening her lips. "Thy aunt is retired? I should go."

"No." He shook his head. "Stay. She is . . . there."

"This is a very awkward arrangement." Maddy made a helpless gesture toward the adjacent drawing room.

"Old . . . *fashion*.   Great   chamber . . . withdrawing room . . . bedroom." He made three marks in the air, lined in a row. "Old lords . . . eating feasting great chamber . . . after eat . . . ah—ate . . . they ate . . . *then* invite . . . friends . . . withdraw private to—drawing." He nodded back toward the drawing room. "It was . . . sign of favor. Good friends only . . . invited. Same . . . the same . . . never changed here. Great Chamber . . . to drawing . . . to bedroom. Old fashion, Jervaulx. Hundreds years."

"Still, it is awkward now. Perhaps thou art weary, and wish to go to bed."

He shrugged off his coat. "Gone days, the best of friend . . . invited . . . all the way . . . come into . . . here." He swept out his coat in a bow. "High honor to . . . you."

"I should depart. Is there another way I might go out?"

He laid the garment over a chair and started to unbutton his waistcoat, then dropped his hand. He looked at her. "Can't . . . fasten."

One button was already undone. Maddy pursed her lips. "Thou canst. Thou ought to begin to try."

"I can't," he said serenely. "You." He came and stood in

front of her, his sleeves white and full, the waistcoat exquis-
itely embroidered with tiny silver flowers, a contrast with
the solid masculine outline of his body.

He was so matter-of-fact that it was hard to be uncomfortable. She reached up and undid the buttons, then loosened
his neckcloth. There were buttons on his cream-colored
trousers, too, but she ignored them. When she finished, he
moved promptly away, leaving her with the waistcoat and
neckcloth.

She relaxed a little more, catching up his coat and carrying the clothes into the dressing closet. When she came
back, he was sitting on the chaise lounge, leaning down to
remove his shoes.

His shirt loose and his collar open, half-dressed and cavalier, he stretched his legs out on the chaise and leaned his
head back. "Tired," he said, and gave a deep sigh. "Plague
of . . . she-dragon."

The last trace of Maddy's unease vanished. "She has a
forceful character," she said with a small smile.

He reached and dragged the desk chair next to him. "You
sit . . . me."

Maddy sat down. Perhaps it was best to stay a while
longer, to make certain his aunt had left. She folded her
hands in her lap.

He looked at her sideways. "Prim . . . Maddygirl." Before
she could prevent him, he leaned over and tweaked her skirt
aside, revealing her sturdy shoes and woolen stockings beneath the elegant blue silk. "Off," he said, and sat up. He
bent down and began to unfasten them.

"Indeed thou *canst* unfasten," she said in accusation.

He grunted noncommittally, holding her ankle when she
tried to pull her foot away. "Let," he said firmly. His hand
was warm and solid on her, unyielding. Maddy bit her lip
and stopped resisting. He took off her shoes and tossed them
one by one away. "Done-up, Maddygirl?" He clasped her
feet within his palms and lifted them onto his lap, rubbing
his thumbs into the arches.

It instantly felt so wonderful and rejuvenating that her protest died on her lips. She tried to remain sitting straight, but the combination of his delightful kneading of tired muscles and the angle of her position would not allow it. "Oh. That is . . . very easing."

He made no answer, looking down at her feet as he rubbed them. Her skirt fell in a sapphire sheen to the floor, rumpling a little as he compressed her heels and then slid his hands up to the back of her ankles.

"Oh," Maddy murmured, with another sigh. She closed her eyes. He kneaded her calves, and then slipped one hand back to her toes, wriggling them apart one by one in a maneuver that was as delicious as it was singular. She gave a breathless small laugh, her eyes still closed. "I didn't know such a thing—felt so agreeable."

"Mmmm." He shifted. Maddy opened her eyes. He was repositioning himself, stretching his legs out on the chaise again. She started to withdraw her feet, but he held them, settling back. He closed his eyes and went on with his smooth massage.

"Wouldst thou prefer that I rub thy feet instead?" she offered.

"No."

Looking at him, she might have thought he was asleep, except that he continued the strong, steady circles with his thumbs against the soles of her feet, then up the sides, and all around her heels. Then her toes again, one by one, until her feet began to tingle with pleasure.

She closed her own eyes again and sat still, allowing herself to be immersed in the sensation. The hearth in his room was of the modern sort, a raised grate that sent warmth to the corners. She let the silk shawl she'd worn all day slip down off her shoulders.

"Could only Rembrandt . . . paint you," the duke said.

She found him watching her. He ran his palm along the length of her leg, a light stroke, from her ankle to her knee.

"This way . . . paint . . . so I can remember."

His hands ceased their motion. The room was silent, except for the slow faint hiss of steam from the coals. In the light of the oil lamp, curves of indigo and cobalt draped down her skirt, rich color against the stark white of her stockings. His hand lay across her exposed leg, motionless.

He was watching it, his face dark and harsh in the lamplight. He looked up sideways at her. "Friend?"

She made no answer, too full of feeling to put words to it.

"Friend you, Maddy . . . always. Don't . . . forget."

"No," she whispered. "I will not forget thee."

He moved abruptly, setting her feet away. She drew them underneath her as he rose. "Sleep here," he said. "I . . . bedding closet."

There was a sleeping cot in the dressing room; Maddy had seen it when she took his clothes. "Oh, no. That would not be fair. I will go when thy aunt is retired."

"Go? Long way, Maddygirl. Dark. Not-alive. Ghost. Stay here."

"Ghost?" Maddy said.

"Bad . . . *ghost*." He looked at her, all pirate innocence. "Didn't tell?"

"There is no ghost."

He made a sound in his throat, the most blood-curdling low moan. Devil lifted his head, looking up alertly from a comfortable curl on the bed.

"There is no ghost!"

"One step . . . one step . . ." Jervaulx stood in half-light, his eyes glittering. "Hall . . . walk . . . slow . . . up the stairs."

She took a deep breath, found her shoes, and stuck her feet into them. She marched to the door. "I shall go back with Lady de Marly."

"She won't like. Want you here. Sleep." He grinned. "Choice. Dragon . . . ghost . . . me."

"There—is—no—ghost!"

He did not say there was, and he did not say there wasn't. Maddy peeked out into the drawing room and found that

Lady de Marly had already gone. The chamber was dark, growing cool, with only the last orange winking eyes of the coals casting a dim light over the carpet. She thought of ringing for Calvin Elder and realized how late it had become. Besides, it was ridiculous and unchristian to fear ghosts. Devil hopped down from the bed and came to her.

"Wilt thou attend me?" she asked the dog.

Devil wagged his tail. He jumped up and put his paws on her skirt.

She looked up at Jervaulx archly. "We'll take a candle."

He bowed and opened his hand. "Fare . . . well."

"Come," she said to the dog, who trotted obediently ahead of her out the door.

Frigid air washed in the drawing room door as she opened it into the corridor. Devil slipped out and disappeared instantly beyond the wavering globe of candlelight.

"Come back!" she demanded in a hiss. Her words echoed, returning as sinister whispers.

The dog, its nails clicking on stone, came back and jumped up on her. She petted it and started ahead. Devil fell away, trotting on again, vanishing. She quickened her steps, squinting into the quivering shadows cast by the candle.

Her shoes, unbuckled, made scuffling clunks against the floor. She stopped once. The corridor was full of reverberations that died away, leaving cold silence. If there were another person in the entire mammoth pile of stone besides herself, there was no sign of it now. Her breath frosted. She turned behind her.

A man was standing there.

She gave a gasp, jumping back, realizing even as she did that it was one of the suits of armor at motionless attention, the flux of her candle giving it the illusion of strange life.

"Devil!" she called softly, urgently, forcing herself to turn her back on the figure.

In a moment, she heard the reassuring click of dog paws, and Devil's familiar white-speckled shape appeared out of the gloom. This time, she bent a little and grasped the animal's ruff, forcing it to stay with her.

They went forward together to the top of the stair. Maddy stopped there. She heard nothing but Devil's tongue as he took advantage of the moment to lie down and lick at one of his paws.

The stairs swept downward in a broad curve, an invitation into blackness. The memory of the duke's chilling moan came to her, so vivid that she whirled around again to see if he had followed her to tease her with it.

The wide corridor stood empty. As Maddy turned to the stair, Devil's ears lifted.

He stood up, staring down into the dark ahead.

Maddy felt a terrible prickle come over her. Her eyes began to water.

The dog leaned over the stair. He bristled. A low, menacing growl rose in his throat. Maddy's breath seemed to leave her all at once.

He leaped forward with a snarling bark.

Maddy broke and ran.

She had her skirts in one hand, the candle in the other. Her shoes slapped, awkward, echoing as if there were something treading sharply after her. Devil came beside her and ran ahead into the dark. She rushed faster, making little whimpers in her throat, feeling the footsteps behind catching up; when she saw the dog scrabbling at a door, she shoved it open, threw the candle onto the stone floor behind her and slammed the barrier shut. She found herself in the duke's chamber. He was turning around, his shirt in one hand. Maddy hurled herself against his bare chest, whirling so that he was between her and the door.

"There's something *there!*" she cried. "The dog—the Devil—there's something in the hall!"

Chapter Twenty-four

"*M*addygirl. Maddygirl." He held her hard, rocking her, chuckling quietly. "It's all right. There's nothing. Nothing there."

In his arms, the convulsive shivers were subsiding. She felt silly even as she clung to him. There was nothing there. Of course there was nothing. "The dog growled," she lamented, her voice still holding a high-pitched break. "He was looking down the *stairs*."

Another shiver took her. She drew in a deep breath, trying to gather her wits. Devil had jumped on the bed and sat looking at her, absurdly unconcerned.

The watering of her eyes had wetted her cheeks. He touched a tear with his forefinger.

"I'm sorry!" she said. "I know there's—nothing there! I'm so—stupid! At night—in my room—I hear footsteps!"

He folded her closer into his shoulder. "Maddygirl. I'm sorry. It's my fault." He hugged her. "Come. Let's go see what it was."

"Oh, no. I'd rather not!"

But with his arm around her shoulder, he took her to the door. Just outside, the candle she'd thrown down lay in the stone corridor, still burning. He picked it up, not letting go of her. The light flared as he held it up high and fed one of the oiled flambeaux to life. He kept her against him, striding across to the next torch and lighting it, illuminating the corridor as they progressed. The dogs ranged ahead and back.

At the top of the stairs, he snuffed the candle against the wall and pulled the last torch from its bracket. With Maddy beneath his arm, the whole staircase lit by the intense flame, they went down.

As bright as it was, the darkness in the hall ate up the light of the single torch. Jervaulx let go of her at the foot of the steps, handed her the flambeau, and went to a huge crank on the wall. He pulled the brake free, and with a clanking of gears, a rope began to pay out from the wheel.

The torch caught the shadow of a mass descending, illuminated the two immense iron chandeliers declining ponderously from above. When they were within reach, he set the brake again and took the torch, walking from candle to candle, lighting the whole range of both pendants. Slowly the great room began to brighten, lighting him as well, the golden blaze on his bare skin, his hair as dark as the deepest corners of shadow.

Finally he stood back, holding up the torch, a pagan god in the barren hall.

"Better?" he asked.

Maddy had long before begun to feel very, very foolish. "Oh, yes," she said in a tiny voice. "Thank thee."

Devil suddenly let out a bark and scrambled after a shadow that thumped down from the minstrels' gallery onto a table below. The two raced across the floor, the tabbycat making a tremendous leap and disappearing into a niche inside the fireplace just an inch ahead of Devil's nose.

"The ghost," Jervaulx said.

A bewildered young footman in his shirtsleeves appeared in one of the arched doorways beneath the gallery. The duke looked toward him.

"We dispatch . . . specters," he said. When the servant came into the hall, he held out the torch. "Snuff them. The candles . . . up . . . the morning."

The footman took the light and bowed. Jervaulx came to her.

"Thank thee. I was silly. Perhaps—I should go to my room now," she said.

He took her around the shoulders and started for the stairs that led to his own. The dogs came, running ahead. Maddy thought of the dark gallery and the halls and stairs between her and the dowager duchess' apartment. She thought of the footsteps. She didn't believe in ghosts, but in a place like this, it was a fine thing to have two dogs and a large, vigorous and very substantial male striding along the reverberating passages beside her.

Ghosts. Christian rested his arms behind his head, grinning up into the darkness of the dressing room. Maddygirl—his prim, righteous, practical Maddygirl—was afraid of ghosts.

Jervaulx Castle had them, of course. Any number. He'd had to lie extravagantly in reassuring her. His favorite was the staghound that slept before the tremendous hearth in the hall on Christmas Eve. He'd seen it himself, when James was still alive, one cold night after Mass. They'd thought it was a stray got in past the gatehouse, but when they'd called out to it, it had risen, and stretched, and loped away to vanish right through the carved wood of the screens passage. The story—that the dog's place of honor by the fire had been earned saving the lord's child from drowning and that the ghost appeared as guardian, a signal that the lady of the castle was soon to produce and safely raise another offspring— he thought the tale overly maudlin for any self-respecting apparition. But it was true that his youngest sibling Katherine had been born that next year, and was still alive and in perfect health at twenty-five—unlike three of his brothers and two sisters not so fortunate. He sighed, thinking of

James. And Clair, and Anne, and sweet William Francis. His mother had her reasons for curdling into a religious zealot. Perhaps they should have left a leg of mutton out to entice the ghostly hound to come more often.

He hadn't told Maddy about the staghound. On his own account, he'd let only one small truth slip—that above the duchess' bedchamber was the Black Guard's Walk. He didn't even have to tell her the story that went with it; he could see that the mere name was enough.

He smiled. She would stay with him from now on.

Maddy snuggled down in the duke's bed. She was in her chemise, having no gown with her, but still warm and secure. Devil and Cass lay at the foot of the bed, breathing soft occasional sighs.

She did not instantly go to sleep, as comfortable as she was. There were several pillows; she'd shifted around among them until she'd found the one she was certain was Jervaulx's. She lay on it, breathing in the scent of him.

Somewhere between upright Archimedea Timms and total wanton surrender to fleshly temptation was someone new to her: a person who liked pretty colored dresses, and having her feet rubbed, and kisses. And a pillow that held the presence of the man who slept in the next room, close enough to come to her aid if she should be threatened by the Black Guard.

Harbored as she was, the trepidation was only a delicious tremor—an excuse to recall how solidly he'd held on to her when she'd burst into the room in her headlong flight. There were no ghosts. Jervaulx said there were not. Devil had growled at a cat, and the duke had lit the whole hall and sent specters into oblivion against his glowing solid reality, his body in torchlight, in the incandescent flame of two hundred candles.

She tried to listen for his breathing from the other room. But of course the door was shut—almost shut; he'd left it open a crack for her, and she couldn't hear anything but the dogs' quiet inhalation.

She gazed upward into the dark. And then she did a reckless thing.

She pushed the bedclothes back and rose, climbing down from the high bed. The last of the fire cast a color that did not light anything, but she remembered the path to the dressing room door. She slipped her bare feet over the floor, feeling her way.

She felt the wall and the doorframe. She stopped.

"Jervaulx?" she whispered.

If he were asleep, it was too soft to wake him. But he instantly said, "Maddygirl?"

She took a breath. "I'm . . ." She could not quite lie and say that she was still afraid. "I'm . . . shaky."

That was true enough. She shivered as she stood there, from cold and agitation.

She heard the creak of his cot. In a moment the door slipped from beneath her fingers and he was there, a warm shadow. He touched her, finding her arm, outlining her, holding her up close against him. "Scare?"

She said nothing, only pressed herself into the embrace. He was still bare-chested, and she felt a surge of guilt for not seeing that he was properly taken care of.

It was a kiss that she'd wanted, and he gave it to her—light and gentle, his tongue briefly tasting her lips. "With . . . you?" he asked, exerting a pressure against her, guiding her into the main room.

Maddy drew back, not certain what she wished, beyond her flimsy pretext, her excuse for carnal kisses. He stood close to her, not quite touching.

"Scared?" he asked, offering her such easy justification. "Want . . . stay with you?"

She shivered again.

He chuckled softly. "Poor Maddygirl. Come here."

So warm and bare and smooth he was as he enclosed her

in his arms—his shoulder, his skin against her cheek. When he prompted her to move toward the bed, she went with him. In the dimness, he knew it better than she: he turned when they reached it and hiked himself up onto the high bedstead. The dogs shifted about, sniffing at Maddy as Jervaulx gave her his hand and drew her up with him.

"Off," the duke ordered them firmly, at which they retreated as far as the foot of the bed.

Maddy could only see him as an indistinct outline of motion against the paler bedclothes as he settled into the bed. He made a luxurious low sound of pleasure. "Warm here . . . *you* . . . Maddygirl."

She was still sitting up among the sheets, nervous and doubtful at the way things had gone beyond her intention. He caught her, drawing her down next to him. His body seemed to come all around hers: her back pressed up against him, his leg raised in the hollow of her knee. He leaned over her, kissed her shoulder and her throat.

He slid the sleeve of her shift downward. His fingers slipped over her skin, drifting to her breast. Behind her ear, at the margin of her hair, he stroked her with his tongue. There was a boldness to his caresses, an intention.

"Thou said . . ." Maddy could hardly find her voice. "Thou agreed—"

All of his movement stilled. His hand rested on her arm.

He made a soft groan. He buried his face in the curve of her shoulder for an instant and then fell back against the bed.

Maddy stared into the dark. She was relieved and disappointed at once, scared of things beyond ghosts.

Suddenly he pulled her into his arms again and held her very hard, rubbing his cheek against her hair. All along her back he pressed into her. She realized with a shock that he had nothing on at all and was in a state of animal arousal.

He relaxed his overpowering embrace. With a deep sigh, he cradled her. His arm lay beneath her head, a solid heat against her cheek.

For a long time they rested that way.

"Jervaulx—" she said into the dark.

"My name." His breath warmed her neck when he spoke. "Christian." He leaned a little closer. *"Wife."*

She felt guilty and ashamed. It was not he who had demanded that the marriage be kept undone. It was not he who had got up in the night and come to her.

He made no other move. Asked nothing of her. Only lay, impassioned, clasping her in the bed.

She knew what she had done. She had already yielded to the weakness of her earthly self. She had given the decision to him—and he, a man of honor, held to his promise better than she held to her truthfulness.

If there were ever, Christian thought, a time for his peers to question his sanity, it must be if they could see him now, with his arms around the woman he'd taken for his wife, ready for her, aching for her after days of teasing contact—and he did not do it.

Chose not to do it. Smelled the smoky-sweet scent of her hair, felt the curve of her body, the trusting delicate girl-softness under a slip of linen—all the blood in his body ran erotic—beat longing—beat *mine, mine, mine.*

He wanted her, craving more than entry; craving full possession.

And she wanted it, too. He could feel it in her: no stiff withdrawal, no animosity. He knew when a woman was hostile to him and when she was playing at indignation—and this was neither. This was just pure hell, that he could give her all the pleasure that he'd spent the past days leading her on toward; that she'd come this far, to seek him and let him lie down beside her; that he had every right.

Every right.

Hang her religion and her Friends. Was it a different God they'd pledged themselves before? Had she married an infidel? A padishah with two hundred wives?

He was just a man, with a pretty good idea of what his sins were. And wanting to have a real union with his own bride was not one of them.

She was his wife. She was his.

He held her tighter and put his face against her. "You tell . . . when to stop," he said, his voice muffled. "You say . . . you don't want."

The flame in her was slow and deep—he was going to incite it with the fire in himself; he was going to make a blaze to burn down cities, to lay waste cathedrals and castles and plain meetinghouses—to make a world where it was only him, and only her, and this bed, and one flesh.

Maddy felt the change in him before he spoke. She felt his body tighten and stir, the muscles in his arm move beneath her cheek. And then he bid her tell him.

Say—when to stop.

He raised himself above her and bent his face to hers.

Say: stop kissing me, stop the whisper of sensation, the touch of thy mouth along my throat. *Say:* stop thy weight, thy hands, up and down; his palms that stroked her arms.

She could not. She could not.

Say stop, because I know thy face so well, even in the dark, thine eyes that turn to mine in bewilderment, in arrogance. They're blue—dark, like clouds that cross the stars; they laugh without words.

No more. Stop now.

No more, no more as he hung over her, tracing lines of hot delight on her chin, to her lips, to her temples and eyelashes.

Teasing-gentle, dangerous. Oh—stop my hands from holding thy face between them, from pulling thee closer to kiss me, thy mouth on mine, deep and passionate.

Stop; it cannot be; we are impossible, an accident of time and place, worlds collided. Stop—thou art so heavy and yet so sweet. So wicked and so sure, kisses at her chin and throat and lower.

Say stop . . .

Now—before he drew her shift upward, bare skin to bare skin, his hand on her thigh, sliding to her hip, her waist. And hard against her, his arousal—inference and theory made real. She had seen babies born; she had nursed male patients; she'd listened, quiet and still as in Meeting, when the married women talked immoderately. And that only made her wonder at what they had not said.

But they would not have said it, not out loud. Not this, his tongue at the tip of her breast, a slow circle that drew her taut. Not this, his hand on her hip, pulling her up against him in the same rhythm that he tugged at her nipple. She spread her hands on his shoulders and whimpered, arching with him.

He responded with a low growl, pressing his body hard to hers. Then he moved back, trailing his forefinger down the center of her torso, her belly, the most intimate curls.

Stop, oh stop—don't follow with thy mouth and kiss me and taste—oh, that thou shouldst know such ungodly pleasures. That I should turn and twist beneath thee, all flame.

She panted with it, this indecent torture. She drove her fingers into his skin, kneading and pulling, asking him to stop, silently pleading, stop thy kisses, stop now, while I want and want and want . . .

He didn't stop; he answered her body, because all her body said yes. He slipped his fingers inside her, strange and lascivious, hot pressure. He bent his mouth again to her breast.

Mindless sensation spread through her. A promiscuous sound came from her throat, a beast's sound. The deep exploration was pain and lust and him, her husband, pushing to discover more of her, to wring soft cries of surrender from her throat.

Stop . . . please . . . stop.

He lifted himself above her. She was open to him, she must say now, say no more, say I do not want thee, I will not have thee, thou must go away and leave me.

He came into her, delicious burn, more hurt; her husband—

all heat and dark fire; her wicked husband, who knew corrupt worldly things, who held her tight and kissed her and kissed her again while it hurt, stretched his beautiful body over hers, pushing harder, creating pain and soothing it at once, more pain, until she cried out with anguish at the peak.

"Oh no—" He was murmuring, kissing her mouth. "Oh no, oh no, sweet Maddy, no—" His voice ached, as if it hurt him too. He was breathing soft and quick, butterflies of caresses at her lashes and cheeks. He held himself over her, wholly inside her, waiting, with a faint, faint tremor in his arms.

She gulped for air, her tense muscles slow to realize that the sharp piercing hurt had subsided.

A long sigh escaped from her. As if that had been a signal, he bent his head and gave her a kiss as heavy and carnal as his body's ownership of hers.

He began to move in her, renewing the pain. Maddy's fingers curled around his arms in alarm. He whispered to her, but she could not understand it; he had gone away into himself, touching her with his tongue, sucking at her skin, as if he could draw her into his mouth as he shoved inside her body.

It hurt, but the hurt was drowned in his sensual drive—the penetration burned so deep that it was pleasure to her. She raised her arms around him to take more of it. He moaned, shaking his head, lifting her with each stroke. He seemed to grow tormented, as if she were not close enough; he wanted her closer; he wanted every thrust to make them one. He arched into her with a sound that shuddered from deep in his chest—a long and throbbing stretch, a shiver in him and deep inside of her—and she felt him, as far in penetration as he could go, flooding her with his life.

She held him tight to her, held him as he shuddered again and again. Her fingers almost could not touch around his shoulders, he was so much larger than she, and yet he dropped his head and rested on her and nuzzled his face into the curve of her throat like a loving child.

"Maddy," he said, between hard breaths, "make you . . . glad. I swear."

She smoothed her hand down his shoulder and his back. She could feel his heart beating. He shuddered again and pushed himself closer to her.

"I'll make you glad," he repeated.

She bit her lip, resting her head against his.

He turned his face deeper into her. "Black Guard won't get you," he said, muffled.

Stop. Oh, stop, say stop, but it's too late.

Too late. Because God forgive me, I love thee more than my own life.

She opened her eyes to morning and close warmth, enfolded in his arms, her hair still pinned up in double braids of the day before.

She lay still, feeling the gentle rise and fall of his chest at her side.

Her husband. There would be no undoing now.

When she turned he was awake already, lying quiet on his side, looking somewhere beyond her. In the dim morning through the drapes, his hair fanned black over the pillow. His expression was austere, his jaw shadowed.

His distant gaze came back to her. Neither of them spoke. The change in things, the profound chasm between yesterday and today lay between them.

He rolled away from her and sighed, locking his hands behind his head. Then he glanced toward her sideways. "Regret?"

The one word held defiance. She looked in her heart for regret. For anger, or repentance. None of that was there. Only dismay, that she had given in to such weakness. Only a growing sense of the enormity of what she'd done.

"I broke," he said. "I . . . agreement."

"I did not ask thee to stop." It was the truth.

He turned on his side. His blue eyes watched hers.

"Wife," he said.

Such an emphatic presence, even to the impression of his body in the bed, that weighted it down and drew her toward him. His knee touched her calf, high up, where no one ever touched her but herself.

"Yes," she said, a bare whisper. "I am thy wife in truth."

He sat up, flinging back the bedclothes, expelling the dogs from their places. Maddy watched him stalk across the rich room, as graceful and barbaric as the tapestries and paintings. Her own blood marked his skin. The drapes rattled as he pulled them wide. Intense sunlight flooded in, outlining him with the glare. Elevated as the room was, all she saw beyond him through the glass was light and sky.

He leaned one arm on the casement. Then he looked back at her, and grinned.

"My wife," he said. *"Good."*

He stood there, relaxed, a half-shadowed silhouette against the streamers of radiance.

His wife.

She blinked and glanced away, because it hurt her eyes to look at him.

Chapter Twenty-five

𝒜 lone with him, uncommitted, she had not made any approaches to the staff; she had lived in his home like a guest, but neither Lady de Marly nor Jervaulx would allow such a dereliction of duty any longer.

"He is the duke; you are his duchess—begin as you mean to go on," his aunt declared.

At her direction, Maddy had sent a request for the quarterly accounts, and sat down with Rhodes and Calvin Elder to review them. A full half-year of pages were laid before her—and Maddy learned for the first time that while the duke's absence had been presented to the staff only as a lengthy illness, Rhodes and Calvin Elder were well aware of the nature of it. Although the word "asylum" was never breathed, she suspected that they had been quite uneasy about their future and who would control it. They were stiff with Maddy, but not uncooperative—and before they departed, Rhodes asked a guarded question about whether there was any idea of closing up the castle at all.

"I don't know," Maddy said honestly. "I'll ask the duke. But he seems very much at home here."

"Pray don't ask, Your Grace! Don't indeed. 'Twas a foolish question." Calvin Elder gave Rhodes a severe glance. "Your talk will run on to absurdities, Mrs. Rhodes. Why should His Grace close the castle?"

Rhodes accepted this rebuke in astringent silence.

Maddy thought it best to meet the matter head on. "Ye have heard, perhaps, that the duke's competence to conduct his business is in question?"

"We haven't heard anything, Your Grace, but that His Grace was ill," Calvin Elder said—a patent falsehood.

"It's true he has been ill. It's true that there is to be a hearing for his competency in several months."

They both looked at her stoically.

"Dost thou believe him to seem incompetent?" she asked the steward.

"Certainly not, Your Grace."

"He cannot speak well," she replied.

"Very true; I've remarked that. But he does not seem anything but able to me."

Maddy thought this was something of a statement of policy rather than of sincerity, but it showed at least where the steward's loyalty lay.

"Yes," she said. "If ye will be patient, and give him time, and listen well, then ye will find that he's quite able."

"Very well, Your Grace."

"I'll keep these to overlook." She drew the books to her. "And I ask each of thee to inform all of the servants beneath ye that I am not to be addressed as Your Grace, but simply as your mistress. I am—I was raised in the principles of the Society of Friends, and I cannot be easy with the other."

" 'Mistress,' Your Grace?"

"Mistress," she said firmly. "Simply that."

"May I request the favor of using the address of 'Madam'?" Calvin Elder asked. "As more in keeping with the honor of the house?"

Maddy looked directly at him. "I think the honor of the house will be better upheld by the conduct of those within it than by how I am addressed." She instantly heard how self-righteous she must sound, and bit her lip. She added, "I don't pretend that I know anything of a household such as this; I'll need your help and guidance. But—I will not be false with ye; I expect that ye will not be false with me. The duke is in real danger of being judged unfit. If that happens, I cannot vouch for what will come after. So perhaps no one will blame ye if ye choose not to obey me now. But as I . . . I am his wife, I must do what falls to me in that regard at present, and in the manner that seems best to me."

"Yes, Mistress," Rhodes said. "There's been things said— we've heard this and that and the other about His Grace, and it's unsettling. I for one thank you for your frankness. 'Tis better to know the worst than to be kept in the dark and wonder."

"Indeed. Thank you . . . Mistress." Calvin Elder gave the lesser address as if it were a strange foreign word, but he gave it.

Maddy had conducted the session with the staff alone, in the duchess' boudoir, but afterward Lady de Marly sat with her in the drawing room to judge the accuracy and necessity of the expenditures. The last quarter to have undergone query had the duke's scrawled notations tipped in, mostly instructions to Calvin Elder about plumbing repairs. The entire expense of the place was staggering. There was a woodman, and five gamekeepers; watermen, lamp-and-candle men, sixteen chambermaids, three carpenters, an upholsterer and someone called a "gong-man." The costs of candles alone left Maddy light-headed: she felt guilty that Jervaulx had lit so many to chase away ghosts in the hall.

She and Lady de Marly were in ready agreement that the amount of ale consumed belowstairs had been overmuch for a household with no visiting entourage—Maddy painstakingly reckoning up the daily demand against the vast number of staff—but when she objected to thirteen pounds for hair powder for the footmen and grooms of the chambers, she found herself immediately at odds with all moral rectitude and virtue.

"The honor of the house," Lady de Marly stated, as if that settled the matter.

"Still," Maddy said, "I think that the custom may be discontinued except on special occasions, and when no guests are present."

"You know nothing of such things, ignorant girl. They would look ramshackle without powder."

"I shall note that hair is to be kept short and neat at all times." Maddy made a memorandum, the way the duke had done, and placed it in the book.

"Humbug! They must be powdered!"

"On special occasions, and when guests are present," Maddy said, adding it to her memo.

"Oh, you are one of those, are you?"

Maddy looked up at Lady de Marly in question.

"One of those soft-voiced, serene girls that just go on chewing their cud and walking straight ahead, say what you may to them."

She smiled a little. "No. I think by nature I'm shrewish and managing, as thou art. But I discovered from my father that a quiet obstinacy is the perfect counter to it."

"Shrewish! Do you dare! Of all the impertinent—"

"You . . . pride in it," Jervaulx said, walking in from his bedchamber. "Aunt."

"Tell this silly chit that the men must be powdered!"

He paused. "Men must . . . what?"

"The menservants," Maddy said. "Hair powder. Thou hast spent thirteen pounds upon it last quarter."

"A pittance," his aunt exclaimed. "They must be powdered. Your consequence, Jervaulx!"

"They might wear powder on special occasions," Maddy said, "and with guests."

"Guests can arrive at any time. Visitors come to tour without notice. You don't understand an establishment of this stature. Jervaulx—I suggest you set your wife in order straightaway."

He looked between the two of them, sober, as if it were a

profound controversy. "Solomon." He brought down his hand in a vertical cut. "Half powder . . . half not."

Maddy made a count. "There are seven of them. They can't be divided evenly."

Her husband did not blink. "Powder half their heads."

She hesitated, and then broke into a peal of laughter. Christian watched her with pleasure. She always laughed as if she hadn't ever had the enjoyment before, as if the very act surprised her.

He would have her painted. Lawrence, he thought, regretting Rembrandt with an inner smile. She wasn't beautiful; she was like the small painting—a moment, a fleeting shade of expression—he would have liked to have it caught, that instant when he coaxed her, when those sultry lashes lifted and the straight-laced propriety changed to something else, when the promise gave way to reality.

He'd learned that a matter-of-fact bearing relaxed her, and from there a gentle tease was most effective: a silly joke more likely to disarm her than gallantry or urgent wooing. Her sense of humor was unsophisticated. The more patently ludicrous a jest, the more likely she was to understand. He wondered if her Quakers ever laughed at all.

He had another item to please her. He held out a note scribbled in Durham's hand. "Father is . . . now coming. To-day perhaps."

Joy blossomed in her face, and instant trepidation. She took the paper from him, read it quickly, and pressed her lips together. "Oh," she said helplessly, "what must he think?"

"He ought to think you've done prodigious well for yourself," Aunt Vesta said, ill-tempered.

"I should not have married without his permission. I should not have taken it into my own hands." A little tinge of panic crept into her voice.

Christian watched the play of emotion in her face. "He will . . . is . . . angry?"

"Oh, no. He would never be angry. He will only be—he

will be so quiet! He will make me cry, because I ought to have been better!"

"Better?" Lady de Marly demanded. "You've made the best match in the country, my girl! I'll tell him so, if he don't know it for himself."

Maddy only clenched her hands around the note. Christian walked back into his chamber, then stopped and turned at the door. "Maddygirl," he said. "I thee wed. Don't . . . forget."

He met her eyes. He wasn't going to beg for her allegiance. He'd made her his own, by law and by physical possession. She was his.

He only hoped to God that Durham had done some bloody persuasive talking to Timms.

Maddy had wished for her father so violently before, and almost as violently wished now that she could have more time before she saw him. She should have written to him, made some manner of explanation. She dreaded his coming.

And yet, when Calvin Elder brought the news that a chaise approached the castle, she rushed down to the gatehouse and was there to see the conveyance roll into the first court.

"Papa!" She was at the window before the postilion had brought the team to a halt. "Oh, Papa."

Durham had come with him; the younger man rose and gave her father his support. Papa negotiated the steps and stood before her, all bundled in a furred greatcoat that diminished him to birdlike delicacy.

"Maddy girl," he said warmly—and she knew he was glad to be with her, at least.

She went into his arms, hugging him close. "Oh, I have missed thee. I have missed thee."

He kissed her cheek, holding onto her hands. "Maddy girl," he repeated, as if it were all that he could say. He stood back from her and reached up to touch her face, smiling a little. "What hast thou done?"

She shook her head. "Papa, I—" She lost her voice. She squeezed his hands very hard. "Nothing will change!" she exclaimed. "Thou art to live here with us, did Durham tell thee? It is—oh, Papa, if thou couldst see it! It's a castle, with great towers and a hall as big as a steeplehouse. I don't—I don't know what I've done! I only knew—thou commanded me to stay with him, and I did, and this has come of it."

He patted her. "Verily, Maddy—I did not command thee. I wouldst not. I asked thee at Chalfont Giles, was it so difficult to stay—and thou answered me that thou couldst not desert him."

"Yes, but thy message—"

"No need to dally," Durham said. "It's bitter cold out here, don't you think, Duchess? Let us—ah! Here's Shev." Jervaulx came across the graveled court. Durham grasped his arm at the elbow, held it for a moment's grip between the two of them. "How do, my man? An old married fellow, by God."

Jervaulx took her father's hand, enveloping it in both of his. "Timms. Welcome. Come in . . . the cold."

Maddy found herself trailing behind as they guided him off between them. She hurried forward. "There are stairs, Papa. Two long flights. Here—now they begin." Amid an echo of footsteps on stone, Jervaulx and Durham escorted her father up. "It's very formidable to see," Maddy said to him from alongside. "They're—oh, they must be three yards wide, and go up beneath arches, with columns at the landing. There is a huge ancient door at the top and a footman to hold it open for us."

"In . . . *powder,*" Jervaulx added firmly.

"So far no trouble with Timms," Durham said after dinner, as he and Christian lingered alone in the Great Chamber with their port. "Told him it was a surprise love match. Swept away, and so forth. Do you think she'll say anything to contradict it?"

Christian considered. He thought of Maddy in his bed, of

ghosts and a shy sudden laugh. He rested his fist on the table and turned his thumb up.

"Ah. Going well, is it?" Durham asked. "Well, I was vague about the details, but I doubt he'll go comparing notes. All he cared for was that she was safe."

"Not . . . angry . . . wed?"

Durham popped a slice of cheese into his mouth and wriggled his fingers. "Bit puzzled by it all, I think. Doesn't say much, or ask many questions. He's a fine old chap. No fool, either, under that hat brim. Just demanded to know whether you meant honorable by his girl. Don't think he gives a candle for the rest. Didn't ask a thing about money nor endowments. Likes you, that's the sum of it. Thinks you're a bloody genius."

Christian made an ironical grunt. "Bloody . . . imbecile."

"Plain as a pikestaff that you're better than when I saw you last. Nearly good as new." Durham lifted his port. "This will pass. Got to. I only hope you won't look back and wish you'd done differently when the time comes."

"*Good* new . . . do you think?"

"Well, listen to you. You'll be putting 'em to sleep in the Lords in a trifle."

Christian tried to imagine speaking again in the House. His pulse rose. "The Lord . . . the . . . can't . . ." It all locked, the very thought of a public address driving him to halting inarticulation. *"Damn!"* He flung himself away from the windows. At the bookcase wall he stopped. He took hold of a pair of pilasters, gazing at the leather and gilt and Latin titles lined between them. Then he dropped his forehead against the shelf edge, the ancient musty smell of books in his nostrils, the wood hard against his head. *"Can't!"*

Durham was silent. Christian stood with his back to the room. He took a deep breath and pushed himself away, turning.

"Afraid." He shook his head and sank into a chair. "Afraid . . . never . . . Durham."

"I don't believe it. Damn it, Shev, I won't believe it! You've come this far!"

"Far." Christian's lip curled in mockery. "Listen . . . me."

"You've got to keep trying. Perhaps if you had a—a tutor of some sort."

"My head. Gone! Try . . . try . . . *no!* Try is . . . make worse. Understand?"

"What, then? You go to ground in this place for the rest of your days? It won't do, Shev. They'll hark in, force you to break cover. There's too much at stake. Manning's been with your mother every day, did you know it?"

Christian's hands tightened on the chair arms. Manning his sister Charlotte's husband, who'd stood with barristers and bagwigs in that room. Watching. Waiting to see him stripped and chained.

A violent surge of anger spiked through him, shame and dread mingling, holding him mute. He worked his hand on the arm, pressing his fingers into the wood until they hurt. "New . . . *hearing,*" he managed at last, as calm as he could make it.

"It's their chance. I called on him myself, just to get a notion how things stood, and I'll tell you, Shev, it chilled my blood. The man's got himself all talked into it, how you've always been erratic and promiscuous; that if you're left free to act, you'll run the estate into ruin, and there's the future of your nephews at stake. The worst of it is, he's made himself believe it. They're not going to give it up. And I've got to warn you—when they heard of this marriage, it was the devil to pay. It plays right into their hands. Don't think because you haven't had word from 'em yet that you won't."

Christian closed his eyes. He could not have spoken if he'd wanted to.

"For Maddy to get a penny—it'll be like stripping the hide from 'em alive," Durham said. "They'll do anything they can to stop it."

Christian nodded.

"So don't say 'never.' You've got responsibilities. To your wife, if nothing else."

He thought of that—beyond himself, to what would become of Maddy if he were to be declared incompetent. If they took him back. They'd set aside the marriage, certainly. His family would never tolerate it.

Yesterday it would not have been such a disaster for her. But today . . .

To lie in the cell, to lie imprisoned there not knowing where she was, what they'd done to her; not even knowing if she was alive. He imagined it, and the nightmare of that place descended to a depth he had not known it could fathom.

Maddy had seen her father settled in and retired directly after dinner. She spent a good deal of time making certain that his chamber was not smoky and that the bed was warmed.

"Thou must not linger overlong with me, Maddy," he chided her softly. "Thy husband will expect thee."

"Oh, no—I'm sure the duke won't mind." She found herself covered in self-conscious blushes. "Lady de Marly and Durham are there."

"Still—perhaps it is thee that he would rather see. Thou hast only been married a week."

"But I thought we might talk—"

"Go away now, Maddy girl." He smiled. "I'm tired and need to sleep."

"Papa," she protested faintly.

He pulled the bedclothes up and closed his eyes. Maddy sat still. After a moment, he rustled the sheets and turned over away from her.

By the time she rang for a footman to take her back through the dark passages and hall to the drawing room, Durham and the duke had come in after their port. Durham didn't linger. When Lady de Marly announced that she would go, he politely rose and offered to escort her.

Maddy was left alone with Jervaulx. Instantly, a desperate

modesty overcame her, an exquisite awareness of him—and herself. She watched him snuff the candles, leaving only the sharp odor of extinguished wicks and the orange light from the hearth.

He went into his bedchamber. The door was open, the room beyond well lit with oil, but Maddy felt bound to her chair. Papa had steadfastly refused to give any opinion on her marriage. She didn't think he condemned it entirely—at least he did not seem disappointed or cross with her—but he was troubled, that she knew.

She sat in the chair, her legs pressed together, her hands holding the silken ends of her shawl clasped in her lap.

Jervaulx came back to the door in his shirtsleeves, a silhouette against the light from his bedchamber. The coals gave just enough illumination to pick out the shape of his face and the pale fall of the lace on his shirt front. He leaned against the doorframe.

Maddy ducked her head and clasped her hands more tightly on the shawl. She heard nothing; only his shadow falling across the light on the carpet told her that he came into the room.

He walked behind her. He began to take down her hair, searching out the pins and letting them fall silently on the floor. Her plaits came free. She kept her head lowered as they tumbled across her shoulders.

As she sat there still, he began to unbraid them. He spread the ends between his fingers, fanning them open, holding them up to her cheeks to stroke her, feathery, tickling, down the line of her jaw, behind her ears. He traced her throat, pushing away the shawl that she held to her.

It slipped from her fingers. Softly the fans of hair caressed her bared shoulders, in circles and arcs, to the nape of her neck.

She felt his fingers work at her buttons—perfectly capable of it, but slow, one by one downward, unhooking her stays, too. Maddy bent her head as her clothing loosened. She breathed deeply.

He moved in front of her, offering his hand. Maddy stood, expecting him to lead her to the bedchamber, but instead he slid his fingers through her braids, releasing the woven strands, spreading them, combing through them.

There was an intensity about him, a strange severity. He never looked into her face. Fireglow traced his cheekbones and his jaw and glinted on his lashes. He worked her hair, worked it all free, fanned it open, a cloak around her.

He put his hands on her shoulders and pushed her dress and underclothes down her arms. Maddy made a faint sound of protest. Not here, in the open room.

Christian heard her, but he did not pause. He couldn't remember when he had first begun to imagine this: her hair around her in fragrant waves, her pale skin a glimpse beneath. It had been somewhere in the nightmare, and while he had her now, had freedom and sense and beauty before him—while he could touch her he would do it in the light, to make it real.

While she stood immobile, he drew her hair forward in a curtain over her breasts. He allowed her that defense, covered her in a sheen of dark gold, while beneath it he took down all her clothes to her waist, sliding the dress and the white plain shift past her elbows and her wrists.

She made another small sound, as if she wished to remonstrate. But her hands were unresisting as he brought them free of the dress. "This is not—" She caught her breath as he rested his palms on her bare torso. "Jervaulx."

"Christian." He put his forehead down to her shoulder, breathing the liberated scent of her. "With other . . . Jervaulx. With . . . alone—Christian." He was exploring beneath the rippled shower of her hair. His hand touched one straining hook. He released it between his thumb and forefinger. The clothes dropped in a bank of silk and linen at her feet.

"Oh," she said, a whimper of excited misery.

Below the dramatic length of her hair, her stockings

showed white down to the tops of her incongruous stout shoes. Christian smiled. Sturdy Maddy. Luscious Maddy. Layers and layers, prim-provocative-puritanical Maddygirl.

He knelt before her and unfastened the shoes, powerfully aware of the whisper of her hair at his temple. Turning his head, he kissed her calf and the side of her knee through the thick cascade. He cupped both his palms around her leg, sliding them up and down the knitted wool, exerting pressure inside her knee to invite her to come to him.

She caught his shoulders, unbalanced. Christian clasped her stockinged foot, delicate and arched as she lifted it free of the rigid shoe. She drew quickly from his hold, setting her foot down amid the puffs and folds of silk, taking her hands from him.

He coaxed the other leg, but this time she lifted free of her own accord—a moment, the white tip of her toe in his view—and then she stepped back swiftly, her hair moving in a wave around her.

He sat back on the carpet in front of the fire, gazing up at her. The temple of her hair made her virginal—her shoulders glowed ivory where the shiny tumble parted over them— nun-like and seductive at once, a living image of bronze and gold.

"Don't look at me!" she said in a strained, small voice.

"Why?" He didn't take his eyes away.

"It is—creaturely."

Christian leaned back, propping his elbows on his aunt's cushioned footstool. "You're . . . beautiful creature."

"No," she whispered.

"Yes."

"Thou art so wicked!"

"To say . . . beautiful? Not to say . . . is lying. Can't lie, Maddygirl. You taught . . . no lies."

She held her arms crossed over her breasts. Her eyes were shadowed in soft radiance.

And then, unexpectedly, she dropped to her knees at his

feet. She shook her hair back, half-revealing herself. The rise and fall of her breathing brought a glimpse of the tips of her breasts.

Sharp desire rose in him. The virginal image fell away like a mask: she was a nymph of fire and shade, offering herself.

"No," she said. "I ought not to pretend." She lifted one hand a little toward him, and let it fall helplessly. "But I don't—I don't know what to do."

He could have taken her down and had her, without ceremony, without regard for anything but the lust that coursed through him. He could have held her beneath him, pinned down on those waves of hair, thrust hard into her with the force of his own desire.

But all the experience was his. She would not admire him for how he'd obtained it, but it was not lack of hunger that held him still: it was the strength of an exhaustive education in the finer points of love.

"Do . . . what you like," he said.

She hesitated. He held quiescent, relaxed, watching her.

She bent her head a little, her hair falling forward around her cheeks. She touched his boot. Christian smiled, observing her: suddenly the sensual nymph vanished and she became plain practical Maddy again—she slipped the trouser strap off his heel, took hold of his foot with both hands and jerked the halfboot loose with a deft motion, out and up, then slid it free, as efficient as any seasoned valet.

He wriggled his toes at her. Primly, she set the boot aside. In a moment, she had dispatched the second and positioned it neatly next to its mate. She scooted forward a few inches, arranged her hair modestly, sank back onto her heels, and drew his feet into her lap.

Christian tilted his head back, gazing up at the ceiling in pleasure. But he didn't want to waste it, not while he had Maddy to look at, Maddy enrobed in her extraordinary hair, rubbing his feet as if it were a task of the most solemn gravity. She kneaded his arches and his heels, and stopped sometimes to turn one foot a little, looking down at it, bending slightly, inspecting, he presumed, to see that she had done a thorough job.

In one of these pauses, he arched his foot and touched his toe to her body, pushing the sheet of her hair aside a fraction. Below her throat, a pale ribbon of light found her skin down the nave of an erotic cathedral. Last night had been all feeling; tonight it was all the sight of her, in glimpses, in secret moments.

He allowed her hair to fall back as she resumed her earnest massage. He wriggled his toes again to get her attention, which seemed to have fixed too intently on the business of kneading.

She looked up. He drew his feet away and propped them flat on the floor, watching her between his knees. It was a dare: she had to come forward to him or retreat entirely.

"This is not equitable," she said, on a plaintive note.

"Why?"

"Thou art . . . dressed."

He smiled complacently.

"Thou art wicked and creaturely," she accused.

He tilted his head to the side and lifted his eyebrows.

"Thou art laughing at me!"

"Not." He stretched his legs out on either side of her. "Waiting."

"Am I to undress thee?" she demanded. "Is that what I'm supposed to do?"

He brought his feet together to her hips, caressing her. "Want?"

Her eyes evaded his. She dropped her gaze to the carpet in front of her. He moved his toes slowly over her bare skin and hair.

"No false . . . Maddygirl," he said gently. "Want?"

She took a deep breath, exhaled it, and leaned forward over him.

It was all Christian could do to hold himself in check. Her position on her hands revealed her vividly, full breasts under a wash of gold that caught the firelight, that was too finely translucent to conceal shape behind it. Supporting herself on one hand, she loosened the buttons on his trousers.

Her hair slid down, unveiling her back and the curve of her buttocks. She made a quick move to catch it back, rising, a sudden vision of everything; her smooth torso, her breasts, the line of her belly and dark crown of curls.

Christian's restraint deserted him. He sat up, leaning on his hands. She seemed startled; she looked at him like a diffident forest creature, drawing back—but he caught her between his legs. He reached up and pulled her down on top of him. He lay back on the carpet, kissing her throat, her breasts, her hair falling all around.

But he didn't want to hurry—he wanted a luxurious, slow bonfire. With an effort, he relaxed his hands, smoothed them down her body that was poised above him. She had not drawn away, not after that first moment: she seemed to wait, not quite meeting his eyes, her lips parted a little.

"Do you know . . . I like . . . lazy." He locked his hands behind his head. "Still . . . wait."

"I don't know what to do," she whispered again, woeful. "Can't think?"

Firelight glistened where she wet her lips. "No. I can't."

"Up," he said. "Up on . . . knees."

When she made no move, he caught her wrists. He pushed her, his palms against hers, until she knelt upright. She tried to pull her hands away, but he knew what she would do if he allowed it.

"Don't hide." He kept them locked with his. "I remember . . . first night I saw you . . . my table . . . all prim stiff proper . . . thee-thou . . . Miss Timms." He smiled. "Oh, Miss Timms. I saw you . . . like this."

Her cheeks bloomed rosy. "Because thou art wicked."

"You say . . . wicked. So bad, Maddygirl?"

She gazed down at him, apparently unaware of the picture she presented and what it did to him—at least, she did not look any lower than his face.

"You tell . . . first saw me . . . what you thought."

She gave a faint breath of amusement. "I thought thou wert a wicked man."

"Despise." He raised his knees beside her and closed them on her hips. "Scorn. Go home. . . . pray."

"I liked thee a little better after thou offered the mathematical chair to Papa."

"Ambition," he said. "Good wife."

That got a real smile from her. He swayed her slightly with his legs.

"Shrewd. Ambition." He let go of one of her hands and swept her hair back over her shoulder. "Beautiful."

She began to breathe more quickly. He touched her, traced his fingers along her waist and up to her breast. He outlined the underswell of it with his forefinger.

"I like that," she said, in a soft, unexpected rush of words.

"So do I," he said solemnly.

Her breast rose and fell beneath his caress. He went slowly, watching her, every stroke reflected in her face. When he touched her nipple, she drew in a sharp breath and caught her lower lip in her teeth.

Christian made a low groan. He pulled upright, closing the space between them. With his tongue he traced the path of his fingers. He rested his hands at her waist and opened his mouth over her nipple, sucking.

She whimpered, arching into him. His hands slipped downward, thumbs sliding over the provocative short curls. She still had the scent of the night before about her, dense with heat and his passion. Dimly he felt her fingers burrow into his hair, drawing him closer.

He pushed his hand between her legs, coaxing them apart, over his, straddling him wide open—prim Maddy, exquisite sensitive amorous Maddygirl, her hair cascading down over one shoulder, her head tilted back and her lips parted, panting.

He made it last. He made it last oh so long, caressing her, teasing her, until her thighs trembled and she gasped each time he touched her. And when he moved beneath her she made a sharp whimper and her eyes sprang open, and she watched him as he did it, easing inside her, pulling her back down onto him.

He lifted his head from the carpet to suckle her. She moved with awkward exquisite jerks, writhing, until he cupped his hands at her buttocks and taught her the rhythm, her hair sliding between his palms and her skin. With a lovely suddenness, she came—with little female cries, like an unquiet dreamer: he brought his arms up around her and held her close for an instant—then with one deep thrust, holding her hips down to take it, he let go of the lust he'd kept dammed inside him.

When it was finished he held her hard against his chest and never closed his eyes—to make it real, and banish nightmares in the firelight.

Chapter Twenty-six

$\mathcal{M}$addy could barely look at Jervaulx the next day, though he did nothing to indicate he remembered her abandon, or even that he'd taken notice of it. She thought he was even somewhat cooler toward her than usual, composed and collected, treating her in the presence of the others with nothing more intimate than common courtesy. His demeanor was all casual detachment—except for one private glance behind his aunt's back: that crooked pirate's smile, swift and secret, blue eyes beneath black lashes, while everyone stood round a roaring fire in the hall and discussed plans for the tenants' Christmas dinner.

Maddy felt herself blush all over, unable even to break the glance. Jervaulx's smile turned into a grin—and then it was gone, and he looked away.

Durham was suggesting a ball, with waltzing, while Lady de Marly asserted that a pair of oxen roasted, a good dinner of three courses—not less than two hundred dishes to each, mind you—and an elevating concert of religious music after had always been quite sufficient, and would be in the future. Papa smiled at both ideas, and Calvin Elder wore an expression of attentive discernment, as if he had participated in such controversies times out of number, but owed it to his position to consider the arguments one more time.

The Reverend Mr. Durham spent no time on rational propositions to counter Lady de Marly. He merely bowed before her, turning a graceful leg, and began to hum as he lifted her hand and drew her into a revolution. Her stick went clattering. She made an irritated exclamation, but her feet moved with a surprising freedom.

"Unhand me, you outrageous boy," she sputtered, pulling away. "You'll break my bones!"

He held her by one hand, steadying her, still humming as he danced himself around her. "A waltz, my lady! *Dum*dum-ta-dumdum-ta-*dummm, dum*dum-ta-dumdum—"

Maddy found herself swept away as unexpectedly as Lady de Marly, her husband's arm around her waist, his hum blending with Durham's, their voices gaining strength. Maddy had no idea how to dance; she scrambled to keep her balance, stepping out by necessity as the duke spun her about the floor.

The humming had become impromptu music, *dum*dum-ta-dumdum-ta-*dummm,* in strong masculine notes that echoed from the walls while the room whirled about her. His hold on her was light and commanding; his coattails spun out and her skirts flared as they turned. Maddy had to keep her feet moving smartly or be flung off them—though each time that it seemed she must be, he drew her into a spin that saved her. When her toe came down hard on his, his only reaction was an emphatic *ta* instead of a dum, a pointed smile and a tighter hold on her waist.

He and Durham came to the end of their musical piece. Jervaulx held her arm up, bowing to her with a flourish. "Duchess! Thank you." As Maddy stood flushed, trying to catch her breath, he looked toward the others. "Can't . . . *dance,*" he said.

"I don't know how," Maddy exclaimed. "Friends aren't to dance!"

The three of them looked at her. She felt absurdly awkward in her everyday shoes, more clumsy even than Lady de Marly under the weight of years.

"It is an idle amusement," she said.

Lady de Marly sighed. "Hire her a master, Jervaulx."

Calvin Elder met a footman hovering at the screens passage and returned to them carrying a silver tray with two letters on it. "The post is beforehand today, Your Grace. Shall I have it sent to your study?" He bowed briefly toward the duke's aunt. "There is an item for Lady de Marly."

"Leave it in my parlor," she said. "Do you suppose that Italian who taught the girls is still in the country, Jervaulx?"

The duke had taken his letter. He broke it open without aid—a small achievement that no one seemed to note except Maddy, not even Jervaulx himself.

"I should be glad to lend myself to the task," Durham offered, "until you can find a master. But we'll need someone to play the instrument."

"I don't wish to learn to dance," Maddy said. "I'll have no occasion for it."

"Best have a violoncello for music, but no doubt we'll only find some widow woman who can play the pianoforte in the village," Lady de Marly said.

"I really don't wish—"

"Humbug," Lady de Marly said. "None of your dissenter faradiddle, girl. If you want to be excused from waltzing, you may do so on the grounds of propriety, but the respectable dances are a requirement. You're no invalid; you'll be expected to stand up with the duke or look no-how."

Maddy would have argued further, but as she started to speak, she glanced at Jervaulx. Her words faded. He stood with the letter in his hand, unfocused, his face white and set.

"What's wrong?" she blurted.

As soon as she had spoken, she wished that she'd kept silent. The others looked toward him. A shade of wariness came into his expression. He said nothing.

"Let me see it," Lady de Marly said, holding out her hand for the letter.

He looked toward her as if he'd forgotten she was standing there. He shook his head.

"Let me see it."

"No. Nothing." He frowned. "Nothing."

"Don't be a fool, boy," his aunt insisted. "What have you there? Let me see it."

He crumpled the paper in his fingers. Without answering he threw it into the fire as he strode across the hall and out.

"Young fool," Lady de Marly said.

Maddy turned on her. "Canst thou not speak to him as if he is a man, and not a wayward child?"

"I speak to him as I always have, miss. Why should I change now?"

"He is changed."

"But the world is the same. Don't discount it." She thumped her stick on the floor. "The world is always with us—and don't you discount it, Duchess."

Christian stood with his back to the parapet, leaning his shoulders on cold stone, the wind whipping up through an arrow slit and blowing his hair against the back of his head. A falcon coasted over Belletoire, rising up above the tower in a hurtling curve, and then tilting into a drift down and sideways. Beyond that, the sky was empty gray.

Christian stared at nothing. It had been a stupid move, of course. Those moments two nights ago had seduced him, the fleeting instants when his speech had been intact. He'd thought, if he just concentrated—

He'd gone alone to write, and known while he was doing it that it was not quite accurate. He saw his mistakes, but when he tried to locate them exactly, they seemed to disappear, only to reappear at the corner of his eye when he looked away. When he'd seen the sheet upside down, folding it, he'd realized how odd it was—all shifted to one side. But he had given it to Calvin Elder to dispatch anyway.

Stupid. Stupid stupid stupid.

He heard footsteps from the open stairwell. It would be

Maddy; everyone else knew he was not to be followed here.
He'd half-expected that she would come, half-hoped it, left
the doors ajar so that she could guess the way.

She stepped out onto the battlement. No cloak. The wind
caught her skirt and blew it around her legs, showing the
stalwart shoes and white stockings.

Loyal-simple-can't-dance Maddy, who would not ridicule
him. Who would not think she had to tell him what he realized painfully well already. Who would know, if he said he
was afraid, what he had to be afraid of.

He held out his hand to her. She hesitated and then took it,
warm bare skin against his. He enfolded her in his arms,
sheltering them both against the castle wall.

She was silent. He put his forehead down to her shoulder.

For a long time, he rested there, hiding. Then he said, "I
was . . . I write . . . Bailey. At Monmouth. Send for here . . .
write settlements." He shuddered, the cold seeping into his
bones. He held her closer to him. "Bailey . . . fifteen
years . . . attorney . . . manage the . . . manage my affairs.
Agent farm . . . buying land . . . election . . . county—the
county . . . all. Everything here." Christian gazed over her to
the long ridge, the shoulder of Jervaulx Castle and the distant rise of mountains behind it. "He doesn't come. He
writes. He will not . . . act." Christian gave a short, anguished laugh. "He will not act."

He turned his head, his lips against her cold ear. He held
her hard because he thought he was going to weep.

She stood steadily. Her hand crept up and found his, locking fingers.

"My write—my letter—it was . . . bad. I think . . . it was
bad. Mistakes. Stupid!"

"Next time," she said, "I will look at thy writing first, if
thou wish it."

A comfortable, unremarkable, Maddygirl answer. She
looked forward, instead of back. Next time. Next time we
will do better.

He was responsible for her. He had to do better. Far better.

He had to be perfect, so no one could doubt him. So no one could steal his life, no one could take her, no one could lay hands on him and lock him back in that place.

"Maddy. Hearing . . . got . . . I . . ." He broke off in frustration. The way his speech disintegrated under attention and strenuous effort terrified him more than anything: he knew that when he was judged again, he would want it so fiercely he would drive it away. "*Fail.* Too . . . strain. Idiot!"

"Sometimes—" She paused, and then said, "Sometimes, thou art capable."

He groaned and tilted his head back to the wall. "Why not . . . now? Hearing—" He groaned again. "Never!"

She lifted her arms and crossed them over his. "I wish thou couldst exercise and drill, to make thee easier."

He could attempt it. But there was nothing that would accustom him to the pressure of unexpected demands, the ordeal of critical eyes on him. Nothing.

He looked out on the empty valley and the ridges: Jervaulx, that he loved, that he had known all his life—a secure and precarious refuge. He was vulnerable here, but he didn't know what else to do, where to go that would be safe.

She touched his hand, folding it into her cold fingers. He turned his face to her throat, kissing her, warming her with himself, burning away fear with the flame that blazed instantly between them.

Lady de Marly waited in the drawing room when they came down from the tower. She stood up, leaning on her stick. "I've had this from your esteemed brother-in-law," she said, brandishing a paper. "Stoneham. It seems that one of them grows squeamish." She held up her lorgnette, eyeing the missive. "He understands that the public nature of a jury hearing would be offensive to you," she read, "and degrading to the family—hah! Degrading! Late for him to think of that! He offers you a trust in lieu of a declaration of incompetence. You're to live on the Cumberland property, with income of four thousand, the remainder of the estate to be put into the hands of trustees. You agree to borrow nothing against it."

Jervaulx made a sound. He took a stride and snatched the letter from his aunt. He tore it in two strips and flung them into the grate.

"You did not allow me to finish," Lady de Marly said coolly. "Stoneham wishes us to know that Mr. Manning in particular isn't fully convinced of the wisdom of a private trust, and prefers the clean cut. He desires that you be declared incompetent and put away—'however painful in the short term,' as I believe it was described. But Stoneham believes that us long as you agree to renounce your marriage to the Quaker in the ecclesiastical courts, the others can be brought round in the matter."

The duke simply stared at her, a look of cold, killing fury in his face.

His aunt did not flinch. "Your pride will not serve you well in this," she snapped. "Think of it, Jervaulx—if you go before a jury and fail—you lose it all. This is an offer. An opening for negotiation."

"Offer!" he shouted. "*Hang* bloody rotting otter—*Damn* bastards! *No!*"

"Make a counter," Lady de Marly said. "You live here. A trust, but you want thirty thousand a year. The marriage is valid, and you require a statement signed by all your relatives that male issue in your line hold the title without prejudice."

He grabbed a poker from the hearth and sent it swinging across the surface of a marquetry chest, smashing candelabra and Chinese bowls to the floor.

His aunt gazed at the shattered and bent remains. "I believe you are mad," she said icily. "Or worse, a fool."

"No . . . *offer*," he uttered. He swung at a needle-pointed pole-screen by the fire, snapping the gilt stave, sending the two pieces toppling on the hearth. "No . . . *trust!*"

"I will not stand here while you bring the place down

around our heads," Lady de Marly declared. She moved toward the door. "We will speak again when you can control yourself."

Jervaulx seemed to have forgot Maddy was there. He muttered, "No, no, no!" in a ferocious undertone, yanking the bell-rope as the door closed on his aunt. A footman appeared. "Calvin!" the duke snarled. "Ledger—in the study!" He turned his glare on Maddy. "You come . . . *me*."

Books loaded the shelves floor-to-ceiling on every wall except the one behind the desk, where a mounted slate was covered with chalked equations. But what dominated the duke's study—standing aimed at a small hinged shutter in the window like an elegant brass lance set at the stars—was a gleaming telescope, some seven feet long, with a horse bridle hung over the wheel that guided the tripod's hinge.

Jervaulx threw himself into the rolling desk chair as if he knew precisely how far it would travel before he turned it, rummaging among the clutter before him. With an impatient grunt, he shed papers, notebooks, a pair of well-worn boots, and three globes—two of earth and one of the light side of the moon—to create an open space on the desk. He glanced at Maddy. "Sit. You . . . hear."

Maddy had to move a stack of journals, a piece of some sort of machinery, and several models of cannon brightly painted in red and black to find a place. She pulled her shawl close in the chilly room. Calvin Elder entered, carrying a fat ledger and a leather packet tied in brown ribbon. "A boy has just brought this from Monmouth, Your Grace. It was not trusted to the post."

"Bailey?"

"Yes. From Mr. Bailey, Your Grace."

Jervaulx gave the packet a caustic look and waved toward the corner of his desk. Calvin Elder set the case atop a file box there. He laid the ledger in the open space the duke had cleared. Thick, the corners worn down to paleness, the book bore a much more ponderous look of authority than the thin household notebooks Maddy had been given to examine. Jervaulx opened it at the marker.

Those four simple words—*He will not act*—had not seemed to Maddy such fearsome news. They touched the duke's pride, brought him face on with harsh reality, but she'd not seen more in them than that. She watched Jervaulx gaze at the ledger page Calvin Elder had marked.

The steward cleared his throat. "I have been most pleased to see Your Grace return to Jervaulx," he said.

The duke made no answer. He just looked at the book, not turning backward or forward.

Calvin Elder stood with his age-gnarled hands locked together, moving his thumb back and forth over his wrist. "I have queried Mr. Bailey for more money, and Mr. Bailey has queried London, and we were informed only that the receiver-general there could not act."

Jervaulx did not even appear to be reading the ledger; he just seemed mesmerized by that one page of it.

"For want of different instruction, I've kept the castle functioning in the usual state," Calvin Elder went on in a voice that began to exhibit an old man's quaver. "With wages drawn from the household funds until they were exhausted. I took the liberty of delaying payment of my own salary last quarter, Your Grace, in order to meet the roll. The supplies I've obtained on account." He was not looking at the duke, but over his head at the slate behind. "I would just like to add that I'm delighted Your Grace is pleased now to overlook the situation, as it has become increasingly difficult to—ah—I'm sorry to say rumors seem to have circulated—" He cleared his throat again. "It's most vexing; it's monstrous; but a number of the tradespeople have become unduly concerned."

Jervaulx suddenly shoved the volume toward Maddy. She leaned forward to look.

The master ledger held triple columns of entries. In the abstruse system of management that appeared to govern the duke's affairs, all income from Jervaulx—farm rents, coal revenues, ground rents, interest on loans—all passed through

Calvin Elder and the attorney in Monmouth, and then went to a receiver-general in London. A receiver-general who was no longer disbursing payments in return.

While the castle bled money on candles, liveries, servants and hair powder, nothing was compensating for it; the place mounted debt as sums beyond imagining flowed into abeyance somewhere in London.

Maddy could not conceive of why Calvin Elder had waited, with the situation in such dire straits, for Jervaulx to initiate an interest in financial matters. It was clear that the steward had gotten too old for his office. But his relief was so palpable, his deference so deep, and the duke's acceptance of it so automatic and unaccusing that it was obvious that, in both their minds, the real accountability belonged to Jervaulx.

But the duke hardly seemed to care for the household expense. The sums that had dazzled Maddy appeared merely to annoy him; he reviewed them briefly with Calvin Elder, nodding at the information that the steward added to fill out details.

No, it was not the stunning total of three thousand pounds of debt on the account of Jervaulx Castle that made the duke's mouth whiten at the corners. It was the packet from Bailey. While Maddy held the master ledger and Calvin Elder pointed out the unpaid charges, Jervaulx kept staring at the packet as if it were a viper on his desk.

In a pause, he merely said in Calvin Elder's direction, "More?"

"That's all that has come in your absence, Your Grace."

"Enough." The duke shook his head and sighed. "You . . . go now."

Calvin Elder bowed and departed, with a look as dejected as Devil's when the dog was shut out of a room.

"Open," Jervaulx said to Maddy, nodding toward the leather packet.

She untied the packet. A stack of letters slid out, bound up in a red ribbon. She pulled it free and set them before him.

Jervaulx read one, slowly. He handed it to Maddy.

Hoare's Bank, in a memorandum dated months earlier, gently regretted that circumstances required some communication with regard to funds, and politely requested same.

Maddy looked up from that. The duke held a paper engraved with the colorful insignia of the Sun Fire Insurance Office. Without expression, he handed that one to her, too.

It was dated much more recently. In an official hand, couched among numerous compliments, effusive apologies, and more oblique references to "circumstances," the directors of Sun Fire were unhappy to communicate that they found themselves obliged to go much out of their usual course and demand immediate repayment of the entire sum of £45,000 lent to the duke.

"Forty-five thousand!" Maddy gasped.

Jervaulx sat still, his forehead in his hand. He didn't even look up.

"Maddy," he said. "I'll write. You . . . see . . . are no mistakes."

The letter to Hoare's—Christian had finally had to give up and let Maddy copy it out for his signature—had been a straightforward instruction to forward instantly five thousand pounds from monies placed to his petty account. To Sun Insurance and his other creditors, it had been a brisk apology and assurance that the matter was to be taken care of directly. To Bailey, it was dismissal, curt.

Too late. Christian sat in his study with the reply from Hoare's. Most awkward, the letter said: certain new rules and regulations, incidental complications, unavoidable delay in complying with Your Grace's recent instructions. Suspicious shades of his mother's work in a prayer for Christian's health and a blessing on his soul from the pious Messrs. Hoare.

No money.

Not one shilling, from a bank where he knew perfectly well he had a running balance of four times his draft. He

stared at the reply until the words seemed to slide together
into strange hieroglyphic madness.

Christian carried, routinely, an encumbrance of six hundred thousand—and would go as high as seven for short-
term bridging. The delicate framework of his enterprise and
income, debt and endeavor, improvements and speculation
and capital in a complex interplay of his own making—it required intense application . . . and a rock-solid confidence in
him by the men who advanced their money with his. Like in-
terlocking arches, like a beautiful tiered aqueduct that could
stand for centuries or fall with a stroke, it all rested on one
vital point.

The keystone was trust, and it was gone.

He ought to have known. He ought to have predicted, but
he'd been living in mist that cleared at its own inconstant
whim.

The structure could never have stood for long without
Christian's attention, but the paralysis of his agents, the letter from Stoneham, Bailey's packet full of demands like the
one from Sun Fire, the hedging reply from Hoare's, the ac-
celerating speed of destruction: he was going down—they
weren't going to wait for a hearing—they were going to kill
him while he sat here hiding at Jervaulx.

Christian walked through the day in silent panic, carrying
the letter from Hoare's, reading it again and again, dream-
like, as if it would be different the next time he looked at it.

Illusion. Everything around him was an illusion of
safety—this castle, that painting, the Aubusson carpets, his
servants. He'd known it, but he did not know what to do to
defend himself.

They could still send him back. They could break him
down and send him back. Maddy's protests would be swept
away in a moment, his aunt's promises forgotten—all mist
and paper. It would take a hearing to strip him of his legal
existence, aye, but it needed no more than physical coercion
to chain him in the nightmare again.

What was to prevent them? What ever stopped anyone

from throwing bothersome relatives into some convenient dungeon?

He looked around at the walls of his castle. He could lower the gates, seal himself in—man the parapets—arm for a siege . . . arm for a siege . . .

A suit of armor stared back at him in an empty corridor. He didn't even know where he was. His mazed brain kept hanging on that vision. A siege; he had to defend himself; they would seize him; what was to stop them? Jervaulx Castle had never been taken in siege or battle, not by Lancaster, not by Roundheads. In the Civil Wars, Parliament had not even attempted to attack a garrison known to be too strong to conquer. He gazed at the suit of armor.

And the answer came.

He had to be too strong. He had to be the duke again, the real duke, not this muddled coward run-hide not-man.

Power was his only true protection—the power to meet force with force—name, influence, fortune, control. He had lost it. No money, no authority, no command—they could come here and take him and send him back to that place.

Mist. He'd been living in mist, with the mad place waiting for him.

Durham exclaimed: "Good God, listen to this. Fane claims there's a story in town that you ain't been sick a' tall—you're just rusticating 'cause you're bankrupt!"

With rheumy sorrow, Calvin Elder intoned: "The wine seller regrets that he cannot provide spirits for the tenants' dinner this year, Your Grace."

Aunt Vesta stared at the London paper with horror. "Merciful God in Heaven. 'Ruined or Mad: What's Become of His Grace?'" She fumbled for her salts, and took a deep grim breath. "In the papers. God spare us, that I should have lived to see this day."

Maddy simply sat in the study with him and wrote his answers to the loan demands. She had quit blinking at each sum that crossed his desk, but she had a new stiffness about her, a chaste sternness that nettled him.

I will not act, Bailey had written, blatant insult.

So I will, Christian thought.

London. Ruined mad idiot, try to save yourself.

"Back home again tomorrow," Durham said cheerfully, over a dessert course of mince pies, plum pudding, jellies and cheesecakes. "The road begins to look familiar. Will you enjoy one of these cakes with me, Duchess?"

Maddy shook her head. She found it hard to eat when she knew that everything on the board was an unpaid obligation, right down to the cook's salary. Ever since she had learned the immense extent of Jervaulx's debts, she had felt ill inside. His income was grand, but his loans were beyond ordinary imagination. The number at the foot of the totaled list was fearful. Tremendous. Fantastical. It made her, a Quaker bred to devout thrift and prudence, almost afraid of him, of the reckless arrogance that could accrue such a burden with no thought for the outcome. She loved him, lay down with him, bared herself to his carnal touch—and yet she found suddenly that she did not know him at all.

She could not sup on such extravagance in the circumstances, not even for one meal. Instead of the cake, she took an apple that she knew had come direct from the home orchard, foregoing the cheese.

The duke, far down the shining table, said, "Tomorrow . . . go I . . . and Maddy . . . Belgrave Square."

She paused in cutting her fruit.

"To London?" Lady de Marly demanded. "And what is the meaning of this mad start?"

The duke's wineglass sparkled as he turned it in his fingers. "I . . . please."

His aunt took her fork to her mince pie, mashing it into tiny bits as if it were an enemy. "I wash my hands of you, boy. Leave me. Put yourself in their clutches. You'd do better to take Stoneham's trust and be done with it."

Jervaulx did not answer her. He kept his eyes on Maddy.

"Tomorrow," he said. "Prepare in . . . we . . . depart morning."

She put down her knife and fork. "I don't think that will be possible for me."

He lifted his eyebrows. "I require it."

The dinner table, Maddy felt, was not the place for discussion of the matter. She lifted slices of fruit onto her father's plate at her left hand. "There, Papa—that is a perfect apple. Wouldst thou have cheese with it?"

In the duke's bedchamber, Maddy discovered that someone had already been put to work packing. An open trunk in the dressing room held shirts and coats, and her gray silk, pressed and freshened as well as it could be. She took the dress out and returned it to the wardrobe.

As she closed the wardrobe door, Jervaulx came in to her. Maddy unbuttoned his waistcoat as she always did, and stepped back. He looked down at her a moment from beneath his black lashes.

"Hungry?" he asked, in a mocking tone.

"No," she said—not quite a lie yet.

"Bread. Water. Apple." He said it bitterly, as if it were an accusation.

"I eat what seems good and proper to me to eat," she answered, turning away. He appeared to have no idea of retrenchment, and not the slightest desire to attempt it. She had ventured to mention a number of savings that might be made at the castle alone, suggestions that had been met with impatient dismissal. Certainly a reduction of staff, even a sale of the contents, would not make much impression on the colossal total of his obligations, but he did not even wish to make a start.

It alarmed and offended her, this manner of going on in luxury and magnificence, when any right-minded person must know that every feeling and effort ought to be strained toward redeeming such an unconscionable folly.

He shrugged out of his coat. He almost laid it over the open lid of the trunk, then stopped. He looked up at her. "Dress?"

"I shan't leave here tomorrow," she said. "Papa will not be ready to travel again so soon."

"You come . . . with me. Father later."

"Papa cannot—"

"Damn Papa!" He tossed the coat and stalked out into the bedchamber. "You . . . *me!*"

Maddy closed her eyes. She searched for inner calm, denying the hurt. When she had some command over her feelings, she followed him into the bedchamber. He sat at his desk, in shirtsleeves and stockings, gazing at the outside of a folded letter.

The lamp lit his face in strong glare and shadow, made his hair and brows black as Satan's. "We *go*. We are . . . Duke and Duchess of Jervaulx. We attend . . . theater. Dance. You have dresses . . . rich. Even . . . I think a ball . . . we hold . . . entertainment. Spend money. Nothing is . . . *wrong*."

Maddy listened to him with a sliding heart. "No. Thou ought not. Thou canst not."

"Must," he said.

"Go to London. Go and see that thy agent pays the arrears— that is right and proper, to pay, and redeem what can be re- deemed, and then live circumspectly whilst thou strivest to repair thy fortune."

He turned abruptly in the chair, confronting her. "Not . . . redeem! Repair . . . not fortune! Repair reputation, do you understand? Confidence! Live . . . vast. Show 'em . . . confi- dent."

"To what end?" she exclaimed. "When thy affairs are in this terrific state? A proper reduction of thy expense, a sin- cere effort to diminish thy debt—*that* is what will inspire their confidence—perhaps even win thee real respect."

"No!" He leaned his head back and groaned. "No, no, no! Stupid . . . worst . . . to pay off—look like . . . trouble—silly simple . . . thee-thou! You don't understand."

She turned and marched back into the dressing room. "I understand that thou art full of deceit!" she exclaimed, unhooking her dress with an effort. "I understand that thou wouldst bear false witness in appearances! That thou hast learned nothing from thy travail! And what wilt thou do with this false confidence if thou canst secure it? Run thyself into more debt?"

"Yes," he said.

Maddy came to the door. She was so full of words that they tumbled together and none came out but the ones that would sting the most. "Thou ought to do as Lady de Marly says, then, and sign a trust, and let better men try to mend thy folly!"

His eyes narrowed. With a menacing grace, he rose from the chair and stood facing her.

"Not . . . better man. I am . . . *Jervaulx*." His gaze raked her, and she realized with horror that she had not even covered herself. She crossed her arms quickly. He made a sound at that, a harsh breath and a contemptuous smile. Sweeping up the satin dressing robe that lay waiting for him on the bed, he shrugged it on. He took up the decanter and glass. With a bow, lazy and cold, he departed.

Chapter Twenty-seven

"*I* should not be here," Maddy said, fretting already when they had just arrived, wandering the blue salon in Belgrave Square as the faint pops and crackles of early Guy Fawkes celebrations sounded beyond the shrouding curtain. "I shouldn't have left Papa again."

Christian made no answer, continuing to sort painstakingly through the stack of unopened mail that had accumulated at his town house. At the top were demands, most new, some duplicates of the ones he'd got at Jervaulx, then a series of solicitous inquiries after his health, sifting down to normal correspondence and invitations six months old.

"Perhaps thou dost not truly need me here?" she asked. "Perhaps, now that thou art settled, I could return?"

"No," he said.

Her talking to him made him lose his concentration. He had to pause and think to recall whose letter he held in his hand and in which pile he should place it on the sofa table.

"Durham can help thee in these matters, surely. Better than I."

Christian turned his head, scowling at the letter. Stafford. Stafford, yes—a decorous wish for Jervaulx's speedy recovery, no hint of the £15,000 mortgage the marquess held on the Gloucester property. A gentleman, but he went into the last pile, the ones who could be safely ignored.

"I really will be of no use to thee. I cannot dance, nor make idle conversation."

"Converse idle—now," Christian said, without looking up.

"Durham could write for thee."

He tossed down the letter he'd picked up. She made it harder, talking, wanting to go, when it was hard enough already. "You stay."

"I ought not to have left my papa."

He hit his hand against his chest. "Husband!"

"Thou art not reasonable."

"Not!" She angered him. What was more reasonable than that he expected her support when he needed it? All these letters and words, all at once—it gave him a headache.

She sat down in a chair across from him, her face shadowed beneath the sugar-scoop bonnet she'd taken to wearing again. "Thou ought to listen to me."

He glared at the stacks of letters. He knew she was unhappy with him; he knew that he could have come to town with Durham and left her to follow with her father at a pace that the older man could tolerate. But Christian had insisted she accompany him. He'd had a foreboding that was becoming a full-fledged suspicion now—that somehow if he hadn't, her arrival would have been delayed, put off and impeded by nebulous complications that he could not even name. He had sensed her resistance from the moment he'd said London; it had increased with every mile closer to town.

"You . . . listen! Must be . . . duke. Show . . . all . . . all well. Disaster, Maddy! This!" He waved his hand over the letters. "Edge . . . the edge of a cliff! Fall everything!"

"I understand that," she said. "I understand full well that thou hast borrowed beyond all sanity." She kept herself upright, with no emotion in her voice.

He heard the disapproval in it, nevertheless, and it infuriated him. "Understand . . . *nothing!*"

He'd though she would, she who'd been with him and knew what he faced if he lost—but all she did was preach of economy and dismissed footmen, until he saw that she did not comprehend at all. The rules of temporal power seemed impossible for her to grasp.

He could not seem to explain it. He could not convey to her the enormity of what tottered, the number of men whose own fortunes stood at risk with his, who would turn on him—if he was not the duke, if he let them see weakness—who would be upon him like wolves on a deer that had stumbled. They were on him already—these polite letters, the growing pressure of the demands.

He should pay them, she said. With what? Sell these paintings, she said. Not enough. Sell this house. Not enough—she frustrated him in her obtuse morality. Even if he did sell up, wasn't it obvious that suddenly advertising to the world that everything he owned was on the market must create a crisis? That the value of his property would plummet?

Sell Jervaulx Castle, she said—and that was enough and more, but the idea was so alien it was meaningless to him. It was entailed, he'd informed her stiffly, on his heir. And then she had called him a wicked selfish man who had run his own son into debt before any son was ever born.

He could not put concepts such as equity and leverage, floating debt and frozen assets into words. Mostly he found that he could not tell her the truth she seemed mercifully blind to—that he would drag her down with him if he failed.

She believed that she protected him. His wife, next-of-kin: Durham had put that notion in her head—and pure simple honest Maddy, she trusted to such flimsy things as law and order.

"Understand nothing." He took a deep controlling breath. "Maddy—when I came of age . . . debt . . . my father . . . two hundred thousand estate—every shilling encumbered!" He set his teeth together. "Today. Value two million . . . income . . . a hundred thousand clear."

"And a debt now that must make thy poor father turn in his grave."

"Loans, yes!" he said furiously. "Risk! I am . . . Duke of Jervaulx! They all know. Not a . . . bloody widow-woman." But he looked at the letters and despaired; he couldn't even read the claims on him at more than a snail's pace. He needed help—and would have cut his throat before he asked her for it now. "You . . . *here,*" he insisted, reduced to that. "Timms . . . come later."

"I should prefer at least to return so that I might accompany him."

"No." She would not come back if he let her go. He felt it in his bones.

"It is only for a very short while, until I can bring Papa with me."

"No."

"I'm sorry that thou wilt not approve, but I must."

"No!" He took a step toward her.

"I will leave tomorrow."

He stood across the room. "I say . . . command!" He stood over her.

High color flamed in her cheeks. She did not look up at him but straight ahead, half hidden by the bonnet. "I am not at thy command."

"Yes! Husband vow. You obey . . . to me."

"I made no such vow." Her voice held dead calm defiance. "I am not obliged to conform to thine every whim. Thou dost not remember what I said." Still she didn't look up into his face. "I doubt thou even listened."

Christian had a sudden sense of having tread into uneasy ground. "I remember." He set his jaw. "Charge . . . God . . . to love. Husband. Wife."

"Helpsmeet," she said, "with no rule but love between us."

Help me then Maddy! I'm afraid. But he turned away from asking it. Having committed himself to a command, he wasn't going to change it to a plea.

The stacks of letters waited, words and words, to vanish and flicker in his head. The vile belittling frustration of it, the slow agony of such an everyday art, with so much riding on it.

"I should never have said anything." She spoke again. "I should never have stood before a false priest to wed thee at all." Her tone was remote and brittle. "I cannot join in such misguided conduct. It is vain and profitless, this foolish profane course of thine."

A sudden and consuming rage overwhelmed him. He would not bear it; he couldn't sit here while Miss Puritan looked down her nose at his bank balance. He hadn't touched her for a week, not since she'd got so thee-thou self-righteous. He wanted to kiss her until she ached and panted and forgot her bloody spotless sanctimony and became what they both knew she was with him. But he looked at her, only looked at her, and she lifted her chin and stiffened herself.

He swept all the mail from the table, tossing it back in the silver basket, heedless of his careful sorting. He left it and walked past his wife. Just beyond her, he paused. He went back to her, yanked at her bonnet strings and stripped the thing from her head.

"Go then!" he sneered. "Go!"

"So I will!" she exclaimed, snatching at her headpiece.

He cast the bonnet into the fire, walked out and slammed the door behind him. If there was anything in the world that he hated, it was pious women.

Maddy jumped up from the chair, snatching the bonnet back from the flames, beating it against the marble hearth.

"Oh, thou!" she cried, between her teeth. He was profligate, arrogant, impossible; she didn't want to be here; she couldn't do what he demanded of her. Dances, theaters: he'd told her what he planned, and she could not do it, but he wouldn't listen.

So much money—she did not know how he could have slept at night. She didn't know *him;* they were too incongruous—*why* did he look at her in that way, promising and threatening at once, and then stay all night in a chair in the drawing room? Why was he not a sober, prudent, right-walking man who would be humble, who would accept what God had made of him? But no, he chose to reign in Hell, like Satan in the poem, and told her she must stand beside him, wife and duchess, defying what his world might think.

Part of her said that she ought to stay. She well knew that he needed someone by him. He could not fare long alone—the Concern laid upon by her Opening seemed yet to hold. But she ought to go; she felt the mortal danger to herself—her love and her hunger for him that distorted Truth, this ruinous attachment to a worldly and carnal man. She was all a-tangle, torn between escaping and remaining, unable to perceive the Light amid her willful, creaturely passions.

If only she could find stillness, be composed in the calm silence of the soul . . . but she could not. The echo of stridency disordered her, the assertive rush of his presence, gone now, leaving the room emptier than even silence alone could make it.

She wanted to go to Meeting. She had not been for weeks. She wished to be still, to listen—but even in that thought was a new and terrible discovery. She was afraid to go now—duchess, wife to a child of the world. She was ashamed to be looked upon by other Friends, having strayed so far out of the Light.

The bonnet was beyond saving. She made a little sound of sorrow as she examined the scorched brim. Fiendish man! She would go back to Papa. Durham could come and stay with the duke.

A firework popped just outside, making her startle. With a hopeless moan, she tossed the bonnet back into the fire. The flames took it, surging up, swallowing the pristine white in a yellow and red and black conflagration.

Vauxhall was cold and damp. Out of season, the minor walks of the pleasure garden were unlit: only the main pavilion was specially opened, illuminated for a concert and pyrotechnics in honor of Guy Fawkes night. Christian stood in shadow, not mingling with the crowd in the grand walk. He wasn't ready to be seen by anyone he knew, though on a wet autumn night such as this, not many in society appeared to have spent their three shillings for admission to view Two Thousand Lamps in Patriotic Colours, Exhibition of Fireworks, Discharge of Cannon and Magnificent Bonfire.

Well enough. If he must make himself a fool, he preferred to do it before strangers. He let the flow of people carry him. Near a food pavilion he hung back in the dark, leaning on a tree and considering trying some Gunpowder Toffee. As he felt for coins, a flirtatious hand caught at the fold of his cloak.

"Preux chevalier," the lady said, veiled and almost invisible in black. "Pray treat me to a hot cider, dear, and let's have a little coze."

It was a cultured voice, low and husky, the familiarity of the approach unmistakably demimonde. Christian looked down at her over his shoulder, not straightening from the tree. The white hand she'd removed from her sable muff still rested on his arm. She tilted her head, nothing but a pale chin beneath the fashionable hat and heavy veil. He had a notion she was smiling under there. He smiled back, ironically, and shook his head.

"Ohhh—you don't look for a lady?" She suddenly contrived a rather transparent French accent. "You, a gentleman *du meilleur rang?* A duke, at least—and you cannot spare a poor girl a little glass of cider?"

Christian's muscles contracted with alarm. He looked at her more sharply.

She took a step back, lifted her skirts, and did a slow twirl, as if inviting him to examine her. She faced him with a deep curtsy.

"Still you do not know, Christian?" she asked, proffering a trim ankle.

He turned and started to walk away. He didn't know who, and didn't care; he didn't know what else to do.

She hurried alongside. "Christian!" She caught him, tossing back her veil. "For goodness sake! It's me."

He stopped. "Eydie." Her name escaped him, one of those words that was there, with no effort—and he wished he had kept on walking.

She put her arm through his and leaned on him. As he stood paralyzed, she rubbed her face on his sleeve. "Oh, Christian—Christian! It's so good to see you!" Her voice had a sudden break in it. She clung to him.

"What . . . you . . ." He couldn't manage more.

"Don't scold!" she said. "I just had to come out! I couldn't bear it. I brought my abigail. She's behind us—there, do you see. I know I oughtn't to be out, but another eight months of mourning—pity me, Christian! It's so wonderful to see your face!" She turned and began to walk, holding his arm. "You can't imagine what it's been like. Lesley *exiled* me! That very morning he discovered; I hadn't one instant to contact you—oh, he was hateful! He frightened me. And Scotland! That horrid gloomy barn of his family's, all the summer and fall. I couldn't even write; I missed you so! They said I must have rest after such a shock—they thought it was Lesley dying of his stupid influenza, but it was you I wanted; it was you I wept for all those dreadful months. No one would say a thing about you—not at the funeral, not after—nothing—all the vicious old biddies, they wanted me to think you had forgotten me! I've just got into town, that's why you couldn't find me—I was locked up like a prisoner, until—"

She stopped abruptly, looking down at his arm, fingering the scarlet lining of his cloak.

"Christian . . . you have a little daughter."

He stood still.

"I told them," she said defiantly. "I had to tell them, or they would never have let me out of that place! I told them she wasn't Lesley's, and you should have marked their faces! They let me go then!"

Christian stared down at her. *"Fool!"* he exclaimed. "You—"

"She has your eyes, and hair black as coal. She looks nothing like Lesley. Or me, for that matter."

Christian took her by both shoulders and gave her a shove. "Self—selfish . . . bitch! *Told?* What of . . . child?"

"I brought her back with me." She cringed away. "Christian, you hurt me!"

He let go, not without another push. "Stupid! She . . . she's *his,* in the law . . . wedlock!" He groaned, turning from her. Lesley Sutherland was dead? And Christian had a bastard daughter, labeled and doomed in another man's family. He felt dazed, unable to command his muscles, like moving in deep cold water.

"Please don't be so angry!" She stroked his sleeve with small petting movements. "Please! You—Christian—she is yours and mine. I thought . . ." Her voice trailed off, and she kneaded and pinched at his coat wordlessly.

It suddenly struck him what she'd thought. His heart began to pound.

God. Of course.

"Eydie," he said. "Eydie."

She leaned against him like a child, her cheek to his chest. "Christian. I love you so."

"I'm . . ." He had to make an great effort. *"Married."*

She looked up. Her face was rounder now, with wide, half-wild eyes, a shocked question.

He nodded in answer.

She pushed back to arms' length, growing white. "That's not true!"

"Yes." Even that word was a battle.

"No! No. You're lying. I haven't seen the papers for months, but I would have heard. I would have heard that!"

He looked at her steadily.

"When! Tell me when!"

He didn't even try; speech was beyond him.

"It is not true!" She pushed him. "You thought of this when Lesley died! You could have come then, but—oh! You blackguard! This is a lie to put me off!"

He shook his head.

"It is! Look at you. Who is she?"

He breathed faster, trying to gather words.

"Look at you—you can't even think of a name! It is a lie!"

He shook his head again.

She took hold of his cloak by both sides. "Christian—you can't be so cruel. You love me. I love you."

"Married," he said.

"I gave you everything! I never denied you anything! Christian—they have put me out, me and the child! As well as put me out! My odious jointure; I'm living on a pittance! I love you, Christian!"

"Think," he said, disengaging himself. "Let . . . think."

"Oh yes." She seemed to hear the desperation in her own voice. She straightened, gazing at him. "Yes, I—I'm sorry. I've . . . it's only that I've missed you so. And you know—" She began to stroke his sleeve again. "Your family was always in favor—your sister Clementia—even your terrible old aunt." She made a teary half-laugh and leaned against him. "Oh! Why did I ever marry Lesley?"

Christian knew exactly why—it was because he'd never offered for her himself and within the scope of polite conduct had made it abundantly clear that he wouldn't, even when they'd dangled and pushed her on him, as they'd always dangled and pushed the best-bred reigning belle on him every Season.

"Go home." Christian took her by the elbow and faced her back toward her maid. "I'll . . . think."

She clung to him, then suddenly reached up on tiptoe and pressed a passionate kiss against his mouth.

"No," he said, setting her away, knowing where she wanted that to lead. He took her bodily to the servant, dropping a half-crown in the maid's hand. "Home . . . *now.*"

"Yes, sir." The abigail took her mistress by the arm, familiar with Christian's generosity.

"When will you call?" Eydie demanded.

He stood looking at her. Then he turned and walked away into the darkest part of the garden.

Christian sat down on a bench well out of the light. A chilly drizzle weighed his cloak down on his shoulders.

Think, he'd said, but the shock was still on him.

A daughter.

It seemed that his whole life was upside down and under threat. He had money, but he could not control it. He had a duchess who thought she shouldn't have married him and an ex-mistress who thought she should. He had a daughter, and she carried another man's name.

He had no doubt the child was his. Sutherland had been out of the country; Christian had been amorous and careless, bedding a willing woman at whim and convenience—God, had that man been himself? So reckless. Not unheeding of consequences, no—not quite that—just cavalier certain that he could deal with any of them.

Now here he was in the ugly midst of one, and he was helpless. If things had gone as he'd expected when he'd first realized Eydie's condition, she would have slept with her husband and lied, Christian would have kept his distance, and the paternity of the child would have gone unquestioned. Even if Sutherland had suspected, it wasn't the most unusual of situations. People might guess; they might even be certain; but it would be tactless in the extreme to throw doubt publicly on the parentage of a child born to a legal union.

Damn Eydie. She shouldn't have declared it to Sutherland's family. If she'd just kept quiet, they'd have accepted the baby as her husband's, probably treasured it under the circumstances. Now—it didn't bode well that they'd sent both mother and child away from the family seat. Eydie was no maternal angel—she already had two sons who never left

Scotland—she hadn't even mentioned seeing them while she was there. Likely as not, as soon as she realized Christian wasn't going to marry her, the baby would be packed off to Scotland to be raised as a pariah.

And there wasn't a damned thing Christian could do about it. He couldn't recognize the child as his—that would be criminal cruelty. She'd be a pariah in truth then, socially as well as privately. He couldn't even contribute secretly to her welfare—at least not now, when he couldn't even convince his bank to honor a draft. And if they got him, if they sent him back . . . powerless . . . the mad place.

He rested his face down in his hands. The fireworks began, cracks and booms and cheers at a distance. A cold drop fell from his hat brim onto the back of his neck, but he sat without moving. He actually said a prayer. It was short and to the point.

Help me. I can't do this alone anymore.
Amen.

Maddy sat in a chair in the marbled entry hall. She had intended to wait only until he returned, and then go. But she was still dressed to travel, still squeezing her hands together, still listening to the mob and confusion that had reigned all night outside. It was after three in the morning.

Please, she prayed. *Please Lord let him be safe. Please Lord let him find his way. Please Lord if it is thy will let him come home.*

Durham was gone out looking in the places he thought Jervaulx might go. They had no servants but two footmen brought from Jervaulx Castle, and Maddy had sent them both out to look, too. She would have gone herself, but Durham had insisted that she stay off the streets—and she had no idea where to search anyway, amid the crowds where squibs and bonfires and flaming Guy Fawkes effigies lit the night.

The noise and fireworks slowly died down, the roar receding to distant pops and shouts. The streets emptied, and still he did not come. Maddy tensed at every sound of a carriage, but none stopped.

She bent over her lap and kept praying. When the front lock fell with a loud click, her head snapped up.

He came in softly. As he lifted his eyes, she saw that he had not expected anyone to be there.

"Thou art all right?" she asked. Her voice came out wrong, a little squeaky.

"Maddygirl," he said. His cloak and hat glistened with mist. He was beautiful, tall and dark, his blue eyes with that faint perplexity as if he could not quite understand what she was doing there.

She stood up. "Thou wilt be hungry. I have a plate warm downstairs. I can bring it up to thee, or if thou dost not mind, thou couldst eat it in the kitchen."

He hesitated, and then laid his hat on the hall table. He dropped his cloak there, too. It slid to the floor. Maddy went and picked it up, shaking out the damp folds.

He touched her as she rose, his fingers closing on her arm. "Maddygirl," he said quietly.

She bit her lip. She had worried so long and hard that it was difficult to hold back tears, foolish as they were. A very small hiccupping sob escaped her.

He took her in his arms and pressed her hard against him.

"I'm sorry!" she mumbled. "I could not leave thee. I could not."

His arms tightened.

"I was so afraid!" she said into the damp lapel of his coat.

He enfolded her, his cheek against her hair. "Don't . . . deserve thee. Maddy. Ask God . . . I . . . but I don't . . . deserve thee."

Chapter Twenty-eight

*H*e let her go back for her father. He insisted. He did not tell her what it cost him, the dread that he had to conquer, left alone within easy reach of his enemies. He kissed her hard and then held on to her shoulders too long. She looked up at him with a fresh concern, and he found the measure of his courage in the effort it took to form a cocky smile so that she would not stay.

He sent her with both footmen in the private carriage they'd brought from Jervaulx. It left Christian in Belgrave Square, in a closed house utterly empty except for himself—an odd sensation, not unpleasant in itself, with food in the kitchen that Maddy had seen to, cold meats and bread, and chocolate over a fire of his own making. Durham had offered to stay, bringing his valet, but Christian was determined to test his limits. If he could not manage a week of looking after himself, in his own familiar house, then he hadn't much hope of reassuming his greater affairs.

After she left, he kept a coal fire going in the back parlor, sipping chocolate and listening to early activity in the mews beyond the garden wall. No one came to his door: he'd not notified his family—not yet, not until he had thought it through. And now there was Eydie—another complication. Amazingly, she'd made no comment on his affliction. Except to accuse him of lying to her, she hadn't even appeared to notice any peculiarity in his speech.

Talked too much, he thought dryly.

So she loved him, did she? He disliked it when women said that to him. Didn't believe it, either—a lesson he'd learned at seventeen, the hard way.

He remembered Maddy, sitting white-faced and sober in the cold marble hall, waiting for him in the hours before dawn.

He would not let her down. He didn't want to make mistakes; he was slow and methodical on that account, but he had put together a plan.

He dressed to go out, getting it all right but the neckcloth, making an impossible disarray trying to tie a cravat. He had to settle instead for a black stock that he could buckle by feel and slide around to the back.

In the mirror, he looked almost whole. If he focused, he could find all of himself, not all at once, quite, but part by part—right hand, right arm, only a little peculiar, not precisely the way he thought he ought to look. He opened and shut his palm in the white glove: the glove in the mirror opened and closed concurrently.

Behind him in the mirror was his desk. Set to one side, under a few papers, was a neat closed wooden box: a writing machine that the engineer Marc Brunel had given him for making simultaneous copies while transcribing letters and drawings. Christian had not used it often. It was a clever feat of mechanics—he admired it for that, and kept it available, but his own handwriting was so illegible that there was little use in reproducing it when he had a secretary to copy out for him far more admirably.

But he had no secretary now. And hideous as his writing had become, he had to attempt it. The machine would save him double the labor, at any rate.

He sat down and opened the instrument. It required a little

setting up; he remembered how to do that—such a lovely small device, perfectly engineered.

Brunel and his son were magnificent. Christian had used their floating docks and tunneling shield, and held a considerable interest in their Rotherhithe tunnel under the Thames—a hell-born high flyer of a scheme that looked to lose thousands for Christian before it began to turn around, if ever—the kind of project that he'd tried and failed to explain to Maddy, that his brothers-in-law hated, that drove his debt and income balance, that could not be allowed to collapse for lack of fresh capital—yes, borrowed, in all likelihood—nor just paid off by letting go a few footmen.

With a renewed determination, he slid papers into place beneath the double pens. He made some circles and scribbles to test the instrument, then wrote *God Bless the King*.

He read it. God Bless the King. All there and correct.

He looked up at the second pen's copy. In letters pushed to one side of the full page, it said *God Bles O King*.

At first he thought it was a malfunction in the machine, but when he looked back down at what he had written, he swore softly to himself. His original was the same: if he looked with care he could see the identical shape and squeezed proportion to the letters, even though it still seemed correct if he only glanced at it.

He leaned over the instrument and wrote it again, this time keeping his eyes on the other pen instead of the one he held. *Guy Fa*—he caught himself beginning to write a *u* instead of a *w,* and drew the letter correctly. Cautiously, painfully, he went on, stopping himself in the midst of misspellings and even completely anomalous words—*Guy Fawkes Time* instead of *Night.*

It was rather terrifying, as if some phantom guided his hand, while he could only compare what it produced with his real intentions by watching what the copying pen wrote.

But it seemed to work, if he could trust what he read on the copy, correcting errors before they happened or at least able to recognize them when they did. He spent five hours at it. When he was done, he had two sheets, identical, both with margins centered evenly when he examined them upside down.

> *Gentlemen,* they read, *this is to inform you that I have made a settlement upon my wife, Archimedea Timms Langland, Duchess of Jervaulx, effective immediately, of the entire sum of my disposable estate and possessions, to be held by her and hers forever, with no sympathy or consent for any other claims by any other person upon it. This settlement shall go forward unless I should be shown satisfactory proof that no question, now or in the future, shall be made concerning my competence or ability to conduct my affairs according to my sole and unhampered judgment.*
>
> *Given proof of such, acceptable to me, I might possibly be disposed to revise the above arrangement.*
>
> *Christian, Duke of Jervaulx*

He thought that was what it said, anyway.

He hoped it was good enough. It had to be. Make them worry, make them stop and think and wonder if he was quite so helpless as he seemed to be.

The clerk in Torbyn's office had never seen Christian. While he wasn't especially lofty about going into the City, normally his business came to him, rather than the other way round, and arrived with scrapings and hustlings of no minor order. This pup merely looked up at Christian from his copying and said, "Good morning. Have you an appointment, sir?"

Christian took off his hat and cloak and tossed them on the desk, right across the poor devil's papers where condensed mist dripped off the capes onto the fresh copy. As the youngster sputtered, Christian flipped his card onto the pile and walked past. He went up the stairs. An instant later the clerk made a sharp exclamation and came pounding behind.

He caught up with Christian at the landing, bowing and

panting apologies. Then the youth went up the second flight half-backwards, still trying to bow, missed the third step, sprawled and picked himself up and bowed again. Christian really felt rather sorry for him.

He saved his true satisfaction for the look on Torbyn's face, and it was no disappointment.

"The Duke of Jervaulx," the clerk announced, opening the door. "His Grace!" he added belatedly, bright red.

Christian paused in the doorway, playing it to the hilt. The land agent who acted as his receiver-general was caught in the midst of dictation—his chair slung back on two legs, his hands locked across his waistcoat, white-haired and pugnacious, a bulldog barking his directions to the manager of some far-off estate.

He did not close his mouth. For a prolonged moment, Torbyn, clerks and Christian held a motionless tableau.

Christian moved first, to keep his advantage. He'd been practicing a single three-word sentence, repeating it over and over all the way to Blackfriars. "Make . . . *outlays,*" he commanded.

He didn't succeed with all three words, but Torbyn's expression changed from shock to comprehension. He rose from his chair.

"Pray sit down, Your Grace."

Christian didn't move. "Now. The checks."

"Bring the duke's box. This is the number." Torbyn pulled a scrap of paper toward him and scribbled quickly. He handed it to one of the clerks. The boy slipped out behind Christian. "You understand, Your Grace, that my hands have been tied without a power of attorney."

Christian had never allowed payments to be made out of this office without his own signature—an old cautious habit learned from his father's mistakes. Legally, Torbyn had not had the power to disburse funds, though Christian didn't doubt that the agent was an old bird wise enough to have reckoned a way to hold things together if he'd had the disposition to try.

"I'm delighted to see you recovered," Torbyn said, when Christian remained silent. "Mr. Manning had given me cause to be greatly concerned."

Outside, some porter whistled sharply. Christian walked to the window, looking down into the traffic. "No concern," he said.

From just below, the boy who must have answered the whistle took off running across the street, stuffing a message into his coat as he went. A moment after, the clerk's feet sounded on the stairs.

The youth entered the office and set a large blue box on Torbyn's desk, a carton that usually came to Belgrave Square once a month for this little ritual of check-signing. The agent opened it and began removing books. "I'm afraid you've caught us flat. We'll have to write out the checks. It will take a little while. Would Your Grace care to step into the parlor with me for a cup of coffee in the meantime?"

"No." Christian didn't want to spend any longer in conversation than he had to do. Damn! He had not thought of this—the checks and counterfoils had always been prepared before, ready for his signature.

"Very well." Torbyn set a chair. "If you would be pleased to sit here . . ."

"No," Christian said. "I . . . must go." He felt his command of his tongue slipping. "I . . . other . . . business."

"If Your Grace will honor us with a few minutes of your time."

"Later." Christian began to move toward the door.

"Not long! Really, not long at all. I'll put both boys on it. Just a quarter hour."

Something in Torbyn's anxiety penetrated Christian's awareness; he thought of the whistle and the messenger boy. He stopped.

"Damn you!" he snarled. He swung back to Torbyn. "Sent for them!"

"Now—just a moment—Your Grace, indeed—I think you ought to consider—"

As Christian pitched books into the box, the agent tried to prevent him. Christian froze with Torbyn's hand on his wrist. He raised his eyes.

"Do you dare?" he asked, deadly quiet.

Torbyn let go. Christian cast the book in.

He had not meant to move so soon, before he was ready, but he pulled the statement he'd written from his coat pocket and laid it on Torbyn's desk. "Convey to . . . Mr. Manning."

He covered the blue box and picked it up, escaping, striding steadily, holding himself back from breaking into a run.

He was committed now. He could not flinch. He walked into Jervaulx House without notice, gambling that Torbyn's messenger had gone to one of his brothers-in-law and not here. It was his mother's at-home day. Well enough: guests would keep her a little in hand. Her butler met him, coming down the stairs.

"Calvin," Christian demanded.

The man turned utterly white. Christian reached out and grabbed his arm before he could retreat.

"Tell . . . *where!*"

"With Her Grace, but—"

Christian paid him no more attention, taking the steps two at a time. He rounded the upper banister and strode into the drawing room.

Ladies sat in conversation, stiff as if they still had backboards strapped to them, their hats all feathered and flowered. He walked toward his mother.

She was talking; it was the silence that he carried with him across the room that caught her notice. As her companion fell mute along with the others, she looked up at him and swooned.

It was a real one, too. Ladies gave little shrieks; Christian caught her as she slumped forward in her chair. He held her back from falling out of it, looking over her at Calvin, who had been gathering cups on a tray at the back of the room.

The faint lasted only an instant. As soon as she drooped,

she began to move weakly. Between him and Calvin, they helped her upright. She clutched at Christian's arm, blinking up at him feebly.

"I'm . . . Belgrave Square," he said. He pulled free, and while his mother made incoherent whispers of entreaty, gave Calvin a long look. "Come?"

"Certainly, Your Grace." He was still supporting the dowager duchess. "I will be there directly."

"I . . . need staff," Christian said.

"I'll see to it, Your Grace."

Christian gave his mother a deep bow, nodded politely at the shocked circle of feminine faces, and got himself out of there.

They arrived at Belgrave Square too soon: Manning, Stoneham, Tilgate and Perceval, with an attorney and Torbyn along for good measure. Their force of six made Christian taut with alarm, but he had a remedy for that, loaded and primed in his pocket, to even the odds.

Calvin had not come yet. Christian saw them from the window of the blue salon. Alone, he waited there, listening to them pound on the door. His lips drew back in contempt as he heard them force it and start to search.

Spurious hospitality was not within his ability, nor his mood. It was Manning who came to the salon, with Stoneham close behind. Christian merely stood watching them, lifting his eyebrows in a show of disinterested amusement at their expressions when they found him there.

Stoneham went squealing for the rest. Christian did nothing as they came in and Manning closed the door. He left the first move to them.

It was somewhat anticlimactic. Stoneham, foppish and nervous, kept fiddling at his excessive sideburns. "You gave your poor mother a sad start!"

Christian leaned against the mantel. "Poor mother," he said dryly.

A silence fell.

"Are you alone here?" Manning demanded. "Where is the woman?"

"*Duchess* . . . do you mean?"

Manning stalked to a chair, a large and florid man with a look of the squire and the hunt about him. "You don't mind if we sit?"

Christian let his mouth curl a little. "Can I stop?"

Manning waved the others down. The attorney, a Mr. Bacon, laid a rolled sheaf of papers on the sofa table.

"Mr. Torbyn says that you took the checks and estate books," Manning said. "I don't think that was wise, Jervaulx."

Christian remained standing, his arms folded.

"We're asking you to return them."

Christian allowed his bitter smile to grow. "Bastard."

Manning took a breath. He leaned forward in his chair. "We're trying to do what's best for you."

Christian let that hang in the air.

"Damn it, we're trying to save what can be saved! But you and your aunt make it bloody difficult." He sat back. "This 'settlement' you claim you've made—you don't really think a court in this country would uphold it?"

Christian inclined his head. "You . . . find out."

"You must face it, Jervaulx. Everything you do now, everything since—since your wit failed—is in question. Including this mockery of a marriage. Do you understand that? I don't think you do. You seem—your aunt spoke of lucidity—but lucid intervals will not suffice to administer the estate in a proper manner. When the hearing goes forward as it ought to have done a month since, the testimony will cover the whole period."

"If." Christian smiled. *"If."*

Manning's voice rose. "No *if!* The hearing goes forward!"

"But, Manning—" Stoneham reached out a hand.

"Perhaps—if I might speak," the attorney said in a conciliatory tone. "I've brought Mr. Perceval's and Lord Stoneham's proposal for a private trust, Your Grace. I would be pleased to do myself the honor of reviewing it with you."

Christian held out his hand. The attorney jumped up and untied the set of papers, giving them over to him.

"The first page is only preliminaries and courtesies," Mr. Bacon said. "So if—"

Christian pulled off the first page and dropped it into the fire.

"That is—" The man looked nonplussed. "If you will turn your attention to the second, you will—"

Christian fed the second page to the fire. He held up the third, smiling a question at the attorney.

"For God's sake, he's an imbecile!" Manning stood up. "You can't expect rational understanding." He moved as if to snatch the remaining papers away.

Christian dropped the whole bundle into the grate. It curled and blackened, and with a puff exploded into yellow flame.

"No . . . *trust*," he said.

"This is futile," Manning snapped. He reached for Christian. "Stoneham! Hold him!"

It was what Christian feared, half expected, and yet when it came it seemed unreal. Manning made a wild grab; Christian jerked back and drew the pistol. Stoneham, who'd made no more than a timid advance, stopped in his tracks. Torbyn had been more aggressive: he was frozen a close foot away, with the attorney sheltering behind him.

Christian meant to order them out, but his blood was pounding in his ears. He could not command a word. They wanted him; they would take him if they could do it. He felt how close it was—how he would wake up in the jacket, with the Ape and the garrote and madness.

"Careful," Torbyn said. "Careful, Mr. Manning."

Manning slowly dropped his hand.

"He's gone mad," Stoneham whispered.

Christian gave an enraged laugh. "Bumble . . . amateurs!" The Ape would have had him, twice over. He felt sickness and fury in his throat.

"Lay it down," Manning said, with a little move of his

head. "Lay it down on the mantel, Jervaulx. It will only make things worse."

"Get out," Christian said.

"We're here to help," Manning answered, with a coaxing reason that put him in more mortal danger than he knew.

"Out," Christian growled.

"Put down the gun," Manning urged.

Christian saw that his brother-in-law was going to force it—Manning either had no idea of what a real madman could do, or was counting on quite enough lucidity for Christian to see the obvious: that he couldn't commit murder in his own salon and get off as a reasonable man.

"Put it down," Manning said "You aren't going to shoot anyone."

Christian knew he should have waited. He should have had Durham. He shouldn't have let them corner him alone. His brother-in-law had reason on his side of a bluff. Christian had the madhouse, had losing his money and Maddy and his mind in that place.

He'd rather hang.

He leveled the gun, an unrifled, short-barreled wickedness that didn't need much aim to take down the nearest man and more. As his lips drew back, Manning seemed to comprehend. He suddenly lost all his color.

"Don't."

It wasn't Manning. It was Maddy's voice, clear and high, a shock like a reveille trumpet in the frozen silence. She stood in the doorway, stern plain propriety and sense in her gray gown, with Calvin and three footmen ranged behind her.

Christian exhaled a long, soundless breath of deliverance. He smiled slowly at his brothers-in-law.

Maddy stood back and lifted her hand. "Ye men will leave now. The duke wishes ye promptly gone from the premises."

Chapter Twenty-nine

*H*e sat in a chair, unloading the pistol, working with slow care, his head turned to see it better, heedful of the percussion cap. When he had it safe, he laid them both aside and slanted a look at her. "You should be . . . at . . . Papa."

"The further away we got, the more I thought—thou needed me more." She lowered her lashes. "I am thy protection. I ought not to have left thee."

He allowed her to think it. He didn't say that he'd have chosen the pistol, Calvin and three sturdy footmen over her for protection any day. He wished that she had not even been there at such an unpredictable moment. It had come down to what he'd known it would: the balance of force against force.

"They wished to take thee?"

"Manning . . . jumps. Stoneham, Perceval . . . not so sure. You . . . Calvin . . . change their minds." He smiled dryly, and gave her that. "Glad you came."

"Yes. I won't leave thee again." She looked shaky in the aftermath. "They will remember it. It was not wisely done of thee, Jervaulx—the gun."

He shrugged. "Defense."

"Peaceful conduct is thy best defense." Her voice was audibly quavering in belated reaction now.

"Easy . . . say!" He stood up and lifted her hands out to her sides. "Great hulking brute . . . as you. Look! Scare . . . little children. Dogs tails down . . . you walk past. Ground shakes. Easy to be . . . peaceful . . . you!"

She swallowed, compressing her lips, humor gaining ground against her nerves. "Thou art buffle-headed."

He was glad to see her. He was so glad to see her. "Aye. My head is . . . buffled." He brought her hands together and kissed the backs of her fingers. "Rest . . . in working order."

Her hands closed, but he held them. Her mouth was barely, shyly smiling; her straight sweep of lashes made a veil of gold over green.

He pulled her a little toward him, hungry with relief and the release of tension, with her unexpected presence. He was still free and alive, and he kissed her, sucked her lips as if he could have the breath from her and held her hard against him. Without words he lifted her. Doors and hall, her mouth, her body in his arms—his bed.

He spent no time on polite preliminaries: he took her with rough vigor, reclaiming what was his, while she twined her hands around him and pulled him down with an urgency that seemed the same.

In the morning, Maddy was put to work over breakfast writing out a pointedly polite suggestion to a partner of Hoare's Bank that he present himself without delay in the duke's drawing room—an objective she was pleased to pursue, since in the meantime they were living off the two hundred eighty-seven pounds left from Jervaulx's buckles, a sum which no longer seemed huge to her but appallingly inadequate to the duke's expense.

As soon as she completed that wording to Jervaulx's satisfaction, she had to write a notice to be inserted in the newspapers that the Duke of Jervaulx no longer chose to honor Mr. Torbyn, land-agent, with the exercise of his business affairs. All queries and interests should hitherto be directed to Belgrave Square, and no expense or commission undertaken save by the duke's personal authority. She was then allowed a respite while the duke went upstairs to be shaved and dressed.

In the back parlor, a comfortable room fitted out in daisy yellow, overlooking a barren garden court and the wall of the mews, she indulged in a second cup of tea. She started a letter to her father, knowing that after Jervaulx returned she would likely have little more time for it.

She was in the midst of the second page when Calvin slipped into the parlor with a silver tray balanced on his hand, closing the door behind him. Maddy looked up reluctantly.

The butler bowed. "The duke is not with you, Your Grace?"

She felt that neither she nor London Calvin quite knew what to do about one another: as something of old antagonists who had found themselves standing firmly together last night, they seemed now in an odd suspension of hostilities that might turn into peace or war at a feather touch. Maddy sincerely preferred peace, so when he addressed her solemnly as "Your Grace," she almost didn't object. It was becoming a true cross, this worldly title, which was what made her certain that she ought to bear the consequences of denying it.

"I wish to be called 'Mistress,' Calvin," she said, in her most amiable manner. "If thou wilt remember, I cannot give nor accept any such compliments as the other."

She fully expected him to stiffen and look down his long nose—just like Calvin Elder's. It was provocation enough, she knew, to set them at odds for good and all. But instead, the dignified set of his jaw seemed to temper a fraction. "I remember, Mistress," he said.

He surprised her with this easy capitulation. "Thou art not offended by it?"

"It would be impertinent of me to be offended by anything you expect, Mistress."

Maddy lowered her chin, dubious.

He made a bow. "After begrudging a proper address to His Grace, if you now set yourself up as worthier of it than he—in that case I should have been offended. However, since you are no more than consistent, I must instead appreciate the reliability of your conduct."

She chewed the end of her quill. "Dost thou like to wear hair powder?"

She startled him with that, she could see. He lowered the tray. "I had not thought as to whether I liked it or not. I suppose . . . it makes the hair unpleasantly stiff, after the paste is applied. And it has to be washed out every evening, which must sometimes lead to colds."

"Well, if thou dost not like to wear it, thou needst not. Jervaulx does not care, and I think it a silly waste of money."

Calvin bowed.

Maddy hid a smile. "Thou ought not to bow to me, either," she said.

He half-bowed, and caught himself. "As you say, Mistress." He straightened. "The duke, I apprehend, has gone upstairs?"

"Yes. Is there something I can do instead?"

"You need not bestir yourself, Mistress. Merely an early visitor for His Grace."

"Oh dear." Her heart dropped. "The dowager duchess?"

"Certainly not. I should never ask her to wait in the hall!" He lifted the tray a little. "I might mention," he added, in a confidential manner, "that I've not known the duke to encourage his mother to call in this house. He goes to her."

"I see." This lack of filial hospitality seemed undutiful, but perhaps not entirely unjustified. Maddy bit her lip. "I suppose—I think perhaps—Jervaulx wishes me to speak to these people." She stood up. "Perhaps I ought to make his visitor welcome, if thou wouldst see him in here to me, until the duke comes down."

Calvin cleared his throat. "You would do well to ask His Grace's desire in this instance, Mistress. May I go and inquire for you?"

"In this instance?"

"In this instance, yes." He shut his mouth up tight, with the look of a man who had spoken all that he was going to say.

"Oh. I hope—thou dost not think it rude to keep the caller waiting?"

"I will inform the duke, Mistress." He made another bow, caught himself in the midst of it again, and closed the door.

She was left perplexed, not knowing if Calvin had some objection to this particular visitor or if he feared that Maddy would disgrace herself and the house on her first trial. She wondered that Calvin had not put this person in the breakfast alcove where Maddy had always waited. It seemed a deliberate indignity to leave him standing in the hall. That, and Calvin's strange attitude, made Maddy tend toward the conclusion that it was the caller who was more questionable than herself.

Just as she was tentatively settling on that, the door cracked. "Christian," said a playful feminine voice. "It's Eydie." The door swung farther open. "Come, I know you're here—"

The caller stopped on the threshold, dressed in elaborate mourning black, her veil thrown back to reveal a delicate face and striking yellow hair in ringlets down her cheeks. For an instant this Eydie seemed startled, taking in Maddy from head to toe. Then disinterest came into her face.

"Ah," she said. "I wish to see your master."

"The duke is upstairs." Maddy kept her voice steady, determined not to make a complete botch of this first encounter with his society. "I'm Archimedea Timms—that is . . . I am his wife." She extended her hand in greeting.

The woman had been looking in her reticule; at the same time Maddy offered her hand, the caller lifted hers. "You will take this—" The lady looked up, arrested in the act of handing Maddy a note with a half-crown prominently displayed under her glove. "What did you say?"

"I am Archimedea." Maddy tried to make her lips form a smile, without much success. "The duke's wife. It is a surprising thing, I know."

Eydie seemed to think it more than surprising. She seemed to think it hilarious. She turned back her head and burst into a high-pitched, nervous laugh. "This is a joke," she said.

"No," Maddy said.

The note and coin slid to the floor. "He's paid you; he's paid you to sit here until I came, and say that to me. It is a joke."

"No. I fear—it isn't a joke."

Eydie shook her head. "Yes. Yes, yes, yes. It's a joke."

Calvin appeared in the doorway. He was rigid as stone, utterly without expression.

"His Grace is not at home, madam," he said to the visitor. Eydie gazed at him.

"He is not at home," Calvin repeated firmly.

She began giggling in the most dreadful way, falling into a chair as if some skittish puppet-master had dropped her. "It is a joke!" She lay back in the chair and kept giggling in that strange manner, growing more agitated. "It is a cruel trick."

"Mrs. Sutherland, I must see you out directly," Calvin said.

"It is *cruel!*" she screamed, throwing back her head. She flung herself from the chair and ran past him to the hall. "Christian!" Her voice and footsteps echoed in the marble stairwell. "Christian, it is cruel! Do you hear me? It is *cruel!*"

Maddy hastened out after Calvin, in time to see Eydie rush halfway up the curving flight of stairs.

"Do you hear me?" she shrieked, holding her skirts high as she ran upward. "It is a *lie!* You are not married!"

Amid the reverberating shrillness of her voice, Jervaulx

strode out to the top of the stair. He was in boots and shirt-sleeves; he caught the wrought-iron and gilt balustrade and held there, his fingers white with the strength of his grip.

"Christian!" She stopped below him. "It is not true." Jervaulx didn't move. He stood looking at her, with stillness setting into every line.

She hung against the inclined rail, curling her hands around it, leaning her head down on her outstretched arms and looking up at him like a puppy crawling forward to beg affection. "Please don't tease me this way. Please tell me."

"True," he said, in a low voice that filled the hall with hushed sound.

Eydie let herself collapse onto the steps, breaking into the same hysterical giggles. "But I gave you everything. Ch-Christian!"

Her laughing sobs echoed against marble. Maddy realized that Jervaulx's valet was standing in the upper hall behind him; all three footmen were in the lower hall and the chambermaid and cook had come to the door of the back stairs: everyone paralyzed and staring.

Maddy picked up her skirt and mounted the stairs. She heard Jervaulx make a wordless sound, but she went to the weeping lady and knelt on the stairs beside her. "Come," she said. She took Eydie's black-gloved hand and drew her up off the cold stone. "Come, thou must not make thyself ill." Eydie was limp, breathing in gasps. Maddy sat on a step, slipping her arm behind the wretched lady, pulling Eydie against her shoulder, rocking her. "I'm sorry. It shouldn't have happened this way. I'm sorry."

The other woman was crying in earnest now, frenzied tears and great gulps of air, like a child in a tantrum. Maddy met Calvin's eye and moved her head, asking him to clear the hall. He looked as if he had just witnessed a terrible accident, moving in a stilted, shocked way to obey her.

"I—hate—him," Eydie mumbled. "I—*hate*—him. I hate you!"

Maddy let her talk, holding her, staring at her own knees

before her and the rich lace on Eydie's black gown. The other woman's hat brim pressed painfully into Maddy's neck.

Eydie whimpered, a long, aching sound of grief. "It should have been me. It should have been . . . me."

"I know," Maddy said quietly. She looked at Eydie's bright yellow curls dangling down and remembered the lock in the watch-case by Jervaulx's bed. "I'm sure it should have been thee."

"What?" Eydie's body convulsed with a scornful sob. "Don't you want him . . . now that you . . . now that you—" She moaned again, pulling away and hunching over her lap, holding her arms tight around herself. "Don't you—want him now?" she said between tears and a bitter laugh.

"I meant—that we are not much like," Maddy said.

"Like!" The lady's shoulders shook. She put her face down in her lap and cried.

Maddy stroked her shoulder, feeling the deep huffing sobs under the exquisite satin.

Eydie dug in her reticule for a handkerchief and held it to her mouth. "You're one of those Quaker people," she said through the linen.

"Yes, I was brought up a Friend."

She rocked herself. "I don't believe it. I don't believe it. I hate you, Christian." She raised her voice to a scream. "I *hate* you, do you hear me?"

No answer came. Maddy didn't look to see if he was still there. Eydie began to weep again, more quietly now, her handkerchief pressed to her face. She shrugged Maddy's hand off her shoulders.

"How did you manage it?" she asked suddenly.

Maddy sat on the stair, gripping her fingers together around her knees. "Manage?"

"How did you trap him into it? And don't tell me silly lies," Eydie cried. "His sister is my friend. She will tell me everything true." She suddenly gathered up her skirt and started down the stairs, as if that thought had impelled her

from grief into action. At the foot, she stopped, then cast a
quick glance backward, above Maddy. An instant later she
had pulled her veil over her face and vanished into the
vestibule. The front door slammed, echoing around the hall.

Maddy sat on the steps. She had to think of each breath,
holding back the shudder that started in her stomach and
tried to work its way outward to all her limbs. When she
thought she had it under control, she rose. She turned, but
she already knew that he was not there: she had seen it in
Eydie's face.

Calvin came quietly into the hall from the back stairs.
"It's my blame, Mistress," he said. "I ought not to have let
her in the door."

"Calvin," she said in a treble voice that almost went out of
her command. "I need to have my cloak."

"Mistress—"

"I must go outside. I have to go outside."

"The garden is—"

"No." She started for the front door. "Away from here."

"A moment, Mistress. His Grace will wish to know."

She opened the door. Cold damp air poured in—it felt
good on her hot cheeks. She did not wait for Calvin or her
cloak, but quietly closed the door, went down the pristine
white steps and began to walk toward home.

Christian heard the front door slam beneath his dressing
room. He didn't move, nor look down on the street to see
Eydie leave. He stood alone in the center of the room, the
sound of her shrieking voice still in his ears.

He stood there for a long time.

The bizarre unreality of it, to stand watching while his
wife went to comfort his weeping mistress. And vile piece of
work that he was, he'd thought: *she doesn't realize.*

If she did or if she didn't, her simple compassion cut him
open—exposed him to himself for what he was: he'd been
furious at Eydie's brass in coming here, enraged into frozen
passion at the scene she made, ready to throw her into the

street—and Maddy, oh, Maddy, she made him feel it, how he'd wounded.

I didn't mean it to come to this: nauseating whine of every thoughtless devil after the fact. I didn't mean it; I wouldn't have done it if I'd known, if I could have foreseen, if I'd just considered, if, if, if . . .

Calvin's light scratch at the door made him turn. He flung it open.

The butler looked like a man facing execution. "Your Grace—" he began.

Christian cut off the groveling before it could start. Too disgusting, to rake down a servant for what was at heart nothing but the devil's luck and the devil's own folly that had induced it. "Where?" he demanded.

"Mrs. Sutherland?" the butler asked.

"Hang Sutherland! Duchess is . . . where?"

"Your Grace—she has gone out. A few minutes ago." As Christian made an exclamation and headed through the door, he added quickly, "Your Grace—I thought it best— she seemed determined to proceed. I sent a man after her with a cloak, and orders to attend her at a distance and send word if she doesn't return directly."

Christian halted. "Yes. All right." Let her calm herself. Give her time. Give her time and room. "Yes. You did . . . well."

The butler cleared his throat and said reluctantly, "Mr. Hoare has arrived to see you, Your Grace. I have put him in the library."

Damn—so soon! Christian wasn't prepared—he'd intended to have Maddy with him, primed to help him if he needed it. Hoare was the lynchpin; if Christian failed here, he was dead.

He pushed a breath through his teeth and picked up his coat. He had no choice. The wheel was turning. He'd set it to rolling and had to ride it now.

Christian entered the double-storied library from its book gallery, where he could overlook the room below. Pausing amid the familiar smell of leather bindings, he swore silently as he looked down upon the men sitting like a pair of misplaced undertakers on a couch still slipcovered in red summer stripes. His summons had been answered by the one partner Christian had the least desire to deal with. Of these two promising scions of the Hoare family, the elder was agreeable enough, but his younger cousin was Religious—not a trait which recommended him to Christian, nor the other way round.

Hoare's had been bankers to the Dukes of Jervaulx for a century. Christian hadn't changed that, though he'd often thought of it when the partners had tilted at him with polite vigor over his schemes—reckless or visionary, depending on whose side held the floor. But Hoare's had stood with the family through his father's decades of real debt, so Christian had kept on with them, impatient though they made him. He wished now that he'd been a little less loyal.

He thought of the letter they'd written in reply to his last draft. Pray for his health, would they? Self-righteous bastards. He'd give them something to pray about.

With a loud, rude step, he went down the stairs and swung to face them from the foot. "Gentlemen," he said, without greeting. "Explain."

They both rose, with murmured good mornings. The religious Mr. Hoare walked forward as if to shake hands.

Christian didn't move. The man stopped, losing momentum before he got three feet.

"I . . . *wait*," Christian said. "Explain."

"If you refer to the delay in—"

"Delay!" Christian cut into the banker's dignified words. He did not dare allow a rational dialogue to develop. "I am . . . my feelings . . . so violent—" He flung himself away from the staircase. "Can hardly . . . speak, sir!"

He didn't want to play up inarticulate fury too far or he would encourage doubts about his sanity. So he stopped at his desk and sat down. This, at least, he'd had time to prepare—

another draft already written out and placed beneath a blank sheet, the whole concealed from their view by a convenient stack of books. He picked up a pen and wrote across the blank sheet—God knew how it turned out, but he didn't stop to check—and slipped the one Maddy had examined for errors from beneath.

He stood up and held it out. "Try again."

The bankers had looked uncomfortable from the start. The elder of the Hoares stepped forward to accept the draft, but his partner said, "I'm afraid there may still be a delay."

"Why?"

"We have instituted certain new regulations."

Christian leaned on his desk. "My money . . ." he said menacingly. "You have . . . lost it?"

"Certainly not!" The elder spoke up.

"To be perfectly candid, Your Grace," the younger Mr. Hoare said stiffly, "your family has given us grounds for concern as to . . ." He found himself swimming in deep water and spread his legs, taking a firmer stance. "As to the propriety of allowing funds to be removed from your account at present."

"Ah." Christian smiled. "No regulation." His lip curled. "Just plain . . . thief."

"Now see here! We are merely exercising due care, as anyone of sense would expect us to do in this uncertain situation."

Christian sat back in his chair, picking up a copy of *The Times*. He held it up in one hand and looked at it consideringly. " 'Bank robbery. Hoare's steal . . . *deposit*.' " He tilted his head in approval. "Clever headline."

They stood like men facing an armed highwayman themselves. Christian lowered the paper and smiled apologetically.

The elder Mr. Hoare folded the draft and put it into his pocket. "Of course that won't be necessary," he said, in a quieter tone than his cousin had yet used. "We had understood that Your Grace was not well, and that communication alleged to be from yourself might not be perfectly legitimate. We wished to exercise due prudence. For myself, I hope it hasn't caused Your Grace offense. If so, we must apologize profoundly—must we not, Cousin Hoare?"

His younger relation begrudged it. His tone still held a grain of defiance. "Of course, we'll be keeping strict account, should there be any inquiry from the Lord Chancellor's office."

"By all means," Christian said. "The money . . . when?"

"I'll have a courier here before noon," the elder said.

Christian pulled the bell for Calvin. He let them stand there until the butler came, stewing in his unforgiving silence. They went out with stiff wishes for his continued health that he answered with no more than a curt nod.

When they were gone, Christian collapsed heavily into his chair. His hands were not quite steady.

Victory.

All on his own, victory.

He wanted to grin and weep at once. He wanted to share it, this charge of elation. He wanted Maddy beside him.

The watermen's calls were all that was tangible about the river—the calls, and the slow current at the bank that fanned the water weeds, a silver surface that vanished into mist a few yards out. The fog had clung to Chelsea all day, swallowing the row of houses behind her and muffling the sound of traffic. Maddy leaned on a rail by the river, huddled in her cloak. The footman from Belgrave Square was still with her, a patient silhouette standing under an awning across the street, just at the edge of the mist.

The light had begun to fail. She knew she would have to do something soon. She could not stay here forever.

A waterman ran his punt up onto the bank, secured it, and dragged out a basket. She watched him hike his pants and make a nimble leap to a set of wooden steps. He climbed up. "Live eels, ma'am?" he asked cheerfully.

Maddy shook her head.

He walked past, holding his burden up for the view of a carriage that Maddy heard coming along the street behind her. "Live eels, then!" he called. "Live-o!"

The steady beat of the horses' hooves advanced slowly. Maddy turned to look as the coachman curbed his team in a jingle of harness. The waterman raised his eels hopefully toward the shining black chariot.

It had a bright, familiar crest on the door. She saw her shadowy footman come forward to it from the mist.

The door opened. Jervaulx stepped down, his cape spreading to show a flash of scarlet. He stood looking toward Maddy.

"Five and a half, Your Lordship," the waterman said, asking an outrageous price. "Alive-o. Look here." He started to open his basket.

Jervaulx glanced at him, then toward the footman with brief nod. The servant forestalled the ecstatic waterman from displaying his wares to the duke, drawing the eel catcher away toward the rear of the carriage. Jervaulx walked toward Maddy.

He stood in front of her.

"Enough," he said quietly. "Come . . . home."

Home, she thought. But this was home, this village and river, these trees, these boats; she knew them all, could have found them in the mist, with her eyes closed. She had lived here all her life.

He looked away from her, toward the river. Then he made a sweep of his hand, dismissing the carriage.

"Walk?" He offered her his arm.

In silence, she turned, resting her fingers lightly on his sleeve. He was warm beneath her cold hands. He put his glove over her fingers, covering them against the misty air.

He always made so it easy to walk with him. Without awkwardness, with a feeling of fitting naturally to her step. They walked until Maddy could no longer hear the soft snorts and intermittent hoof thumps of the waiting horses.

"Wast thou engaged to marry her?" she asked.

The muscle in his arm tightened a little beneath her hands, the only sign of change in him. "No."

"She said—that it ought to have been her."

He didn't answer.

"Beside thy bed, thou hadst a lock of her hair."

He was gazing at the pavement ahead, a hard, silent set to his mouth. He didn't deny it, nor repent it.

"And dost thou love her, then?" she asked at last.

He stopped, taking both her hands in his. "No, Maddy. No."

She drew away, hugging herself, facing the river. "If that is true—and thou received her token—verily, thou art a wicked man."

"Yes," he said, on the harsh note of some emotion she couldn't identify.

She watched a white cat, a pale indistinct shape that prowled among the beached punts. The water lapped softly below, blurring into the dusk.

"Come," he said. "Dark."

She didn't move. The cat placed a paw upon the prow of a boat, then made a quick silent leap inside and vanished under the seat.

"Thou art a stranger to me," she said painfully. "I do not truly know thee or what thou art."

Jervaulx spoke in the hush. "I am . . . ashamed, Maddy. To . . . the deepest . . . pit of my soul. All I can . . . say. Can't go back. Can't . . . change it."

The white cat emerged in the stern of the punt. It mounted a coil of rope, lay down and curled up there. She felt Jervaulx, unmoving, behind her.

"Come home," he said. "Maddy."

Wretched Eydie—to have given a lock of her hair to a rake. To fall in love with him, and end in hopeless weeping on his staircase. It was like a cautionary tale in a sermon-book. Maddy could draw the proper moral from it.

"I'm afraid," she whispered. "I'm afraid of what thou wilt do to my soul and my heart."

"Your heart . . . is precious to me," he said quietly.

She bent her head. She turned around without looking at him and took his arm.

Chapter Thirty

"_L_ ike . . . the opera?" he asked, holding her hand as she came down from the carriage in Belgrave Square.

"I've never seen it."

"Tonight," he said. "You wear . . . blue."

Calvin met them at the door. He took Maddy's cloak, started to bow and stopped himself. "I've seen to it that there's a good fire for you, Mistress. I'll have a tray of tea sent up. Do you like strawberry jam and clotted cream? I've just brought up marmalade from the pantry, too, if you're partial, or I can see about—" He cut himself off suddenly, as if realizing how anxious he sounded, and gave Maddy a stiff nod. "I wish to apologize again, Mistress, for my negligence."

"There is no blame to thee," Maddy said.

The butler looked as if that were little comfort to him, but he said no more. As she went upstairs, all the servants were quick to jump to their tasks, and the chambermaid, whom Maddy had barely seen, shyly said that she had put a hot brick in the bed, in case Mistress wanted to rest a while before supper.

Maddy lay down gratefully, still chilled through by the

mist. It was the duke's chamber, but he had stayed below: she had the sinful luxury of it alone, except for the faint scent of him all around her.

When she opened her eyes, it was after dark. In the light of a shielded candle Jervaulx sat by the bed, watching her. He was elegantly dressed, turned out in midnight blue and white by his valet in a way Maddy had never been able to manage.

"The opera." She pushed up, with a little spurt of apprehension. The theater, and dances, and fine clothing, all the things of his world—the time had come to face them.

"Supper—" He nodded toward a large tray, already set with a table and chair by the fire, "Then dress." He laid a box on the counterpane beside her. He stood up and walked to the door, paused with his hand on the knob, and nodded toward the box. "For your hair," he said, and left her.

Maddy sat up and opened the box. It was a string of pearls, like her mother's, only larger and more luminous in the candlelight, with a diamond strung between each pearl.

She pressed her lips together. A vain, frivolous, expensive thing—sparkling, pretty. She tried to be on guard, to barricade herself against him, but he sought out her weakness unerringly. Not the gift, no. Not the lavishness of it, not even the unexpected beauty of the jewels.

For her hair, he said. He remembered that, and stole through her defenses simply.

They arrived late. Christian had calculated it. The Haymarket was brilliant but lonely for the space of the performance, gaslight gleaming on the rows of waiting carriages, on harness and coach lamps.

After the money from Hoare's had arrived, it had taken less than half an hour to have a job team and livery put to his town carriage. The world was open to him again. He'd begun spreading coin around like a wealthy Cit, a hard cash liberality calculated to impress the most dubious creditor. Not paying off too many of his existing tickets—just making new purchases with sterling, to give them something to think about.

He'd sent Calvin to Rundell and Bridge for the pearls, dispatched a footman to spend two hundred pounds at the silversmith's, had the cook make lavish purchases from Harrod's and the wineseller, and, through Calvin, made some special arrangements with a nurseryman—all paid in advance.

Maddy had worn the pearls. He hadn't been at all sure that she would do it. He didn't know how to treat her, how to penetrate the mist of reserve that still cloaked her. Sweet words and expensive presents—they were all he could think of, and he knew what she'd likely label them: falsehood and immorality. More time would have been better, but he had no time. He needed Maddy, tonight, beside him.

The light from the theater's Corinthian portico flooded down on her as she descended to the walk, making her simple toilette rich with color: the blue dress and her ale-gold hair, the subtle luster of pearl against a sparkle of diamond. She was arresting, he thought, though no one could describe her as conventionally beautiful. She had a chaste and spartan aspect rather than pink blowsy charm. Not Aphrodite, but prudent Athena—of the sage owl, and the golden bridle that tamed Pegasus.

The nearly empty vestibule, the dim corridors, even the growing sound of music did not prepare Maddy for the burst of light and color that struck the eye as she entered the duke's box. With her ears full of song, she could only gaze at the sweeping tiers of boxes in red and gold, rising up to the roof, full of people leaning aside to their companions or forward over the rail, looking down on the stage and the massed audience on the floor of the theater.

And the stage—Maddy took one look and quickly averted her eyes. The people dancing across the boards were not dressed! She heard a rumble growing from the spectators, a new note of disturbance amid the music and the audience hum. The people on the floor two tiers below were turning, looking up; the occupants of the opposite boxes were staring and directing spyglasses—all at the place where she and Jervaulx sat alone.

She dropped her eyes to her lap, unable to look anywhere: not at the indecency onstage, not at the audience.

"Chin . . . up," Jervaulx said, without turning to her.

She raised her chin.

"Thank you," he said. "Watch the . . . perform. The stage."

"I—they are—oh dear," she said, obeying him in that too, appalled by the girls in pink tights, their ankles and calves in full view, their legs showing clearly through diaphanous skirts. "This is dreadful."

"Watch," he said.

It was not without a certain lurid fascination. The unclad figures alternately leapt and cavorted about the stage, and stopped, poised, to sing at the top of their lungs. Maddy knew little more of music than a few Christmas carols and street songs she'd heard, but she understood from reading the papers that the opera was an elevated branch of art. Certainly it was loud—and not many of the spectators seemed concerned about talking over it.

Indeed, she heard voices through the curtain enclosing the back of their box, where Jervaulx had left a footman who held his line firmly in a not-very-discreet controversy over whether he ought to allow the petitioners outside to enter. Jervaulx never moved a muscle, though he must have heard it clearly, too.

Maddy could not help herself; she could not watch the deportment onstage and began to look at the audience below. There she had another shock, coming to the slow realization that unaccompanied men were strolling and sitting down with women they didn't appear to know—holding their hands, even putting their arms around them. One scarlet officer's coat caught her eye as he stood up.

"There is Colonel Fane," she said.

As she spoke, the colonel turned and looked directly at their box. He smiled and bowed, drawing the attention of everyone on the benches around him.

Jervaulx gave a nod back, the only sign of recognition he'd made to anyone. The officer left his seat and began to make his way up the aisle.

A few moments later, the duke rose and held back the curtain himself. Colonel Fane walked into their box.

"Ma'am!" He grinned and bowed to Maddy, lifting her hand. "It's a pleasure to see you again; in such looks, too! And Shev—deuce take you, why didn't you tell me you was back in town?"

"Haven't . . . long," Jervaulx said.

"May I call on you, ma'am?" Fane asked, sitting down beside Maddy and leaning toward her.

"Thou wouldst be welcome to call."

He shook his head, smiling. "I vow, I dote on that way you talk." He looked over her head at Jervaulx. "I'm going to become her cicisbeo, I warn you."

The duke lifted his brows.

"My siso—? What is it?" she asked.

Colonel Fane stood up, lifting her hand for a kiss. "Why, your lover, ma'am. And now I must go, before my poor heart is in shreds—or your husband calls me out. Farewell, my stern Helen. I die for you."

Before Maddy could quite digest this extraordinary speech, he was gone. She lowered her face, aware of people all over the theater staring at them. She stole a look from the corner of her eye at Jervaulx.

He gazed at her somberly. Then he smiled, an intimate look that cut down her heart without mercy. "I . . . must shoot him?"

She took a deep breath and lifted her head. "Thou needst not be concerned," she said quietly. "I do not trifle with love, Jervaulx."

His face went still. Maddy looked away from him, watch-

ing the cavorting actresses as they rushed here and there
about the stage, warbling like delirious larks.

Holding out his hand, he stood. "Long enough. Let us go."

As a bachelor, Christian had not been much troubled with
formal calls on himself. More usually, he paid them, doing
the civil in return for dinners and parties, nursing his interests, business or otherwise, flirting or paying his respects as
required. But this morning the cards piled up on the silver
tray in the hall. A stream of carriages stopped, one after another, for a few moments outside the house in Belgrave
Square, and then continued on, their occupants turned away
from the door. Every hour, Calvin delivered a new batch of
cards to the library.

Maddy, sitting across from Christian at his desk, read the
name on each card aloud. Then, according to his nod, she
dropped it into one of two matching jade bowls appropriated
from the ornamental console tables for the purpose. Between influxes of cards, she took dictation of checks and letters while he worked over the ledgers. And every half hour,
Calvin came again, with a new bouquet of flowers for her.

It had begun before breakfast, this steady delivery of
Christian's tulips, daffodils, sweet-smelling hyacinths, carnations and picotees, auriculas—some cut, some in Dutch
pots, some in baskets, each one a little larger than the last,
until the library was a garden and the flowers overflowed
into the salon next door.

To his consternation, Maddy appeared utterly unim-
pressed. She had accepted the floral presentations without a
word all day, quietly directing Calvin to set them aside. But
when two footmen and the nursery boys, heralded by the exquisite scent of southern climes, dollied in a pair of huge
tubs planted with orange trees in full bloom, she finally put
her hands over her mouth and closed her eyes.

"What art thou about?" she cried through her fingers.

"There is a message, Mistress." Calvin produced a note.

"The nurseryman will call at your convenience, and inquire as to what plants you will wish to have set in the back garden, and in the orangery to be built for you there."

She made a little moan behind her hands and rolled her eyes toward Christian.

He wasn't quite certain if this were success or disaster. As the servants quit the room, he went to one of the trees and plucked a blossom. She was watching him over her hands, impossible to fathom.

He took a deep, sensual breath of the flower, rotated it in his fingers, and strolled to her. He paused, as if considering what to do with it, and then stuck it behind his own ear.

"Pretty?" He put his hand to his head, turning it to show his ear better.

She giggled, a woeful sound, as if it were choked out of her and she could not help it. Poor simple-hearted Maddy-girl, to laugh at that. Poor buffle-headed Christian, to be reduced to it. His experience was broad, but he found it wasn't deep enough to make him adept at soothing the aggravated sensibilities of a Puritan lady.

"I know what thou art doing," she said.

"Primp . . . myself pretty."

"Thou art pouring the butter-boat over me. Giving me jewels and flowers."

He shook the blossom from his ear and let it drop into his hand. "Is it working?"

Her cheeks pinkened. She dropped her eyes. "Working to do what?"

"Turn up . . . sweet."

"To what end?"

He shrugged. "So . . . don't have to sleep . . . in the dressing room."

She looked around at the flowers that covered every table and cabinet. "This expense . . . only for that?"

With the blossom caught between his middle fingers, he caressed it lightly over the back of her hand. "Only?"

She blushed vividly. "It is thy house. I never said thou

shouldst sleep here or there or anywhere. It isn't my place to say."

"Your place to say . . . you want me there." He slowly circled the petals over her skin. "With you."

"Oh." Her breathing had become agitated. "Is it?"

"You say. You tell me . . . you want me."

She watched the flower. "I don't know," she said miserably.

"Don't know, Maddygirl?" he asked softly.

"Oh, why art thou so—so carnal?" She snatched her hand away. "I ought not!"

Christian felt an immediate rise of his spirits. Here was something perfectly familiar—a lady who ought not but very likely would. On that note, he made a strategic withdrawal. He could be patient. "Very well," he said with dignity, and left her, walking round his desk to sit down before the ledgers again.

He bent over the books. After a few moments of silence, he looked up. "One other. Another thing . . . too. In a month, we will have . . . a ball for five hundred." He pushed the jade bowl with the largest number of cards in it toward her. "Invitations . . . to these."

He didn't come that night, as he had not the night before. Maddy was left alone in his bedchamber to contemplate a ball for five hundred people, and what he said it was her place to tell him.

She wanted to be angry at him for these outrageous new extravagances. The flowers, the jewels—they were sly worldly tricks. He had admitted it outright, guileless, with an orange blossom behind his ear—*Is this working?*—stealing from her the immunity of virtuous indignation.

She felt herself slipping, sliding into his net.

In the morning, they worked together again in the flower-filled library to unravel his affairs. He labored with a concentration that clearly wearied him; by noon his speech had deteriorated, and he slammed the books closed impatiently.

"Perhaps thou ought to rest," she said, when he had been trying to give her the amount of a payment and had to recalculate it three times. "It is difficult for thee."

"Not . . . difficult!" He threw himself back in his chair. "Simple. But it . . . it is . . . slips . . . it goes away. As if . . . try to work and . . . listen to . . . talk. Can't . . . both." He leaned his head back and put his hands over his eyes. "I'm not . . . stupid."

"I didn't say thou art stupid," Maddy murmured.

He sighed heavily, dropping his hands, still staring at the ceiling. "I feel . . . stupid." He groaned. "Bloody damned idiot."

She sat looking down at her lap desk. She fiddled with the corner of the paper, rolling it up, and then unrolling it. "Christian," she said, watching her fingers. "Wouldst thou please come tonight?"

For a moment he didn't do anything. Then he steepled his hands and lifted his head from the back of the chair, resting his chin on the tips of his fingers, gazing at her.

"Why wait?" He smiled. "I'm here . . . now."

Maddy's eyes widened. She looked at the paper, and back up at him uncertainly. "Thou art giddy."

He laughed, low and soft. Maddy thought it prudent to set the lap desk aside. She stood up, tucking papers into neat piles. When he rose, she almost dropped an inkpot, fumbling.

He caught it from her fingers and set it safely down. "Giddy?" he asked with amusement.

"I believe Calvin has a luncheon prepared—"

"Later."

"It is time for eating, Jervaulx. It is daylight. I did not say to thee—" She lost the tail of her sentence as he came behind her and brushed his lips across the nape of her neck.

"Want me, Maddygirl?" he murmured.

She shuddered with the exquisite hot tickle. "It is *daylight!*" she exclaimed, her voice high and faint.

He gave that rich, soft laugh again, his breath warm against her skin. "Didn't ask . . . time of day." He traced his finger down the line of her throat to the buttons at the back of her neck. Maddy felt the first one pop open.

"Calvin!" she said desperately. "He'll be coming in!"

He unbuttoned another button, placing a kiss on her exposed nape.

"Thou art weary!" She seemed rooted to the spot, feeling the electric caress flow down her body to melt in heat and carnal places—the tips of her breasts, and lower, lower. "Thou shouldst . . . thou ought to . . . rest."

"No answer yet," he said, loosening all the buttons and the ribbons of her corset, finding the opening in her camisole. "Want me, Maddy?"

"Thou art—" A scratch on the door made her give a small helpless whimper of panic.

"Yes?" Jervaulx said toward the door. He held her still with his hands on both shoulders, pressing her dress together with his thumbs.

Calvin stood in the entry. "Luncheon, Your Grace."

"Serve here," Jervaulx said, expressionless. He dropped one of his hands, running his finger up and down the open slit in her dress, bright erotic sensation against her spine.

Maddy flushed, staring at Calvin, unable to move or speak. The butler merely bowed. "Directly, Your Grace," he said, and withdrew.

"There," she said, trying to shrug her dress up from where Jervaulx was drawing it down off her shoulders. "Now showest sense! He will be back—in a few moments—no! No, thou must not—not here!"

Her bodice fell loose. He held her against him, kissing the curve of her shoulder through her thin cotton camisole. His hand explored upward beneath her open corset, skimming over the cotton. His palm grazed her nipple through the fabric: a sweet shot of delight. She sucked in her breath.

"Want?" he murmured close to her ear.

"They'll come," she moaned. "They'll come, they'll come."

His arms tightened. "Want me?"

Noise at the closed door brought her to panic. She began to push at him, but he held her harder. He drew her back into the deep narrow space between a bookcase and a cabinet, half-hidden. Then he let her go, leaving her standing in brazen undress. As the door opened, he moved in front of her and pulled a book down from the shelf.

He stood perusing it, his back to the room, obscuring the servants from her view. She heard the rattle of trays and dishes, saw around him the flash of white stockings as a footman passed the place where she hid in broad daylight. She feared that she must certainly be visible, though she herself could see nothing past Jervaulx's broad shoulders.

He turned a page. "Here," he said, as if he'd just discovered some passage he'd been searching for. He looked up at her with laughter brimming in his eyes. "Hamlet. 'Lady, shall I lie in your lap?'" Maddy squeezed back against the wall, pressing her lips together, frowning at him with frantic severity. His look changed to exaggerated innocence. "'I mean, my head upon your lap?'"

"Don't!" she whispered furiously.

He grinned at her. "Right here . . . in the play. I only . . . read it."

She heard the door open and close. For a long moment Jervaulx stood watching her, holding her trapped by modesty and by himself, solid barrier to escape. Maddy listened for any sound, and then mouthed *Are they gone?*

He turned his head, looking over his shoulder, first one way, and then the other, theatrically. He looked back at her. "Don't know. Better stay . . . here."

She gave him a push. The book slid down; he held it out behind him and let it fall with a flutter and thump as he leaned forward to kiss her mouth. He caught her body in his hands, his thumbs passing provocatively over her breasts, caressing the tips, back and forth. The feel of it drew a liquid arching, a breath and a pressing flex of all her muscles toward him.

"Want me?" he whispered, licentious, the Devil at her ear in full daylight: a man's firm elegant hands on her body, blue eyes and long dusky beautiful eyelashes.

She whirled, her back to him, pressing her fiery cheek to the smooth cool leather of the library wall. He stroked the naked skin of her back, pushing her undergarments aside. He ran his hands over her torso, up beneath her arms: creating delight and embarrassed agony as she could not stop the shivering of pleasure. "It is day," she moaned, hiding her face, pressing it to the leather-covered wall. "Thou shouldst not."

He ceased his touch on her bared torso. But he didn't move back; he moved closer, holding her against the wall. She could feel the crushed lace of his shirt against her skin. His scent mingled with the smell of leather. He began to draw her skirt up in his hands.

"Oh, no," she cried, muffled. "No, no—it is indecent! Christian!"

He closed his teeth on her shoulder, his pressure against her more urgent, his body pinning hers to the wall. She tried to thrust back from it and only brought herself closer to him. He kissed her all along the curve of her throat and shoulder, kissed and nipped and sucked at her skin, pulling her hands down and back away from the wall until they fluttered helplessly without purchase. Her skirt was caught up between them; she felt shamelessly exposed, her legs and stockings uncovered to her garters.

But he didn't stop there. He pulled her petticoat and dress higher, cupping her hips and her buttocks with his bare hands. He made a rough, ardent sound near her ear. He bit her, hurt her, kneading her body in his palms, but it was sweet pain and sinful ecstasy. She felt him release his own buttons; his hard male part pushed and pressed, and she began to pant in desperate guilty excitement.

Like stone melting, her body slackened, her legs allowed him between. The sound of his breath was caustic, an animal engine, brushing heat across her nakedness. He pressed her hips, a rash hard grip of his fingers, making her close her legs on his shaft.

He forced his hands between her body and the wall, dragging her skirt up in front. He caught her wrists. "Touch me." He brought her fingers to the place between her legs, to hot moistness and his smooth head. "Yes," he groaned, moving suddenly, demandingly against her. "Yes—yes—Maddy."

With their hands entwined, jammed to the wall, he slid his fingers against her private place, massaged and teased and pressed deep in rhythm with the thrust of his body against her. His man's part moved between her legs, an unimaginable pleasure, a sensation that flowed to her breasts, made the nipples full and tender, like flame pushed against the cool leather. Wet hot dew spread over her fingers and his: she molded her hand to the head of his arousal, taking deep and lurid satisfaction in the sound she drew from him.

"Want me?" His voice was grinding, insistent, taut with extremity. "Maddy . . . inside you."

She bit her lip, her face turned aside to the wall. "I want thee," she said, on a sob. "I want thee."

And he showed her how, then. How to bend and submit for him, in bondage to him, in daylight, sinking together on their knees to the floor, with him deep inside her, over her and around her, his hands holding her breasts, his mouth against the nape of her neck—lost in him and in his coupling with her. She cried out with violent joy at the height, her voice mingling with his masculine groan: the two of them no more, and no less, than every wild creature that God had made of clay to walk the earth.

He bought her a carriage. Two carriages, one with a team of four white-stockinged chestnuts and one with a pair of cream-colored ponies—for the park, he said, as if she were ever going to go driving there in it.

Maddy told him that she did not want such things. She insisted that he put a stop to his ill-advised purchases and gifts. He bought her an antique marquetry cabinet from a selection that the dealer fetched to Belgrave Square, and began to redecorate the back parlor, a perfectly smart and comfortable room that had hardly seen a year's use, transforming it into an outlandishly expensive boudoir full of gilt and red satin.

Maddy berated him for wastefulness. He purchased her a small magnificent Rembrandt by private treaty, the complement of the one in his bedroom at Jervaulx Castle, a study of a serious youth who looked as if he might be the brother of that mischievous girl. Maddy read afterward in the newspaper that the duke's offer had been so generous, it had forestalled the painting's scheduled auction at Christie's, sending the cognoscenti into paroxysms of jealousy.

She lived in misery and delight in the small world of the duke's house. They were never at home to callers, nor went out except at dusk, conveyed by a carriage to some secluded country lane beyond the city, where Jervaulx stretched his long legs into a walk that had her striding to keep up. Around a corner, or beside a shaggy hedge, with the dim autumn sunset casting shadows across mats of fallen, frosty leaves, he would stop and kiss her—and sometimes more than that. He touched her often; he looked up across the library desk with a smile that knew too much of her. She felt utterly owned by him. The gifts were nothing; it was her own hunger that enslaved her—she *wanted* to be touched; she wanted him to take her, in any way, any place and time, with no care for modesty or decent conduct.

She wanted simply to look at him. Every dispute over his spending was doubly painful, because he wouldn't even quarrel now. He either went away, driving out alone, leaving her bereft amid the splendor, or he seduced her. Like Eydie, she was lost to him—only worse—worse in her need, in how deeply she had surrendered herself; she would do anything he guided her to do and take pleasure in it. She was terrified of him—this power that he held, and still she gave it to him, heart-glad and wretched.

She was defenseless. She thought of Eydie on the stairs. His coaxing skillful caresses, his worldly sophistication; she thought that there must have been others and would be others again, locks of hair and painted miniatures and pain.

She ought to go. Leave this place. Anyone could do such work as she performed for him, a clerk, a secretary; she ought to get away, go to her father and save herself while she had yet enough shame left to understand what was becoming of her. But she was responsible still—just this morning she'd had a letter from Lady de Marly. Maddy had read it, and then burned it, to hide it from Jervaulx, so that he would not see what his aunt had written.

His mother wanted him confined again immediately. The power of this iniquitous jade who claimed to be his wife must be broken. So far, Lady de Marly's barrister had persuaded the dowager duchess to delay an unwilling detention, avoiding a fuss that was likely to become mortifyingly public, perhaps even scandalous—attempting to confine a man not yet certainly judged incompetent. But as a result, pressure for a hearing had grown to intense proportions. The attorney was having serious difficulty preventing a date being set. The family were beside themselves at the duke's rate of expenditure and his dismissal of the land-agent who'd handled his affairs for years. Maddy, Lady de Marly made no bones to tell her, was considered the sole source and spring of this bleeding discharge of money, painted in the halls and offices of Chancery in the lurid shades of an avaricious, opportunistic harpy who had complete control of the mindless wreckage of the Duke of Jervaulx.

This picture was such a reverse from the real truth that it had choked an awful laugh from her. But it came as no surprise. She wasn't at all sure herself that Jervaulx had competent control of his affairs—there was no saying what his situation must appear to an outside party. Certainly she might reasonably be supposed the guilty party. She thought it one more cause to leave him, but Lady de Marly ordered—

begged, actually begged—Maddy to do all in her power to make him reduce his expenses to a reasonable level, specifying a figure that would have seemed to Maddy monstrous a month ago, but appeared quite modest now.

She despaired of being able to do it. Jervaulx was not even paying the arrears of his loans—though he dictated polite letters in response to all, he'd settled only the most desperately threatening claims. With all of his labor over the figures, Maddy did not see where he was making any progress—she'd begun lately to suspect that he was instead hoarding money, neglecting payments so that he had an even greater income than before.

They had argued about it again just this morning—or at least Maddy had argued; Jervaulx had merely scowled at her until he lost his patience and came around the desk and began to kiss her.

Fortunately, Durham arrived, putting a stop to that more effectively than Maddy ever could herself. She was not asked to accompany Jervaulx and his friend on this first round of selected calls they planned to make, a society custom which intimidated her extremely. Durham, who didn't seem to have a glimmer of her feelings, apologized to her for being left home.

"You'll be out and about at such stuff before you know it," he predicted optimistically. "As soon as this ball gets you popped off official."

"Oh," Maddy said. She glanced at Jervaulx. "It is for that?"

He swept a bow. "Introduce my duchess."

"Bowl 'em over," Durham said. "Only way to do it. Take your fences head on. Nerve and pluck will carry it. Not the height of the Season, but with nothing else going forward, you'll have 'em here bag and baggage. Hunting's been so slack, even your Melton men may forgo the chase a day or two for this."

"Sacrifice!" Jervaulx said dryly.

"Shev don't like to fox-hunt," Durham confided to Maddy. "Not modern enough. He prefers shooting, as more scientific."

The duke seemed to find that a sour thought. "No more," he said. "Couldn't hit . . . broad barn now."

"It'll pass," Durham said insistently. "See how you're improving."

Jervaulx didn't answer that, but stood at the door, a grim statue, waiting for his friend to shake hands with Maddy. As they went out, he was saying, "We don't stay . . . only five minutes. Damned short, Durham. Understand? So I don't . . . talk."

Calvin appeared a few moments after they had departed. "I'm to help you with the invitations, Mistress, so as to get them out by tomorrow. The stationer has sent materials." He laid a packet on the desk and produced a small pair of scissors to clip the string.

Maddy sighed. Clearly, whatever his creaturely talents, patience was not one of the duke's virtues.

It seemed hours later, and her hand and back were aching from transcribing the letters of the morning and the invitations of the afternoon when a footman scratched on the door.

"The nurseryman, Mr. Butterfield, and his gardener Mr. Hill," he announced.

In spite of the flowers that still filled the library, delivered fresh every day, Maddy had completely forgot the appointment Jervaulx had made for her with the nurseryman. But Calvin had risen, and the footman was already showing the two men into the room. The second wore a Quaker's hat and plain coat.

"Thou misspoke my name," he said, turning from the footman to Maddy. "It is Richard Gill."

Chapter Thirty-one

$\mathcal{M}$addy felt a great wave of humiliation. She sat rooted to her chair, covered with it, breathless as if she stood upon a platform and heard her offenses cried in the public streets.

Mr. Butterfield bowed low, and gave a cheerful smile as he bounced his portly figure upright. "It is an honor to serve you, Your Grace. I hope the flowers and plants have been satisfactory?"

She nodded. Like a creaky pull-toy, she stood up and held out her hand to Richard. "Friend," she said.

"Archimedea," he answered, just touching her hand and dropping his away, while the nurseryman looked on in surprise.

"We're already acquainted," Maddy said to him. "I'm—" She did not say that she was a Friend. She couldn't, not now. She had no right. "I have met Richard Gill before."

Mr. Butterfield was all smiles again. "How fortuitous. Gill has been with me just a short while, but perhaps you know he has come directly from Mr. Loudon, Your Grace?"

"No," Maddy said mechanically. "I didn't know that."

"Ah. But you're familiar with Mr. Loudon's work?"

"Mr. Loudon—" She found a kernel of intelligence to cling to. *"The Suburban Gardener?"*

"Indeed, Your Grace. The premier horticulturist of our day—*The Suburban Gardener and Villa Companion, An Encyclopedia of Gardening,* the *Gardener's Magazine*—a fit successor to Brown and Repton, I assure you. And Gill here comes with Mr. Loudon's highest recommendation as designer and florist. He is an expert in botanical science, and can aid us in planning an arboretum and garden in the most forward style. Beautiful to the eye, educational to the mind, and most importantly, uplifting to the spirit. I hope he will be acceptable to you?"

Richard merely looked at her, his clear-eyed gaze steady, killing in its lack of accusation. Maddy could barely meet it for an instant. "Yes. Acceptable. I'm sure Richard is acceptable."

As soon as she said it, she thought of Jervaulx, who would likely not think it acceptable at all. But she could not say that, nor find the words to turn off smiling Butterfield and the whole opulent project. The nurseryman was clearly elated over his commission.

"Well, then—" Butterfield turned to Richard and took a notebook and sketchpad from him. "Shall we take a look at what we have?"

The space between the house and stables was no larger than her garden in Chelsea had been, paved and bleak and new. Between walls that had no softening cover of trailers or trees, nothing provided ornament but a single wrought-iron bench. Butterfield made a judicious moue of his lips. "There's a service basement beneath the pavement?"

"Yes." Maddy was familiar with the kitchen and cellars from her first day alone with Jervaulx, and cravenly glad to have something impersonal to talk about. "It goes through to the mews."

"I'll have to have a look at the foundations before we begin. It won't take a moment. Gill—you'll attend the duchess.

If Your Grace will please to let him know any particular plants you may have a fondness for. No, no—no need to stir! I'll find someone to show me down."

He was darting back into the house before Maddy could realize that he meant to leave them alone. She lifted her hand—but he was gone.

She stood looking at the handsome French door where he'd disappeared into the house. In the alley behind the stables, someone was whistling. She hung immobile in the powerful silence that prevailed inside the barren court.

"Why?" Richard asked.

Maddy had to turn to him. She kept her eyes down, staring at the raw pavement.

"Did he force thee? Archimedea—" His quiet voice had a terrible undertone of emotion in it. "Thou could have come to me. Surely thou knew it."

She shook her head quickly, helpless to explain.

He walked away to the wall. "The Lord required of me to watch over thee, and to the grief of my soul, I failed in it."

"No, Richard—it was not thy failing."

The white stone outlined him, square-shouldered, faced to the wall, dark severity against the stark light. When he turned, Maddy averted her eyes again, unable to meet his. He came closer to her.

"No matter that he took his way with thee," he said low, his tone burning with intensity. "I would have asked consent of Meeting to make thee my wife."

"Wife!" She looked up at him, staring.

"I still will do it, Archimedea, if thou will repudiate this fearful error." Beneath the shadow of his hat, his face held a steadfast purity of purpose—almost innocence, it seemed, compared to the muddied turmoil of her own spirit. "It is my blame."

"Thou art too good," she said wretchedly.

"Come back with me. Leave here; leave this corrupt place and come back now."

Maddy stepped away from him, feeling her heartbeat

quicken. She'd known she was sinking in this slough of worldliness and carnal love—how far, she had not realized until he offered his hand to pull her free. "I've married him," she said uncertainly.

"An unbeliever. An ungodly man. 'Duchess,' they call thee! 'Your Grace'!" He made a grimace of disgust. "Married. Oh, Archimedea, can thou name it that? How, married? Not in the Truth, in the Light, with thy Meeting's consent and thy father's. It is no marriage. Thou are no more than whore to him!"

A small sound escaped her as she pulled her shawl tight around herself and turned her face away.

"No—that was not justly said." He laid his hand on her arm. "The shame is not thine. It belongs to me. I came back—and they had taken thee away. And every day and night," he said fiercely, "I've scourged myself for leaving thee one hour, for one minute. I knew it unsafe!"

"But—my father wished it."

"Thy father! God forgive him if he wished such a thing!"

She half turned. "Thou wrote it! That Papa wished me to go with Jervaulx!"

"I never wrote to thee any such nonsense!" he said vehemently. "Nor would have, even if I could have seen thy father and he commanded me to do it!"

"Even if—" Maddy had the ends of her shawl gripped in her hands. "But—thou saw him."

"No. He was not there when I went, not at the hotel. I ought to have come back to thee instantly, but I waited late for him to—"

"Richard!" She brought the shawl up to her cheeks and pressed it there. She broke away suddenly, walking three paces from him. "Tell me—" She spoke, facing away, with desperate deliberation. "Thou went to my father that day, and sent back a note, in the depth of the night, with instructions to me—to go wherever the duke's friends sent us to hide him."

Richard's silence seemed to grow and grow, becoming a thundering in her ears. Maddy turned back to him.

"Tell me! Didst thou write it?"

Slowly, he shook his head.

She felt a weakness come over her. Her mind could not seem to get round the knowledge, but her body had already begun to tremble. Richard caught her hands. "He's the devil!" he exclaimed. "Thou *must* come—"

Voices sounded from within the house: the nurseryman's, and Durham's. The glass door opened and Jervaulx stepped out, turning from the others behind him.

The brief echo of cordial voices went silent except for Butterfield's blithe monologue. "—adequate support for beds, and I have an idea of bringing up pipes and using steam from a boiler to heat the greenhouse. If Your Grace . . ." His voice faded away as he seemed to realize no one was looking at him.

Richard did not release her hands. He held them harder. "Come with me now, Archimedea," he said, calm and steady. "Come away."

Jervaulx strode toward them. Maddy had a sensation of terror; she tried frantically to speak, to disengage her hands, but she was too late. Jervaulx grabbed Richard, a grip that pushed him; in the opening space the duke's leather-gloved fist came up fast. Maddy flung herself forward to prevent it. In the power of his onslaught Jervaulx's shoulder impacted her with a brutal jolt. It propelled her off her feet: Richard's hands jerked from hers; she heard his agonized cough and hit hard stone, a flash of hot black sensation in her head and arm.

Her vision wavered. She lay stunned, curling up against the shock of pain. Jervaulx dropped on his knees beside her. "Maddy . . . Maddy," he was muttering, leaning over her with such a look in his face that she managed to find her breath to speak.

"Don't. I'm all right." She tried to sit up.

"Calvin," he shouted, sliding his hand beneath her head. He bent down close to her. "Still, still . . . Maddy . . . hurt."

Durham was there, and the nurseryman. Past Jervaulx's shoulder she saw Richard climb to his feet and stagger a little. Durham steadied him and let go, leaning over Maddy. "Damn it to hell—is she badly injured?"

"No!" Maddy tried again to push herself up, but her arm kept collapsing under her. "No. Only—the wind knocked out of me."

Calvin came running up. "Doctor," Jervaulx snapped. He put his arm around her shoulder, holding her against him.

"I don't need a doctor." She tried to pull away, but all her strength had left her. She could not seem to get her breath back. When she moved her arm, an excruciating spasm went from her wrist to her shoulder. A wave of nausea washed over her. In spite of herself, she had to rest back against Jervaulx's support.

He stroked her forehead and put his face down next to hers. He didn't say anything, but in each breath there seemed to be the half-shape of a word: her name, and sorry, sorry, sorry.

"Richard?" She tried to sit up a little more, with her weight on her other hand. Her voice came out all trembly. "Art thou hurt?"

He came within her view. "I'm well enough," he said tightly, but his face was white, and he held one arm across his midriff.

Jervaulx looked up at him. *"Gone,"* he said. "See you again . . . horsewhip."

Richard stood unmoving. "I will not leave her alone with thee."

Maddy felt the tightening in Jervaulx's body.

"Your Grace!" Butterfield said, thrusting forward. "My most profound apology for the unspeakable insolence of this man. I'd no clue as to the revolting nature of his character, none whatsoever. From this moment, Richard Gill is no employee of mine, nor will he have a letter—from me or anyone else if I can help it!"

"No," Maddy moaned. "Please." She struggled, pulling free of Jervaulx, holding her arm against herself. Her hip ached. She held out her uninjured hand to Durham, who bent instantly to help her.

"Sit down here, ma'am," he said.

As Maddy hobbled to the garden bench between him and Jervaulx, the chambermaid brought forward a vial of hartshorn. "Thank thee," Maddy said gratefully. The pungent scent seemed to clear her head a little. She sat cradling her injured arm. "Butterfield," she said, lifting her chin with what firmness she could muster. "I wish to have a greenhouse—the duke has promised it to me, and I won't have it designed or supplied by anyone but Richard Gill."

Richard said, "I will not enter this house while thou remain here, Archimedea."

She looked up at him, biting her lip against its quivering.

"Come with me," he said.

"No," Jervaulx said.

Richard ignored him. "If thou can walk to the bench, thou can walk out of here."

"No!" Jervaulx took a step forward.

The Quaker turned. "And what will thou do to prevent her? Use a horsewhip?"

He spoke in his quiet voice, with nothing of malice in it—and yet the effect upon Jervaulx was like a whiplash itself. He stood stock still. Then he set one shoulder to the wall. For an instant he was a casual picture, a careless aristocrat—until he turned his face to it, leaning his forehead into the stone.

Maddy closed her eyes. She would not cry. No, no, she would not.

"Come along, Gill." Butterfield's voice made a sharp little echo in the court, but she didn't open her eyes.

Nothing moved. She kept her eyes squeezed shut.

"Gill!" Butterfield snapped.

Richard spoke her name, firm and quiet. She knew it was the last time he would say it.

A liar, a villain, a haughty violent reckless man of the

world. He was growing worse instead of better. Richard was asking her to leave him, supplying a steadfast will to take the place of her own.

But she couldn't move. Not the tiniest, least certain of moves could escape from her frozen frame.

And she heard the sound of Richard's footsteps, turning and walking away.

Until the closing door went to silence, she did not open her eyes. When she looked up, the court was empty but for Jervaulx, and Durham standing with his hand on the door. "I think you ought to come inside, ma'am, and lie down."

"Ye tricked me," Maddy said. "There was no message from Richard. My father never told me to stay with thee."

Jervaulx pushed away from the wall, with a bitter half-laugh. "Bastard . . . *Gill.*"

"It was my idea," Durham said quickly. "I must take full blame, and beg your pardon, ma'am, from the bottom of my heart. It was bad, very bad. But—" He was crimson to his hair. "Do let us help you inside, where you may be comfortable!"

Maddy stood up. Her stomach still felt strange and weak. Her arm seemed made of india rubber. When she moved it past a certain angle, she sucked in her breath as agony shot through her.

"Maddy," Jervaulx said, his voice harsh, as if he was angry with her. He put his arm around her waist with a gentleness that belied it, careful not to touch her injured limb. With the black dizziness threatening, she took the necessary steps quickly, passing through the door into the back parlor, where Durham hurried to throw a pillow on the sofa. A footman and the maid hovered inside, and Calvin came from the hall.

"I've sent for a physician." He had a lap robe and another pillow. Maddy, grimacing, let him adjust them around her. "There—Mistress—no need to sit up. Keep the arm quite still."

"Go away," Maddy said feebly. "I'm all right."

Calvin didn't take offense. "Here are the salts, next to your hand."

"Go away," she said again. "Everyone."

"Yes, Mistress. Just call out when you want us." The butler withdrew with the other servants. Durham, bowing, followed them out with alacrity.

"Go away," Maddy said.

Jervaulx didn't move from his place. He stood with his hands locked behind his back, staring out at the barren garden court.

"Please," she said.

He turned his head, as if he heard her. But he did not go.

It was only a very bad sprain, the doctor said, and immobilized it in a sling. He had her moved into bed, and put her to sleep with laudanum.

During the examination on the couch in the back parlor, she had made no sound in spite of his manipulations, until he'd asked her how it had happened. "A fall on the stairs?" he inquired cheerfully.

"Outside," she said in a dull voice.

"A stumble, then? What was the cause?"

Maddy was silent. *I did it,* Christian thought, and felt himself crumbling inside.

"A little spell of light-headedness, perhaps?" The physician was one Christian had never seen before, a benign, schoolmasterly sort. He seemed inclined to prod. "Have you been feeling any faintness lately?"

"I just . . . fell," she said.

"You must try to be more careful of yourself," he said. "I expect you haven't been married long? This kind of seemingly minor accident can sometimes have more serious consequences. I must appear to be a little indelicate, now, and ask if there is any chance that you may be with child?"

Oh God. Christian closed his eyes.

Maddy didn't answer. The doctor peered over his glasses at Christian, brows lifted in a silent masculine inquiry. Christian gave a terse nod.

The doctor patted her uninjured hand. "I think we will move you into bed, young woman, and just keep a close eye on matters, in that case." He smiled. "Here, here—don't start to weep now, my dear, after you got through all my poking and prodding so brave! I've seen nothing so far to cause us any concern. Nothing at all. Poor thing—you've been a Trojan, haven't you? Let's have you upstairs where you can go to sleep snugly."

He marshaled Calvin and a footman to take her up. By the time the doctor came back down, Christian was pouring his third brandy. He turned around as the door opened.

The physician came in and sat down unceremoniously with his bag, pulling out a notebook. "The arm has suffered an uncomplicated wrench of the ligament. The bone doesn't appear to have been injured. It'll be mightily painful, but time and stability are the answers to that." He made a calculation, and frowned over it. Then he looked up at Christian. "Sit down, sir. Sit down. I want to talk to you. Would you describe your wife as of a nervous disposition?"

Christian sat down. He thought of Maddy—staunch Maddygirl.

Not nervous. No. He shook his head.

"The present state of her emotions is not steady. Quite possibly it's the distress of the injury, although she bore the examination with the greatest fortitude. You'll forgive my directness—lability of the emotions might also be an early sign of pregnancy, which concerns me, with this fall. She was not forthcoming about either the fall or her menses. Were you present when she had the accident?"

Christian looked at the Oriental carpet between his feet, and nodded.

"Did she appear pale, or in any way faint?"

He stood up, walking. Going nowhere, just walking the room.

"Sir—I'm a physician," the man said evenly. "I realize these matters seem—"

"I . . . did it." Christian stopped at the window, staring out. There was a short silence. "You caused her to fall?"

He turned to the doctor. "Yes."

The man nodded slowly, without taking his eyes from Christian. "I see." His face had grown more grim. "You don't feel that any disequilibrium of hers contributed, then."

"No," he said.

"She told me that you have only been married for a few weeks?"

"Month."

"With what little information I could coax from her, I calculate that she's just barely late. I could wish this fall had not occurred at such a time. If she begins to bleed, we'll hardly know if we've lost something, or if she was barren, but I don't scruple to say, sir—my instinct as a physician tells me that you're a father."

Christian took a deep drink of brandy.

The doctor stood up. "I'll look in this evening. I'm Beckett, by the way. Only just moved into the neighborhood last week. I'm afraid your man brought me along so quick that I didn't properly learn your name."

"Jervaulx."

He offered his hand. "Well, Mr. Chervo." He gave Christian one merciless shake. "I'm not going to mince words. I advise you to practice a more careful tenderness with your wife, and not cause her any more falls, sir."

Maddy had never been an invalid in her life. She was angry at this doctor, who must make such a matter of it. He was even worse when he'd come back in the evening. He'd begun calling her "Your Grace" by then, clucking over her like a hen with one chick: chiding her for not taking the laudanum he'd left, for getting out of bed to sit up, for any movement whatsoever—not to protect her arm, but to prevent this imminent tragedy he seemed convinced must occur.

And to her great exasperation, she did begin to bleed in
the night. She slept little—propped up against pillows to
support her arm. Her unfortunate timing could not be hidden
from the doctor when he arrived in the morning. He shook
his head with a mournful regret, prescribing complete bed
rest for three weeks. He didn't even inquire about her arm
before he went out.

Maddy pushed her feet from beneath the bedclothes. She
held her aching arm against her in the sling, sitting up on the
edge of the bed, her feet resting on the bedsteps.

Ignorant man! Trying to make a tremendous fuss, so that
he might up his fee over nothing more than a wrenched
muscle.

The bedchamber door opened. She saw Jervaulx's white
ravaged face.

"It isn't true!" she exclaimed. She gripped her injured arm
to her. "It's only what happens every month—thou didst not
cause it, dost thou hear me?"

Her voice had risen. For no reason at all, she began to
weep, watching his taut face blur until she couldn't see it.
She shook her head fiercely and reached out her free hand.

"Christian—thou didst not cause it."

He came. He took her hand and held it in both of his, staring down at it. She pulled away.

"Dost thou hear me?" She swallowed tears and shook her
head, over and over. "It's too soon for him to know. I would
feel differently. Thou didst not make it happen."

He didn't look up at her. He stood by the bed, unmoving.

She took an indignant breath. "It is all stuff and nonsense.
Thou ought not to pay him for anything more than putting
me up in this sling."

His lashes lifted. For a long moment he scanned her face,
and then he turned away and leaned against one of the white
pillars near the foot of the bed, staring out the far window.
"I . . ." The muscles in his jaw clenched; he tilted his face up
to the ceiling, pushing air harshly through his teeth. He
shook his head.

She couldn't look at him. She sniffed and wiped hard at her eyes, unable to stop the absurd tears.

"Leave," he said suddenly. "Want?"

He was watching her with intense question.

"I can't leave," she said dully. "We're married. Thou canst not be alone. I have to stay with thee."

"Want to leave?"

"My arm hurts. I wish to sleep."

"Gill?" he said through his teeth. *"Gill?"*

The tears just kept coming. She gave a resentful sob. "At least he is a decent man! Not a liar, or a spendthrift or a savage."

Jervaulx put his arm around the column, holding onto it. He gave a short, ugly laugh. "Savage . . . idiot."

She was glad that her arm hurt so badly that she could not reach out to him in response to the bitter penitence in his face. She was horrified at herself; she should have left with Richard, but she had just sat there, frozen, as if someone else were going to make the decision for her. "He doesn't go about hitting people, anyway," she snapped. "He doesn't give preposterous balls for five hundred guests."

"He's a pious . . . mule. You would never . . . go with him."

"I wish thou wouldst leave me alone!"

"You would never go with him," he said, more strongly.

"Go away!"

"Quaker . . . tiresome . . . holy . . . mule."

"What dost thou know of it?" she cried. "He is a better man than thee! What dost thou know of good and right?"

"I know . . . you," he said.

She fell back on the pillow and curled up around her aching arm, hiding her face from him. "Leave me alone," she sobbed. "Go away and leave me alone."

Chapter Thirty-two

$\mathcal{W}$ithout making an issue of it by stealing off and locking doors, Christian moved Brunel's writing machine into the game room and began to take occasion to polish his play. After a week Maddy was already up and about the house, against the doctor's orders, but even females inclined to deprecate the Vice of Idleness, Christian suspected, would not find much to interest them in a game of billiards.

The first time, he'd actually played a ball or two, attempting a few strokes before he gave it up, depressed. Another pleasure forfeit to his mazy brain: his fine true table and favorite ivory-handled cue were no remedy for losing the pocket when he focused on the ball—that sensation of something there and not-there, odd and scary, and not overly beneficial to one's aim. He sighed and scattered balls, laying the cue across the cloth. Pushing back the spirit decanters on the buffet, he'd set up his writing machine out of sight of the door if it should open.

Eydie, it appeared, was determined to create the maximum amount of difficulty without inconveniencing herself. No, she would not accept any sort of trust for the child; she knew all about that sort of thing, and detested having Fridayfaced solicitors always in her house picking at her private concerns. Yes, she certainly would send the babe right back to Scotland if it pleased her; no, she did not like the idea of a discreet arrangement with the Sutherlands to safeguard the child's welfare—why, she wrote plaintively, could he not just send the money directly to her? She was like to think he did not trust her!

He didn't. His sympathy for her had vanished in this donkey's performance. Wounded her he might have done, but she'd known the rules of the game as well as he. No one had forced her to play. He didn't pursue this unpleasantness for her sake.

Something strange and painful had happened to him. "You're a father," the doctor had said, and Maddy had reached out her hand and wept—and by no logical sequence of thought that he could identify, Christian had come to a grim determination to do right by this unseen and unwanted daughter of his own.

It was a delicate matter. He had nothing really to offer but financial support, and at the moment not even that in any significant amount. His income was strained to the limit against far more immediate problems, and he was already forwarding a sum weekly out of cash—household expenses and wages for a wet nurse that Eydie had complained she couldn't afford. One presumed that ladies of her station couldn't be expected to take the economical way out of that, he thought cynically. But it wasn't an infant's nominal keep that occupied him. The sort of long-term commitment that he envisioned—nurse, governess, schooling, a Season and a substantial dowry—required arrangements outside of all previous settlements that encumbered his estate, a secure and concealed source of income that couldn't be rooted out by his family should he chance to hop the perch untimely.

There was the rub. Nothing he had now would answer the purpose, and he had yet to be able to finance fresh undertakings—not with whispers of the competency hearing spreading around him like ripples round a pond. And if he dared to wait until after . . . if he lost . . .

There would be an end of it, if he lost.

He stared at the writing machine. He was safe, for as long as he could command his bank account. He'd heard the growing panic under the censure in Maddy's voice and understood better than she that he gambled with gunpowder. Every penny he spent now told against him in Chancery if it came to that—and told against her too.

He'd tried to live in the moment, to keep feeling what it felt to be here and now, at liberty, alive. He was not what he'd been. Sometimes the losses caught him like an unexpected slap across the face—small things stinging as hard as the bigger ones: the defiance of his bankers made him angry; the confused wobble of a billiards ball made him want to weep.

Durham said he was getting better. Christian held on to that like a lifeline, and at the same time didn't trust it. Better, yes. Good enough, he did not know. The standing up, the test, knowing that everything—everything—counted on his erratic wit—God.

At any odds, the price of failure was too high. He didn't intend to wager on his own flawed mind. He didn't intend to submit to any hearing.

Everything he did, his calls, the opera, his purchases, the heady amount of cash he'd managed to gather by a calculated rearrangement of his loan payments—it all culminated in the ball. The ball that was to introduce his duchess to society. And what was more, make him safe from the mad place for good.

But preparing for it was almost more than he could manage alone. Writing and reading, tickets for wallpaper, caterer's bills, cases of champagne and his account balance in daily fluctuation, available cash pushed to the limit, trying to keep it all in his head because he couldn't trust it to notes, his wretched woolly head that went clear and then foggy, chasing after words and intentions that slipped away and left him lost.

Claiming stubborn ignorance of such worldly depravities as balls, Maddy had refused to help with any of it but the loan payments, and Christian had paid all of those that he intended to pay. He could not spare more—another point of discord between them.

Her injury had forced him to postpone the event a fortnight beyond his intended date. There was no objective disadvantage to that as far as he could reckon; it merely made the theme something more of Christmas than before, and the strain of anticipation two weeks more tense. He used Durham to spread word of Maddy's accident to excuse Christian's minimal appearances in public. He went back to the opera twice, once alone, once with Durham and Fane, and made a few more calls with them in circumstances that he knew would not require much conversation. He carefully controlled his exposure, and so far it had seemed a success.

Durham was confounded by it. He came to sit down at breakfast with Christian and Maddy while he regaled them with the latest.

"It's extraordinary," he said, bringing Maddy more tea from the urn on the sideboard. "I mean to say, you'd think the man was Lord Byron warmed over, only for standing there looking intense and keeping his mouth shut." He arranged her cup for her. "Milk, my darling?"

"Yes, thank thee. Thou ought not to call me that."

Durham and Fane had begun a battle of endearments over Maddy, having survived her gentle censure for the incident of the faked letter. Christian bore the brunt of her reproach—an injustice, he thought sullenly, if she knew how little he remembered of the ruse. That night of their escape was an incoherent jumble to him. Durham had masterminded all the details, but it was only Christian that she called a liar to his face.

But then, everything seemed to be his fault these days, according to Miss Thee-Thou Pinchpenny Archimedea Timms.

"You'll have to keep a sharp watch on the ladies with this

fellow," Durham advised her, disposing himself at his ease in a chair.

"Will I?" she asked, looking down at her tea. Her fingers moved restlessly, smoothing over and over the porcelain handle. Christian watched them, tried to memorize them. If he lost, if they sent him back—she wouldn't be there.

"The females seem to love it." Durham shook his head. "A look of torrid mystery, rumors of a dangerous tendency to become wild under a full moon, a simple 'yes' or 'no' in answer to everything—Lord, I intend to give it a try myself. They'll be swooning at my feet. God knows they're swooning at his. What do you think?"

Fane came in, and stopped dead. "What's wrong with him?"

Durham abandoned his sultry pose. "I'm practicing pentup passion."

"Well, don't." The colonel bent over Maddy and lifted her hand. "How do you do this morning, angel?"

"Thou shouldst not call me so," she said, which was what she always said. "I am much better. I can move my fingers with no hurt at all, and I slept last night without the sling."

Fane listened to this report gravely. "In high gig then. Will you come driving with me in the park?"

"After . . . the ball," Christian said.

"Spoiler," Fane grumbled.

"A veritable curmudgeon," Durham said. "Rot me, there's nothing worse than a jealous husband."

Christian made the appropriate dry smile, but he *was* jealous, though he'd have choked on it before he'd admit it to his friends. He was jealous of their ease with her, jealous of the simple way they could kiss her fingers—touch her— something he had not done since that moment when she'd sat on the edge of his bed, bound up and hurting by his own hand.

And he was madly jealous of Richard Gill, a phantom presence between them. Christian had swallowed all his rage and pride and summoned the nurseryman Butterfield to make certain he didn't dismiss his pious mule of an employee, blaming the incident on that universal and transparent case, the "unfortunate misunderstanding." Christian had done that for Maddy, and made certain that she knew about it, expecting the reward he surely thought he deserved for the bitter pill it was—to leave the Mule unpunished for openly trying to seduce Christian's wife into leaving him in his own back garden.

It had been his first conscious foray into being a better man, and all it had garnered him was a modest, "Thou didst right, then."

Christian set his teeth together. He didn't think he liked being a better man. He thought that if he couldn't banish the hallowed specter of Richard Gill soon, he was going to take a rapid turn for the worse.

Jervaulx had selected the fabric and design for her ball gown. Maddy had known perfectly well that she must have one, but in a perverse reaction to the curl of inward pleasure she experienced at the idea of a special gown, and in full accord with the trepidation she felt about the ball itself, she had met with the couturiere only with the greatest reluctance, and had refused to give any opinion at all as to what she liked of material or pattern.

That hadn't appeared to concern Jervaulx. He attended the session in the back parlor, examining fashion plates and dolls as if he were a master of it. Maddy secretly inclined toward the vivid, peacocky colors of a green silk trimmed in purple, as pretty as an exotic flower and just as opulent, shown in the picture with three rows of flounces at the hem, puffed sleeves and a trailing boa in transparent purple, but of course she would never have said so. She couldn't imagine herself wearing it in any case—but she thought it very taking.

The modiste was clever enough to push that particular plate back into view several times, offering samples of possible fabrics, but Jervaulx didn't even glance at them. He'd held a scrap of colorless material in his hand, sifting through the plates impatiently until he got to the bottom of the stack and sat back.

The French madame returned to the purple and green combination, holding it up to Maddy's face, making a small frown and shaking her head. "No," she'd said. "It will not do. It will swallow her up whole."

Maddy held herself aloof. She was not disappointed. Her days alone in bed, protected by her injury from his lures and temptations, had given her time to meditate on her weakness. She had erased all that part of herself, the part that turned to color and idle mirth and to him.

Jervaulx picked up one of the fashion dolls, turning it over in his hand. Suddenly he reached for a pair of scissors and began snipping at the trim, ignoring the modiste's faint "oh." The ruffles fell away until the gown that was left seemed as simple as Plain Dress, except for the wide, low scoop of neckline. The original design had had a broad trim of lace to border it; Jervaulx cut that away in the center, leaving only a sort of lace shawl over the full sleeves. He laid the drab scrap of cloth on the doll and handed it to the couturiere.

She examined it for a moment, looking up at Maddy with narrowed eyes. Then she pursed her lips and lifted her brows. "If it is what you wish," she said.

Jervaulx only nodded, and left Maddy to be measured.

That had been when her arm was still completely immobile, and an awkward, painful process it was. Now that her injury allowed more freedom of motion, Jervaulx had informed her at breakfast, the modiste required another fitting.

Maddy reluctantly presented herself at the appointed time. The bland fabric that he'd chosen had extinguished her one pleasure in the gown—all it was now was a concrete reminder of his uncontrollable intemperance and the approaching trial of the ball.

The assistant helped her out of her day dress, as her arm was still far too sore to be very useful. With a mutter of disapproval, the modiste unbuttoned Maddy's corset and chemise. "It is too high to the neck—it will show." Before Maddy realized what the woman was about, she had stripped the undergarments down to Maddy's waist.

Maddy sucked in her breath and crossed her arms over her breasts—and of all moments, Jervaulx chose that one to walk into the room.

He glanced at her, meeting Maddy's horrified gaze without a flicker of reaction. While they tied the bustle, he sat down in a chair, relaxed, like a detached connoisseur in watching women dress.

The gown came down over her head. She hadn't expected it; she'd been caught up in her mortification at his entry and the pain the quick movement to cover herself had caused. Maddy made a little whimper as the assistant caught her hand, trying to bring up the sleeves.

"Careful!" Jervaulx said sharply, and the modiste and assistant murmured profuse apologies. They began to work with more gentleness, allowing Maddy to adjust her arm in stages to get it through the sleeve. This required that she stand quite exposed before Jervaulx, and he didn't have the decency to avert his eyes for an instant. By the time the gown was adjusted, she felt hot all over with embarrassment.

The assistant held the gown together in the back, pinning it very tight, since she had no corset. "Your arm down, madame, if you please to try it," the modiste requested.

Maddy opened her elbow in increments, biting her lower lip. Jervaulx bent his head a little, resting his mouth on the back of his hand, looking down for the first time.

"Ah." The modiste stood back. She had a slight, acerbic curl to her mouth. "I see what you are about, Your Grace."

Jervaulx lifted his eyes. He looked at Maddy from hem to head, a slow appraisal that brought blood brimming to her cheeks.

He nodded.

The assistant hustled to carry the cheval glass around in front of Maddy, and she saw herself for the first time.

She was shocked. The drab scrap of fabric, the fine, stiff,

scratchy material that poked and abraded her bare skin—in the glass it shimmered with color like a faint prism, metallic threads interwoven with silk to make a silver tissue that caught the light and held it, transparent flame.

The plain cut of the dress, with no frills, only the half-shawl of Venetian lace, drew the eye instantly to the neckline that dropped off her shoulders and swept low across her breasts, voluptuous and yet stark. The sleeves echoed her simple dresses, stopping just above her elbows, but full and glittering, radiating light.

It was blasphemous, a deliberate transformation of Plain Dress into sparkling provocative luxury.

"I cannot wear this!" she exclaimed.

"Madame," the modiste said quietly, "it is magnificent."

Maddy looked at Jervaulx. "I cannot. Thou must know!"

He smiled, saying nothing—that maddening perceptive smile, as if he knew her better than she knew herself.

"I cannot!"

The modiste bent to shake out a fold of the skirt. "If it does not please madame, then I will take it back. I think of a half dozen clients now who will—"

"Not back," Jervaulx said. "She wears it." He reached beneath his coat and brought out a box of a sort that was becoming all too familiar to Maddy.

"Oh, no," she said, eying the jeweler's case. "I don't want it. I don't want these ornaments. Canst thou not understand that?"

Jervaulx stood. He opened the case, and Maddy gave a moan of dismay. The modiste and her assistant were not so ungenerous; they inhaled in unfeigned wonder at the sight of the flashing tiara with three stones the size of wren's eggs, holding all the color Maddy had secretly wished for: a green blaze of emeralds framed by curling vines of amethysts, pearls and diamonds.

Maddy had begun to learn something about money and what it might buy—and this, she knew instantly, was no casual gift of a pearl chain, or even an orangerie. This was something that would ransom princes and adorn queens, the size of the stones alone a declaration of sovereignty.

She stepped back as he lifted it to place it in her hair. "Where didst thou come by this?"

She had a hope that it was a family piece, some ducal heirloom that he meant his duchess to wear on her debut, but he only said, "Bought. Think I . . . stole it?"

"Jervaulx!" she cried. "More? When thou art—"

A warning in his sideways glance stopped her. She gave another whimper as he slid the silver comb beneath her coiled braids. "Why, why, why?" she moaned. "Thou must know I despise such things. Where is thy sense?"

"A small purchase," he said.

"Small! Oh, thou art infamous! When thou ought to be paying—"

He put his forefinger against her lips, smoothing them in a sensual touch. She jerked her face away. She couldn't let him touch her, couldn't give in to the rush of love and yearning, the sensation he aroused so instantly.

He lowered his lashes, withdrawing. "Perhaps you don't like." His voice had taken on an undertone of cold mocking command. "But you will . . . show grace . . . to His Majesty."

She stood motionless. "To—whom?"

He moved back and sat down in the chair, stretching out his legs. He observed her with a critical eye, then turned to the modiste. "Your opinion?"

The woman surveyed Maddy with professional acumen. "Unusual, Your Grace." She nodded slowly. "Memorable."

"The king?" Maddy asked in a small voice. "Dost thou speak of the king?"

He held out his hand, and the modiste hurried forward to take the tiara from Maddy's hair and convey it to him reverently. The jewels disappeared again into the box. The duke went to the chamber door.

"Jervaulx," Maddy said tremulously. "Dost thou mean to say—the king is coming to thy ball?"

He looked back at her and shrugged. "Perhaps," he said.

The door closed behind him. *"Quelle chance!"* The modiste clapped her hands together. "Oh, madame," she breathed. "It is the *coup de main*. His Majesty comes to your debut!"

From Christian's single planted hint, the talk spread. He did not risk any further appearances in public; he let Durham and Fane act his point-guard, bringing back reports of what was said by whom.

God only knew if he'd cut his own throat by making this final stake. It had taken all the cash he could lay hands on— exhausted his liquid income, drained dry his account at Hoare's, provoked another visit from Mr. Manning and friends that had been barred at the door by Calvin and a set of footmen carefully selected for their formidable size and robust constitutions.

Poor old King George had been discreetly peddling the tiara, a bauble once given by Bonaparte to the Empress Marie-Louise, at the outrageous price of fifty thousand pounds for years. There's been no takers: His Majesty's royal whim wasn't trustworthy enough in political matters to make it worth the cost—but Christian had paid it, reckoning that with the completion of the Brighton pavilion giving way to a princely passion for creating Gothic glories at Windsor, an infusion of hard cash, instead of another tiresome creditor, would be powerfully welcome to the king.

Acceptances for the ball had already been copious enough, but the prospect—the great question—of His Majesty's appearance had the effect of stirring a hornet's nest. Ridiculous the king might be, fat and gouty, ever more secluded, a target of easy scorn—but let it chance that the monarch might condescend to attend a social gathering, Christian thought dryly, and the old beguiling perfume of royalty turned out to be more than a fading whiff.

It was power. If he managed to anoint himself with that influential cachet, then his brothers-in-law would find themselves members of the wrong club entirely. To publicly insist in the courts that His Majesty chose to honor idiots and mad-men with his friendship was to go beyond the pale. Against the king's indulgence, pushing forward a hearing into Chris-tian's reason became a gaffe of grandiose proportions. George could stop them with a word, if he cared to utter it.

The betting book was open at White's, and Durham claimed that he'd witnessed a debate at Brooks's of three hours' duration: Jervaulx's stubbornly progressive politics, anathema to the King, versus the still-amazing fact that back in '20, Christian had gone dead against his party and public opinion, supporting George's attempt to rid himself of his sordid queen when even the Tory peers had slunk away. As it happened, Christian had taken that particular position on a bet that he could do it and still walk into Whitehall without being pelted with rotten eggs—which he'd lost—but nobody beyond he and Fane and Durham were privy to that.

And half in spite of himself, Christian had always liked George. It required a private acquaintance to see the sincerity, the good heart and clever humor beneath the self-indulgence, the man inside the sad shell he'd become. He'd a child's tem-per and a talent for extravagance, no restraint and no judg-ment, but he'd transformed the face of London with his elegant taste, and dispensed old-age pensions to such diverse personages as Coleridge the poet and Phoebe Hessel the woman soldier; he kept his ministers poring through the crim-inal lists to find condemned prisoners who had no other advo-cate in order to consider their cases for mercy himself; he donated his library—after the Emperor of Russia had offered him a hundred thousand pounds for it—to the nation.

George had his moments. Christian just hoped to the devil he was going to be one of them.

Even with Calvin and the new secretary to do the foot-work, he was nearly spent by the end of each day with the effort of the preparations, tired and angry and lonely when he faced the dressing room and single bed. He and Maddy didn't speak at all now. He couldn't put a moment to when it had happened; a slow barrier of silence had just seemed to grow between them as her arm healed and the ball drew closer. Durham and Fane made breakfast conversation, and at midday Christian took a tray in the library with his work.

Dinner was agony, alone at the table with her. He fell to solving mathematical equations in his head, to give him something to do besides watch her pick at her food like a caged and unhappy bird.

He was losing her. She was deliberately going away. Her body was here, but his Maddygirl, who laughed at foolish jokes, who looked up at him beneath sultry lashes—she was disappearing before his eyes, transforming into this ghastly severe gray ghost-creature.

He never touched her. He never tried. At first it had been because he'd not wanted to hurt her again, but as she'd healed the stiffness had grown in her. She moved away when he came near.

She paralyzed him into a frozen courtesy. He would not be a savage. Instead he worked, and tried to savor the transitory moments of autonomy, and longed for just an hour of no words, no future, nothing but her body and his own in raw and primitive communion.

By the morning of the ball, Durham reported that word the king was dropsical had sent the odds at Brooks's to seventy-to-one. Christian tried not to think about it. He wasn't certain Maddy was going to hold up on him. She looked almost ill at breakfast, picking at her food while Christian and the secretary went over details.

"Gown?" he asked her. "Here and fits?"

"Yes," she said, staring at her buttered eggs as if they spelled out D-O-O-M in large letters.

"Gloves?"

"Yes, I have the gloves."

He tilted his head. "Your arm . . . hurts?"

She stirred the eggs with a broad knife. "No. It's all right."

Maddy, he wanted to plead, *don't do this to me. I need you now.*

But it was impossible. The constraint between them had reached incurable proportions. She left him at an utter loss. He could not touch her, he could not depend on her; he had himself only to get through it.

She lifted her head suddenly. "Jervaulx," she said, with the air of having taken an irrevocable decision.

He closed his hands hard and looked up at her.

"Thou ought to understand that I cannot curtsy nor give vain flattering titles to the king," she declared. She flung a look toward him, as if she expected a battle, and then, shying from it, pushed her chair back and bolted from the room.

Oh, excellent, Christian thought, dropping his head back on the chair. I'm looking forward to it.

Supper would be served at midnight in the dining room. Christian intended to place a quartet of musicians on the library gallery for the card players. He'd had the blue salon cleared for dancing and the real orchestra. Some of the best furniture from the salon had been moved to the back parlor on the ground floor. That room was unrecognizable now, after the refitting, transformed from the most casual to the most magnificent chamber in the house in a scheme of pure white and gold, expanded with mirrors, accented with a vivid red and blue rug, and porcelain dragons writhing up the tall pair of candelabra standing to either side of the new crimson sofa.

That sofa appeared ominously empty when Christian made his inspection. The whole room looked precisely what it was: a shameless grovel to a king who couldn't climb the stairs—therefore bring the ball to him. There was a chair for his mistress Lady Conyngham and accommodation for the favored Dr. Knighton, space enough for anyone His Majesty wished to honor by calling them down from upstairs, and another set of musicians who would wait in the adjacent breakfast alcove until—if—His Majesty appeared, at which time they would play Italian airs.

Christian leaned on the doorpost. Behind him, a footman made a polite cough. Christian turned. He accepted the note offered, hiding the further sinking of his mood as he recognized the telltale wafer. With a sigh, he walked across the hall to the billiards room, poured himself an early cognac, and broke the seal.

Your Grace, Eydie wrote—intending a pointed sarcasm, he supposed—*I have received in the post an Honorable offer of Matrimony from Mr. Newdigate of Bombay. In view of his steady devotion to me since before my marriage, his substantial prosperity and the generosity of his proposals, and my Understanding that I can no longer expect worthy treatment from those of whom I deserve better*—"better" being underlined three times—*I am inclined to accept him. Therefore I will be departing for Calais directly. Mr. Newdigate kindly forwards Sufficient funds for my own travel, however he is not aware of a Package which I must perforce leave behind me, as I am completely without means to convey it to Scotland. As you have indicated your Keen Interest in this parcel, I leave to you how it may best be disposed. I do hope your little Quaker nurse does not prove a horrid Embarrassment to you at your party, my dear. Your sister tells me that you are not well—I wonder that you have undertaken to entertain at all. Do you think it quite wise?*

The pert tone of this missive made him set his teeth. Well enough if Eydie had dug up a nabob for herself, but he had no time for it now. He'd have to make the arrangements to return the babe to Scotland himself, as it was obvious Eydie would not lift her finger. At least she didn't seem inclined to drag the child off to India—clearly the nabob wasn't to be imposed upon by any such tedious details as deep mourning or infants.

He set up the writing machine, but scrawled only a brief reply, watching the copying pen for mistakes. It was so short he could hardly botch it even the first time. He pulled the sheet free and dispatched it.

Chapter Thirty-three

$\mathcal{M}$addy was standing in a robe, staring listlessly out the window of the spare bedroom where she was to dress when she saw the hackney draw up before the front steps. As the cab's door opened, she sucked in a horrified breath at the sight of a Friend's hat and dark coat.

The maid was already laying out the silver gown. Maddy hastened back from the window, slamming the shutters. "Quick—something—" Her day dress had been left downstairs. "Help me put it on!" She snatched up the ball gown and thrust it at the startled maid. A minute later, barely buttoned and hooked, Maddy was rushing down the stairs.

She reached the hall just as a harried footman laid aside a tray of glasses to answer the bell. "It will be for me," she said, desperate to think of somewhere to hide him—why, oh, why had Richard come now of all times! The back parlor was impossible, the breakfast room full of Italian musicians, Calvin's buttery stocked to the ceiling with crates of champagne—she thrust open the door of the billiards room. "Show him in here." She stepped through and closed herself in.

There was a murmur in the vestibule, and then the footman held open the door. "Mr. and Mrs. Little, Mr. Bond, Mr. Osborne."

Maddy had a moment of strange suspension. It was not Richard.

She stood facing the elders of her own Meeting, with her heart withering in her breast.

The footman closed the door. Maddy's lips parted, but no sound came out.

"Archimedea Timms," said Elias Little, "we are come in concern to see thee here in the house of an unbeliever."

The other three stood somber, looking at her in the silver ball gown that mocked Plain Dress.

Elias spoke quietly. "We ask thee, hast thou wedded this man?"

She had known this would happen, that they would come to tell her, but she had not known how it would feel. She had not known what it would be to face them, these people she had loved, who had been as good as family to her. Constance Little was already weeping, silently, her hands twisting in her apron.

Maddy blinked. She turned her face away. Wordlessly, she nodded.

"Oh, Maddy," Constance said in a whisper.

It was as if they had not quite been able to believe it before. Elias glanced around the rich leather and gilt appointments of the room. He gazed at the billiards table, his kind face furrowed with distress.

"It is a real sorrow to Friends," he said, in his great soft voice that she had heard roll out so often on First Day. "The Meeting has directed us to visit thee, and bring thee to a sense of thy wrong. According to the good order of Truth, a Friend ought not to be unequally yoked to one of the world, nor make a motion toward marriage without the consent and approval of Meeting." Elias held out his hand, touching her wrist, speaking more gently. "Archimedea, these are not aimless regulations, but protection for thee, that thou dost not run into the enemy's snare. A young person may be hasty, and mistaken in the Way, and therefore the matter is brought before Meeting and declared unto Friends, who are able in the wisdom and power of God to see into it, whether it is in the Light. Dost thou understand this as the Truth?"

She swallowed. "Yes." Oh yes. She understood.

"And yet thou wast not governed by it. Thou took not counsel of the Lord, nor of Friends, but only thy own willful way."

She half-opened her mouth, and then pressed her lips closed. She did not speak.

"Understanding this, thou wilt know why we are come."

Maddy made a small sound of misery. She turned her back on them.

There was a faint rustle of paper. Elias cleared his throat. "Archimedea Timms, because thou hast from a child been used to go with thy father to Meetings, and taken the outward character of our profession, bearing the name of Quaker, and because thou hast run out from the Truth and married a man of the world, a necessity lies upon us to give forth this testimony against thee, that thou art not at all—" There his deep, soft voice faltered. " —not at all owned as one in fellowship with us."

The tears began to fall, dripping down in hot salty grief to Maddy's chin.

Elias took a deep breath. "Furthermore—because it be well known to many that thou hast had the name and appearance of a Friend, and art reputed by the World's people a Quaker, for the safety and honor of the Society, we direct thee to publicly clear truth by drawing up a paper making it known that thy unequal marriage was not taught nor countenanced by Friends, and to copy it three times, and deliver said copies one to Meeting, to be read out, one to him called a minister who performed the marriage, and one to the newspapers, in order that thou may not under the name of Quaker deceive the world."

Maddy closed her eyes. The newspapers! It was because of Jervaulx, because he was a duke and so everyone must know. She put her fingers up and wiped her eyes, turning quickly. "Let me do it now, then."

If she waited—if she stopped and thought—she was afraid she would not have the courage. She cast a wild look around the room, turning from Constance's tears. There— the duke's writing machine—she pulled open the little drawer on the closed box and found pen and ink. There was no paper; she opened out the box and caught the pieces that fluttered free.

The topmost was already used, scrawled *Send the parcel to me* in Jervaulx's imperfect handwriting. Maddy scratched through that so hard that the tip of the pen broke.

"Archimedea," said Elias, "thou ought not to write in an immoderate spirit. Thy words must be acceptable to Meeting."

Maddy dropped the pen. She sat down on a bench. "I should not have done it." Her face wrinkled up. She could not keep control of tears, or the low mourning note in her throat. "I want to go back." She rocked, weeping, and looked up. "Oh, Constance, I want to go home! Can't I go home anymore?"

Constance rushed to her, taking her hands, kneeling. "Maddy, dost thou wish to come back? Thou canst come to me! Clear Truth, and come and live in the Light."

Maddy looked up past her toward Elias in a wild and sudden hope.

"Thou knowest that we bar no one from Meeting, Archimedea," he said. "But thou canst not manifest the appearance of a Friend and be wed to this man of the world. We could not be easy in such a thing."

"But I could come back?"

"I cannot speak for Meeting," Elias said. "We're only given to say that the paper must be written."

She bowed her head. "Yes. Yes, I'll—"

The door to the billiards room opened suddenly. Maddy jerked upright, clutching Constance's hands.

Jervaulx stopped, with a look of blank startlement. He

seemed slow to retrieve his focus; for a long moment he just gazed at Elias Little.

Then he found Maddy; he looked at her hands locked with Constance's and the scatter of paper on the sideboard. A wariness came into his face.

Maddy slowly let go of a breath as she realized he was not going to explode. She disengaged her hands from Constance's. "Jervaulx," she said, lifting her chin, "these are Friends who have come to speak to me."

He said nothing, only stood there with that guarded look.

"This is my husband," Maddy said quietly.

He was dressed in formal coat and black breeches, his shirtfront all lace with an emerald pin glittering in the folds—tall and still, not a little Satanic in his looks: the model of a carnal pleasure-seeking man.

"Speak what?" he asked, with a hint of challenge.

"We come to testify that Archimedea is no longer in our fellowship," Elias said somberly, "because she has gone out of the Truth and wed herself to thee."

Jervaulx looked to Maddy's tear-stained face and back at Elias. "You cause . . . to cry."

"It is a heavy thing that we do."

The duke surprised Maddy. Instead of erupting into a temper he only said, "Finish?"

The elder nodded. "We have said what we were directed to say."

Jervaulx stood back and held open the door.

Constance turned. She gave Maddy a quick hug. "Come to us," she murmured, before she hurried past the duke out of the room. The others followed more slowly. None of them looked back or said anything.

Maddy was left in place, facing him.

He walked to the sideboard, gathering up the broken pen and papers. He collected it all and put it away, closing the box, crushing the sheet that she'd scratched over. He looked up at her sideways. "Not sorry . . . Maddy," he said with cool defiance. "You weep . . . but I am not sorry."

* * *

At dusk, he looked down from the library window and saw her in the empty court, kneeling near the wall, her head bowed, as if she were praying. He made a wordless mutter toward his secretary and left the room. In the garden court, he found her on her knees in the biting cold, dressed in her old drab Quaker clothes, pulling at tiny weeds along the base of the wall with her fingernails.

"Maddy," he said, brought up short in his irritation, confounded by this strange task. "What are you doing?"

She sat back on her heels and looked up at him briefly, then went back to her meticulous weeding. "I wish to make myself useful in some way."

He stood watching her. "Not now. You . . . dress. Don't have to. . . . useful."

She bent closer to the ground, digging at mortar with her bare fingers.

"Don't," he said sharply, disliking to see her at such work.

"Thou dost not permit it?"

"No. Maddy—' "

She rose, and sat down on the iron bench, looking at her lap.

What's wrong, what's wrong?—but he was loathe to know.

"I would like something to do," she said, her breath frosting as she spoke. "I'm not accustomed to idleness."

"The ball—"

"Oh, yes," she said lightly. "Hast thou made a note in thy accounts? 'One duchess, in ball gown, to be stood at the top of the stairs to receive.' " She shook her head. "I am no duchess. I won't belong there."

"Maddy." He reached out to touch her, but she suddenly stood up and walked away.

"I don't belong *here*," she said, facing away from him.

"Need you . . . Maddy. If you want something . . . task . . . the ball—"

"I know nothing of that!" Her voice was resentful but subdued, half lost as she continued to look down. "Thou hast thy secretary. Thou dost not need me." She picked at the edge of her sling. Her voice broke upward. "Thou dost not need me."

He gazed at her, holding himself in check. "What do you want . . . instead?"

She bent her head a little, not answering.

"Quaker?" he asked softly. "Gill?"

"I don't want to forget what I am," she said with a strange intensity. "I don't want to."

His body tautened. He opened and closed his fist. "My wife. I need now . . . tonight . . . stand with me."

"Tonight!" she said in scorn. "There are other things in the world besides thy frivolous ball. There are other things besides making thyself the great duke again!"

His control was cracking; he breathed softly through his teeth. "Where's your dress?"

"I'm not going to attend," she said. She lifted a finger in dismissal. "It's a creaturely amusement."

"Amusement?" he uttered viciously. "Think I do it . . . for *amusement?"* He caught her arm, thrust her back to face him. "What happens . . . when I'm not the duke?" He gripped her hard. "What happens . . . to you . . . I'm there again?" Shaking her, he shouted, "Lunatic! *Lunatic,* Maddy! Suppose you can stop? You can't. I can't. King! The king can stop, if he will." With a low violent sound, he let her go. "Never go back . . . I will not lose . . . you! Lose all! I—will—be—the—duke!"

He pushed away, turned and left her in the vacant court. At the door, he stopped and looked back.

"Save us. That's what I do . . . tiara . . . king . . . frivolous ball. *Save* us!" He jerked his head toward the house. "You want . . . useful. All right! Useful. One duchess! Receive! Silver dress! Understand?"

She was gazing at him, unmoving, as if he were someone she'd never seen before. He glared back at her. She moistened her lips. "It is . . . to save thee?" she repeated.

"Both. You and me. Go . . . *dress*," he snapped, and slammed the door.

At the top of the staircase, in a hall that smelled of evergreen and ladies' perfume, so full of noise that the wall of sound seemed tangible, Christian shook hands. There was no need to speak; no one could possibly hear what he said. A footman at the base of the stairs bawled the names of the guests as they mounted the step, but no one could hear him, either.

Maddy stood beside him, the tiara flashing green fire every time she moved her head. She had come back to life, his Maddygirl—serious still, but sometimes she gave him a look beneath her lashes, an anxious question, as if to ask if they were succeeding at what they did.

He could tell that her injured arm hurt her. She held it against herself, trying surreptitiously to support it, no doubt as aware as he that every moment she was under the scrutiny of endless eyes. Christian waited until a brief pause, a distraction produced by a lady catching her hem on the stairs below. He took Maddy's elbow and steered her away from the hall where they'd been posted for an hour, and into the blue salon.

The press of guests cleared magically at their passage, moving back from the center of the room where the rugs had been taken up, obviously expecting him and Maddy to open the ball. But he could not, not until the king arrived. Christian passed right by the waiting orchestra and began a circuit of the rooms.

He'd found that the social commonplaces were easy, so ingrained in him that he could speak them without hesitation, like the words to an old song too familiar to have meaning anymore. The noise helped: in the library the quartet was barely audible above the talk. He didn't stop anywhere longer than it took to pause and accept mechanical congratulations, enduring the curiosity and exchanges of looks that he knew trailed behind them.

It was just one more gamble, waiting to begin the dancing. Every minute beyond midnight made it more obvious. 'Til half-past, he reckoned—he could wait that long. If His Majesty hadn't arrived by then, he'd put all his blunt on a losing card.

At least his brothers-in-law weren't here to see it in person. He'd invited his family—but of course they had not come, nor acknowledged it. Not with Maddy in his house, not with their attorneys trying to have him stripped to nothing.

She walked beside him, a silver Galatea, life turned to sculpture instead of the other way round. She did a strange thing with her grave reserve—she embarrassed them. Christian could see it. They had come to sneer at her—that one night at the opera and the rumor mill had done its work fortune hunter, Quakeress, elevated demimondaine; one could only guess, and she didn't give them a clue.

He came across Fane near the end of the circuit and caught him away from the army coterie, drawing him into the open dressing room, where flowers and a few chairs made a quiet but public nook amid the slow current of guests. "Rest." He handed Maddy into a armchair. She clung to him a moment, her only sign of dismay, but he bowed. "A glass," he promised. "Fane will stay."

"Honored to do so," Fane said instantly.

Christian went to dispatch a footman to them, and check for any word of the king.

"You're monstrous comely tonight, my love," Colonel Fane said, bowing to Maddy.

A couple stopped beside them. "Indeed! A rara avis," the man agreed, sweeping a bow.

"Your gown is—so unusual, duchess," his partner said, in a tone that might be a compliment or an insult. "Is it Devey?"

"Devey?" Maddy repeated.

The woman gave her a patronizing smile. "Madame Devey. In Grosvenor Square." She fanned herself with a spread of feathers. "This is such an interesting new idea, to put back the dancing. How late it seems! Is it after midnight yet?"

The colonel dug in a pocket beneath his brilliant scarlet coat. He dug deeper, frowning a little.

"Twenty-five past," the other man said, consulting his own watch.

"Will we begin soon, duchess?" the woman asked sweetly.

"I don't know," Maddy said.

"Ah! Well! We must not monopolize you, ma'am." With a light laugh, the woman bowed and drew back. "Magnificent decorations."

As the couple drifted away, Colonel Fane grinned. "Regular cat-party." He was holding his watch, still digging deep in the pocket of his coat. "Confound it, look here what I've found. There!" He pulled his hand free and held it out. "Caught in the lining, by George!"

Maddy looked down into his open palm at an opal and pearl filigree ring of distinctive design.

"Your wedding ring, ma'am," he announced proudly.

She frowned at it.

"Hang me for a half-wit—no wonder I didn't have it at the ceremony. This coat never left London." He lifted her hand, and closed her fingers over the ring. "There now. Better put it on, so you don't lose it."

Maddy had long since given up trying to keep Jervaulx's signet on her hand. She bit her lip, and then slid the opal onto her finger, where it fit with chance perfection.

The tiara had given her a tremendous headache. What anyone saw in this unpleasant form of entertainment, Maddy could not fathom: a huge, hot press of overdressed people with nothing to do but talk to one another at the top of their lungs and drink. The laughter had grown giddy, and people were complaining. She'd been asked five times if His Majesty was expected, and had answered honestly that she didn't know. She suspected that the guests wished to ask much more than that, but either Colonel Fane or Durham, sometimes both, was always at her elbow, fending off the most pointed inquiries with their singular blend of nonsense and wit.

She'd learned from Durham's observations, and dedicated herself to brevity in conversation. It didn't seem to work quite as well for her as he'd claimed it did for Jervaulx—people looked at her in very peculiar ways—but she told herself that she did not care. She did not wish them to like her, nor befriend her, which was well, because they did not.

A tipsy woman in a purple dress pressed up to Maddy from behind, stumbling against her. The lady's gloved hands clung painfully to Maddy's sore arm, while a painted mouth opened and smiled, too close.

"Pardon me!" the lady cried. "I am so clumsy!" She took Maddy's hand. "It is a lovely ball, dear. When is the dancing to begin?"

"I don't know," Maddy said, but her questioner was already gone, leaving a folded note pressed into her hand. She opened it.

Upstairs, was all it said, scribbled unevenly.

Maddy didn't know why Jervaulx could not come for her himself, instead of sending a drunken lady as a messenger, but she told Colonel Fane that she was wanted. He nodded affably, a little worse for all the champagne himself, and escorted her through the crowd to the back stairs.

At quarter before one, the vultures arrived. Calvin brought word to Christian that Mr. Manning and Lord Stoneham had entered without announcement. Come to gloat, Christian thought. He'd been aware of a subtle outflow of people in the past few minutes. He could hardly blame them. They'd got what they'd come for, a view of him and Maddy—and still the dancing had not begun. The midnight supper was waiting, and people were beginning to look at him and speak in lowered voices.

Durham drifted past in the crowd. He smiled, holding a glass of champagne above the feathered headdress of a countess who was prattling to Christian about some daughter of hers that he didn't remember. Durham didn't say anything. With the subtlest of moves, he simply shook his head.

Christian gave it up. He bowed to the countess and went to look for his wife.

Maddy climbed the back stairs alone. On the upper floor, the music from the gallery was much more audible, while the sound of the guests faded to a dull roar. She paused in the hall, and then went to the open door of the spare room where she'd dressed.

"Jervaulx?" She peeked around the door. At the sight of two of the duke's brothers-in-law, Maddy looked quickly for the duke and did not find him.

"Ma'am. Do come in. We'd like to talk to you."

She pushed the door wide. "Where is he?"

The ruddy-faced one leaned over and caught her wrist, drawing her inside. "Jervaulx? Why, downstairs with his guests, I suppose. I don't believe we've ever been properly introduced." He closed the door. "I'm Manning. This is Lord Stoneham."

Maddy glanced at the other man, who was smoothing over and over at his ample sideburns. He bowed quickly.

"Let me speak directly to the point," Manning said. "We're here to make terms with you."

Maddy stood silent.

"Come, Miss *Timms*." He put a sarcastic emphasis on her name. "You must know by now that this wild grasp at the king isn't going to answer."

Still she said nothing.

"He isn't going to come, ma'am. You've bought that vulgar trinket on your head for nothing, if you thought you purchased His Majesty's protection along with it. He is notoriously erratic, my dear. A shrewd cast, and one that might have saved you—but I'm afraid it appears as if it won't."

She sank down slowly in a chair, watching him in fascination. "Saved me?"

"If you thought yourself made safe by quashing all hope of a hearing—then indeed—had the king cared to bestir himself this evening, you were saved, weren't you? But he has not."

She clasped her hands in her lap, staring at them, feeling the weight of the tiara on her head. "Perhaps—he might come yet."

"Unlikely. You hold your orchestra silent for nothing. But there's no need to dwell on that. Let us talk business. You wear the tiara—you know what it's worth. You may have it."

She kept her head lowered. "I don't understand."

"Miss Timms, I shall lay the facts before you. We have investigated this so-called wedding, and discovered your ploy. Farce, I might better call it—since only a man who'd gone simple in the head could possibly have tumbled for a pack of country yokels hired to pound at the door."

Maddy's chin came up abruptly.

Manning smiled. "Ah, yes. We've found you out, you see."

"Hired—to pound at the door?" she said in wonder.

"Spare us your histrionic talents, Miss Timms. We can produce the fellows in court. I take it this damned Kit Durham is in it with you hand and glove, but what you must realize, ma'am, is that there is no marriage. The law requires the approved Church of England ceremony and no duress. Quite aside from Jervaulx's incompetence, and the sham pursuit, we have a witness who can testify to the irregularity of the ceremony itself. It has a very ugly smell, Miss Timms. Very ugly. There are heavy penalties for the sort of trick you've tried to pull."

"I hired no one," Maddy said. "I—"

"Don't think to succeed at making Mr. Durham your scapegoat. Your dirty work he may have done, but I'll see to it—I'll see to it personally, Miss Timms—that you suffer all the penalty you deserve, should you push me."

"Manning," the other one said, with a plaintive note. "Let me talk to her. Try to understand, Miss—ah—ma'am. We're awfully upset. We hate dragging this through the mud, but you really ought to think a moment. That's why we're here, you see—we don't want to carry it all the way, but you're forcing us into such an unpleasant position, with all this spending and these balls and things. Please think about it."

"What—do ye want me to think about?"

"Cutting your losses, ma'am," Manning said harshly.

"And ours," Stoneham added. "Don't make us go so far as a public hearing. The family name, ma'am! Have a little pity. Just give him back to us, so that we don't have to take it to the courts."

"Where you will lose everything, Miss Timms. Everything, once he's declared incompetent. And I don't scruple to say that it is *you* who tell against his wit the heaviest—his marriage to such as you, and the deranged actions he's taken under your power—dismissing Torbyn—that gun—the tiara—this bungle of debts—this very ball, madam, at such a time! I'll admit that he might fool the casual eye, but all this will come out in court, and then you're gone—with nothing. Except perhaps a place on a convict transport."

"But we don't want to take it that far," Stoneham pleaded. "We're prepared to be generous. Very generous. We'll do anything to avoid a hearing."

She shook her head, trying to comprehend. "But—do ye say—you don't want a hearing?"

"Of course we don't want a hearing! And we'll pay you. The tiara, as Manning says. Take that."

"Why?" She was bewildered.

"Miss Timms, I beg you not to waste our time by playing the dunce," Manning said. "If you agree not to contest a nullification of the marriage, then we are prepared to let you keep the tiara."

Maddy sat still, gazing at him. "It can be nullified?"

"Indeed it can. And will be, whether you like it or no. Your only decision is whether or not you wish to be sensible and take what you're offered, or make us wrest it from you by force."

"I had not thought . . ." She stared into space. Her voice

dropped. "But—can it be nullified—" She moistened her lips. "After . . ."

"Ah! The lady blushes," Manning said unpleasantly. "The more fool you, then. Did you think a consummation would protect you? The marriage was illegally conducted. It was induced by fraud. The duke was not in his right mind. It can be nullified."

"But you see, you save us going into all that, if you will cooperate," Stoneham said. "If you will agree to an annulment, say, on the grounds of non-consummation, it's all much simpler. None of this hearing business."

"And if you're breeding, which I may sincerely hope for your sake that you're not," Manning added, "a stipend can be privately arranged for the child. It's better than you will get in the other circumstance."

She stood up suddenly, walking away from them, from their falsehoods and terms and manipulations. She saw herself in the cheval mirror and stood looking at the silver, unfamiliar figure there. "Ye would not have a hearing, then," she said, and the stranger in the mirror seemed much more confident and sophisticated than naive Maddy Timms.

"Are you looking for certain safety from the law, madam?"

She stared at the silver figure, and turned. "If I am to agree to a nullification, I must know that there is to be no hearing. Ever."

"You have our word on it," Stoneham said eagerly.

Maddy looked at him and at Manning's sturdy belligerence. They were not Friends; she could not trust them.

"I'm not decided. I will consider it," she said. The ball gown swished around her as she turned to leave.

Manning caught her arm. "You haven't long, madam," he said. "My patience with this situation is worn quite thin."

She pulled herself free of him, moving toward the door.

"And don't think to try to spirit him away again," Manning said behind her. "I warn you—you'll catch cold at it this time."

* * *

Christian couldn't find Maddy. As he worked around a chattering couple by slipping into the recess of the bay window, he paused. He looked down at a man standing below in the light of a streetlamp.

Christian's hand closed convulsively on the drapes. He flung himself back, ramming into a guest behind him. The man began to apologize, but Christian muttered, pushing away, walking into the crowd.

It was the Ape down there.

Christian was having trouble breathing. He plunged through the guests, ignoring the commotion. At the top of the stairs, he grabbed a footman. "Outside! The man . . . shaved . . ."

The servant blinked at him in confusion. "Your Grace?"

"Rid of him!" He gave the man a shove toward the stairs. With a look of uncertainty, the footman bowed. He turned and descended. Christian watched him go out, then pushed back to the window. He looked down.

The liveried servant stood talking to one of the guests' coachmen. The man shrugged. No one else stood on the walk.

A hand descended on Christian's shoulder. He jerked and swung around on his assailant in berserk reflex—saw it was a Whip MP and barely controlled his reaction in time. The man smiled and waved his glass of champagne, launching into a voluble discourse on Catholic emancipation. Christian stared at him, unable to master a word. He glanced past the politician and saw the blood-man's back, familiar Quaker coat, terrible—pausing for an instant by the far door, and then passing on through, lost in the crowd.

The politician hesitated, squinting at Christian. "I say. You look jolly queer, my man. Do you think we had better open this window?"

Chapter Thirty-four

*I*n the cold dimness of the duke's stable, a row of eight perfectly-matched shapes marked the hind stockings of the new team. The horses shifted, with alert chinks and deep draughts of air, scenting the intruder as Maddy paused, adjusting from the ball noise and the shadows of the garden court to this deeper darkness.

The material of her dress caught what small light there was, shimmering. She took her skirt up in her hands and walked to the coach at the end of the aisle, then turned and walked back again, trying to be sure, to find the Light and certain answers.

It was only another sign of how far she had strayed, that it was so hard to reach a state of inner calm, to listen for the still, small voice. She had lost the way of it; for a long time, she hadn't been to Meeting, she hadn't prayed: she knew she had not even really tried. All those nights of worry had been only that—worry, and misery, and wishing that things were not what they were. All willful stubborn resistance to the Truth.

She did not belong here. She had stayed—why? Richard had begged her to leave, her own elders had hinted that she might return—and still she was here.

Because Jervaulx needed her.

Because they had made the marriage irrevocable.

But he did not need her, and the marriage was not irrevocable.

Gradually the arched windows looking out on the alley took shape. The rumps of the cream ponies made dim pale shapes—beyond them in the row two stalls stood black and empty. As her vision grew sharper, she could see the faint gleam of the town carriage, and the other vehicle beyond that. Something brushed up against her skirt and made her jump, but it was only a cat, purring loudly.

Marriage that was no marriage—a wedding that had been a farce, a trick; quick anger rose in her and she pulled the opal ring from her finger. It had never left London, Fane had admitted—and Maddy remembered, vividly, Jervaulx saying that he'd just given it to the colonel before the ceremony. Lies and falsehoods. Hired yokels, to pound at the door! To make her think he was in danger, to use her, to ruin her life because he thought of no one and nothing but himself.

He had needed her then, that badly.

She stopped at a window and stared out into the mews. The other stables were dark at her level, the only light falling down onto the cobbles in misty squares from the grooms' quarters on the floors above.

The marriage could be nullified. She might go home. She might even do him a service by it—removing the terrible stain on his sanity of marriage to a Quaker. They promised no hearing, ever, if she left him. She had felt the hate in Manning—perhaps she would draw it away with her, the way a fox drew the hunters from her young.

She paced the aisle again, past the stolid rumps of the horses. She could not trust those men. She could not take their word. That much Jervaulx's world—Jervaulx himself—had taught her well.

She remembered the night she had left him here, and grown more uneasy every mile until she had turned her back on her father and returned here to find Jervaulx cornered by them. Surely that disquietude had been the clear voice of God in her heart, telling her what she must do.

If she were not here, his legal wife, what was to stop them from trying that again? But if she was not his legal wife, then what was to stop them anyway?

How could she ever leave him, knowing what they could do, by force or by law or by guile?

How could she stay?

She pressed the ring between her cold hands, and lifted them to her mouth. How had she come to this—that she loved him outside of all reason and right?

Elias Little could tell her. It was because she had run out of the Truth into self-will and carnal temptation. She had not turned to Friends, she had not listened to Richard's counsel at the coaching inn, she had always and ever taken the part of a wicked and worldly man.

But he needed her.

But he didn't.

Outside, a new lamp flared, and the rumbling scrape of a door brought the stable across the way to life. Voices spilled into the alley, and the wide door stood open to a vacant carriage house.

A figure that had been invisible sprang into view at the edge of the light and moved into the shadows again, the hooded and shawled outline of a woman. Maddy watched through the window for a moment.

"What d'you want?" one of the grooms called toward the shadow, and got only a muffled negative in reply. "Move along, then," he said. "Our rig's back."

There were always ragged people and beggars in the square; it was one of the painful ironies of this place, something that Maddy had not directly confronted. She felt her failure sharply now, a convenient blindness thrown in high relief against the background of the ball, the laden supper table and the drunken laughter.

Iron hooves echoed in the alley. The returning carriage clattered down the cobblestone, activating a quiet bustle.

Coach lamps reflected against the upstairs window panes
while the driver backed and cornered his pair with a seasoned deftness. When the vehicle was angled halfway toward the door, the footman swung down from behind. He
took a lamp from its bracket, carrying extra illumination to
the grooms who efficiently unharnessed the team.

The frosty puffs of their breath mingled with the horses'
steam. One by one, the grays were led off. The grooms came
back to grab the shaft, and with a low call and a running
heave, pushed together to roll the carriage in.

The footman made a quick check around the cobblestones
with the lamp, throwing brief light on the beggar woman's
silent figure. He didn't seem to notice her. His breath shone
bright for an instant as he turned inside and gripped the door
handle. The big barrier rumbled closed.

The alley lay dark and silent, with only the murmur of the
party drifting out over the barren cobbles.

Maddy stood at the window. All the heated blood of her
pacing had cooled; she shivered even in the shelter of the
stable. Though she could not see the beggar, she was powerfully aware of the woman standing invisible in the shadows.

Taking a deep breath, Maddy rubbed her cold arms. She
unlatched the stable door and let herself out into the alley.

The woman rose, coming toward her instantly, as if she
had been waiting. "What am I to do?" she asked.

Maddy halted, startled at being addressed so boldly. "Art
thou hungry?" she asked, standing a few feet away.

The hooded figure came forward. She too stopped, with
an equally shocked expression: a girl much younger than
Maddy had expected, with fresh plump cheeks and red-
rimmed eyes. "Oh," she said, dropping a quick curtsy. "Forgive me, mum. I didn't mean—I thought you—I was told to
wait here. Excuse me." She shrank back toward the dark,
clutching her bundle close to herself.

"Art thou hungry?" Maddy asked again. "Wilt thou come
into the kitchen?"

"Oh, no, mum! I was told not to come in!"

Maddy moved forward, puzzled. "Thou needn't fear me. I'm—I am the mistress here. If I say it is all right for thee to come, then it is."

The girl suddenly stopped her retreat. "Oh, mum—you're the housekeeper?" she exclaimed in vast relief. She dropped a curtsy again and came close, holding out a note, still clasping the bundle tight against her. "If you please, mum, I was told to go here, and say to His Grace that the parcel from Mrs. Sutherland is come."

Maddy took the note. It was not sealed; the girl held the paper out open to show her the writing. *Send the parcel to me,* it said, in his conspicuous hand.

"Oh," Maddy said. "Well, then. Thou must bring it in There is no need to wait out—"

A low wail issued from the bundle in the girl's arms. She hiked it up onto her shoulder, crooning softly, and glanced up at Maddy with an apologetic smile.

For one moment, Maddy stood motionless. She felt as if she were hung at the top of a great fall—not thinking —not breathing.

Then she whispered, "From Mrs. Sutherland?"

The girl curtsied. "Yes, mum."

Maddy began to shiver. The cold suddenly took hold of her. She clutched her arms around herself. "A parcel? Is that the parcel?" Her voice was shaking hard. "Is that—the parcel?"

"Yes, mum." She smiled again, with a tinge of sadness. "Aren't they awful, the nobs, to call it so? It's a sweet little girl. I'm wet nurse—I lost me own boy two months back."

This simple confession broke the dream-like suspension that held Maddy. The fall began, the real fall, a plummeting, nauseating descent into comprehension.

Eydie. Mrs. Sutherland.

They had been lovers.

They had a child.

"Are you all right, mum?" the girl asked.

Maddy blinked. She could not stop the shivers that racked her. Water had come to her eyes. She saw the girl through a slur of light and dark. "I'm all right," she said, in a ghastly voice. She cleared her throat. "I'm all right."

They had a baby; he had done—with her—with *Eydie* . . .

All his kisses. He knew so much; he knew everything— and Maddy, besotted, bewitched—she had thought it wicked to keep a lock of hair and a miniature.

She'd been blind. She was blind and dazzled and utterly lost. She heard the fragile whimper of the child and instead of righteous repugnance felt only a surge of love and pain and misery that drowned her—because it was his, because it belonged to him, and she loved even dishonor and iniquity if it was his.

"You're colder than us, mum, shakin' so. Should we go in, then?"

"I—"

With a clash like a fire alarm, the stable bell began to ring madly. Maddy and the girl both leaped back as lanterns flashed and grooms seemed to come running from everywhere. The baby began to wail. Behind the girl, a sharp blaze of light appeared at the end of the alley. A pair of horses came trotting under the arch, their riders emblazoned in scarlet and gold, carrying torches, posting ahead of a coach that wheeled smartly around the corner. The coachman was seated on a sumptuous blue and purple hammer-cloth: bewigged and epauletted, royally turned out. The king had come.

On the front walk, Christian was in a silent tumult, elated and distracted, supporting His Majesty's painful progress from the curb to the stairs. Christian was on one side—and Wellington on the other.

Wellington, for the love of God. Christian found himself in the middle of politics—he might use the king; so the king might use him. Christian hadn't spent much of his concentration on the newspapers, but he'd followed enough to know that strong currents were running, and likely to sweep the present ministry away. And there was no other interpretation for a public healing of the breach between George and the Iron Duke than to pave the way for Wellington to assume the premiership.

They chose Christian's ball to advertise it, a stroke of brilliant luck, but he had no time for contemplation. He'd no idea where Maddy had gone—she ought to have been at his side to greet the king at his carriage—she ought to bc here now at the door—she ought to *be* here—God damn her, *where was she?*

George got one swollen leg up onto the second step, gripping hard on Christian's left arm. Wellington on the king's other side took his turn, bracing His Majesty's all-too-majestic bulk. The strong scent of hair oil rose from the shiny curls of George's nut-brown wig, mingling with the heavy perfume of his pocket handkerchief. Christian turned his face away for a covert breath of cold fresh air, and then glanced up. Heady relief flooded him.

She was there, standing in the open doorway, with Calvin and a pair of tall footmen behind her. The tiara flashed; hcr cheeks were red spots in white, her lips absolutely bloodless. He hoped to God she wasn't going to faint.

He grinned at her, to give her courage, and looked down to his work without waiting for a reaction. The royal attendants swarmed forward, and he lost her as thcy reached the door and George stepped through. The king patted Christian's arm. "Thank you, thank you, dear boy. I can make a go of it from here, eh? Where's my stick?"

The king leaned on his cane. There were guests in the hall—those who knew they had the entree had taken initiative to come downstairs. George shook hands all around, with every sign of pleasure, while Calvin and the footmen kept him discreetly steered toward the room prepared for him.

Christian could hear the reaction to Wellington. It rose up the stairs like a breaking wave, turning a dull rumble to a roar. Hang 'em. Hang 'em all—the Ape and the blood-man and Manning and his family.

Wellington stood back from the king while His Majesty

was occupied. Christian, no favorite of this high Tory war-horse-hero, felt himself raked by those famous bright blue eyes that had assessed whole battlefields at a glance. The Iron Duke bowed. "His Majesty commanded me to attend him tonight. I hope it's not an imposition?"

Christian offered his hand. "It is . . . an honor," he said, and meant it. He saw the other man's quick perception of his speech. "I'm different," he added bluntly, judging that Wellington, with his ear in the upper reaches of government, would be no stranger to Christian's debacle in the Lord Chancellor's office. He gave a slight dry smile. "You of all . . . know trial by fire . . . changes."

Wellington gave him a hard, quizzical look as they shook hands. Christian endured it. He'd won through his own particular inferno—he didn't reckon he had to look away on account of his politics.

Wellington lifted his brows. "Any hope of a change in your liberal opinions?"

Christian shrugged. "Wrong fire."

The commander snorted. "You're your own man, at least. I give you that." He smiled grimly. "A *visage de fer*. It's the only choice in life, eh?"

Christian opened his hands, indicating the ball around him—his own face of iron. Wellington, no fool, inclined his head with a look of acknowledgment. He put his hand on Christian's shoulder and gripped hard before turning back to the king.

George had made the parlor and sofa at last, sinking down with a creak of corset stays. He called to Christian, smiling like a rosy-cheeked obese cherub. "Won't you bring your duchess to us?"

Christian turned. Maddy had been hanging back near the door, half hidden among the guests and court attendants while Lady Conyngham and Knighton were seated.

He held out his hand. Maddy did not look up at him, but came forward and stood before the king. The hum of conversation in the room grew quiet.

"Archimedea," Christian said. "Duchess of Jervaulx."

She offered her hand, without nodding or curtsying. "I welcome thee here," she said gravely.

George gave a burst of a laugh. "My dear! A Quaker indeed! They had told me so, but I could scarce believe it." He took her hand, kissed and then held it. "I've a great fondness for your people, a very great fondness. Good, kind, honest people. Schools. Bibles. Banks. You are a credit to them."

In a small, steady voice, she said, "I must tell thee that I am not esteemed a Friend any longer."

He patted her hand. "Your marriage, is it? Ah, me—the principles of religion are sometimes a weight upon us, are they not? But you have a consolation in this fine husband of yours." He looked past her at Christian. "You must remember my friendship, dear boy. I am at your service whenever you choose to call upon me."

Christian bowed. It was only with an effort that he kept himself from laughing out loud in elation. The king . . . and Wellington.

Damn their eyes—let them try to touch him now.

He opened the ball merely by taking Maddy to the head of the room, bowing to the guests and to her, and signaling the maestro to begin. The deuce for excuses and explanations. The whole world could think what they pleased of a duchess who did not dance.

There was a moment as they walked off the ballroom floor, while the sets were forming and everyone turned toward the dancing, that Christian found himself and his wife unobserved in the stairway hall.

He was so full of success that he gripped her ice-cold hand in his, drew her to him and kissed her amid the sweep of music.

He inhaled night air, an island of crisp cleanliness in the heavy, perfumed atmosphere. She had not once looked directly at him, but he didn't care; he felt crazily invulnerable now; he felt that nothing could go wrong.

For a grim moment it seemed he'd been mistaken. She was stiff, repulsing him with a sharp withdrawal. He let go of her. She stepped away and looked back at him, his Maddygirl, his sparkling wise Athena, silver and beautiful to him even in her astringency. She stared at him through the lashes that turned her green eyes to gold, chaste and sensual at once, setting the current moving fast and hard in his blood.

"I love you," he said under his breath, the words riding the music. He knew she could not hear them. He didn't want her to hear. He didn't want her answer to it, not tonight, his night, when everything, even his flawed self, was a victory.

"Thou wilt be safe now?" she asked, standing clear of him.

Christian made no move closer. "The Ape . . . here," he told her.

Her hands closed. She made a convulsive step toward him, and stopped.

"The Ape," he said. "Doctor . . . from the madhouse. Calvin found them . . . skulk bastards . . . among the guests."

Her body was tense, her hands white fists against the silver gown.

He smiled slyly. "Arrested now. Trespassers. Thief."

"Arrested?" Her eyes widened in stupefaction. "Cousin Edward—thou hadst him arrested as a *thief?*"

"Chain up . . . toss in the watch house." His lip curled in satisfaction at the thought. "See how they like it." He could see that she wasn't entirely delighted; she was staring at him with an expression he could not interpret. He shrugged. "Maybe tomorrow . . . maybe a week . . . withdraw the charges. I'm a better man. For you. Let 'em go."

Something in her face altered. The severity left her. She reached for him, embraced him, her hands rising up and pulling him against her as she lifted her mouth to his.

Christian made a sound of excitement and pleasure, answering. She came into his arms with a willingness that shocked him, opened her lips and kissed him frantically, as if she had never done it before and never would again, as if there were no one to see, no one to stare. He forgot the ball and the music, lost himself in the feel of her, her body against his with a new urgency, a promise that he found himself hard pressed to postpone.

"Maddygirl, Maddy . . ." He made himself set her away. He felt his own foolish smile, but he couldn't help it; he was so glad; happier than he ever remembered being in his life.

She held her lower lip caught in her teeth, watching him intensely. She looked almost ill with the paleness and color flaming in her cheeks.

"Soon," he said, touching her hot face. "First . . . get rid of the king." He ran his finger down her nose and kissed the tip of it. "Then only you . . . and me."

She lowered her lashes. Without a word, she slipped her hand from his and turned away to descend the stairs.

His Majesty, damn him, lingered until six. By that time Christian saw it all through a dizzying haze of exhaustion. He was exhilarated almost to euphoria: he didn't trust himself to do anything properly, but somehow, minute by minute, he got through.

Maddy amazed him. A hundred times he looked at her and thought she was beautiful. In her silver simplicity, in her sober grace, she anchored him. He was proud of her: she hadn't curtsied before the king; she hadn't given up her integrity—she didn't fail her honesty or herself one inch. She even spent a half hour talking to Wellington, by God—no doubt canvassing him on the political disabilities of Nonconformists. The two of them were a pair, both so dignified and serious—she made Christian smile.

He could look about him and see any number of women he might have had for a wife, but none he could imagine at his side through this. The devil that she could not dance. It only made her more unique.

He kept watching for Manning and Stoneham, but never saw them. It didn't matter; it was only that he would have enjoyed seeing their faces. By dawn, when the last of the carriages rolled away from the door in the frigid light, leaving a house that smelled of stale wine and perfume, he wanted only to lie down and let blessed unconsciousness take him.

He watched Calvin close the door and stoop to pick up a broken plume from the floor. Maddy had disappeared some time ago—for that he didn't blame her. He could hardly see his own hands, he was so tired.

He climbed the stairs, past the salon where the extra staff had already arrived and begun sweeping. Another floor seemed almost too much, but the dressing room where he'd been sleeping for the past month was full of chairs and flowers.

His valet appeared from the back stairs. Christian shook his head, dismissing the man. He leaned on the newel post and looked up. One more flight. And Maddy would be there, in the guest room. He wanted to lie down with her and go to sleep. Enough of the strange distance between them.

That kiss. His pulse warmed. Tonight—

Actually, it was morning. He smiled to himself, pulled his neckcloth free and climbed the stairs.

In the upper hall, a fan of early light spread on the rug from the open guest room door. He hesitated outside it, trying to gather his muzzled wits. It seemed suddenly a little embarrassing, after so long, just to walk in upon her. Perhaps he could pretend that he'd forgotten to order two spare rooms made up. Perhaps he could just kiss her again—arousing thought—just take her down on the bed and kiss her. The spirit was willing, anyway.

He heard a soft female murmur from inside. With an effort, he put his body in motion again, pushing away from the wall.

"Maddygirl?" He looked in the doorway, a little sheepish, without excuse or rationale—not precisely one of the proverbial lords of creation.

The guest room, fitted up in stylish feminine taste, was all sunny pink chintz undimmed by any use. In a diminutive puff of an upholstered armchair sat a girl Christian had never seen before.

She held a baby—the source of the murmurs—that batted with awkward arms at the ribbons on the girl's cap.

For a moment he had the odd sensation that he had walked somehow into the wrong house. The room was unfamiliar, the girl a stranger, and the baby . . .

He gazed at them.

"Damn!" he exclaimed, and went two paces into the room. On the bed lay a metallic shimmer of fabric, Maddy's ball gown, with the tiara and a sealed note atop it. He whirled on the girl. "What's the meaning . . . *this?"*

The baby stopped babbling at the sound of his voice. The girl, who had not yet moved, moistened her lips and said, "The mistress told me to wait here for Your Grace." She rose, adjusting the child against her shoulder, and curtsied. "This is the little girl, sir, Mrs. Sutherland left yesterday, and said I was to bring her to you."

Christian grabbed the note and ripped it open. His right hand was awkward, shaking; he tore the paper half down the middle and then couldn't seem to get the parts together. He couldn't make his brain decipher it. He heard himself making distraught noises and swallowed against the panic, leaning over the dressing table, smoothing the page flat, but the words just slid and tilted as he looked at them. *Christian.* He read his name. He saw letters that said things, things he didn't want to hear. *I must leave thee now. It was wrong. Thy world, the wedding, illegal, nullify. Thy daughter.*

He closed his eyes, hanging his head over the note. All his breath had left him, like a great blow to his chest.

"Go . . . out," he said. "Next room. Away. Go away."

"Yes, sir." The girl passed him quickly. He heard a door open and close.

Maddy, he thought. Maddy, Maddy . . .

Christian yanked the bell-rope. He would go after her. Bring her back. Explain. He started out of the room to the stairs, slamming the door behind him.

In the other room, the baby instantly began to wail. The sound stopped him dead. He had a wild thought that it was all a mistake, that Maddy must listen to him if he could say that it was a mistake. The baby was Eydie's; she ought to have taken it, but there'd been this misunderstanding—unfortunate—unfortunate—misunderstanding.

He threw open the bedroom door. The girl looked up wildly as the baby's howl burst on him. "I'm sorry!" She shifted the child in her lap. "I won't let her cry! She's very good, Your Grace!"

Her look of terror made him halt on the doorsill. Just as abruptly, the wail ceased. The girl had the infant supported, sitting halfway up against her, revealing the small face.

The baby whimpered. A pair of tear-filled button eyes gazed at Christian, fixing him with anxious concern. Its forehead puckered in a tentative question, like some omnibus passenger who's just got down and found himself stranded at the wrong stop.

And with an uncanny sting of recognition, a revelation, Christian saw his own self. Not in the round, featureless infant face, the indistinct thatch of hair; not in the physical shape of it that could have been any baby in any random cradle. What he saw was that small worried bafflement: the dawning knowledge that the world was a strange and capricious place, the slightly foolish, helpless sensation of having perhaps just walked into quicksand.

He knew it, that feeling.

His hand opened. He let go of the door and took a step nearer. The round, unblinking eyes followed his motion with ardent perplexity. The baby gazed at his shirtfront and his black coat, regarding him as if he were an object of great but unfathomable importance.

She looked up into his face. And then her sudden smile broke out glowing, the way a lover would turn to discover him in a crowd. *You're here!* The silent message lit her up like a candle, caught him up instantly in it too. *At last you're here!*

The infant arms flailed, and she began to coo excitedly.

Christian backed away, shocked at the sensation that seized him.

"The deuce take you," he said low, and the baby laughed at him.

"Sir?" His valet's voice behind him made him jerk around.

With a wrench, Christian focused on the man. "Duchess . . ." He realized that he would have to suffer the whole house knowing. Anger rose in him. "When she left! Find out."

"Your Grace—the cook said that Mistress departed through the kitchen two hours ago, and forbid anyone to follow her."

Christian knew where she'd gone. To her Quakers—the dark thee-thou sobersides who'd been here yesterday.

Or to Richard Gill.

Silent violence exploded inside him. Let her go, then! Let her go; let him have her. Christian struck the door with his forearm, sending it slamming back to the wall and bouncing off. The baby began to wail again.

"Hush, hush," the girl urged, and it screamed louder. She stood up and hiked it onto her shoulder. The infant kept howling. "She'll quiet when she's put down," the girl said over the wails. "If I could just put her down somewhere. I've been carrying her all the night."

"Put down then!" Christian waved at the bed. "There."

He reached for the bell-rope as she obeyed him. This baby, this damnable baby—Richard Gill—Maddy . . . Maddy . . . she wouldn't have to put up with the Mule's byblows, would she? Pious prick, he wouldn't know how to—

Christian flushed with rage, thought and image freezing him.

His; she was his wife. He wouldn't suffer Gill to touch her. He yanked the bell-pull. "My cloak," he snapped at his valet. "Call up the carriage."

*   *   *

Beneath one of the long arched showrooms of Butterfield's
Lambeth nursery, flanked by rows of potted flowers, Christian stood waiting, his foot propped on the end of a bench.
He leaned on his knee, slapping his riding whip lightly
against his leg as the Quaker came toward him down the
length of the greenhouse.

Gill stopped. Christian did not straighten, only looked at
him sideways.

The last echo of the gardener's footsteps died away down
the arched cavern. He returned Christian's look with a restrained, slightly questioning expression—no triumph, no
defiance—and Christian knew she was not here.

He dropped his eyes, his fingers loosening on the whip.
With the tip of it, he nudged between the blossoms of the
pink-and-white carnation, staring in silence at the petals. He
had a great urge to cut the whip across, snapping the blooms
off all the flowers in reach.

He did not do it. He put his head down and rubbed his
hand over his eyes.

"She has left thee," Gill said.

Between his fingers, Christian saw only the black silk of
his full dress against a background of gay peppermint-
striped petals. He moved the whip, stirring the foliage. He
thought that the scent of humid soil and carnations must
make him ache with shame and anger for the rest of his life.

"She has not come to me," the Quaker said. "Does thee
know what Meeting she attended?"

Christian shook his head.

"I can learn," Gill said. "I will send thee notice that she is
safe, if thou wish it."

Christian felt himself left outside a high wall, the gates
closing, dark-coated sober figures drawing them shut
against him.

Maddygirl, he thought helplessly. Maddy.

She had gone through of her own will and left him here.
He could not learn her ways, he could never be the man she
would esteem; evidence enough of that wailed at the top of

its lungs in his guest room. His life repelled her—it was this serious God-fearing gardener, this plain modest pursuit of virtue that she wanted.

He looked at Gill and thought: you will never make her laugh, will you?

You'll be kind and constant and wise—wiser than I am—and she'll respect you. Damn you. Damn you. A better man.

Christian threw back his cloak and stood straight. He turned away. He stopped as he pushed open the door, holding the whip and his hat in his hand. "She's afraid of thunderstorms," he said, something that Gill might never find out for himself.

And ghosts, he thought as he stepped into the early frost—but he did not give Richard Gill that hint.

Full morning shone through the crack in the guest room curtains, casting a bar of bright light across the bed and the pillows that bolstered the baby. Christian leaned one hand on the bedpost.

He glanced at the girl sitting in the corner, noticing for the first time how weary she appeared.

"Eaten?" he asked her softly.

"I nursed her and cleaned her just a half hour ago, sir."

He hadn't even thought of that. "You . . . I meant."

She said quietly, "Last night. The mistress bade me eat when we come in."

"Go down now."

"Oh, sir—I can't leave her alone."

"I'm here."

"You, sir?" In the darkened room, she looked more than a little dubious.

"Ten minutes," he said. "Eat!"

She dropped a bow and scurried to the door.

Christian closed it. He went to the foot of the bed and stood looking down at the infant as it lay in the middle of the bed on its back. He'd wakened it; the small arms waved, and a whimper bid fair to become a cry.

Arrangements. Scotland. He'd have to write the Suther-lands. It made him tired to think of it, trying to write. It made him tired just to stand up.

The girl seemed responsible; perhaps she could be paid to escort the child. The whining sound it made rose, like a creaky door, and it began to bawl in earnest.

He shoved away from the bed and went to the curtains, pulling them closed, so that the bar of bright light vanished. In the deeper darkness, the baby still cried, not screams, but a forlorn baaing sort of sound, like a sheep out on the hills.

It had only the girl's shawl overtop it. He thought the room was cold without a fire and shrugged out of his coat. As he laid it over, the button eyes turned toward him. The crying stopped, replaced by that pucker of befuddled worry. He stood back, and it began to sob again.

Fed, clean, warm: he didn't know what the devil more an infant required. Picking up, perhaps—not that he was going that far. He should have called another maid; he wanted to lie down before his body and his brain collapsed in weari-ness.

He thought of leaving it here—it looked safe enough. He could lie down in the bed next door. The girl would be back in a few minutes.

It just kept crying: long, fragile, lost-soul sobs. He leaned over it again, trying to see if there was something truly wrong or if this were only some female trick that they all knew from the cradle.

It looked at him, weeping as if the whole world were just too miserable to bear. The bed gave beneath his weight, and he sank down onto his elbow.

The baby closed its mouth, staring at him with hope and small hiccups.

"Jesus," he said. He lay down on the bed, pulling the pil-low under his head, and drew the whole bundle of coat, shawl and infant up against his shirt. A tiny hand closed tight on the lace. One sob erupted, and then changed mid-breath to a soft sigh.

Women, he thought sardonically, sinking in the bedclothes, with sleep revolving and closing in his head. He
moved one finger, feeling a cheek as soft as down.

What's your name?

Ask the girl. Remember that . . .

Maddy . . .

It was wrong. I must leave thee now.

Don't cry. Don't cry, little girl . . . I'm so tired. I never deserved you, did I? Maddy . . . but I loved you.

I always loved you.

Chapter Thirty-five

*E*lias Little had fetched Papa back. It was not thought advisable for Maddy to go on the journey or be brought into contact in any way with the world she had left. She submitted herself to the wisdom of Meeting, living retired with the Littles in Kensington until the sublease of the Chelsea house should fall in and she and Papa could return home, for it was conspicuously apparent that they would never be welcome with Cousin Edward again now that he'd finally been released from his ignominious imprisonment.

Her father was very subdued. In earlier days, Maddy would have thought he was unwell, he was so quiet, but she knew it was the havoc she had made of his life and her own that oppressed him. He did not even speak much to Elias; almost as if they were somehow set at odds after a lifetime of fraternity. When the solicitor came to consult upon a nullification of the marriage, it was Elias and Constance who sat with her through the ordeal of explanation. Papa did not even enter the room.

The most difficult part was that she could not do as Jervaulx's brothers-in-law had wished and say that the marriage had not been consummated. The case must rest upon the irregularity of the marriage itself and the fact that neither side would contest a nullification. Maddy was aware that letters were sent and attorneys advised, but she saw none of them. Elias and the elders directed the worldly business; she had only one task—to write her letter of condemnation of her actions.

It was the most difficult thing she had ever done in her life. She had not wept; since the moment she had left Belgrave Square, she had not—but when she sat down with pen and paper, everything went to a blur and she could not even see to write. She had attempted it several times, waiting until she felt herself more steady, closeting herself in the late afternoon, rising early in the morning—she even went to write it straight from the silent hours of mid-week meeting for worship, and drenched the paper with the most copious tears of all.

At dinner that night, Elias carved the roast. "I was visited by the solicitor today," he said, lifting a piece of meat onto Maddy's plate before he passed it back to her. "He has received firm word that the Duke of Jervaulx does not desire to lay any obstacle in the way of canceling the error."

That was how they spoke of it, as "the error." Maddy looked down at the food on her plate. No one said anything else. She picked up the old steel cutlery with its white horn handles and pushed a bite of meat onto her fork. But she could not eat it.

The plain life, the simple waiting upon silence and God— she fit into it so easily again, helping Constance with the washing, attending worship, accompanying the older woman on her visits to the sick and the troubled. Everything was simple: it was right to rise early, work hard, speak little; wrong to be lazy, dishonest, creaturely. Wrong to think about him.

She felt at home, and yet remote from home. She did not miss the servants, the carriages, the gilt and rich furnishings— she did not even miss the pretty dresses, when she thought of how ill she became them compared to the bright-plumed ladies who had danced in Belgrave Square.

She only missed one thing, and that was a part of her soul left behind.

In strange irrational moments, she would suddenly find herself imagining that she ought to help him to button his waistcoat, that he would want her to write out his letters—things he hadn't even needed done for him since her arm had healed. She heard footsteps on the stairs and her head lifted—but they were never brisk enough, impatient enough. She pressed her fingers over the filigree ring—a small stolen treasure, her one theft. She walked the hedgerows and stopped and hugged her arms around herself, her face turned upward to the winter sunset and to him—as if he were there, as if she could feel him again, just once again.

But he did not desire to lay any obstacle in the way. She took the bite of roast and made herself swallow.

He had needed her, and now he did not. For a little while, their lives had crossed in time and place, and gone apart again. He was the Duke of Jervaulx. She was a scandal in her Meeting. She attended under a cloud of censure, one of them and yet not, her name an item of public interest in the newspapers, causing bitter humiliation to the Society.

She was grateful that Elias and Constance and some other weighty Friends spoke on her behalf, testifying how she had been in fallacy but had turned from it, and would walk henceforth in the Light again. And everyone awaited her letter of self-condemnation. It was not a thing said aloud, but if the words she wrote were strong enough, if it showed a real and absolute longing to clear Truth, Friends might be convinced to relent in their disfavor and receive her wholly again into the Society.

"How does thy work proceed, John?" Constance asked Papa.

He rubbed his chin. "Slowly. It goes slowly in these latter days."

Maddy said, "Thou hast not wished me to transcribe for thee."

"I'm not certain that I intend to publish the paper."

She turned toward him. "Not publish it?"

"Maddy girl," he said quietly, "thou knowest that all the credit is not mine to claim."

"Not all, but—" She stopped.

"Shall I publish with his name connected? I had not thought thou wouldst like it." He smiled his sweet, sad smile. "And to tell truth, I have come across a complication in the proof that is beyond my ability alone."

She bent her head over her plate. It was not fair. Papa had spent so long and worked so hard. It should not come to naught because of her mistakes.

"Wilt thou have some of this savoy, John?" Constance changed the subject, helping Papa to the dish. "Friend Gill brought it to us this morning. He says that the sea-kale has come into the market, at a shilling and sixpence the basket."

"I wish he'll find us some asparagus," Elias said. "Or grow it, alongside those flowers of his."

Constance made a little smile. "Archimedea must ask him. He will do it for her."

"Now, Constance," Elias reproved her gently. "Thou art beforehand."

Constance, unrepentant, put some of the savoy onto Maddy's plate. "It will all be settled happily," she said. "I feel in my heart that it will."

"Hast thou continued to write thy paper, Archimedea?" Elias asked.

"Yes," she said, stirring the savoy aimlessly on her plate, cutting it across, and across again. "I am not finished."

"We will pray together tonight," he said. "Perhaps that will help guide thee."

"Yes," Maddy said.

The error would be repaired. He did not wish to put any obstacle in the way of it.

She remembered him at that last moment—she would never forget him—sly confidence, brilliance and command; stars and infinity, a world beyond reach. *A bon chat, bon rat,* below the phoenix rising. Self-possessed, audacious, sanguinary in his revenge. Like the good cat, lazy and playful, powerful and unforgiving, he turned the table and bedeviled his tormentors—tossed them in jail, almost let them free, withdrew and renewed allegations, had them up to face a grand jury before he liberated them again at his whim. Poor Cousin Edward, Maddy thought, would never be the same plump secure rat again.

He was the Duke of Jervaulx. He had lovers. He'd defeated his affliction by his own strength.

You *come,* he had said to her, so many times. She could almost hear his voice.

But it slipped away from her even in imagination, the one last thread that tied her to another life. She would write her paper. It was time.

With Elias and Constance after supper, she sat in the austere parlor and listened to the elder's deep resonant voice in prayer. She heard all the things that she should write. Afterwards, she wrote them, without tears.

Christian sat with the post, flipping invitations one by one into the fire. He paused at a letter from Scotland and set it aside. He sat looking at it unopened on the desk. Then he broke the seal and read it.

He rose, and went upstairs.

In the yellow room, a cradle had the warmest spot, carefully screened from the grate. Jilly glanced up from it. "Oh, Your Grace—she's just woke up and all ready to see you."

He nodded. The girl curtsied and left, quietly closing the door behind her.

Christian did not go up to the crib. Instead he leaned against the bed, watching from a little distance. Diana had not noticed him: she lay on her back, kicking at her long linen shirt and playing with her feet. She now had a white embroidered cap and tiny beribboned slippers, collars and bibs, a silver rattle, a soft ivory brush and comb—all the proper equipment, he was informed by Jilly and the various females in the house.

"Little girl," he said softly.

She turned at the sound of his voice, something that she'd only just learned to do. The bewildered frown creased her forehead as she looked for the source.

Christian walked to the top of the crib. She began to smile before he got there, breaking into frenzied batting with her arms and legs when he leaned over her upside down. She squealed with delight when he rubbed his nose against hers. Her fists banged his cheek and jaw. He twitched his head and made a sound each time she hit him, a game she seemed to find rousing.

He pulled back and stood over her, offering his forefingers. She grabbed them immediately, arching her head back to look at him.

"Cold in Scotland?" he asked her.

She puckered up her forehead quizzically.

"Warm clothes," he promised. "I'll send. Dresses. Money. Some pretty things."

Toys for her birthday. He wondered if they would give them to her. He would not be able to write her or hear of her. They made that clear. He was to pay for her support, confidentially, and do nothing that would cause the family further embarrassment.

It was the best thing, of course. The best thing for her.

To stand aside, silent, as he was standing aside for the nullification of his marriage. That too, the best thing. He seemed to have become something of an embarrassment to everyone.

He pulled his fingers from the baby's grip and went to the door. She turned her head, following his motion. The little pucker of uncertain worry clouded her face.

The best thing.

He looked back at her in dumb despair and silently closed the door.

Twelfth Night came and went, with no cake or games. He found reasons to put off sending Diana: the holiday, the weather, the need for a few more warm clothes. She had a wardrobe that any femme fatale might envy, created by her own modiste, the cook's sister's cousin, in consultation with Cook and Jilly. Calvin had contributed a length of embroidered muslin that had somehow leaped into his basket while he was ordering the spring liveries. Durham brought blue ribbons, to match her eyes.

Christian drove slowly down Oxford Street at night and made the carriage wait on him as he walked among the gaslights, buying shawls and wool and velvet. He did not want her to be cold. Above all, he did not want her to be cold.

When it became obvious even to him that no infant could possibly make use of so many clothes at once, Jilly packed the lengths of fabric away in a trunk. Christian thought he ought to look into arranging for a post-chaise and escort for the journey north, and didn't find the opportunity.

On a day in January, Calvin brought an unkempt boy into the library, where he stood chafing at his fingerless mittens while the butler said solemnly, "A Young Person, Your Grace, from the Lancasterian School, to speak to you."

"Please sir," the boy said, before Christian had done more than lift his eyebrows. "I'm a monitor at the school. Friend Timms teaches us arithmetic. I'm to say from him that—" He closed his eyes to recite. " 'I would ask a moment of thy time to scrutinize a problem. May I come to thee?' " The boy opened his eyes. "And if the duke says no, then I'm to beg pardon for Friend Timms and go right away, and if the duke says yes, he may come, then I'm to tell him that Friend Timms teaches on Fourth Day—that's Wednesday, sir—and Friend Timms can call after that in Belgrave Square at two; that's the only time he can come alone, and the duke will know why. And that's all, sir." He let go of a breath, relaxing his hands.

Christian had been doing nothing, just sitting and watching the blank wall of the garden court. Inside him, a small bittersweet spark came alive.

"You go the coach house," he said to the boy. "Look at the carriage. Remember it Wednesday, at two o'clock . . . it waits near the school. You find. You take Mr. Timms to it . . . so it brings to me."

"Yes, sir!" The boy bobbed his head.

Christian felt nervous as a girl as Calvin ushered Timms into the library and got him settled. "You're well?" he asked, standing back aloof when the butler departed.

Under the low brim of his beaver hat, Timms turned toward the sound of Christian's voice. "I am well in body," he said evenly.

Christian could not tell if there was accusation in his tone. He worked the fingers of his right hand. The room seemed to grow heavy with silence.

"And Maddy?" he asked, very low

Her father smiled faintly and shook his head. "I do not know."

Christian walked to the desk where Timms sat and pulled up the chair on the other side. "What problem . . . do you want me to look at?"

Timms had brought no papers or carved figures. He briefly described an equation so straightforward that Christian didn't even have to write it down. He suggested an obvious redefinition of the problematic variable.

"Ah." Timms gave another faint smile, as if the answer were more ironic than pleasing. "Of course."

Christian waited for the other man to present his real challenge. Timms said nothing.

"You never came . . . only for that," Christian said at last.

"I thought it might take a little longer," Timms said wryly.

So Christian would have wished. He asked, "The paper goes . . . otherwise?"

"I have not made progress," Timms said. "I fear I was much caught up in thy fine mathematical library at the castle, and indulged myself there."

"Will you stay to dinner?"

"I cannot. My daughter does not know that I am come here."

Christian pushed away from the desk suddenly. He walked to the window. "She would be . . . angry."

"Not angry, perhaps. I don't wish to distress her further."

"Distressed?" He closed his eyes.

"Tomorrow is Monthly Meeting. She's to read her paper there. Meeting has required that she send a copy also to the newspapers and thy friend Durham, that performed the marriage."

Christian turned his head. "Her paper," he said. "What paper?"

Timms rose, his hands resting lightly on the edge of the desk. "Come thee to Meeting, friend," he said, "and thou wilt hear."

Maddy walked every morning with Constance to the work-house, where they took food to the old ladies and the children. She went this morning just like any of the others, though it was the day of her disgrace, when she was to be censured in Meeting.

Their route was along the back of the village, past fields and nurseries. Across a plot of winter-plowed soil, a strange image was visible well before they reached the institution, at the corner where the lane turned into the workhouse court.

The jersey cow was tied to its barren tree, munching at a pile of hay: a daily sight on this spot. But today, in the middle of the dirt lane next to it stood two bewigged footmen in white livery, flanking the bizarre apparition of Lady de Marly seated in a gilded chair, her feet placed delicately upon a matching stool. A closed carriage waited beyond, completely blocking the way past.

Constance only said, "What can this be?" and kept walking toward the waiting troop. Maddy's feet went slower and slower. She finally stopped, twenty yards from the barricade.

"I think I must go back."

Constance looked at Maddy, her round, soft face as tranquil as the jersey cow's. "It is only worldly persecution," she said, so calm that Maddy took courage. "We will simply walk on."

They continued, coming closer to Lady de Marly, until Maddy could see the carved jade bottle of salts that lay in the old lady's lap.

"How very touching." The aged voice rang clear and hard in the empty air. "We're going about our little charities, are we?"

Maddy made no answer. She started to swerve past, but a footman stepped into her path.

"We *will* speak, Duchess," Lady de Marly said. "Here and now, or at another imminent time and place."

Maddy moved away from the footman. "I am not a duchess."

"No. 'Twould appear you are a coward merely." The duke's aunt was wrapped in rich shawls, her lap covered by a fine woolen rug, her hands thrust into a sable muff.

"Come, Archimedea," Constance said, turning to the side.

"Why not let her listen?" Lady de Marly asked. "If I'm the Devil come to tempt her, is she not strong enough to resist?"

"Thou art not the Devil, but only another trouble to her," Constance said. "She has trials enough to bear today."

"No." Maddy was stung by the suggestion that anything Lady de Marly could possibly offer as temptation might be enough to overcome her vocation as a decided Friend. "Let her speak, then. She has nothing to say that will disturb me."

"Jervaulx is not well," Lady de Marly murmured.

Maddy turned quickly, her throat closing. "Not well?"

Lady de Marly chuckled. "And you say I can't disturb you."

Blood prickled in Maddy's cheeks. She felt it rush in her head, a beating fever that was too visible.

"It is by the grace within her that Archimedea is concerned for the welfare of a fellow creature," Constance said.

"Is it indeed?" Lady de Marly commented, with dry amusement. She leaned forward, adjusting a shawl behind herself in her gilt chair. "He's well enough, girl—well enough to damn my eyes for a meddler. I had to locate you on my own resources. You know what my interest is." She fixed Maddy with a penetrating eye. "Is there any expectation?"

Maddy understood her. She thought of the "parcel," the bundle in the girl's arms, his own blood, left to bide in an alley. But such a child as that would not answer for what Lady de Marly demanded.

"No," she said, briefly. Absolutely.

The old woman gazed long at her. Then her mouth pursed, and she sighed. "Well, then. That is that, I suppose."

"I am moved to speak Truth to thee," Constance said, with a firm pitch in her voice. "Whilst I earnestly desire that all blessings may come to thee and thine, I would have thee understand that this marriage was an ill-done thing. A terrible thing, to force Archimedea to wed out of unity. I would have thee know what courage it has taken, and will take, for her to return to her covenant with God."

"Ah, yes." Lady de Marly nodded toward their baskets. "Carrying your little loaves and fishes to the poor."

"Thou mockest what thou dost not understand."

"No doubt you know God's mind better than I," Lady de Marly replied, "but I understand your Archimedea pretty well. She's no courageous saint." She looked at Maddy. "Are you, girl? Not at all. You're only afraid of the real task that God chose to set on your plate." She pulled her hand from her muff and groped for her stick, poking it at Maddy's basket. "This doesn't take much thought, does it? A kindly gesture, oh, yes—but does it put menfolk to work?"

"It is for children, and the elderly. I have not the means to put men to work," Maddy said, "or I should do it."

"Oh, you foolish girl. You foolish girl. You don't know what you had. You were too afraid to take your hands down from your eyes and look." She carefully set her feet on the dirt and pushed herself up. The footman moved swiftly forward and supported her to the carriage door. She stopped and turned back to Maddy, leaning on her stick. "You will feed— how many? Ten, out of those basins. Think of it, girl. When you might have fed ten thousand, if you'd only had the nerve."

* * *

"Will you go to Brooks's with us?" Durham came up the stairs two at a time. He dangled a tiny mirror tied to a string. "For the ravishing Diana." He handed it to Christian, following him into the guest room. "The ladies like to get an early start on their toilette. What do you say? Fane's to meet me as soon as he's off duty."

Christian tried out the mirror on Diana. She burbled and grabbed it. He played tug-of-war with her. "Not today," he said.

"When?" Durham said. He strolled to the window and leaned on it, looking out. "Someday, do you think?"

There was a definite you-can't-put-it-off-forever tone under his lightness.

"Not today," Christian repeated. He looked sideways. "Durham. You had a letter from Maddy?"

His friend ceased the restless tapping of his fist against the shutter. He didn't turn around. "Something . . . yes—I think I had something," he said vaguely.

"Something?"

"Some sort of letter. I don't know. Certain you don't want to go to Brooks's, old man?"

"Tell me . . . what it said."

Durham was still looking out the window. "A lot of spiritual this-and-that. Very Quakerly. I didn't really read it too closely."

"Quakerly?"

"Listen, it was a rubbishing letter. I'm off, if you don't think you'll come."

"She reads it out today to Quakers. And it goes in . . . newspapers."

Durham turned from the window. "Then, old man, I'd heartily advise you not to purchase a paper." His expression belied his flippant tone. Thrusting his hands in his pockets, he walked out of the room. "Come along to the club, if you should change your mind."

Chapter Thirty-six

*C*hristian had let himself in the door hardly knowing what to expect: an inquisition, a tribunal, some silent worshipful gathering. What he found was rather more like a restrained board meeting without a chairman. In the large stark room they sat on benches and took no votes; anyone appeared welcome to speak: clumping and shuffling echoed off the floorboards and the roof as members stood up one by one to intonate their feelings, and then at length someone would make a statement that drew general approval and it went down in the record.

Christian had not sat, but remained by the door. The row of men on the raised dais across the front of the room had looked askance at him when he'd entered. None moved to evict him, but one continued to stare at him gravely—he recognized the head of the dour group who'd come to see her at his house. Christian stared back, not moving.

There was only one female present. She sat alone on one of the forward benches, just below the dais, facing front—a white bonnet and shawl over black, anonymous. Finally a lull came in the meetinghouse, with only the scratch of the secretary's pen as he completed the latest minute.

"Is Archimedea Timms in attendance?" a quiet voice asked.

Christian felt a sinking scarcity of breath as she rose. He could not see her face, but she was shaking. From where he was, he could tell it.

She stood with her head bowed, her back to the room.

"Archimedea Timms," one of the men in the front gallery intoned, "thou hast been summoned here in the matter of thy marriage by a priest to one of the world, and certain other miscarriages. Friends have asked thee to clear truth by writing a paper of condemnation of thy actions."

The congregation made a soft noise of agreement.

"I ask thee now to read it out," someone said from the pews.

Christian took hold of the framing of the door behind him, gripping it hard.

With her head still down, she lifted the paper in her hands and began reading, her voice trembling and low, unintelligible except for the sound of it, a sound so familiar and sweet that he felt it like a physical ache.

"Friend," a man in the back complained loudly, "thee must turn and speak clear."

She was still for a moment. Then she turned to the room. "I do not doubt —" she said downward—and then, as if determining to face them truly, she lifted her eyes.

Over the heads of the congregation, her look came instantly to meet his.

Her lips had parted to speak, but she did not. Light from the high round windows fell down on her, white bloodless stillness.

He looked at her, defiant.

Say it, he thought. *Say it to me, if you can say it to them.*

She seemed to lose the sense of things. Her gaze faltered away from him. She cast an unsteady glance back and forth over the rows between them, a hunted, searching look, as if she thought she would see something, as if she could not recall what she was to do.

"Archimedea." The large, low-voiced man who'd visited her spoke. "Thou must go on."

The paper lay in one of her slack hands, resting against her black skirt. She lifted it. It shuddered like a broken bird's wing as she looked down at it blindly. "I do not doubt—" she said in a shaking voice. She stopped and visibly gathered herself. "I do not doubt—it's being right for me to suffer— and I—am content that it should be so—" She raised her head and her voice came clearer. "—for it is awful to me, that though I have walked among Friends I was not one of them, for if I had been, I would never have done this thing— and if I had taken counsel of the Lord, or of Friends, I would not have done it." She wet her lips. Her words took on a new, higher quaver. "When I was in the steeplehouse before the false minister, I said there that I had received a charge from the Lord to love him, and I called him husband, but that was contrary to Truth, and when I was there I said I was his wife, but that was contrary to Truth, also." She was gazing now at a back corner of the room, a distant look, away from the paper, away from him. Tears began to slide down her cheeks. "I knew when I had done it that I had done a dreadful thing," she said, "and that I ought to disown it, and I told him so, but I had not the courage to act even when the Light from above seemed to beat upon me. The visitation was strong, but my will was stronger. I—"

She paused. She was weeping openly, standing before them all, a single lonely figure with the paper slowly disintegrating in her restless hands. She pressed her lips hard together, and her gaze wandered up to the ceiling and down to the floor and everywhere but at anyone who watched her.

"I went," she said in a slender voice, "to his house and lived in it an abandoned woman—"

Christian made a sound, letting go of the wood and stepping forward, but she did not stop.

"—among luxuries and selfish, earthly satisfactions and comforts, and even when I knew that I was not married in Truth, and was steeped in the sins of fornication and carnal pleasure, still my will was stronger, and I could not and would not comply with Gospel order, but ran further into the enemy's snare, and returned to him even as I tried to free myself by withdrawing to my father."

Christian was shaking his head. He looked at her, willing her to look back at him, shaking and shaking his head no.

"I have said often in my heart that I loved him, and that it must be Truth, but it was an illusion of imagination or the suggestion of Satan and not the blessed influence of the Holy Spirit," she said, going on relentlessly in that high quivering tone, "and I know that to be so because I had a sense that I was doing what I should not and when I saw Friends afterward I was ashamed to look on them." She stood with tears streaming. "And I am sorry. I am unworthy. I have disowned this thing I did and I beg Friends will not cast me off, for I have turned my back on him." She blinked, an empty look at nothing. "I feel deeply the weakness of my nature." She bowed her head. "And I wish now—to sink down in the light and live according to Truth."

"Truth!" Christian exclaimed, the word ringing loud in the silence.

He made her look at him at last, she and everyone else. He stood square in front of the door, out of place—dressed wrong, angry, humiliated—only Maddy was as human as he amidst the rows of sober faces.

"Truth!" he shouted, staring at her, a mindless echo of himself, the only word that came. His voice went around and around the bare cavern of the room.

Upon the gallery, the low-voiced man rose. "Friend," he said to Christian, "we feel a tender compassion toward thee, but we must inform thee that thou art out of the Divine Life, and an intruder upon this Meeting."

Another stood, in the pews. It was Richard Gill. "We desire thee to depart."

Christian gave a wild laugh. He walked down the center aisle and snatched the tattered sheet from Maddy's hands.

"Who wrote this?" He held it before her in his fist.

She looked at him as if he were a delusion, as if he spoke in some mad babble that she could not understand. Her expression enraged him. Blank scared pain, stupid weak, not *you*, not Maddygirl, lies lies *lies!*

He glared back with the paper crushed in his hand, felt the Quakers behind him, saw her in front of him, standing there lying false pious speech wrong! *Wrong!* He had to tell her that. He tried to tell her and hit the wall—the bars, the jacket and chains and words throttled before they ever got to his throat, words imprisoned in his brain.

It happened; he lost it; he'd known it would vanish when he most needed it. They were staring; he was a circus freak *shrinking shriveling can't talk lunatic Quakers judgment thee thou stare!*

But in his furious desperation he held his ground. He stood there pulsating with shame and ferocity, breathing like a jungle creature, a miserable mad idiot standing in front of them.

Quakers! Quakers pious *Richard Gill!*

"Better!" The word slammed through, a shout. He spread his arms. "Look! Me! Can't talk *sinner!*" His voice battered the bare walls of the room as he pointed at Gill. "Think he's . . . *better?*" He sneered at the Mule. "Think you . . . so holy . . . deserve . . . my *wife?*" Turning his back, he lifted the paper toward the solemn men in the galley. "Who wrote this? You?" He brandished it at the sober faces. "Or you? Not her. Not her . . . say I'm—*enemy.*" Christian shook his head and made a disbelieving groan. "Maddy . . . 'fornication'?" He was halfway between a laugh and tears. "I called it . . . love for you. Before God . . . love . . . honor . . . my wife . . . cherish all my days. I said it. Still truth, Maddy. Still the truth . . . in me, and always."

She stared at him, standing straight and fixed. The tears dripped down her face.

"Helpmeet!" he shouted at her, at the blank weeping facade of her. "God . . . a charge . . . *love!* No rule but love! *Duchess!*"

Her lips moved. She moistened them.

"Think . . . *not?*" he demanded. "Think you're a meek mild little Quaker?" His reckless laugh at that echoed to the rafters "Stubborn . . . self-will . . . pride opinionated *liar!* Won't curtsy to the *king,* damn you! Walk in madman's cell—head up . . . no fear . . . I could have killed you, Maddy. Killed you a hundred times."

"It was an Opening," she whispered.

"It was . . . *you,*" he said. "Duchess. You . . . took me out of there. You married . . . duke. You said . . . no powder on the footmen." He pointed at the floor. "You tell me now—go down on my knees, and I will do it. The Devil's gift." His mouth curled. "Not pearls, flowers . . . gowns. Something unholy in truth. I give you . . . selfish arrogant bastard . . . what I am, and all I can do. I give you . . . my daughter . . . because I'll keep her . . . because I'll ruin her name to please myself . . . because only you—only you, Duchess . . . understand why I do it. Because only you . . . can teach her courage enough . . . teach her not to care . . . the scorn . . . what they say. Only you . . . can teach her to . . . be like you. A duchess." He opened his hand and let the paper fall to the floor. "A duchess inside!"

With one sweeping fierce look at the rows of Quakers, he turned away and strode down the aisle.

He stopped at the door and looked back. "I'll wait outside . . . five minutes!" he snarled. "You . . . *come!* Or never!"

Across from the meetinghouse, in the shadows of a small churchyard—a tree and some old graves squeezed between buildings—Christian held to the railing. He was still shaking: the reaction had hit him the instant he'd walked out of the door, wild aftereffect, outrage and dread coursing through his veins. Traffic bustled in the street. Only the tiny churchyard and the meetinghouse stood without life and motion, facing one another like islands of hush amid turmoil.

He waited much longer than five minutes. He waited, with

diminishing hope, for full an hour, and then two, knowing he
should go, knowing the futility of issuing stupid ultimatums,
finally knowing that, foolishly, he was waiting for a glimpse
of her—one glimpse—just one more before she was gone
beyond his reach.

Gripping the rail, he watched the traffic press on in a busi-
nesslike stream. A canvas-covered wagon lumbered along,
drawn by two oxen, in no hurry, but plowing steadily forward. When it had moved past, he saw her standing on the
steps of the meetinghouse.

The iron points of the railing made blunt pain against his
thumbs. No one else came out. He frowned, unable to be
sure of her expression beneath the bonnet, only certain that
she was alone.

She seemed to search, turning to look up and down the
street. He saw her descend the steps and walk toward him.

A paralysis seized his limbs. He only watched her; he
could not move or speak as she stopped at the curb, waiting
for a gig to rattle past. She picked up her skirt and crossed
the street.

He pressed his palms down on the pointed shafts. The
wrought iron separated him from her as she stopped on the
walkway. She lifted her face. It was marked with tears, but
without sadness. In the little dusk of the churchyard, the
white brim of her bonnet seemed to catch the light and make
her glow.

A terrible uncertainty rushed over him. He let go of the
railing and walked a few feet away, back into the churchyard. He didn't want to know. He didn't want to hear that the
source of that illumination in her was an accord with her
Quaker meeting.

"The child." His voice came out harsh, echoing and alien
in the narrow churchyard. "Eydie's and mine." He looked up
at her with a curve of his lips that was not humor. "That
is . . . what's called 'fornication.' "

"Yes," she said, standing still on the outside of the railing.

He felt a compulsion to tell it all, every skeleton in his

cupboard, so that she could not say he was false again. He looked down on the faded lettering of a marble slab. "Sutherland . . . the family knows . . . she's mine. They don't like it, but they will . . . take her." He shrugged. "She has a pedigree. She does not ever . . . need to know." He smiled fiercely at the gravestone. "If I am the unnamed benefactor."

He could not look at her. It was too hard. His shame—his mistakes—his sins. He had driven her away with them long before he had ever met her. She was luminous and calm, unworldly. The aura of tranquility about her made him bleed inside.

"Thou wilt keep her?"

"My daughter," he said bitterly. "My bastard daughter. As well brand her . . . by name."

"Yes," she said. "But thou wilt keep her?"

He bent his head. An unexpected strangeness gripped his chest. The lichens on the gravestone began to slide into the letters. He blinked and laughed. "I just think . . . 'she'll be cold, and they won't care.' " From where he stood the sound of traffic was like a distant grinding, queerly softened, as if from some other world. "I didn't know . . . it would be so hard." He wiped the heels of his hands over his eyes. "Maddy!"

With a jar of the gatelatch, she came inside. She walked to the tree and stood before him, serene and upright, a fine ruthless angel. She would come to tell him, of course. She would not shrink from it or slip away quietly just to save him pain.

"They will . . . have you stay a Quaker?" he asked dully. "Your paper passed?"

"It was not Truth," she said simply. "And I have come to thee."

The sound of everything still receded, falling away and away from him. "To me?" he repeated numbly.

Her mouth took on a faint, wry curve. "Thou art my husband, and I am thy wife—helpmeet, with no rule but love between us." She touched his sleeve, lightly, like a school-teacher's admonishment. "I will repeat that last part to thee every morning."

He caught her hand, gripped it. The words in him were like birds dashing themselves against glass.

"If thou wilt have me," she said at last in the silence, diffidently. "My paper—I stayed to rewrite it, and read it again, to speak the real truth—that we have no resource but our Lord and Master who speaks to our souls by His spirit, and He alone can determine for us what our service shall be— and when, and where, and how it shall be performed." Her fingers twisted in his. She lifted her eyelashes. "It's been longer than thy five minutes."

He still had no command of himself, no way to answer but to go down on his knees and press his face against her body, with a groan that was yes and yes and I love you and are you sure?

He felt her fingers push through his hair. She lowered herself, sitting on the marble slab, her hands on either side of his face. Her eyes were level with his.

"Not Gill?" he asked painfully. "Not . . . better man?"

She watched her hands as she smoothed his hair. When she didn't answer, he made a low miserable growl, shaking her slightly.

"Thou hast not guessed it yet?" She smiled. "I fear I'm only good enough to be thy duchess."

"You . . . make me . . . better."

"Oh, I will try." She played with a lock at his temple. "But thou art the duke, a bad wicked man, and I love thee too well to make thee something different."

"Bad wicked . . . idiot," he said wryly.

"No," she said. "A star that I could only look up and wonder at. Thou perceivest my true covetous nature—I'm glad thou fell, and I can hold thee in my hands."

He gave a hoarse laugh. "Tinsel . . . star." He looked down at her lap. "Don't deserve you, Maddy, but too . . . reprobate to give you up."

"There," she said. "We are equal in selfish iniquity."

He laughed again, ironically. "Not quite. Not quite, Maddygirl." He found his fingers locked with hers and the ambush of stinging heat in his chest and eyes.

After a little silence, she said, "What is thy daughter's name?"

"Diana." He swallowed and cleared his throat. "Diana Leslie Sutherland. The—her—family christened her." He shook his head. He was still staring at her lap. "Maddy. Do you understand how it will be? They will . . . look down. Talk about her. About you. They . . . will be cruel."

She made a little disdainful flick of her fingers. "I will teach her how to care for such worldly trifles."

He lifted his head. "Will you?"

"Oh, yes," she said, with a peaceful certainty.

A strained laugh escaped him. "Upside down, Maddy. You turn . . . my world upside down."

She lowered her eyes. Her fingers found his again and slid between them. "And thee with me." She held their hands together. "I've been afraid of that. That with thy kisses, thou canst make me—wanton. And—jealous—and fearful that thou wilt not save them all for me."

He looked at her pink cheeks, her lower lip worried between her teeth, and saw that she was serious. He leaned forward, his lips close to hers.

"Maddy," he whispered. He brushed the corner of her mouth.

Her hands gripped his hard. She turned her head and met his kiss with sudden greedy recklessness, unschooled and ardent. He pulled her toward him until their bodies pressed together and her legs enclosed him. He searched deep inside her mouth and felt her respond zealously, just as fervent in her passions as in her virtues, little thee-thou duchess.

She made him smile—a hard thing to do in the midst of a highly erotic kiss. He had to break away and lower his face.

Her back stiffened. "Thou art laughing at me!" she said, trying to pull her hands free.

"Loving you." He retained them, grinning at her, changing his method to light butterfly touches of his tongue across the soft curve of her chin and cheek beneath her bonnet. "Kiss you." He caught the tie and tugged it loose, tossing the stiff cap away. "My love." He held her cheeks between his palms. "My sweet life. Three horses own—two coaches—velvet—chambers—cushions—bed . . . my kisses. All my kisses. All to be . . . for thee alone."

Epilogue

Having missed their Christmas dinner last year, the tenants of Jervaulx Castle appeared determined to double their celebration for this one, and the duke full glad to triple it. In the Great Hall, two days before Christmas, on a wooden floor put down over the stone, it was feasting, drinking, music, dancing, reveling and kissing from noon until half past midnight. Even Maddy was put up to dance, against her laughing protests, carried bodily onto the floor and left there in the center, with Jervaulx facing her. He led her through the stately steps of a quadrille with Durham and Lady de Marly, to music and vast merriment—but it was friendly laughter, growing to a roar when Jervaulx took her by the shoulder and the top of the head like a solemn puppetmaster and rotated her back from a turn the wrong way.

At the end of it, he bowed to her. Maddy, with a shy smile, put out her hand to shake his. He accepted it gravely, and then pulled her up to him and kissed her, in the middle of the hall and everyone, with frenzied applause and music beating in her ears: a long, hard, branding kiss, a hot silence of their own amid the clamor.

"Now," he murmured next to her ear, "we make . . . a graceful exit."

She kissed her papa, and even got a peck on the cheek from each of the duke's family, his mother, his sisters—and from Lady de Marly a snapping complaint that it was high time the duke and duchess withdrew: Maddy had allowed this nonsense to go on much too long. They left her tapping her stick to the music and leaning over to Papa, informing him that he was old and ought to go to bed.

"Come with me," Christian said to Maddy, leading her away from the staircase out the other end of the hall. Maddy went gladly. All the passages were lit with flaming torches, smoky and bright, until she and Christian came to the quiet apartment set aside as a nursery.

He opened the door softly. Jilly sat up in the anteroom with a shielded lamp, all dressed and hopeful. She jumped to her feet and curtsied. Christian nodded at her, and she broke into a grin and curtsied again, hurrying out of the room to join the party. When she was gone, Maddy watched him look through the open door into the darkened bedroom beyond.

She'd tried, in the past year, to live according to the Light, even amid the grandeur and luxury—and found in full Lady de Marly's meaning when she'd spoken of nerve and courage. It had not seemed difficult, on a small income, to know what was right to do. She'd kept enough for her and Papa to live upon, and what little was left—and it was little—went to collection at Meeting.

Now, with so much, it was daily a decision: what was necessary, what was frivolous—one might dismiss half the footmen, but as Jervaulx noted dryly, he would then be paying for their support on the parish. It was so much gray—so little black and white; for a year she'd spent more of her time questioning herself and how she lived in Truth than she had done altogether in her life. She had her own projects, and the ones she had pressed upon Christian—his Good Works, he called them, winking at her as he wrote the checks—huge stunning checks that were a weight of responsibility she quailed under.

But it was not all uncertainty. She had her one confidence: the service that she knew with every fiber of her heart she'd done as it had been meant to be done.

Whatever the future, whatever the world might call disgrace—Diana was a gift, and if she grew up seeing what was in Christian's face as he looked in on her asleep, she would always believe it.

He pulled the door closed to a crack and came back to Maddy. The distracted cast had vanished from his eyes somewhere in the year gone, so gradually that she could not tell when. He was not what he'd been, to his own agonized impatience—meaning, Maddy thought wryly, that what had used to take him a moment to analyze or say or decide now took him two—and he could only deal with one topic instead of several at a time. But he looked at her with full perception. She did not appear to confuse him at all as he carefully released the pearls in her hair and took down the braids.

He drew his fingers in a whisper across her cheeks and down her bare arms. "I've seen this gown before," he murmured.

"One ball gown is enough," she said firmly, as he worked at the hooks of the silver dress.

"But think of the starving seamstresses."

"Thou shouldst not mock. It's true that many starve."

"So don't order a new dress," he said into the curve of her shoulder. "Just send them . . . some of my money."

She put her hand against his cheek, feeling the hard shape of it. "Better that thou shouldst speak to the government and pass a law to see them fairly paid."

He lifted his head. "Of course. I'll . . . pass a law. How simple . . . in the land of Free Trade."

She smiled at him, tracing the faint scratchy groove of muscle from his cheek to his mouth. "I have some numbers from—"

He put his face down against her throat and groaned.

"We'll speak of it tomorrow," she said.

He groaned again, slipping his hands up beneath her breasts, pushing her backward. Jilly's bed was narrow and soft. When he kissed her, she forgot gowns and laws. When he came into her she held him hard and close—this was hers, outside of all worldly concerns. This was sweet unity and kinship, her charge to love, strong and overflowing joy in every part of it.

In the dawn of Christmas Eve day, the Great Hall was a disaster of littered benches, burned-out candles, fading mistletoe and dragging red ribbons. The Yule log still burned in the mammoth fireplace, warming a deserted room. Christian smiled at Maddy's exasperated face when she caught sight of Devil atop a long table, gnawing on a ham hock trapped between his front paws. Cass was demurely lapping at melted ice in the big silver wine cooler that stood in the middle of the floor.

He whistled. Cass came, but Devil only looked up at him and went back to work.

"What dog is that?" Maddy asked in surprise.

Christian turned. On the hearth lay a huge staghound, its rough gray fur almost lost against the daylit silvery stone.

He took her around the waist and guided her toward the staircase. "Just a dog."

"I never saw it before."

"It doesn't come in often."

"Oh." She mounted the step, glancing back. "I suppose someone let it in last night. It's certainly a large animal."

"A good dog," he said, following her. "Never bites. Loves children."

"Ah. Maybe when Diana is a little bigger—" She yawned. "She could have it for a pony."

Christian stopped, pulling her against him. He leaned back on the curving wall of the stairwell. As he bent his head to kiss his wife, he could just see beyond her to the hearth.

The staghound rose. It stretched and turned to glance at him for a moment.

He closed his eyes in the kiss. When he looked up, there was a flash of plumed tail disappearing from view: Devil's or Cass's or imagination, it was impossible to tell.

But Christian knew. Maddy stood in his arms, her cheeks flushed, bemused and sleepy-eyed. She leaned her head against his chest and yawned again.

He smiled down at her. He knew. A buffle-headed bad wicked man he might be—but he could recognize a miracle when he saw one.

OH! THE SCANDAL!

A runaway heiress, a letter that was never meant to be sent . . .
A celebrity in disguise, a womanizing duke . . .
There are *such* goings on in the Avon Romance Superleaders. . . .
It's as shocking as the headlines you read in the gossip columns!

*But there is much more than mere scandal; there
is love—sometimes unexpected, sometimes unpredictable . . . and* always *passionate! These new love
stories are created by the best and brightest voices—
Cathy Maxwell, Patti Berg, Eloisa James—and there
is one of the most beloved romances ever, as created by
Laura Kinsale.*

*So don't miss the scandal, the sizzle . . . and the chance
to read about some truly handsome men!*

WAYWARD HEIRESS BOLTS TO SCOTLAND FACES RUIN IN EYES OF SOCIETY!

**"I'm furious!" states her father. "I've arranged a
perfectly good match for her, and the ungrateful chit
repays me by doing this!"**

In *New York Times* bestselling author Cathy Maxwell's *Adventures of a Scottish Heiress*, Miss Lyssa Harrell takes one
look at her proposed husband and runs as fast as she can—
to Scotland and the protection of her mother's family. But
before she reaches the border she's tracked down by Ian
Campion—a powerful soldier-turned-mercenary hired by
her father to haul her home. But before he can get her back
to London, the two begin a romantic adventure they never
expected . . .

It was Abrams who broke the somberness of the moment.
"Let us not be too grim, eh?" he said. He rose, offering his
wife a hand up as he did so. "The future can wait until the
morrow. Tonight, I need my sleep."

Madame nodded. "You are right, my son, and very wise.
Come, Viveka. You will dream tonight and, in the morning,
tell me every detail. Then perhaps we shall know more."

"I don't know if I'll be able to sleep," Lyssa answered.

"Keep the card close," Duci advised. "Your Knight will
protect you."

She said the words in earnest and yet they sounded
strange, because, for a moment, it had been the Knight that
had frightened Lyssa. Her uncertainties dissipating, Lyssa
laughed at her own gullibility. Neither Reverend Billows nor
her father would be pleased.

Madame rose. The Gypsy gathered the cards while her

husband put away the folding chair and the reading table. No one seemed to notice that Lyssa still had the Knight of Swords. She stole a look at it and then turned to secretly tuck it into her bodice—

And that is when *he* appeared.

He stepped out of the darkness into the waning firelight, as if appearing out of nowhere.

For a second, Lyssa thought her eyes deceived her. No man could be so tall, so broad of shoulders. Smoke from the fire swirled around his hard-muscled legs. His dark hair was overlong and he wore a coat the color of cobalt with a scarf wrapped around his neck in a careless fashion that would have done any dandy proud. His leather breeches had seen better days and molded themselves to his thighs like gloves. A pistol was stuck in his belt and his eyes beneath the brim of his hat were those of a man who had seen too much.

Here was her Knight come to life.

He spoke. "Miss Harrell?" His voice rumbled from a source deep within. It was the voice of command.

Lyssa lifted her chin, all too aware that her knees were shaking. "What do you want?"

The stranger smiled, the expression one of grim satisfaction. "I'm from your father. He wants you home."

Ian was well pleased with himself. His entrance had been perfect—especially his waiting until *after* the card-reading mumbo jumbo. At the sight of him, the self-styled "Gypsies" turned tail and scattered off into the woods. They knew the game was over. But best of all, the headstrong Miss Harrell stared up at him as if he were the devil incarnate.

Good.

This task was turning out to be easier than he'd anticipated.

With a coin slipped here and there in the dark corners of London, he'd learned of a wealthy young woman who had hired some "Gypsies" to transport her to Scotland. Supposedly, the heiress was to stay hidden in the wagon, but after a time, she had felt safe enough to show herself along the road and thus became very easy to track. More than one person, upon seeing the miniature, told Ian that the young lady's red hair was a hard thing to forget—especially among dark-haired Gypsies.

Now he understood why they had felt that way. Here in the glowing embers of the fire, the rich, vibrant dark red of Miss Harrell's hair with its hint of gold gleamed with a life of its own. She wore it pulled back and loose in a riotous tumble of curls that fell well past her shoulders. It was a wonder she could go anyplace in Britain without being recognized.

And her clothing would catch anyone's eye. It was as if she were an opera dancer dressed for the role of "Gypsy" . . . except the cut and cloth of her costume was of the finest stuff. The green superfine wool of her full gypsy skirt swayed with her every movement. Her fashionably low white muslin blouse was cinched at the waist with a black laced belt and served to emphasize the full swell of her breasts. She must have had some sense of modesty, because she demurely topped off the outfit with shawl of plaid that she wore proudly over one shoulder.

It was a wonder she didn't have hoops in her ears.

Her awestruck silence was short-lived. She tossed back her curls, ignored his hand, and announced, "I'm not going with you."

"Yes, you are," Ian countered reasonably. "Your father is paying me a great deal of money to see you home safe, and see you home safe I will. Now come along. Your maid is waiting at an inn down the road with decent clothes for you to wear."

Her straight brows, so much like her father's, snapped together in angry suspicion. "You're Irish."

Ian's insides tightened. Bloody little snob. But he kept his patience. "Aye, I am," he said, letting the brogue he usually took pains to avoid grow heavier. "One of them and proud of it."

She straightened to her full height. She was taller than he had anticipated and regal in her bearing. Pride radiated from every pore. A fitting daughter to Pirate Harrell. "I don't believe you are from my father. *He* would *never* hire an Irishman."

"Well, he hired *me*," Ian replied flatly, dropping the exaggerated brogue. He rested a hand on the strap of the knapsack flung over one shoulder. "The others couldn't find you. I have. Now, are you going to cooperate with me, Miss Harrell, or shall we do this the hard way? In case you are wondering, your father wants you home by any means *I* deem necessary."

Her eyes flashed golden in the firelight like two jewels. "You wouldn't lay a finger on me."

"I said 'by any means I deem necessary.' If I must hog-tie and carry you out of here, I shall."

Obviously, no one had ever spoken this plainly to Miss Harrell before in her life. Her expression was the same one he imagined she'd use if he'd stomped on her toes. The color rose to her cheeks with her temper. "You will not. Abrams and my other Gypsy friends will come to my rescue. Won't you, Abrams?" she asked, lifting her voice so that it would carry in the night.

But there was no reply save for the crackling of green wood in the fire and the rustle of the wind in the trees.

"Abrams won't," Ian corrected kindly, "because, first, he knows he's not a match for me. I have a bit of a reputation for being handy with my fists, Miss Harrell, and that allows me to do as I please. And secondly, because he's no more a Gypsy than I am. Are you, Charley?" he called to "Abrams."

"Who is Charley?" Miss Harrell demanded.

"Charley Poet, a swindler if ever there was one. You probably think Duci is his wife?"

"She is."

Ian shook his head. "She's his sister. And your fortune-teller is his aunt, 'Mother' Betty, once the owner of a London bawdy house until gambling did her in."

"That's a lie!" a female voice called out to him. "The house was stolen from me!"

"Is that the truth, Betty?" Ian challenged. "Come out of hiding and we'll discuss the matter."

There was no answer.

The color had drained from Miss Harrell's face, but still she held on to her convictions. "I don't believe you. I've been traveling with these people and they are exactly what they say they are—Gypsies. They even speak Romany."

"Charley," Ian said. "Get out here."

A beat of silence and then sheepishly, Charley appeared at the edge of the woods. He was slight of frame, and with a scarf around his head Ian supposed he could pass for a Gypsy. "Tell Miss Harrell the truth," Ian said with exaggerated patience.

THE D——OF J——TO DUEL AT DAWN
NOTORIOUS NOBLEMAN TO CHOOSE HIS WEAPON AND DEFEND HIS HONOR

Friends are concerned that this "brilliant" and "dangerous" man may tempt fate once too often.

Who could ever forget the first time they opened the pages of *New York Times* bestselling author Laura Kinsale's *Flowers from the Storm*? It's one of the greatest love stories of all time.

If you haven't yet experienced its powerful magic—and the exquisite love story of London's most scandalous rakehell and the tender woman who saves him—you are in for an experience you'll never forget.

"How long ago did you lose your sight, Mr. Timms?" he asked.

Maddy stiffened a little in her chair, surprised by such a pointed personal question. But her papa only said mildly, "Many years. Almost . . . fifteen, would it be, Maddy?"

"Eighteen, Papa," she said quietly.

Jervaulx sat relaxed, resting his elbow on the chair arm, his jaw propped on his fist. "You haven't seen your daughter since she was a child, then," he murmured. "May I describe her to you?"

She was unprepared for such a suggestion, or for the light of interest that dawned in her father's face. "Wilt thou? Wilt thou indeed?"

Jervaulx gazed at Maddy. As she felt her face growing hot, his smile turned into that unprincipled grin, and he said, "It would be my pleasure." He tilted his head, studying her. "We've made her blush already, I fear—a very delicate blush, the color of . . . clouds, I think. The way the mist turns pink at dawn—do you remember what I mean?"

"Yes," her father said seriously.

"Her face is . . . dignified, but not quite stern. Softer than that, but she has a certain way of turning up her chin that might give a man pause. She's taller than you are, but not unbecomingly tall. It's that chin, I think, and a very upright, quiet way she holds herself. It gives her presence. But she only comes to my nose, so . . . she must be a good five inches under six foot one," he said judiciously. "She appears to me to be healthy, not too stout nor thin. In excellent frame."

"Rather like a good milk cow!" Maddy exclaimed.

"And there goes the chin up," Jervaulx said. "She's perhaps a little more the color of a light claret, now that I've provoked her. All the way from her throat to her cheeks—even a little lower than her throat, but she's perfectly pale and soft below that, as far as I can see."

Maddy clapped her hand over the V neck of her gown, suddenly feeling that it must be entirely too low-cut. "Papa—" She looked to her father, but he had his face turned downward and a peculiar smile on his lips.

"Her hair," Jervaulx said, "is tarnished gold where the candlelight touches it, and where it doesn't . . . richer—more like the light through a dark ale as you pour it. She has it braided and coiled around her head. I believe she thinks that it's a plain style, but she doesn't realize the effect. It shows the curve of her neck and her throat, and makes a man think of taking it down and letting it spread out over his hands."

"Thou art unseemly," her father chided in a mild tone.

"My apologies, Mr. Timms. I can hardly help myself. She has a pensive, a very pretty mouth, that doesn't smile overly often." He took a sip of wine. "But then again—let's be fair. I've definitely seen her smile at you, but she hasn't favored me at all. This serious mouth might have been insipid, but instead it goes with the wonderful long lashes that haven't got that silly debutante curl. They're straight, but they're so long and angled down that they shadow her eyes and turn the hazel to gold, and she seems as if she's looking out through them at me. No . . ." He shook his head sadly. "Miss Timms, I regret to tell you that it isn't a spinster effect at all. I've never had a spinster look out beneath her lashes at me the way you do."

WHERE IN THE WORLD IS JULIET BRIDGER?
CULT MOVIE STAR-TURNED-NOVELIST
LEAVES PARTY SAYING SHE IS
"SICK AND TIRED OF CAVIAR!"

**"One minute she was enjoying the party,"
said her personal assistant, Nicole, "the next
she was driving off wearing her designer gown."**

In Patti Berg's *And Then He Kissed Me* blonde bombshell
Juliet Bridger has had it—too many cocktail parties, too
many phone calls from her jailbird ex, too many nasty items
in the gossip columns. So she disguises her identity and
runs . . . straight into the arms of Cole Sheridan, a small
town vet with troubles of his own . . .

He moved to the passenger door, rested on his haunches, and
peered at the woman through the window. "What's the problem? Out of gas? Engine trouble?"

"I have absolutely no idea." She scooted as far away from
the window as humanly possible, as if she thought he might
punch his fist through the glass, latch on to her, and drag her
out through the jagged shards—then eat her alive. "If you
don't mind, I'd appreciate it if you'd go away."

Ungrateful female.

"You gonna fix the car yourself?"

"That's highly unlikely."

"You expecting a miracle? A heavenly light to shine down
on this junk heap and make it start?"

"I expect no such thing." She sighed heavily. "Look, you
could be the nicest guy on the face of the earth; then again,
you could be Ted Bundy's clone."

"I'm neither," Cole bit out, her frostiness and his annoyance getting the better of him.

"Okay, so you're not nice; so you're not a mass murderer, but my dad taught me not to talk to strangers and, believe you me, I've watched enough episodes of *Unsolved Mysteries* and *America's Most Wanted* to understand not to accept help from people I know nothing about. Therefore"—she took a deep breath and let it rush out—"I wish you'd go away."

That would be the smart thing to do. Get the hell home before Nanny #13 walked off the job, but he couldn't leave the woman in the middle of nowhere, alone and stranded. Not in this heat.

"Look, lady, this hasn't been the best of days. My frame of mind sucks, and I'm in a hurry. Trust me, killing you doesn't fit into my schedule."

"All it takes is one quick jab with a knife or an itchy trigger finger and I could be history."

"I haven't got a knife, haven't got a gun, and I'm almost out of patience. If you're out of gas, just say so. You can sit right there, safe and sound behind locked doors, while I siphon some gas out of my truck and put it in your tank."

"The car's not out of gas. It simply backfired and died."

"Considering the lack of attention you've given the thing, I'm not surprised."

Even through her rhinestone glasses, he could see her eyes narrow. "I just bought the *thing* three days ago and before you tell me I got screwed, I already figured that out. Now since you're in a hurry and I'm not"—she attempted to shoo him away with a brush of her hand—"I'll wait for the cops to come by and help me."

Damn fool woman. "This isn't the main road and it isn't traveled all that often. If I leave, you could sit here for a day or two before someone else passes by."

She glared at his unkempt hair, at the stubble on his face, at his white T-shirt covered with God knows what. "I'll take my chances."

"You always this stubborn?"

"I'm cautious."

"Foolish is more—"

"Do you have a cell phone?" she interrupted, holding her thumb to her ear, her little finger to her mouth, as if he were some country bumpkin who needed sign language to understand the word "phone."

"Yeah. Why?"

"Perhaps you could call a tow truck."

"This isn't the big city; it's the middle of nowhere. There's one tow truck in town and it could be hours before Joe can get away from his gas station to help you."

"I'll wait."

"It's gonna be one hundred two degrees by noon. You sit in your car for a couple of hours you just might die."

"I get out of my car, I might die anyway."

He didn't have time for this. "Fine. Suit yourself."

Cole shoved away from the MG. Getting as far away from the crazy woman as he possibly could was the smartest thing to do. As bad as this day had been, he was sure it would get far worse if he stuck around her any longer.

He was just opening the door to his truck when she honked her horn. The squeaky beep sounded like a chicken blowing its nose, and the ghastly noise rang out four times before he turned. The confounded woman wiggled her index finger at him from behind her bug-spattered windshield, beckoning him back.

Shit.

Cole glanced at his watch. He glared at the woman, then, shaking his head, he strolled back toward the car and stared down at the face peering through the window. His jaw had tightened but he managed to bark, "What?"

She smiled. It had to be the prettiest smile he'd seen in his whole miserable life—but it was also the phoniest. "You will call a tow truck, won't you?"

Leave it to a woman to use her feminine wiles to get what she wanted. Leave it to a woman to be a pain in the butt.

LOVE LETTER GOES ASTRAY.
MEMBERS OF THE *TON* ARE AGHAST
AT SUCH IMPROPER DISPLAY OF AFFECTION.

**"I never thought Henrietta could inspire such passion,"
said her bosom pal, Lady Esme Rawlings. "Especially from
a man like Simon Darby. He's so cool on the outside, but
clearly there are unseen fires burning there."**

In Eloisa James' *Fool for Love*, Lady Esme Rawlings thinks she
can manage her friends' romances, so she concocts a plan to
have a love letter—proported to be written by the inscrutable
Simon Darby—"accidentally" read aloud at a dinner party.
Now, the only way the reputation of her friend Lady Henrietta can be saved is to marry Mr. Darby . . . quickly.

Slope played his part to perfection. Esme waited until after
the soup had come and gone, and fish had been eaten. She
kept a sharp eye to make certain that Helene and Rees weren't
going to explode in a cloud of black smoke, because then she
would have to improvise a bit, but besides the fact that Helene
was going to get a stiff neck from looking so quickly away
from her husband, they were both behaving well.

The roast arrived and Esme sent Slope for more wine. She
wanted to make certain that her part of the table was holding
enough liquor to respond instinctively. Mr. Barret-Ducrorq
was ruddy in the face and saying bombastic things about the
Regent, so she thought he was well primed. Henrietta was
pale but hadn't fled the room, and Darby showed every sign
of being utterly desirous of Henrietta. Esme smiled a little to
herself.

Just as she requested, Slope entered holding a silver salver.

Speaking just loud enough to catch the attention of the entire table, he said, "Please excuse me, my lady, but I discovered this letter. It is marked urgent, and feeling some concern that I might have inadvertently delayed the delivery of an important missive, I thought I would convey it immediately."

A little overdone, to Esme's mind. Obviously, Slope was an amateur thespian. She took the note and slit it open.

"Oh, but Slope!" she cried. "This letter is not addressed to me!"

"There was no name on the envelope," Slope said, "so I naturally assumed it was addressed to you, my lady. Shall I redirect the missive?" He hovered at her side.

She had better take over the reins of the performance. Her butler was threatening to upstage her.

"That will be quite all right, Slope," she said. Then she looked up with a glimmering smile. "It doesn't seem to be addressed to anyone. Which means we can read it." She gave a girlish giggle. "I *adore* reading private epistles!"

Only Rees looked utterly bored and kept eating his roast beef.

" 'I do not go for weariness of thee,' " Esme said in a dulcet tone. " 'Nor in the hope the world can show a fitter love for me.' It's a love poem, isn't that sweet?"

"John Donne," Darby said, "and missing the first two words. The poem begins, 'Sweetest love, I do not go for weariness of thee.' "

Esme had trouble restraining her glee. She could not have imagined a comment more indicative of Darby's own authorship. He actually knew the poem in question! She didn't dare look at Henrietta. It was hard enough pretending that she was the slowest reader in all Limpley Stoke.

" 'Never will I find anyone I adore as much as you. Although fate has cruelly separated us, I shall treasure the memory of you in my heart.' "

"I do not believe that this epistle should be read out loud,"

Mrs. Cable said, "if it truly is an epistle. Perhaps it's just a poem?"

"Do go ahead," Rees said. He appeared to have developed an active dislike of Mrs. Cable. "I'd like to hear the whole thing. Unless perhaps the missive was addressed to *you*, Mrs. Cable?"

She bridled. "I believe not."

"If not, why on earth would you care whether a piece of lackluster poetry was read aloud?"

She pressed her lips together.

Esme continued dreamily, " 'I would throw away the stars and the moon only to spend one more night—' " She gasped, broke off, and folded up the note, praying that she wasn't overacting.

"Well?" Mrs. Cable said.

"Aren't you going to finish?" Mr. Barret-Ducrorq said in his beery voice. "I was just thinking perhaps I should read some of this John Donne myself. Although not if his work is unfit for the ladies, of course," he added quickly.

"I believe not," Esme said, letting the letter fall gently to her left, in front of Mr. Barret-Ducrorq.

"I'll do it for you!" he said jovially. "Let's see. 'I would throw away the stars and the moon only to spend one more night in your arms.' " He paused. "Sizzling poetry, this Donne. I quite like it."

"That is no longer John Donne speaking," Darby remarked. "The author is now extemporizing."

"Hmmm," Mr. Barret-Ducrorq said.

"Did that letter refer to a night *in your arms*?" Mrs. Cable asked, quite as if she didn't know exactly what she heard.

"I fear so," Esme said with a sigh.

"Then we shall hear no more of this letter," Mrs. Cable said stoutly, cutting off Mr. Barret-Ducrorq as he was about to read another line.

"Ah, hum, exactly, exactly," he agreed.

Esme looked at Carola, who turned to Mr. Barret-Ducrorq and sweetly plucked the sheet from his stubby fingers. "I think this sounds precisely like the kind of note that my dear, dear husband would send me," she said, her tone as smooth as honey and her eyes resolutely fixed on the page, rather than on her husband. "In fact, I'm quite certain that he wrote me this note and it simply went astray."

Esme could see that Mrs. Cable was about to burst out of her stays. Henrietta was deadly pale but hadn't run from the room. Tuppy Perwinkle was torn between laughter and dismay. Darby looked mildly interested and Rees not interested at all.

Helene raised her head. She had spent most of the meal staring at her plate. "Do read your husband's letter, Carola," she said. "I think it's always so interesting to learn that there are husbands who acknowledge their wife's existence."

Esme winced, but Rees just shoveled another forkful of beef into his mouth.

Carola obediently read, "'I shall never meet another woman with starlit hair like your own, my dearest Henri—'" She broke off.

All eyes turned to Henrietta.

"I'm sorry! It just slipped out!" Carola squealed. "I truly thought the letter must be from my husband."

Henrietta maintained an admirable calm, although a hectic rose-colored flush had replaced the chilly white of her skin.

To her enormous satisfaction, Esme saw that Darby was looking absolutely livid.

Mrs. Cable said, "Who signed that letter?"

Carola didn't say anything.

Mrs. Cable repeated, "*Who* signed that letter?"

There was an icy moment of silence.

Esme said gently, "I'm afraid it's too late for prevarication, Carola. We must look to dearest Henrietta's future now."

Mrs. Cable nodded violently.

"It is signed Simon," Carola said obediently. She looked straight at him. "Simon Darby, of course. It's a quite poetic letter, Mr. Darby. I particularly like the ending, if you'll forgive me for saying so. After all, we have already read the letter."

"Read it," Lady Holkham said in an implacable voice.

" 'Without you, I will never marry. Since you cannot marry me, darling Henrietta, I shall never marry. Children mean nothing to me; I have a superfluity as it is. All I want is you. For this life and beyond.' " Carola sighed. "How romantic!"

Then Henrietta did something that Esme had not anticipated, and which was absolutely the best of all possible actions.

She slid slowly to the right and collapsed directly into Darby's arms.